STAR TREK®
MIRROR UNIVERSE
OBSIDIAN ALLIANCES

STAR TREK®
MIRROR UNIVERSE
OBSIDIAN ALLIANCES

Keith R.A. DeCandido
Peter David
Sarah Shaw

Based upon *Star Trek* and *Star Trek: The Next Generation*®
created by Gene Roddenberry

***Star Trek: Deep Space Nine*®**
created by Rick Berman & Michael Piller

***Star Trek: Voyager*®**
created by Rick Berman & Michael Piller & Jeri Taylor

POCKET BOOKS
New York   London   Toronto   Sydney   Stratos

POCKET BOOKS, a division of Simon & Schuster, Inc.
1230 Avenue of the Americas, New York, NY 10020

This book is published by Pocket Books, a division of
Simon & Schuster, Inc., under exclusive license from
CBS Studios Inc.

ISBN-13: 978-1-4165-2471-7
ISBN-10:   1-4165-2471-1

This Pocket Books trade paperback edition March 2007

10 9 8 7 6 5 4 3 2 1

POCKET and colophon are registered trademarks of
Simon & Schuster, Inc.

Designed by Lauren Simonetti
Cover art by Tom Hallman

Manufactured in the United States of America

For information regarding special discounts for bulk purchases,
please contact Simon & Schuster Special Sales at 1-800-456-6798
or business@simonandschuster.com.

The war was a mirror; it reflected man's every virtue and every vice, and if you looked closely, like an artist at his drawings, it showed up both with unusual clarity.

—George Grosz

The Mirror-Scaled Serpent

Keith R.A. DeCandido

Acknowledgments

As always, primary thanks have to go to my editor, Marco Palmieri, who came to me with this crazy idea in the first place. Thanks also to Paula Block and John Van Citters at CBS Consumer Products, Margaret Clark, the editor of the other volume in this two-book trip to the alternate universe, and my noble agent, Lucienne Diver.

Secondary thanks to Jerome Bixby, who first gave us the Mirror Universe in "Mirror, Mirror" on *Star Trek* in the 1960s, as well as Peter Allan Fields, Michael Piller, Ira Steven Behr, Robert Hewitt Wolfe, Hans Beimler, and Michael Taylor (who penned *Deep Space Nine*'s various MU episodes) and Manny Coto and Michael Sussman (who wrote *Enterprise*'s "In a Mirror, Darkly"), and also the late Mr. Piller once again, along with Rick Berman and Jeri Taylor, who wrote "Caretaker," the first episode of *Voyager,* from which I poached rather liberally. In addition, I must give thanks and praise to the other authors of this six-novel/two-book magnum opus: Greg Cox, Peter David, Kevin Dilmore, David Mack, Sarah Shaw, the aforementioned Mr. Sussman, and Dayton Ward.

Tertiary thanks to the actors who played this story's characters (or at least versions of them) on-screen: Karen Austin (Miral), Robert Beltran (Chakotay), Wren T. Brown (Kohlar), David Clennon (Crell Moset), Roxann Dawson (B'Elanna), Martha Hackett (Seska), Marva Hicks (T'Pel), Jennifer Lien (Kes), Robert Duncan McNeill (Thomas), Colm Meaney ("Smiley" O'Brien), Kate Mulgrew (Kate Janeway), Gavan O'Herlihy (First Maje Jabin), Tricia O'Neill (Kurak), Ethan Phillips (Neelix), Robert Picardo (Lewis Zimmerman), Richard Poe (Evek), Tim Russ (Tuvok), Jeri Ryan (Annika Hansen), Garrett Wang (Harry Kim), and Time Winters (Gul Daro).

Thanks also to the usual reference sources, especially *Star Charts* by Geoffrey Mandel, the *Star Trek Encyclopedia* by Mike and Denise Okuda, with Debbie Mirek, and the online resource Memory-Alpha.org. Perpetual thanks to the Forebearance, in particular GraceAnne Andreassi DeCandido, a.k.a. The Mom, for their continued wonderfulness.

Finally, I must thank them that live with me, both human and feline, for all their continued support.

Historian's Note

This story is set between the events of the third-season *Star Trek: Deep Space Nine* episode "Through the Looking Glass" and the fourth-season episode "Shattered Mirror," before the Terran rebellion took Terok Nor.

Dedicated to the memory of Michael Piller

1

Kes tried to screen out the voices in her head.

The blinding, agonizing pain made that rather difficult.

Sunlight shone through a slit in the top of the door to the room. *Room, hah!* In truth it was a closet, and not a very big one. There was just enough space for Kes's small form and one of the Kazon-Ogla. All the light Kes ever got was that sun shining through the slit, and that for only a few hours a day.

She loved it, though. She knew from the voices she heard in her head that the slit was intended to torment her, to give her a glimpse of what she was missing. But even that brief glance at the sun was the most beautiful sight in the universe for someone who had never seen it in person before.

The voices in her head were coarse and rough and full of greed and avarice. The Kazon-Ogla under the leadership of First Maje Jabin were not particularly refined or pleasant to talk to, but that was as nothing compared to their thoughts.

There was Raltik, who wanted to rape Kes until she talked. Kes knew every aspect of her body that he desired, every part he wished to violate. He, at least, was the only one who felt that way, as the other Kazon found Kes's pale skin and smooth hair to be repulsive in the extreme. For Kes the feeling was mutual, especially after exposure to Raltik's thoughts.

There was Nauris, who hated Jabin and whose aspirations to replace him as first maje were stymied only by his inability to come up with a good plan to remove him.

There was Garthik, who brought her two buckets every day—one with a soppy gruel for nourishment, one for getting rid of waste. Garthik never said anything, but he looked forward to the day when Kes mixed the two buckets up, which he thought would be hilariously funny.

There was Kabor, her torturer, who had found ways of inducing pain in Kes that she had never imagined. Ever since he broke her arm in several places, her entire left side flared with pain every time she shifted her position. Her right hand was useless and throbbed constantly. And her vision had remained blurred for the last day or so.

Then, of course, there was Jabin himself, who was single-mindedly determined to find a way to the underground city of the Ocampa, to see if the legends of the paradise beneath the surface of this world were true.

Kes knew that they were, of course, because she had left that very paradise of her own free will. There had to be a universe beyond the enclosed spaces the Ocampa had lived in under the Caretaker's protection for so long. To most Ocampa, that protection was like a blanket that kept them warm and comfortable, but to Kes, that blanket was smothering. She had found a gap in the security field the Caretaker had placed for the Ocampans' protection and had come to the surface—only to find that someone wanted in as much as she wanted out.

For months they beat her, they questioned her, they hurt her. She had lived a life of peace and harmony for all two years of her life, and had never known pain beyond the occasional stubbing of her toe.

Now, pain was almost all she had.

That, and the thoughts of the Kazon.

Were they any other thoughts, she would have welcomed them openly, cheered to the heavens for them.

The legends are true!

Jabin wasn't the only one who wanted proof of old stories. Many Ocampa believed that they once had far greater gifts of the mind than the simple transmittal of thoughts. Ever since she had come to the surface, ever since Kes had tried harder and harder to retreat from the pain and the agony and the suffering that Kabor inflicted on her, she had found her ability to read thoughts improving.

The sun sank below the slit. Kes's leg had fallen asleep, so she shifted her position. Pins and needles shot through the limb, and then agony sliced through her left side. She let out a wail of anguish that she knew the Kazon wouldn't hear through the big metal door.

One other thing distracted her from the thoughts of the maje's people and the pain, but she didn't dare dwell on it—on him—too often, for fear of letting hope become too strong.

Neelix.

When she had come to the surface, it was in the hope of finding new people to experience. Neelix had been exactly what she had been hoping to find.

She had not been expecting the Kazon.

Unfortunately, Neelix had not been back for some time. He had tried to ingratiate himself with Jabin, but his efforts had failed, and Kes had not seen him.

Kes would have cried, but she had no tears left. She could not let herself think too much of Neelix because there was a very real chance he would never come back.

And why should he? She was just some strange alien, short-lived by his standards—how amazing, she had thought, when Neelix had told her that his life expectancy could be measured in decades rather than years—and probably not worth his time. Neelix had a whole galaxy to explore. Why would he risk his life for her?

Because he loves me. He said so.

Don't think about that.

Don't think about the pain.

Don't think about Kabor coming back.

That, unfortunately, left her with little to think about.

Then she felt it.

Kabor and Jabin. Both were awash in anticipation. Kes did not think that boded well for her.

The door squeaked open loud enough to make shivers race up and down Kes's spine and her teeth rattle. She winced, causing her vision to swim again. The afternoon sun that had moved beyond the slit shone right into her face. She closed her eyes against it, unable to lift her left arm, unwilling to lift her right and risk further injury to her fingers.

Kabor came in and knelt before her, a huge grin on his face.

Jabin's deep voice echoed in the small room. "Where is the entrance to the Ocampa city?" It was the same question he always asked. It was the same question she never answered.

Kes opened her eyes and stared at Jabin, backlit by the sun so she couldn't make out his harsh features, which she saw as something of a kindness.

She said nothing.

Jabin folded his massive arms over his chest. Kes saw thoughts of pleasure and eagerness far beyond what she normally felt from him. He said, "Every day, I have come to this door. Every day, I have asked the question. Today, the answer will be different. You see, we have obtained this device."

Kabor held up two items. In one hand was a small square piece of metal, which he affixed to Kes's forehead. Four pins pricked her skin and skull, and she found herself blinking uncontrollably.

In the other hand was a large square box with a lever in the center. Kabor moved the lever one notch to the right.

Pain! White-hot agony coursed through every fiber of Kes's being. It felt as if every limb was being dipped in liquid fire, every cell was being boiled, every molecule was being electrocuted, every atom was being vaporized.

It went on forever. It was over in an instant.

Kes collapsed to the floor, falling onto her left side. Oddly, *that* was when she screamed, as much out of habit as anything. Certainly, the pain she felt when she fell on her broken arm was as nothing compared to what she had just experienced.

"Where is the entrance to the Ocampa city?"

Jabin's words barely registered on Kes's ears. Her breathing was labored, and sweat poured down her face. After she landed on her broken limb, she didn't move, and that kept the pain down, somewhat. The memory of her earlier agony, however, would not leave.

Still, though, she said nothing. While her people often frustrated and annoyed her, they were still her people. Under no circumstances would she expose them to these animals.

When her silence—aside from her labored breathing and the occasional moan—went on for ten seconds, Jabin nodded to Kabor. The lever, Kes now noticed, was back at its original position.

Kabor moved it two notches.

Nonononomakeitstopmakeitstopithurtsithurtsithurtspleasenononono nothepainthepainitwon'tenditneverendsithurtsnonononononoNONONO!

Without knowing how she got to this position, Kes found herself facedown on the floor of the room, the cold metal pressing on her injured head.

Her vision swam. Everything hurt—her *hair* hurt.

It wouldn't end.

It would *never* end.

Kes could not have that. Could not stand that. Could not bear feeling the pain any more. Could not fathom the notion of seeing what the third level might have in store for her.

"Where is the entrance to the Ocampa city?"

Her voice slurred with suffering, Kes said, "You'll never know!"

Then the pain came back, but it was only in her mind. White-hot spears shot through her skull and screams tore through her very being.

The anguished cries, however, were not her own.

Neelix had a plan.

He wasn't sure if it was a good plan. In fact, he was fairly sure it was an awful one.

Unfortunately, it was the only plan he had. As he applied braking thrusters to his ship in order to land it on the Ocampa homeworld—a safe distance from Maje Jabin's camp, since the plan called for approaching the Kazon-Ogla on foot—he wondered if perhaps he should wait another day or so, see if he came up with a better scheme.

But no, he knew that to be unlikely. Nothing he found in that debris field near the Caretaker's station prompted any better ideas, and he had to face the fact that the longer he waited the less the chance Kes would hold out.

She was a beautiful, noble flower, his Kes, and she had great strength, he knew. But she could last only so long against the maje's importunings, especially after he overheard that communiqué about the Haakonian interrogator that Jabin had purchased. He couldn't risk Kes being exposed to *that*.

Nor could he simply walk away. Well, yes, he *could* walk away, but he wouldn't.

Kes was all he had left.

His family had been killed, his people subjugated, his home lost to him forever. He had only his ship and a galaxy to explore.

But he did not want to explore it alone. Kes had to be by his side, or it meant nothing.

He landed his ship, stepped out of the hatch, closed it, activated the security system, prayed it was working right while confident that it really wasn't, and then began the slow walk to the Kazon camp.

Meek and supplicating. That's the way to go. Jabin likes it when people bow and scrape to him. The only other thing he respects is force, and I don't have that. So I will cater to his every whim, appeal to his baser nature, and ingratiate myself with him. I'll even offer to perform such menial tasks as, say, bringing the prisoner her food. . . .

The sun was starting to set, which was why Neelix had chosen this hour to enact his rather pathetic plan. This late, the sun was merely exhausting, not ruinous, and it took a whole minute for sweat to start stinging Neelix's eyes, as opposed to the immediacy of such an event at midday.

Neelix had no idea why the Caretaker did what he did for the Ocampa. Legend had it that he drove off invaders who had destroyed the surface, and then built them the underground city and protected them against further invasion. According to another story, the Ocampa were chosen for some great task that the Caretaker was preparing them for.

In truth, Neelix didn't much care one way or the other. He just wanted his love back. She would only live a few years, and he could no longer bear the notion of not being with her for even another hour.

It took Neelix several seconds to realize that he was almost on top of the maje's camp, and he had yet to encounter a single Kazon. At this point, he should have at least encountered a sentry or two. But he didn't see anyone.

Until he tripped over him.

Spitting sand out of his mouth and rubbing his arm where he'd landed on it, Neelix clambered to his feet to find a dead Kazon on the ground.

At least, Neelix was fairly sure he was dead. He wasn't breathing, and he was bleeding from his ears and nose.

And eyes.

Clutching his stomach with his bruised arm, Neelix turned and ran. He had never seen anyone bleeding from the eyes before, and he decided he could live a happy life without ever seeing it again.

As it happened, that desire was stymied a few seconds later, many times over.

The camp was littered with corpses.

Kes . . .

He ran toward the place where they kept Kes. Whatever had happened here had happened suddenly. The Kazon were all over the place, some holding weapons, some next to each other, some on their sleeping mats, some eating, some with readers next to their hands.

All bled from the eyes, as well as the ears and mouth.

Neelix had seen many things in his life, including the most vicious weapon he ever hoped to see, but not even the metreon cascade unsettled him the way this killing field did.

I must find Kes.

He arrived at Kes's cell to find two Kazon on the floor, just as dead as the others. One Neelix did not recognize, in part because he was facedown.

The other was First Maje Jabin. Neelix had dreamed of standing over Jabin's corpse someday, but this . . .

"Neelix?" The voice was cracked and broken and beautiful.

Peering into the cell, Neelix saw his love on her knees. Her left eye was red, her left arm hung at an odd angle to her shoulder, and blood was caked under her nose.

"Kes? Are you all right?"

"I killed them, Neelix."

Then she fainted.

It was several minutes later that Neelix began carrying Kes back to his ship. The delay was due to his having to spend those minutes throwing up.

The metreon cascade had killed Neelix's entire family, the final blow that allowed the Haakonians to conquer the Talaxians. Neelix had left his home then, putting Talax behind him.

But even the radiation poisoning that resulted from the cascade didn't leave quite so . . . disgusting a corpse as whatever Kes did.

Assuming she really did kill them.

That was, however, the least of Neelix's concerns. Right now, he wanted to get himself and Kes as far from Ocampa as possible.

Luckily, Kes was light. He was able to carry her limp form over his shoulder. Taking care not to trip over any more bloody Kazon corpses, he gingerly made his way across the desert to his ship.

Setting Kes down gently, he opened the hatch, not remembering until after he did so that he hadn't deactivated the security system. However, it didn't activate. It didn't matter much in this case, seeing as how all the potential security risks on the planet were quite dead, but Neelix made a mental note to have words with the dealer he'd bought it from at his next opportunity.

He placed his love gently in the only passenger seat, not wanting to do any more damage to her broken limbs. She moaned and awakened as he was going through the startup sequence.

Abandoning the preflight checklist, he leaned over her. Cold sweat pooled on her forehead.

I did it. I killed them all.

Neelix almost fell backward in his chair. That was Kes's voice in his head! *She's never been able to do that before!*

Her eyes fluttered open. "I can do it now, my love." Her voice was a ragged whisper, and she began to cough, causing her entire body to shiver. When she was done, he heard her next words in his mind: *I can speak with my thoughts and hear the thoughts of others.*

His intended response was interrupted by the beeping of his ship's alarm.

Peering down at his console, he swallowed. "I would love to discuss this wondrous new ability with you, my sweet one, but I'm afraid we have bigger concerns. Jabin's mother ship is approaching the planet—and I suspect they will not be especially pleased by your recent foray into mass murder."

You don't approve of what I did.

"My dear Kes," Neelix said as he finished off the preflight checklist and began takeoff, "I approve of anything that removes you from the custody of that foul Jabin."

"You're lying," she said aloud, her voice slightly less ragged. "You hate what I've done. It reminds you of what happened to your people." She leaned forward in her seat. "Neelix, I'm so sorry—I didn't intend—"

"It's all right," Neelix said quickly. "We can discuss it later. Right now, we need to escape from the Kazon-Ogla."

★ ★ ★

Neelix had purchased his ship for a fair price, and it had served him well, problems with the security system notwithstanding. But it was not as fast as a Kazon mother ship, and Neelix had barely left orbit of Ocampa when Jabin's comrades came looking for him. And the fact that they broke orbit only a few minutes later, on an intercept course for Neelix's own ship, meant that they had a good idea who was responsible for the massacre of their people.

"I'm going to try to lose them in the debris field," Neelix said, and set course for it.

They're expecting that.

Kes's thoughts turned out to be accurate, as the mother ship had cut him off, forcing him to either stand to or head to the Caretaker's station. The latter course of action was, of course, utter madness. The Caretaker was powerful and not to be trifled with. Everyone stayed away from that station for good reason.

But just at the moment, Neelix had better reasons for getting as far away from the Kazon-Ogla as possible.

As he steered his ship toward the Caretaker, his communication system rang out with a message from the Kazon: *"You will not escape us so easily, Talaxian. We know you're responsible for what happened to the first maje, and you will pay!"*

Wonderful, Neelix thought, *they think I killed Jabin.*

"I'm sorry, Neelix."

Unable to take his eyes off the scanners, Neelix said, "It's all right, Kes—truly. What's done is done, and at least now we are together. Assuming, of course, that we—"

And then he saw it . . .

. . . Kabor's sessions of torture . . .

. . . Jabin's endless questions . . .

. . . the agony in her arm . . .

. . . the blinding pain of Jabin's final interrogation tool . . .

. . . the despair that Neelix would ever come to rescue her . . .

. . . and at last, he understood. Kes had no more choice in lashing out at the first maje and his people than a trapped animal did in snarling and biting at the hunters who trapped it. The difference was, Kes's long-dormant Ocampa gifts had come to the fore, and so her snarling and biting had somewhat more consequence.

Still, at least Neelix now had a better grasp of what his dear one was going through.

I love you, Kes, he thought fervently, and he knew she heard it. Now he was more determined than ever to get them out of this. Neelix's ability to escape death had become legendary. He was sure he'd survive this time, too.

Then another alarm went off, and this one Neelix had heard only once before: when he had purchased the ship. "If you hear this," the dealer had said while activating the alarm manually, "head for the exits as fast as you can. This one'll only go off if the ship's not for the galaxy much longer."

"What is it?" Kes asked.

Squinting at the scanner readouts, Neelix said, "I don't know. The ship isn't recognizing the energy it—"

Then everything went white.

2

Chakotay gritted his teeth as the *Bak'rikan,* the *Galor*-class vessel commanded by Gul Evek, bore down on his ancient flitter. Dubbed *Geronimo* by Chakotay, her captain and pilot, the flitter was operated by a ragtag group of Terrans and Vulcans who had dedicated their lives to the express purpose of making life miserable for Evek's superiors. Right now, *Geronimo* was getting its shields pounded by the shots Evek managed to get in.

To Chakotay's relief, the shots were few. His evasive maneuvers were fairly nonstandard—mostly by virtue of his making them up as he went along—and so Evek's gunner had a hard time anticipating them.

The *Bak'rikan* fired again, and several consoles sparked. Not able to take his eyes off the display, Chakotay yelled out, "Damage report!"

From his left, Tuvok spoke in his usual calm voice: "Shields at sixty percent." They'd been under fire together on any number of occasions, and the ebony-skinned Vulcan's equanimity had always come to Chakotay as something of a balm.

The woman on Chakotay's right, however, had none of that calm when she almost shouted, "A fuel line has ruptured. Attempting to compensate—"

Her words were cut off by Evek scoring a direct hit. The *Bak'rikan* had strafed the area with disruptor fire, forcing Chakotay to maneuver around in such a way that he was a sitting duck for that last shot. He let out a curse his father had cautioned him to use only in the most dire of situations. *Under the circumstances,* he thought, *I don't think Kolopak would mind. . . .*

The screams from his right continued. "Dammit! We're barely maintaining impulse. I can't get any more out of it."

"Be creative," Chakotay said without looking at her. He needed more than thruster power to get where he wanted to go. They were at spitting distance from the Badlands, and once there, they'd be home free—but not if he just had thrusters to work with.

"How am I supposed to be 'creative' with a thirty-nine-year-old rebuilt engine?" Her urgent words were a trifle extreme, even in these circumstances. Chakotay supposed she was simply feeling the pressure of being trapped between two worlds—that fact often informed her behavior far more than immediate circumstance.

Then the screen lit up with the boxy face of Evek.

"Rebellion ship, this is Gul Evek of the Alliance vessel Bak'rikan. *Cut your engines and prepare to sur—"*

Chakotay angrily cut Evek off. "Seska—"

The Cardassian woman to his right said, "I know, I know, be creative." She let out a breath. "Thanks for taking that *tralk*'s face off the screen."

Grinning, Chakotay said, "My pleasure." Seska had been one of Evek's most trusted officers, which had made her defection to the Terran rebellion all the more meaningful. While her knowledge of Alliance protocols, patterns, and strategies made her an invaluable asset, they also made the rebellion in general and *Geronimo* in particular a rather big target. Evek didn't take kindly to defectors.

On the other hand, because his pride was so damaged, he was unlikely to call for reinforcements, and because his reputation was likewise damaged by Seska's defection, he was unlikely to get them if he called for them.

If we can just make it to the Badlands. The rebellion's bases were located on several planetoids in the Badlands. Alliance ships powerful enough to shield against the storms were too big and unwieldy to maneuver. Flying in the Badlands required finesse, a quality one didn't generally find in the average Klingon or Cardassian soldier. It was one of the things that had kept the rebellion going.

"Shields," Tuvok added, "at fifty percent."

"Let's cut weapons power," Seska said suddenly. "It's not like we're making a dent in their shields."

Tuvok dryly said, "Considering the circumstances, I'd question that proposal at this time."

While Chakotay valued Tuvok's propensity for prudence, now was *not* the time. "Do it—take weapons offline. I need thirty seconds of full impulse to get into the Badlands."

To his credit, Tuvok didn't argue further, but followed orders. "Disruptors offline."

Having spent the last several minutes engaging in ever more ridiculous evasive maneuvers, the last thing Evek would have expected was the flitter to go in a straight line. *At least I hope that's the last thing he'd expect,* Chakotay thought worriedly as he input the course and then sent the flitter rocketing straight for the Badlands.

Born on a world populated by Terrans from the Americas, Chakotay's home had managed to stay off the Terran Empire's sensors. They had formed the colony in the early twenty-second century to get back to their roots after centuries of oppression on Earth, and a small collection of agrarians were simply not worth the trouble for the Empire to conquer. However, after the Empire's fall and the rise of the Klingon-Cardassian Alliance, they became very much worth the trouble, as the Alliance saw any Terran world as a viable target and a fertile source of slaves.

Chakotay's people had never taken kindly to being subjugated, and the man himself had eventually started resisting his overseers. Thanks to a now-deceased fellow Terran named Benjamin Sisko, he had the means to put actions to thoughts. Sisko had purchased the flitter from one of the contacts he'd made during his time in service to the Bajoran Intendant, and Chakotay and his hand-picked crew had made as much trouble for the Alliance as they could, putting Seska's intelligence and Tuvok's computer skills to good use—not to mention those of his two crack engineers, who were probably cursing his name belowdecks at the moment. Their most recent mission was for Sisko's successor as leader of the rebellion, "Smiley" O'Brien: assembling parts and power sources for equipment with which to build a warship whose designs O'Brien had stolen during a trip to a parallel universe.

Taking a second to glance to his left, he asked Tuvok, "Are you reading any plasma storms ahead?"

Without hesitation, Tuvok—who had, no doubt, done such a check in order to warn Chakotay to avoid them—said, "One— coordinates 171 mark 43."

"That's where I'm going."

Chakotay didn't look to see if Tuvok reacted. All he said was, "Plasma storm density increasing by fourteen percent—twenty— twenty-five—the Cardassian ship is *not* reducing power. They're following us in."

Smirking, Chakotay said, "Gul Evek must feel daring today." He set a course that would take *Geronimo* near Tuvok's plasma storm.

Out in open space, Evek had the advantage. Chakotay's flitter could fit in Evek's cargo hold, with plenty of room to spare, and the *Bak'rikan*'s greater size made it hard for Chakotay to harm it and to avoid its multiple weapons arrays.

But here in the Badlands, size was not a benefit. Chakotay's more maneuverable vessel allowed him to cut it fine with the plasma storms that wracked the Badlands. The *Galor* class had speed and power, but it had the agility of a wet sponge.

The *Bak'rikan* started to take evasive action. Chakotay saw why a second later: A tendril of energy had flashed out from one of the plasma storms. Chakotay also took evasive action, and was well away from the tendril in seconds.

The Alliance ship wasn't so lucky. The tendril struck it right in the nacelle. Chakotay couldn't help but shake his head at that. Had the *Bak'rikan* stayed on course, it would have sustained only minor damage to the middle of the hull.

"Typical Evek," Seska said disdainfully. "He never knows when to stop. Only a fool would take a ship that size into the Badlands."

"Anyone's a fool to take a ship into the Badlands," Chakotay said ruefully. "Let's try to—"

Suddenly a flash of white light blinded Chakotay. A second later, it was gone, and Chakotay was blinking blotches of color in front of his eyes. Next to him, Seska was doing the same. "Report!"

Tuvok, whose nictitating membrane—the so-called "inner eyelid"—had protected him from the blinding light, answered with dispatch. "Some kind of coherent tetryon beam."

"Source?"

"Unknown—but I am now reading another vessel."

Chakotay blinked. "What? Where'd it come from?"

"That is also unknown. The ship matches no design in the computer's database, nor do I recognize it."

The latter fact, Chakotay knew, was of more use than the former. Their computer had limited storage space, and ship recognition beyond what the Alliance was flying these days wasn't a priority. But Tuvok had been a personal slave to a Klingon named T'Kar before joining the rebellion, and that Alliance official had been part of the Obsidian Order, the Alliance intelligence-gathering organization. Although as a mere Vulcan slave, he hadn't seen any classified data, Tuvok was exposed to plenty of other information, including data on ship types.

"Chakotay," Seska said, "a plasma storm is heading right for it."

"The wavefront will intercept us immediately following," Tuvok added.

Before Tuvok could finish his sentence, Chakotay had started plotting a new course on the fly, trying to stay away from the other plasma storms, and also out of Evek's path, while not being hit by this wavefront. He barely found a course to take in time to avoid it.

The shield alarm beeped as the explosion of the unfamiliar vessel struck them. Chakotay hadn't even noticed that the ship had been destroyed, so focused was he on avoiding its fate.

"That's odd." Seska was frowning at her console. "I'm reading a communication from near the debris of that ship. I think it might be a distress signal."

Tuvok said, "Sensors are reading two small, cylindrical objects in the vicinity of the explosion."

"I'm changing course," Chakotay said, marrying thought to action.

Seska put a hand on Chakotay's arm. "What are you doing?"

"You said it was a distress call." Chakotay spoke without looking at her.

"I said it *might* be a distress call. We can't just—"

"Those are escape pods," Chakotay said. "We've got to try to rescue them."

Tuvok said, "That course of action would be unwise. The ship was of unknown design, and the communication's true nature is also unknown. It could be a trap. The logical course of action—"

"If we don't take them, the Alliance will. I won't let that happen to *anyone* on my watch if I can avoid it."

Unbidden, images of his sister Sekaya flashed before his eyes: growing up together with her under Kolopak's stern yet indulgent tutelage, learning the old ways of their people; both of them being taken by Klingon foot soldiers when the Alliance invaded their homeworld; Sekaya defying the soldiers, and being beaten for her trouble so hard that her left eye never closed properly again, and her speech was slurred for the rest of her days; in the dilithium mines on Drema IV, both of them being worked to the bone and beyond, Sekaya's once-happy face stunned into obedience, her once-proud voice unrecognizable.

One day, she fell over, exhausted. The Bajoran overseeing the mine blew her head off without a second thought, the disruptor making her skull explode. Chakotay later strangled that Bajoran, having sworn an oath on Sekaya's dead body that the monsters who killed her would be destroyed.

Chakotay would do whatever he could to keep the Alliance from gaining another victim.

"Scans show one life-form per pod," Tuvok said. "Two different species, neither recognized by the computer." He looked over at Chakotay. "The *Bak'rikan* is changing course to intercept the pod farther from us. At best, we will be able to rescue only one of these aliens."

"Then we'll rescue one of them," Chakotay said. "Can we get a transporter lock?" he asked Seska.

The Cardassian woman just stared at him for several seconds, before finally looking down at her console.

I am going to hear about this later, Chakotay thought. Seska had a certain focus, and she didn't like anything to get in the way of the rebellion's mission to bring down an Alliance that she saw as corrupting the soul of Cardassia.

But the Alliance corrupted souls of all kinds, and Chakotay would fight to keep as many of those souls out of their hands as he could.

"I have a lock on the life-form," Seska said.

"The other pod has disintegrated," Tuvok said. "However, sensors detect an Alliance transporter trace in the debris. It is logical to assume that Gul Evek has brought the alien on board." Before Chakotay could comment on that, Tuvok said, "Plasma storm, bearing directly on the *Bak'rikan.*"

"Beam the alien on board and then beam the pod into the hold," Chakotay said as he watched a wavefront strike Evek's engines.

"Significant damage to *Bak'rikan,*" Tuvok said

At the same time, Seska said through gritted teeth, "Energizing."

I'm definitely *going to hear about this later.* Chakotay glanced back at the two-person transporter platform in the rear of the flight deck just long enough to see that their guest was humanoid and appeared to be alive. Then he piloted the ship away from Evek, who was retreating out of the Badlands, prompting Chakotay to go farther in.

"Pod is aboard," Tuvok said.

I'm sorry, Chakotay thought at the other pod's occupant. *I wish I could've saved you both.*

"*Bak'rikan* is leaving the Badlands, on a course for Alliance space," Tuvok said.

"About time," Seska muttered. More clearly, she asked, "Can we go home now?"

"Uhm—exc—excuse me?" a voice sounded from behind Chakotay before he could answer.

Chakotay turned to take a closer look at their guest. Years in the mines had exposed Chakotay to a goodly number of the Alliance's subject species, and the last year in the rebellion had done the same for his knowledge of those outside the Alliance's sphere of influence, and none of them looked like this little person.

He was quite small—about the size of a Ferengi—and seemed male, judging by his build. The top of his head was covered in dark spots, and his skin was yellow at the temples. He had a fairly long mane of hair and a few tufts under each cheek. As for the alien's face, he had a bulbous nose, beady little eyes, thick eyebrows, and pale skin (apart from the spots). He was also bleeding from a gash on his forehead. Chakotay reached under his seat for the first-aid kit.

"My name's Chakotay. This is my ship—*Geronimo.* We rescued you from capture by the Alliance."

"Well, I—I appreciate that, Captain Chakotay, truly I do. And—and the technology you used to bring me here—it's like nothing I've ever *seen.* But I—I *must* ask—were you able to rescue the other pod?"

As he moved to apply a bandage to the alien's forehead, Chakotay said, "I'm afraid not. The occupant of that pod is in Alliance hands now."

"Thank you," the alien said as Chakotay applied a bandage. "I'm—I'm sorry, but what is this—this 'alliance' of which you speak?"

Seska said, "If you ask me, Chakotay—"

"—you think he's a spy," Chakotay finished. "If he is, we'll beam him back out there. What's your name, alien?"

"Ah—I am called Neelix, and I must once again ask about this alliance." Neelix was starting to sound a bit more coherent, probably by virtue of no longer being in a ship coming apart at the seams. "You see, the occupant of the other pod is someone rather dear to me, and I went to a great deal of trouble to rescue her from the Kazon-Ogla, and—"

"Who are the Kazon-Ogla?" Chakotay asked.

Neelix laughed at that. "Oh, very droll, Captain, very droll. As if anyone from this region of space doesn't know the Kazon. Although"— and now he looked thoughtful— "I must confess to not having seen creatures quite like you before, and I do not recognize your technology, either, especially that miraculous teleporter of yours. Are you strangers to this space?"

"You're the one who's the stranger, friend." Chakotay wasn't liking the sound of any of this. From the looks of it, this Neelix, whoever he was, was very lost. "As for the person in the other pod—if it *is* someone dear to you, you'd best pray to whatever gods you worship that the Alliance is quick with her."

Before the conversation could continue, the intercom beeped. *"Flight deck, this is engineering."*

Touching a control to complete the comm, Chakotay said, "Go ahead, Annika."

"Chief, Kate wants to know if you're going to be abusing her engines further, or can she take the deuterium injectors offline for a bit."

Chakotay bit back a response, having long since given up explaining to Annika Hansen how much he hated being called "Chief." In truth, he suspected that she continued to do so precisely *because* it annoyed him. There were times when Chakotay believed that he kept Tuvok around because he was the only member of the crew who *didn't* give him a hard time.

Annika went on: *"We're also going to have to leave the Badlands in order to do it—the plasma storms are playing merry hell with the things."*

Smiling, Chakotay asked, "Why doesn't Kate ask me herself?"

"Because she's up to her arms in plasma conduits, and she doesn't trust herself to say something she won't regret later. She did ask you not to take the ship into the plasma storms until she could realign the injectors and warn you of dire consequences should you not heed her sage advice." Chakotay could almost hear Annika Hansen's mischievous smile.

"When she climbs out from under the conduits, tell her to take it up with Gul Evek. If he hadn't come after us, we wouldn't have had to go back into the Badlands so soon."

"It was Evek after us? Again? Doesn't he get tired of losing?"

"No," Seska said, "it just makes him more determined."

"He must be the most determined gul in the Alliance."

Chakotay sighed. He didn't particularly want to exit the comparative safety of the Badlands. But he also didn't want to argue with Annika—or, through her, Kate. From the sounds of it, his engineer was already pissed at him. There was no percentage in tempting fate with the woman primarily responsible for maintaining *Geronimo*'s engines. *Besides, if I countermand her now, I'll be sleeping alone tonight, and that simply isn't going to happen.* He set a course. "All right, we'll head out of the Badlands, but let me know the instant we can go back in. Evek might try to sniff around again, and I'd rather be elsewhere."

"Won't be more than an hour, Chief. Out."

Tuvok put in, "Exiting the Badlands."

Chakotay nodded as the storms cleared and the stars could be seen through the viewport. "Holding position."

"Oh, *no.*"

The shock in Neelix's voice caused Chakotay to turn back to face the small alien, who was staring at the viewscreen with eyes as wide as they could go. "What is it?"

"The stars—they're—they're all *wrong!*" He shook his head and looked away. "No, no, it simply cannot *be.*" Looking up at Chakotay, he asked, "Captain, may I see your local star charts?"

"Don't let him, Chakotay," Seska said.

But again, Chakotay ignored the Cardassian woman and called up the local charts on the screen.

Neelix peered at the display. "No, no, no, no, no, no, this is *all* wrong. Where's Oblissa or Rectilia? The Vidiian stars—no, no, this is *wrong.*"

Frowning, Chakotay said, "I don't recognize any of those names, Mr. Neelix."

The alien seemed to be ignoring Chakotay, preferring to mutter to himself. "Nothing is where it should be. A red giant where the Komar Nebula should be—a stellar nursery where I know for a fact that Trabar is."

"I believe I have a theory," Tuvok stated suddenly.

"Of *course* you do," Seska said with a sneer. "This is *pointless.* We should beam him into space and get on with our mission."

"What's your theory, Tuvok?" Chakotay asked, studiously not looking at Seska.

"You will recall that I detected a coherent tetryon beam. Tetryons do not occur naturally in the Badlands. However, it is possible such a beam could be part of an interstellar transporter."

Chakotay frowned. "That sounds a little far-fetched."

"Actually, it isn't." To Chakotay's surprise, those words came from Seska, who spoke them with what sounded to Chakotay like the most extreme reluctance. "I remember reading a report about some attempts being made by Alliance scientists to produce an interstellar transporter, one that would work over many light-years. Tetryon particles were part of that."

Tuvok went on. "If Mr. Neelix is speaking the truth, it is possible that he was brought here by an interstellar transporter, which would account for his lack of recognition of the local stars, as well as his inability to recognize so common a piece of technology as a transporter."

"The Caretaker," Neelix whispered.

"The what?" Chakotay asked.

Waving him off, Neelix said, "It's a long story."

"We've got time. It'll take my engineers at least an hour to realign the injectors. It might even be less, but we're not going anywhere until they're finished. So you have that amount of time to give me a good reason not to beam you back out into space to die."

At that, Neelix's eyes went wide. "You wouldn't—"

"Mr. Neelix, all of us on this ship are on the run from a very large interstellar empire that wants nothing less than our violent deaths. We have limited resources, and in all honesty, I need a compelling reason to waste food, air, and a bunk on you."

Neelix took a long breath. "Very well, Captain. If I could trouble you for something to drink? Some fruit juice, perhaps, or—"

"Give him some water," Chakotay said to Seska.

Seska glowered at Chakotay for a second, but then Neelix surprised all of them by saying, "Water? You have *water?*"

Frowning, Chakotay said, "Of course we do."

"That's incredible!"

Seska had gotten up and gone to the port-side water spigot. Grabbing a plastic cup, she poured it full of water and handed it to Neelix. The alien admired the cup for a moment. "It comes from the walls. *Amazing.*"

Tuvok raised an eyebrow. "Curious."

Neelix drank it down and then set the cup aside. "Thank you, Captain. That you would provide so valuable a commodity to an unfamiliar alien bespeaks a nobility that belies your intention to kill me. When you hear my story, and learn of the wonderful woman these alliance people have captured, I'm sure that you will come to my aid."

"I doubt it," Seska muttered.

3

G ul Evek, I think you should come down here right away."
Evek looked up at the communiqué from the Klingon
doctor and sighed. The very sound of the woman's voice irritated
him. "Doctor, can't this wait?"

"No."

Snarling, Evek rose from his command chair. Of the glinn at
the helm, he asked, "Estimated time to Elvok Nor?"

The helm officer took several seconds to reply, a lapse in discipline that Evek once would have severely punished. "Maybe
thirty hours or so. Give or take. Uh, sir." That last was added as
afterthought.

Letting loose with another, louder snarl, Evek departed the
bridge. He didn't bother to instruct anyone to take command of
the bridge. He didn't trust any of them to do a proper job, and
better no command than bad command.

*I could enforce discipline, but what would be the point? They've sent me
the worst of the worst.*

Damn that woman!

As he traversed the corridors of the *Bak'rikan* to the infirmary,
he cursed Seska. She had been his right hand, his first officer, his
most valued subordinate. And she betrayed him—not just with
her defection, but with her constantly aiding the thrice-damned
rebellion to cut away at the Alliance.

Suddenly, the rest of Evek's crew was reassigned. After what
happened with Seska, he was told that it would be best if his crew
was split up, to make sure that they could be kept under surveil-

lance individually, rather than be able to gather in a group and possibly spread the contamination of Seska's sedition further. Had Evek been in any position to argue, he would have pointed out that, if the rest of his crew was also made up of turncoats, then sending them to other posts would just make the situation worse—but then, that was not why they were reassigned in the first place. . . .

"Ah, there you are," Doctor B'Oraq said as Evek entered the infirmary. "You're not going to believe this."

And then the final insult, a Klingon physician. Such a concept was practically a contradiction in terms. True, B'Oraq had actually studied medicine on Cardassia, but she still came from a medical tradition where the treatment of a wound was to hack off the injured body part with a *d'k tahg* and the treatment of a disease was to kill the patient.

Unwilling to look for long at the auburn-haired Klingon woman who now occupied his infirmary, Evek instead turned his gaze to her patient. It appeared to be a female of some kind, with the smooth face of a Terran or Vulcan, but with ears of a type Evek had never seen on either species. "What is she?" he asked.

"I have no idea. Her life-sign readings don't match anything in our computers. And yes, I checked twice."

"No doubt a computer malfunction," Evek said dismissively.

"I don't think it is. Her DNA sequence isn't like anything I've ever seen."

Impatiently, Evek said, "Doctor, I fail to see how—"

"The fact that she's an alien isn't why I called you down here," B'Oraq said quickly, tugging on the auburn braid that hung down over her left shoulder, one of the Klingon's many annoying habits. Evek listed breathing at the top of that particular list.

"Why, then?" Evek folded his arms.

"When I scanned her brain, I found tremendously elevated levels of psilosynine—that's a neurotransmitter that is produced in telepaths."

Evek's arms dropped to the floor. He'd been mostly ignoring B'Oraq's words, instead coming up with entertaining ways of skinning the doctor alive, but the word *telepath* caught his attention. "Are you saying—?"

"That she's a telepath? I don't know. More tests need to be run, but I don't really have the facilities here. She's sedated right now while her injuries heal—she's been beaten *very* badly—and I'd rather not wake her up and find her reading my thoughts."

Nodding, Evek said, "Run the tests you can here."

"I already have—the brain scan I did was the extent. If this was a Klingon ship, I could map the brain more thoroughly, but *Bak'rikan* doesn't have that equipment."

"*Some* Cardassian ships do," Evek said bitterly.

"Either way, we need to get this woman to a facility that can examine her properly and determine if she really *is* a telepath. If she is . . ."

B'Oraq didn't need to finish that sentence. The Terran Empire had wiped out every known telepathic species in the quadrant a century ago. A true telepath would be a valued commodity, one the Alliance would reward the procurement of.

"Are we on course for Elvok Nor? They have a much more complete infirmary there, and Doctor Dorkan is a fine—"

"No," Evek said. "That is to say, we *are* currently on course for the station, but we will not be for long. Gul Jasad is in charge of Elvok Nor, and he would quickly take the credit for the discovery of this alien."

Again, B'Oraq tugged on her braid. "I have a suggestion that you probably won't like."

"Then don't bother telling me," Evek said, and turned on his heel.

"You could set course for Ardana."

Evek stopped in his tracks. He knew that Ardana was a former subject world of the Terran Empire, and was once the prime source of zenite for the Alliance before it was mined clean, but little else beyond that. "Why would I do that?"

"Because there is a research facility on Ardana. Some of the top minds in the Alliance are working there, including Crell Moset, Kurak, and—"

Evek turned around. "Kurak is a Klingon name. You expect me to believe that one of the top minds in the Alliance is a *Klingon?*"

"Believe what you want, but the head of the base is a woman named B'Elanna. She's an old friend of mine, and—well, let us say she is one who can sympathize with your own position. She used to be the Intendant of Cestus III, until she failed to quell an uprising. Her mother is a high-ranking adviser to the Regent, so she was spared the usual fate of such failure. Instead, she was exiled to an outpost of scientists. I can assure you, she would be a valuable ally."

For several seconds, Evek said nothing. Finally, he asked, "Why are you suggesting this? What good would it do you?"

B'Oraq had mostly been avoiding eye contact; Evek had been doing likewise. Now, however, she stared right at him. Evek tried to return the stare, but found himself looking away. "I grow weary of being part of your punishment, Evek. I didn't study medicine on Cardassia in order to serve on a Cardassian ship and aid in the embarrassment of a disgraced Cardassian gul. I studied so I could bring better medicine to Klingon worlds. I would have thought our alliance would bring about shared practices, but such has not been the case. Klingon medicine is barbaric—you've said so yourself, mostly about my own work, despite the evidence to the contrary— and my desire is to improve it. I can't do that while wasting away serving as an object lesson to you for being too incompetent to hold on to your officers."

Evek strode forward and raised an arm as if to strike the doctor. "How *dare* you?"

Her smile grew wider. "Oh, *do,* Gul. Strike me, so I may challenge you."

"This isn't a Klingon ship, woman—your tiresome notions of duels and honor do not apply here."

"They apply to me. Section forty-seven of the treaty signed by both our peoples seventy-five years ago states that any Klingon officer who is challenged on *any* Alliance vessel will be subject to Klingon rules of conduct. If you strike me, I have the right to challenge you for your command." She stepped close to him. The scent of her breath was vile, doubtless from that wretched raw meat she insisted upon eating right there in the mess hall, and Evek's stomach roiled with nausea. "I am quite proficient with the *d'k tahg,* Evek, and as a doctor I know *precisely* where to strike to cause the most pain. You cannot afford to deny me my rights under Alliance law, not in your current state of disgrace. And when I kill you, I will claim the telepath for myself."

Evek was sorely tempted to go through with it and damn the consequences. The worst that could happen was that he *would* lose and finally put an end to an existence that had been a misery.

No—I am no Romulan who falls on his sword as if that meant something. One thing Cardassians and Klingons—and Terrans, if it came to that—shared was a loathing for suicide. His ship was named *Bak'rikan*: "no surrender." Once a symbol of his tenacity in battle, it now represented his stubborn refusal to let his disgrace ruin him.

He lowered his hand and turned toward the exit to the infirmary. "I will consider it," he said as he left.

As he walked through the corridors of the ship he still stubbornly thought of as his, he imagined he could hear B'Oraq laughing at him. While he could not afford to challenge her, he couldn't afford to simply accept her offer at face value, either.

Soon, Evek arrived at his quarters. They were, naturally, the largest on the ship—one of the few remaining perks of being a gul that Evek was permitted, these days. The walls were decorated with paintings by a Vulcan artist by the name of S'larok, whose works had been personally looted by Evek from a storehouse found in a raid on Betazed. There had been rumors of a resistance movement building on that barren world—this was years before the current rebellion had commenced—and the *Bak'rikan* had been sent to investigate. They had found no rebels, but did find a cache of magnificent spacescapes that had been missed by the Terran *voles* who had overrun Betazed after its people were exterminated. Evek had been surprised to find such compelling art from so bland a species as the Vulcans—they made excellent slaves, but had no aesthetic sense. Evek's own sense of aesthetics was never well cultivated, either—he appreciated good art and fine poetry, but had no talent for them himself.

Staring up at S'larok's rendering of a nebula, Evek considered B'Oraq's words. The painting was called, prosaically, *The Agosoria Nebula*. To Evek's spacefarer's eye, the rendering looked nothing like the cloud in question, but S'larok had captured the turbulence and beauty of the nebula, even if the details weren't accurate. It was a level of interpretation one didn't often find in literal-minded Vulcans.

He sat at his desk and called up Alliance records on Ardana. Moving past the history of the world, including the construction of their "cloud city" above the surface and the now-dormant zenite mines below it, he came to the purpose of the base established on that cloud city many years ago: scientific research. One of the projects on which they were working was an attempt to re-create the research begun by a Terran woman named Sisko on a transpectral sensor array that could work in the Badlands. *Would that they had succeeded in that,* Evek thought bitterly. *Then I would at last have Seska back in my thrall.*

Briefly, Evek allowed himself the pleasure of imagining what he would do to Seska once he had her back again. She had always been fond of her long tresses, so they would be the first to go. Perhaps having her hang from the ceiling and then removing an eye . . .

Turning back to the task at hand, Evek studied some of the other projects under way at Ardana, including those of a Terran scientist named Zimmerman, who was doing research into the possibility of genetically engineering telepathy.

As B'Oraq had told him, the head of the research station was a Klingon listed as B'Elanna, daughter of Miral. He called up her record, and was intrigued to see that she had no father listed. Given the Klingon predilection for familial accountability, this was rather a large gap.

Evek thought about his standing orders: Any discovery of a telepathic species was to be reported to Alliance Command immediately. But where would that get him? B'Oraq, the incompetent wench, wasn't even sure this alien woman *was* telepathic. If he brought her to Elvok Nor, there were only two options. The first would be that Jasad would take credit for discovering the telepath and leave Evek out of it. Jasad was far too much of a glory hound for it to be otherwise. Besides, the *tralk* had gone on at great length the last time Evek was at Elvok Nor about how loyal his people were, and how *they* would never betray *him*.

The second option would be that this strange-eared woman would turn out not to be a telepath, thus cementing Evek's opinion of B'Oraq as an idiot and also making Evek out to be a fool in front of Jasad.

Under no circumstances could Evek afford the second option.

This should be an easy decision, Evek thought as he got up and started pacing his quarters. But Evek couldn't get past his distrust of Klingons. He had no illusions about this so-called Alliance. As far as he was concerned, the Cardassian Union had subordinated itself to those Klingon demons, allowing themselves to be ruled by their mad Regent, all in the name of conquest. And yes, it was only due to their combined efforts that they had been able to overcome the Terran Empire, for, as weakened as it had become under Emperor Spock, even going so far as to call itself a "republic" toward the end, the Klingons and Cardassians were only a match for its military might combined. But in the decades since, the luster of Cardassia had been dimmed. More worlds were controlled by Klingons than Cardassians, and the Regent's council had far more Klingons on it than Cardassians—supposedly to be more representative since, despite their generally lower life expectancy and warrior lifestyle, the Klingon population was greater than that of the Cardassians. The only realm in which Cardassians had superior numbers was in the Obsidian Order, the Alliance intelligence agency, but Evek hardly saw that as a good thing. The Order was made up of the vermin of the galaxy, and if he had his way, it would have been abolished centuries ago.

Evek, however, was in no position to do anything about the state of the galaxy. Thanks to Seska's betrayal, he wasn't in a position to do much of anything.

But if I have control of a telepath, that would change everything.

He stared up at *The Agosoria Nebula* once again. *If a Vulcan can be interpretive, perhaps a Klingon can be trustworthy.* It was easy enough to read between the lines of B'Elanna's service record: falling from Intendant of a planet to supervisor of a small research facility was a significant career setback. It was as much a show of no confidence as Evek's own complete turnover in crew. *Right now, the only person I can trust is someone with as little to lose as I.*

Opening a channel to the bridge, Evek said, "Helm, course correction. Set course for Ardana, and execute at maximum speed."

"Sir?" The helm officer sounded befuddled. *"I thought we were going to Elvok Nor."*

"We were. We are no longer. Are you questioning my orders, Glinn?"

The helm officer actually hesitated at that. *"I guess not."*

"Then follow them. And maintain comm silence. Any unauthorized transmissions will result in the offenders being put to death. Out." Evek cut the connection.

Evek doubted that such a threat would do any good. He knew that many of his crew were spies for Alliance Command, or for ambitious glinns and Klingon officers. His actions would no doubt be reported. But that was a risk he had to take.

That was also why he opened a secure channel to Ardana himself, bypassing a communications officer he could not afford to trust.

4

Tuvok listened intently to the words spoken by the alien who called himself Neelix. As the tale progressed, and as Tuvok examined his sensor readings, the star charts *Geronimo* had available, and the navigation information programmed into the escape pod, whose computer the Vulcan had accessed, Tuvok came to a realization.

I must convince Chakotay to mount a rescue mission.

To Tuvok's chagrin, he knew that it would not be an easy thing to accomplish. Gul Evek would no doubt bring Neelix's paramour to an Alliance facility—Elvok Nor and Terok Nor were the closest—and penetrating such a facility would not be easy. True, a rebellion cadre had managed to rescue Professor Jennifer Sisko from Terok Nor only a short time ago, but that was mainly due to the presence of an alternate-universe version of Professor Sisko's former husband Benjamin posing as the one Tuvok was familiar with. That deception had been necessary, though O'Brien had revealed the truth to the rest of the rebellion after the alternate Sisko had returned to his own universe. A second raid was in the planning stages, but Tuvok measured its possibility for success at only 11.3 percent, and it was that high only because they had Professor Sisko working for them.

But it was imperative that the Alliance not acquire the services of a telepath, especially one powerful enough to psionically kill as many as Neelix claimed.

Chakotay put Tuvok's own thoughts into words: "So you're saying that this Kes of yours is a telepath?"

Neelix considered. "I suppose that word would apply, yes. Her people, the Ocampa, have always been able to communicate via thought, but none have been able to do what Kes did today."

"But there *are* no telepaths!" Seska said with a snarl. "Chakotay, he's obviously lying."

"What do you mean there are no telepaths?" Neelix asked.

Tuvok quickly answered. "The Terran Empire, which ruled this region a century ago and has since fallen, engaged in a campaign to wipe out all telepathic species in the known galaxy."

Chakotay added, "Betazoids, Kazarites, Ullians, Letheans, Selelvians—all gone."

"Why would they do that?" Neelix asked, aghast.

"Terrans themselves," Tuvok said, "are generally not capable of telepathy. They felt that a subject species with that ability would have an insurmountable advantage against them. Therefore, the Empire eliminated all telepaths as a preemptive strike."

"So," Seska said, "you can see why we don't believe you."

"Do not presume to speak for all of us," Tuvok said. "I said 'known galaxy' for a reason." He called up the star chart he wanted. "Mr. Neelix, does this chart look familiar to you."

Neelix peered at the screen. "Why yes—yes, it does."

Turning to his shipmates, Tuvok said, "While Mr. Neelix told his tale, I downloaded the information contained in his escape pod. While the pod's computer is small, it does contain an impressive navigation computer—necessary for it to serve its function as an emergency escape. This is the most recent local star chart in the computer's memory."

Like Neelix, Chakotay peered at the screen. "I don't recognize those stars."

For so accomplished a pilot as Chakotay, Tuvok knew this was no small admission on his part. "There is no reason why you should. While I cannot provide precise coordinates, I estimate that they are located over seventy thousand light-years from our current position."

The flight deck was silent for a few moments. Tuvok knew that most non-Vulcans needed time to process information so far out of the range of their experiences.

"The Caretaker," Neelix whispered.

Chakotay turned to their visitor. "That's the second time you've mentioned this Caretaker. Supposedly, you were heading for its station when you were being chased by these Kazon. Who is he?"

"Assuming it is a he, the Caretaker is a being who takes care of the Ocampa, hence the name. He provides the security field that Kes escaped through and that the Kazon-Ogla were trying to penetrate. He also—" Neelix hesitated. "He has been searching the galaxy for ships. Many vessels have appeared in Ocampan space that are from other parts of the galaxy."

"It is possible," Tuvok said, "that the interstellar transporter this Caretaker is using to bring ships to Ocampan space works both ways, as it were, and brought Mr. Neelix here."

"All right, fine, so he's from another part of the galaxy," Seska said. She turned to Chakotay. "What does it matter?"

Chakotay rubbed his chin. "If this Kes is a telepath, it matters a lot. Can you imagine what the Alliance could do with her? It'd be better than that transpectral sensor array they were trying to get Professor Sisko to build—they could just fly in with her and find us. Not to mention interrogations . . ." He shook his head. "Unfortunately, we still can't effect a rescue."

"Why not?" Neelix sounded quite indignant.

"Because we don't know where Evek took her, and there's no way we can follow him—especially since we're late getting our cargo back to base."

"Flight deck, this is engineering."

Tuvok noted that this time it was Kate Janeway herself who was contacting Chakotay. Based on his own readings of Terran interaction, this meant that she was no longer carrying the same anger toward the captain as she had been when she delegated the task of talking to the flight deck to Annika Hansen.

"Go ahead, Kate."

"The injectors are fine. We can go home." And then she cut off the transmission.

Tuvok amended his conclusion. *Still* some *anger, it would seem.*

"Good," Chakotay said, even though Janeway could no longer hear him. "Setting course for base." Without looking behind him, he added, "Mr. Neelix, we'll take you back with us. After that, we can figure out what to do with you. But you can consider yourself a guest of the Terran rebellion until further notice."

"Thank you, Captain Chakotay." Neelix sounded subdued. Tuvok supposed that to be inevitable, given the alien's present circumstance.

After removing the star chart from the viewer, Tuvok did a sensor sweep to make sure they were not being followed. "Sensors read clear," he said when he was finished.

As they traversed the Badlands toward the rebellion base, Tuvok mused on how he was to convince Chakotay to mount a rescue mission without telling him the true reason why.

Tuvok considered the possibility of revealing the truth, but he dismissed it immediately. While the rebellion's cause was just, there were few in its ranks whom he could consider trustworthy. After all, many were former criminals and slaves, not ones to be trusted with the details of a particular raid, much less Tuvok's true purpose.

This was not to say that Tuvok did not support the rebellion. Indeed, he and his co-conspirators had been working for decades to bring about just such a revolution. It came sooner than expected, but it was still all part of the long-term goal.

But if the Alliance gains possession of a true telepath, then all our goals will be for naught.

Tuvok was one of a relatively few Vulcans in the rebellion. Indeed, it had taken some doing to convince Captain Sisko and the others that his desire for change was genuine. Vulcans were the servants to the Klingons and Cardassians, thralls who fetched and carried and collated and did all the menial work that required a modicum of intelligence. The Alliance respected the Vulcans' mental discipline—

—not realizing that their mental discipline was far greater than was generally known. Vulcan telepathy was the most closely guarded secret in the galaxy, one preserved even after the fall of the Terran Empire—or, rather, the Terran Republic, as it had become by then. Now, carefully seeded throughout the galaxy, were millions of telepathic sleeper agents, enacting the late Emperor Spock's long-term, posthumous goal of a truly democratic galaxy.

The truth about Vulcans *had* to be kept secret in order for the plan to have any chance of success. So Tuvok retained his cover, including the rather distasteful fiction that his wife and children were murdered by the Alliance. In fact, though his son Sek had died of an infection several years earlier, despite the impressive efforts of a Cardassian physician to save him, his wife was alive and well. So were his other children, who were serving in the houses and workplaces of prominent Klingons and Cardassians, amassing intelligence. Some of it had proven useful to the rebellion— in fact, the location and security codes for the supply depot they had just raided for equipment to use in building O'Brien's warship had come from Tuvok's daughter Asil—with the rest being collated for the future.

However, that future would be bleak indeed if Kes got into Alliance hands. If she was commandeered for their use—or worse, if Alliance scientists learned how to replicate telepathy in other species—then Chakotay's fear that telepaths would be used to seek out the rebellion would be the least of it. Vulcan agents would very soon be exposed. It was, of course, possible for Vulcans to shield their thoughts from other telepaths, but complete blocking of all thoughts would stand out as much as seditious thoughts would, and an incomplete blocking risked leakage. Besides which, no Vulcans had *had* to shield their thoughts in over a century, and that lack of practice could prove fatal.

No, the risk was far too great.

As *Geronimo* landed on the planet that served as the rebellion base, Tuvok started formulating his strategy. His first step would be to talk to Kate Janeway. . . .

Chakotay, having left Seska to take Neelix into the cave system the rebellion used as its HQ, tried to approach Kate in the *Geronimo* engine room after the ship had landed, but Annika blocked his path. "I wouldn't go in there if I were you, Chief."

Normally, Annika's blue eyes were full of mischief, but right now they were deadly serious, which meant Kate was in one of *those* moods.

But Chakotay didn't care all that much. If anything, that made it more fun. "You're not me, because if you were, this would be *your* ship and *you* could go as you please. Now get out of my way."

Without waiting for a response, Chakotay barreled past the long-haired blonde and headed straight for the warp core.

"Your funeral, Chief," Annika said. "I'm gonna go find Harry."

She's sleeping with Harry *now?* That didn't bode well. Annika went through lovers the way Chakotay went through underwear. In fact, given their laundry and resupply difficulties of late, she probably went through them *more* often. However, Chakotay didn't see Harry Kim as being the type to take the inevitable dumping as well as the last ten men and four women did.

As expected, the lower half of Kate Janeway was visible jutting out from under the plasma manifold. Her legs wiggled a bit, and Chakotay paused to admire her rear end as it squirmed inside her coveralls.

Wearing a feral grin, he said, "Captain on deck."

Her muffled voice replied, "Whoop-de-do."

Five seconds passed, and then she crawled out. Her elfin features were smudged with sweat and dirt, and her red hair—which she kept cut short for practical reasons, a lesson she had tried and failed to impart to Annika—was flying out in all directions. "You're still here?"

"I said captain *on* deck, I never said I was leaving."

"You're gonna *be* on the deck in a minute. Didn't I tell you going into the Badlands before I could realign the injectors was—"

"—a bad idea, yes. Unfortunately, Gul Evek had other ideas. Trust me, if we hadn't gone into the Badlands when we did, misaligned injectors would've been the least of our problems."

She got nose-to-nose with him—or as close as she could, given their differences in height. "Oh, please, you've been dodging the Alliance for a year now. And Evek's got all the brains God gave a *glob* fly. You could've gotten away from him with one hand tied behind your back."

"I didn't want to take the chance. Besides, I trusted you to keep the ship together. Are you saying you can't handle a little trip to the Badlands just because some injector's offline? That's not the Kate Janeway I hired. Maybe I should let Annika take over."

She laughed viciously. "Go ahead! It'll be fun to watch the ship explode as soon as you go to warp."

"Face it, she's twice the engineer you'll ever be," Chakotay said with a sneer.

"She'd be lucky to be half the engineer I am. Maybe I should let her take over. There's plenty of people in this rebellion who need a good mechanic. Smiley can't be everywhere, after all."

"Why don't you go ahead and do that?"

"Maybe I will!"

"Good!"

"Good!"

Then he grabbed her by the shoulders, pulled her close to him, and kissed her with violent intensity, his lips pressed hard against hers, their tongues snaking around each other as he pressed her close by grabbing the back of her head.

She wrapped her arms around him and tightened her grip, pressing their bodies together. Frantically, she started unfastening his shirt. He in turn started clawing at her coverall, to very little effect. She had gotten his shirt off, and he stood there bare-chested, still kissing her while trying and failing to get the coverall off.

With a sigh of frustration, she broke off the kiss. "Oh, for crying out loud." She undid two flaps and the coverall dropped completely off her shoulders and fell to the floor with a *whump.*

He smiled appreciatively at her naked form as he removed his pants.

Chakotay had no idea how they wound up, twenty minutes later, under the matter/antimatter reactor, which was clear on the other side of the engine room. All he remembered was a hungry exploration of Kate's flesh, smooth but for the calluses on her hands and feet from her time in the mines on Cestus III. One of the many things he loved about sex with Kate was that wonderful contrast of hard and soft.

They lay quietly together when they were both spent, a tangle of arms and legs, breathing heavily and drenched in sweat.

After a few seconds, Kate clambered to her feet. "Next time, Chuckles, listen to me when I tell you something, all right?"

She padded across the engine room, grabbed her coverall, climbed into it, and walked out.

Smiling contentedly, Chakotay lay against the reactor until a crick started developing in the small of his back, and he finally got to his feet.

Just as he located his pants and started putting them on, a familiar voice said, "Chakotay, you in here?"

"In here, Harry."

The squeak of his leather outfit heralding his arrival, Harry Kim entered the engine room. "I put the prisoner in—"

"Prisoner?" Reaching down to pick up his shirt, Chakotay paused at that word. "Neelix isn't a prisoner."

"That isn't what Seska told me. She said he was a prisoner, so I threw him in the cell."

Chakotay let out a long breath that was half snarl. *Damn that woman.* "The man was just thrust seventy thousand light-years from home, had his ship destroyed, and saw the love of his life captured by the Alliance. He's a *guest.*"

Harry's hard face didn't change expression. The scar that ran down from his forehead, past his left eye, and down to his chin seemed to flare a bit. "Do we know all this for sure?"

"His story was pretty convincing, and Tuvok backed it up with some pretty solid astronomical evidence."

"I can make *sure*."

Shaking his head, Chakotay said, "No." He had no doubt that Harry's infamous interrogation techniques would get the whole truth out of Neelix, but there wouldn't be much of Neelix left when he was finished. Besides which, Chakotay had an instinct about the alien—he was fairly sure the story Harry would get would be the same as the one Neelix told on *Geronimo*. "Get him out of the cell and let him join the others."

"I don't think that's a good idea."

Is my entire crew going to get in my face today? "I don't really give a damn what you think, Harry. Neelix is another victim of the Alliance, nothing more, and I promised that he'd be our guest. You and Seska have made a liar of me. Now I'm perfectly happy to choose to lie, but you made that choice for me, and I don't appreciate it. Do we understand each other?" Without waiting for an answer, Chakotay pulled his shirt on and said, "Get him out of the cell."

Harry's face had yet to change expression. "You're the boss," he said blandly, and turned on his heel and left, the squeaking of his leather echoing and fading.

The "cell" was simply another cave, one smaller than the others, with only limited access. It had gained its function by remaining a piece of hollowed-out rock without the various bits of comfort and decoration that the rebellion had added to other caves over the last year or so. But still, after all he'd been through, Neelix deserved better.

I wish I could rescue his woman, too, but that's a forlorn hope until we get some clue where she is. Still, Neelix was an experienced pilot, and that alone would make him a useful commodity.

First things first, though—O'Brien needs these supplies. He made his way to the cargo hold.

5

B'Elanna, daughter of Miral, seriously debated the efficacy of jumping atop the hardwood table and slitting the throats of the three scientists seated opposite her. They were the three project managers of Monor Base, the scientific think tank the Alliance had set up in the largest building of Ardana's Stratos City, and B'Elanna knew she would derive tremendous pleasure from seeing their broken corpses lying at her feet, the taste of their blood on her lips.

Well, the taste of Kurak's blood, anyhow. B'Elanna had never tasted Cardassian blood, never having had the opportunity to kill one, so she couldn't say how Crell Moset's blood would taste. As for Zimmerman . . . She snarled. Just thinking about killing Terrans made her ill after Cestus III. Not that she could afford to kill Lewis Zimmerman in any event. He was, after all, as valued a scientist as a Terran *could* be, so she could not kill him without sufficient cause, and *he annoyed me* didn't qualify. Miral's intervention likely would not keep her safe a second time.

Besides, the table was priceless, one of the few remaining pieces made from the extinct *doci* tree. Cleaning blood off it would cost a fortune, especially if it got in the decorative carvings.

So she listened to the blather of Moset's report. Or, rather, the elderly, stooped Cardassian gave his report, and she managed to keep her eyes open.

She did not manage to keep her temper, however, once Moset said, "If I may turn the supervisor's attention to the diagram showing our progress—"

B'Elanna did not look at the diagram Moset called up on the screen. Instead she got to her feet and said, "Enough! I do not wish to see diagrams! I wish to know one thing, and one thing only: Can your researches provide the Alliance with anything *practical*?"

Moset seemed to shrink in his chair, and he ran his hand through his iron-gray hair. "Er, well, not as yet, Supervisor, you see—"

"Silence! That question only required a yes or no answer. From now on, Doctor, you will speak when spoken to, and answer only the questions asked. I grow weary of your delays and your toadying. Get me results, or get out of my sight."

"And I grow weary of *you,* halfbreed."

B'Elanna looked down to the other end of the table, where Kurak sat, a sneer on her face. The supervisor grinned. While she could not kill Zimmerman or Moset without cause, she could kill a Klingon just for looking at her the wrong way.

"You have something to say, daughter of Haleka?"

"Yes." Kurak got to her feet also and walked around the table, behind the cowering Moset. "You are unworthy to run this base. Indeed, you are unworthy to *live*. You should've been drowned at birth like all halfbreeds."

Kurak now stood face-to-face with B'Elanna, her brown eyes blazing. B'Elanna's own eyes did not, she hoped, give away too much of her glee. She hadn't had a good fight in ages. True, Kurak was no warrior, but B'Elanna knew she came from a House that had served the Alliance, and the Klingon Empire before it, for centuries. She could not have lived in the House of Palkar without some martial training.

Aloud, B'Elanna said, "Regardless of who my father may have been—"

"Your whore of a mother slept with so many Terrans, did she, that you don't even know?"

Don't even care would have been a more accurate phrase. Miral loved sleeping with Terrans, as they were so wonderfully fragile, and one of them had been careless enough to impregnate her. None of them had names, though; Miral wasn't much for conversation in the bedchamber. B'Elanna continued, "You will find that my heart is still Klingon."

Unsheathing a *d'k tahg,* Kurak smiled and said, "I will make that determination for myself when I cut it out of you."

"Excuse me?"

Both women looked over at the seat across from Moset, where Lewis Zimmerman sat.

"Since this is obviously between the two of you, I wonder if I might be permitted to return to my lab? Like Doctor Moset, I can report no progress since the last staff meeting, and unlike him, I can admit it freely. I might, in fact, make better progress if I wasn't constantly being interrupted by staff meetings. So may I be excused to get back to work while you two try to kill each other?"

B'Elanna was torn between anger at the Terran's effrontery and admiration for his gall.

But before she could say anything, Kurak screamed and attacked with a surprisingly swift lunge that B'Elanna was barely able to parry with her gauntlets. Silently grateful that she had had the foresight to at least armor her wrists—the only part of her body that had such protection, which was more than Kurak had, an advantage B'Elanna planned to exploit—she pulled out her own *d'k tahg.* It was Miral's, originally, and was still identified with her House, but it lacked the symbol that would have indicated that Miral had a daughter. B'Elanna never knew why Miral had never made the addition—it wasn't as if she didn't acknowledge B'Elanna, and she had interceded on her daughter's behalf after Cestus III when the Alliance would have put B'Elanna to death, or worse—but it was simply the latest of her mother's personality traits that B'Elanna expected never to comprehend.

The first three slashes B'Elanna made were not ones she expected to strike, and indeed Kurak dodged them with ease. She was simply trying to get her bearings.

Kurak was laughing at her. "I've waited a long time to slay you, halfbreed."

"Words won't kill me, Kurak—and neither will you." B'Elanna

made an obvious lunge with her blade, which Kurak dodged in an equally obvious manner—one that left her right side open to a left roundhouse kick to her stomach that knocked her sideways and resulted in a crack of bone. B'Elanna immediately followed that up with a right kick to Kurak's face, and then stabbed downward with the *d'k tahg*.

However, Kurak managed to raise her arm to grab B'Elanna's wrist with her right hand before the blade struck, then slashed at B'Elanna's face with her own *d'k tahg*. B'Elanna dodged it by leaning her head back, then she head-butted the scientist, causing Kurak to let go of B'Elanna's wrist. Kurak then let loose with a side kick that send B'Elanna sprawling.

Both women clambered to their feet and faced each other. Kurak's right eye was covered in blood; the spiked soles of B'Elanna's boots had done their job well. Kurak was also breathing heavily and favoring her right side, the signs of at least a cracked rib.

B'Elanna remained unbruised and uncut. Until that desperate side kick, Kurak had been woefully unprepared for anything other than knife strikes during this duel, making the all-too-common mistake of thinking that a knife fight meant one fought *only* with knives. The first lesson Miral had taught her when her mother showed B'Elanna how to fight as a child was that the entire body was a weapon. A *bat'leth*, a *d'k tahg*, a *mek'leth*, a *tik'leth*, a disruptor, a ship's gunnery—all of those were simply tools to aid that weapon.

"I will *not* be killed by the likes of you!" Kurak screamed as she wiped the blood from her eye with her sleeve.

"You're as poor a prophet as you are a scientist," B'Elanna said as she feinted with a strike at her face, which Kurak raised her arms to block, then attempted a strike at Kurak's stomach, which the scientist managed to dodge.

Don't get overconfident. B'Elanna could hear Miral's voice. *They'll underestimate you because you're a halfbreed. Your weak crest and smooth nose will give that away immediately. But just because they don't expect you to have skill doesn't mean they won't.*

The fight continued for a time after that. B'Elanna could not judge how long, as she was completely caught up in the feints and blocks and strikes. Now that she knew how B'Elanna would play it, Kurak was careful not to leave herself open to a kick or punch.

Suddenly, Kurak sliced at B'Elanna's face with a speed and precision she hadn't shown, drawing blood at last. It trickled down B'Elanna's cheek into her mouth; she found the salty taste invigorating, and it gave her a desire to taste Kurak's. She deliberately slashed wild, leaving an opening that she hoped Kurak would take advantage of.

Kurak did, letting loose with another side kick that B'Elanna managed to roll with only because she was expecting it. *Like any good scientist, she observes the data and adjusts the hypothesis to compensate. A pity this lesson will do her no good.*

Stumbling to the ground, she reached with her left hand into the hidden compartment of her right gauntlet for her weapons. They were of Terran design, originally, called *churIQen,* and another gift from Miral, taken off a former lover who tried and failed to escape using the circular bladed weaponry of his ancestors. Miral killed the lover and kept the weapons.

As Kurak charged toward B'Elanna's prone form, B'Elanna grabbed three of the *churIQen* and flung them. They struck the scientist's belly with three squelchy *thunk*s. Kurak stumbled, then, and B'Elanna administered the final blow by stabbing her in the left eye, killing her instantly. True, the *churIQen* would have given Kurak the slow, agonizing death she deserved, but slow deaths meant one's opponent was still alive to try to kill you. B'Elanna preferred her foes to be deceased as quickly as possible.

Looking over at the table, B'Elanna saw that Moset looked horrified and frightened, and Zimmerman looked bored.

"Well," Zimmerman said with a roll of his eyes, "*that* was edifying."

Moset said, "That wasn't entirely fair, was it? You were to fight with daggers, not those other weapons."

B'Elanna grinned. "I'm alive. She's dead. You can't get any more fair than that." She bent down and yanked her *d'k tahg* out of Kurak's skull. Then, for good measure, she stepped on Kurak's head, smashing her face to a bloody smear on her spiked boot.

To the two Klingon guards who stood at the door, she said, "Dispose of this."

"Actually—" Zimmerman started, holding up a finger, then cut himself off and lowered his hand. "Never mind."

"Speak, Terran."

"It's nothing, Supervisor. I was *going* to suggest that I might be able to use her corpse for my own work, but stepping on her head like that likely means any cranial matter is so much mulch."

Zimmerman's project was an attempt to engineer telepathy in either Klingons or Cardassians, or even Terrans, thus far with no success. Any time someone died on Ardana, or anywhere nearby, Zimmerman had requested the corpse, as any brain gave him more material to work with. He had an entire shelf filled with jars containing brains suspended in a green liquid of some sort. B'Elanna had always found it rather disconcerting, especially given the stories Miral had told her about the conquest of Triskelion.

Aloud, she said simply, "I doubt *this* one's brain would have done you much good. Now return to your labs. We've seen precious little results out of this base, and we're likely to see less with her dead—not that I regret her passing, but she will be difficult to replace. Go!"

Moset couldn't leave the room fast enough and was gone in almost an instant. Zimmerman pushed his chair back slowly and sauntered out.

The two guards carried Kurak's corpse out the door, leaving B'Elanna alone in the meeting room. She took a long breath through her nose and then exhaled through her mouth, feeling better than she had in months.

In truth, better than I have since being exiled to this place.

She turned and retreated through the rear door to her office. Like all the spaces in the Monor Base building, it was unnecessarily large. It had a wooden desk, made of the still-common *gnari*-tree wood, but with decorative legs of the same design as the table in the meeting room; a small wooden chair that always put a crick in her back; two doors; and a huge window that took up an entire wall.

That last was its one good feature, as it provided the view. Stratos City was built among the clouds above Ardana. B'Elanna could see the planet from the magnificent view half a *qell'qam* above the surface. The Ardanans had built this place centuries earlier, the overseers living up here while the workers mined the zenite. When the planet was conquered by the Terran Empire, they kept the arrangement, except an imperial governor ruled from the cloud city rather than the Ardanan high adviser and council. Power returned temporarily to the Ardanan council during the brief, misbegotten reign of the Terran Republic, only to be taken forcibly by a Cardassian gul named Monor when the Alliance moved in.

By that time, there was very little zenite left. The Terrans had been efficient in bleeding the planet dry. Since they had an entire facility in the sky, the scientifically minded Monor had converted the building where the council did their business into a place for pure research. Thus was Monor Base born.

Once Monor died—of old age, in his bed, to B'Elanna's disgust—Ardana's importance dimmed accordingly. Its remoteness made it an ideal research base, but without Monor's support, it became a true backwater. The population shrank to a mere few thousand, and supervision of the base soon became a death assignment. It was the post you were given when you did something horribly wrong but you couldn't be killed due to mitigating circumstances. In B'Elanna's case, Cestus III went horribly wrong, and Miral's pleading on her behalf to the Regent provided the mitigation.

Pure research made B'Elanna's crest ache. But better here than dead. Dead warriors could not regain their honor.

And B'Elanna had quite a bit to regain.

The wheels had, of course, already been set in motion. She had several plans in place, some of which might fail, but at least one of which was bound to succeed, and then she would be back in a position of power.

Her personal comm beeped. *"Supervisor, this is Vralk."*

Vralk was one of the operations officers, an imbecilic young Klingon whose only skill lay in pushing buttons. "Yes?"

"The Bak'rikan *has entered the system, and Gul Evek is hailing you."*

"Put him through." Evek had already talked to her once, saying he was on his way to Ardana with "an interesting specimen" for Monor Base, though he could not divulge specifics over subspace. B'Elanna had doubted very much that the disgraced gul could make good on that promise, but she had no justification for turning him away, either. So she gave him permission to come. At worst, it would be a distraction. At best, it could provide her with another plan.

Evek's rectangular features appeared on the screen. She had read over his service record after he called the first time. A good career for many years, with many successful campaigns, until his first officer, a glinn named Seska, defected to the Terran Rebellion right under his nose. That was the other reason why B'Elanna was willing to listen to Evek—they had something in common.

Unbidden, she recalled the ruins of the capital city of Cestus III. The Terrans had called it Kirk City, after one of their ship captains; the Alliance had renamed it Gorkon City, after the Klingon Regent who forged the Alliance. One of the Terrans, an old woman who had been one of the biggest troublemakers in the mines, and was only alive because her quotas were always exceeded, had led B'Elanna and her guards into a trap, sacrificing herself so that the other Terrans could escape.

The old woman had survived the collapse of the administration building, as had B'Elanna, and the latter's final act as Intendant of Cestus III was to interrogate the old woman. Typically, she didn't break, finally dying without providing a morsel of information beyond her birth name, which B'Elanna didn't care about and had already forgotten, and the names of her comrades who had left Cestus in a stolen planet-hopper, a list B'Elanna already had.

She was recalled to Qo'noS, then, and brought before the Regent, who demoted her from Intendant to supervisor and assigned her here, where she spent her time being bored by scientists and keeping an ear out for information on a select list of Terrans, in the hope that someday she could take revenge.

"Supervisor, we are on approach to Ardana now. We should be in orbit in three hours."

Evek's voice startled B'Elanna out of her reverie. "So I've been told."

"With your permission, I will beam to Monor Base personally, along with my, ah, cargo. I will explain all then."

"Very well—you will be taken to my office in three hours. I look forward to meeting you," B'Elanna lied. Then she cut off the transmission, having no desire to talk to Evek any longer than necessary.

She rose from her chair, restless after her duel with Kurak and feeling the need to play with her favorite toy. It wouldn't do to meet with Evek while bursting with nervous energy. If she was to use him and his "cargo," whatever it was, she needed to be focused. Right now, her brain was going a *qelI'qam* a minute, thinking about Cestus III, Miral, the Regent's penetrating stare, Moset's whining, Kurak's pulped face, and the taste of her blood.

One of her office doors led to the meeting room, the other to a lift that she ordered to the lower levels of Monor Base. Most of the crew of the base lived elsewhere in Stratos—there was certainly plenty of room—so B'Elanna had taken over the entire bottom three levels of the building for her own amusement.

She arrived at the seventh of nine levels. Like most of the spaces in Monor Base that hadn't been converted to a different use, this level was all wide, twisting hallways, giant archways, and open spaces decorated with abstract art. B'Elanna went through the room with the Kang Chair, the one with the spiked slab, the one with the branding irons and the brazier, and the one with the snakepit, before arriving at her goal: the room with the rack, where her favorite was currently stretched out, asleep. Or passed out.

Either way, he was unconscious, which B'Elanna found unacceptable.

For several seconds, she simply stared at his prone form, arms up over his head, legs fully extended, bound at the wrists and ankles by Vulcan *ahn-woons*—not the purpose they were designed for, but B'Elanna saw no need to preserve Vulcan traditions. The device itself was of Terran design, and also was being used for a contrary purpose: it had been designed as a tool for punishment and for extracting confessions. The one history on the subject B'Elanna had read—a present from Miral when she was younger— had indicated that it was meant for interrogations, but B'Elanna knew better than to think that such a device would provide truthful answers. It was used to bend the will of the victim.

In the case of the rack's current occupant, that bending had already taken place. He was B'Elanna's, body and soul.

As she stared at his peaceful face, B'Elanna cursed her mother. She had many reasons to resent Miral, not least being her very existence as a halfbreed in a galaxy that did not appreciate such things.

Today, though, she particularly resented her mother for passing on her proclivity for Terrans.

B'Elanna simply couldn't help it. Ridged faces repulsed her on a physical level. With day-to-day dealings, she was fine, but when it came to her bedchamber, she could not bear to touch or kiss or bite a face unless it was smooth. That left out many of the galaxy's species, including the two that made up the Alliance.

Just like Miral, B'Elanna found she preferred Terrans for their combination of smoothness and enthusiasm.

Her favorite was particularly energetic. He had sandy hair, a long face, and eyes as blue as the sky. She had had many lovers, of course, but she always came back to this one long after others had been discarded.

She backhanded him across the face.

"Huh—? Wha—?" He looked back and forth, straining against his bonds for a moment before realizing where he was. He looked at B'Elanna and said in Klingon, "Oh—sorry. Guess I fell asleep." He smiled up at her, his blue eyes twinkling. "What's on the menu for today, mistress?"

B'Elanna smiled. That was what she liked to hear. Another reason why this one was her favorite was because he was so eager to please.

She looked up and down his naked body. While she liked a smooth face, she had less concern for the rest of the body, and his was covered with scars, bruises, and many brands.

His right calf, though, was mostly untouched.

Undoing the four *ahn-woon*s, she said, "Come with me." He got to his feet, stumbling slightly as his legs had to adjust to supporting his weight again. "Move!" she snapped, and he hobbled through the doorway, past the snakepit, and into the next room, the one with the branding irons and brazier. The latter cast a warm glow from the rocks that were perpetually kept alight. Only one slave charged with maintaining it had been foolish enough to let the rocks cool enough to stop glowing, and she was left to lie in the brazier for three days. It had then taken two more slaves several days to scrape the melted flesh and bone off the brazier's bowl.

To her favorite, B'Elanna said, "Heat it."

"Which one?" There were six of them, each in the shape of a different Klingon character.

B'Elanna pondered for a moment, then said, "You told me once that you had a name when you were a boy. What was it?"

He hesitated.

She smiled. Another reason she liked this one was that he never made a mistake twice. "This once, I won't punish you for using your name."

"Thomas, mistress."

"*tlhomaS*." B'Elanna rolled the word around in her mouth. "I don't like it."

"I'm sorry, mistress."

"You should be." She picked the brand that had the character for the *tlh* sound, which was the closest Klingon equivalent to the first sound of her favorite's offensive name. Removing it from the metal wireframe holder, she handed it to him. "Heat this one. You will wear it on your left thigh."

"Whatever you say," he said, taking the brand and going to the brazier. With a practiced hand, he placed the brand into the brazier, holding it far enough up the handle to keep it from hurting his own hand. Sometimes, B'Elanna instructed him to hold it closer to the brand, but she wanted his hands unblistered today. True, they only had three hours, but her favorite was rather good with his hands, and B'Elanna decided she was in the mood to be physically handled.

She removed her gauntlets and then the rest of her clothes while the brand heated up. He finished at the same time that she did, and he calmly walked over to hand her the brand.

Taking the brand, she shivered with anticipation.

6

The rest of Chakotay's day had not been a pleasant one. He brought the raided supplies to O'Brien, only to have to listen to Smiley complain that what he'd brought wasn't what he needed, that it was the wrong model of plasma manifold, that the duranium was entirely the wrong thickness, and then suddenly say, "Never mind, never mind," and casually dismiss Chakotay.

"You're welcome," Chakotay said snidely, and left O'Brien to his tinkering.

He checked the cell to make sure Neelix wasn't in it—he wasn't, but Harry and Annika were, in a position that Chakotay had been trying and failing to get Kate to try for months. To his amusement, while Annika's face was flushed and suffused with pleasure, Harry's face retained the same stoic, unchanging expression it always had.

Quickly taking his leave, Chakotay went to the cavern that served as a mess hall. Neelix was sitting alone, and Chakotay felt the need to check on the alien, so he sat across from him and inquired after his state of mind. Neelix immediately began pestering him with a dozen questions, all of which Chakotay felt dutybound to answer. After all, he had offered Neelix their hospitality, and the poor bastard *was* marooned thousands of light-years from home, so Chakotay could hardly refuse to help him—

—at first. Chakotay considered himself a patient individual. He hadn't made his escape from Drema IV for almost a year after Sekaya's death because he was willing to wait for the right moment. But after enduring an hour filled with endless political

questions, numerous descriptions of Kes that bordered on the ha-
giographic, a lengthy treatise on the Haakonian-Talaxian war, and
the recipe for something called *darvot* fritters, his patience was
at an end, and he suddenly and impolitely excused himself. He
promised himself as he all but ran out of the mess hall that he
would apologize later.

Retreating to the small cavern that he and Kate shared, he saw
that Kate was already on their pallet, fast asleep. Not bothering
to undress—one learned quickly in the mines that one may be
woken up at a moment's notice and not given sufficient time to
dress, so you'd best be dressed already, and that was a hard habit
to break—Chakotay clambered into the pallet next to Kate.

"Oh, good, you're here," Kate said.

Chakotay cursed to himself—he was usually quiet enough to
allow her to continue sleeping. "Sorry." *I must really be tired.*

"That's all right, I wanted to talk to you anyhow, so it's just as
well you lumbered in here like a *targ.*"

A response died on Chakotay's lips. After Smiley and Neelix,
he didn't need this, and didn't have the energy to start an argument. He lay on his side, back to Kate. "Whatever it is can wait
until morning."

"No, it can't."

Closing his eyes and counting to ten in his head, Chakotay
said, "It'll have to. I'm going to sleep."

A foot collided with the small of his back. "Like hell you are.
We're going to talk, and we're going to do it now, since you were
the one who woke *me* up. I would've been happy to wait until
morning, but now it'll take me at least half an hour to get back to
sleep, so I may as well get this over with."

Surrendering to the inevitable, Chakotay rolled over to his
other side so he faced Kate. *Damn, she's beautiful.* Those penetrating eyes, that proud nose, that firm mouth, those sharp cheekbones. She was a perfect physical specimen.

"Are you listening to me, Chuckles? This is important."

If only we could do something about the personality. But no, that wasn't fair. The physical beauty was nice, but it was as much her fire that Chakotay was attracted to as her physical form. If he just wanted someone with good looks and no personality, he could make a play for that Jadzia woman that Sisko used to dally with. As it was, he was content to let that idiot Bashir have her. Chakotay preferred his women to have substance.

"Yes," he said, "I'm listening for as long as I can keep my eyes open."

"I was talking with Tuvok earlier."

That surprised Chakotay. Kate had never had much use for the Vulcan in the past. "What about?"

"Neelix's woman. He thinks we should try to rescue her, and I agree."

Chakotay blinked. "You do? Why? For that matter, why does *he* think so?"

"He said she has psionic potential."

"More than 'potential.' Neelix said she wiped out an entire settlement of aliens. Kizon, or something like that."

Kate sat up about halfway, supporting herself with her right arm. "Can we really afford to let something like that fall into Alliance hands?"

"Little late for that, Kate—she's already in Alliance hands."

"Then we need to get her back." She sat upright.

Chakotay sighed. "Look, I agree that the Alliance having access to a telepath is bad for us. And I admit, I feel sorry for Neelix." Chakotay shook his head, amazed he actually said that after the way he had spent the last hour. "I can only imagine what it would be like to be stuck thousands of light-years from home—and to have your lover taken on top of that. But I don't see what we can do about it."

"We rescued Jennifer from Terok Nor, we can do this."

Now Chakotay, having given up on his admittedly unlikely plan of falling asleep while Kate was haranguing him, sat up next to her. "That was different. We knew where Jennifer was, and we had that other Sisko. But we don't know where Kes is." He cupped Kate's face in his hand. "I'm sorry, Kate, but until we know *where* she is, the whole question is moot."

"We know where Evek *probably* went."

Chakotay shook his head. "We didn't get a solid enough fix on him when he left the Badlands. He could have gone to either of two Alliance bases—or somewhere else altogether. We just don't know."

Kate started to say something, then stopped. "I guess you're right." She let out a long breath. "But I want to *do* something. Raiding parties for Smiley's toy ship are all well and good, but stealing a telepath out from under the Alliance's nose . . ."

Nodding, Chakotay said, "I know, believe me. I bet Seska would especially like to take her away from Evek. But unless we find out *where* she is, we're stuck." Then he grinned. "But if you're looking for something to do . . ."

At that, Kate shook her head. "You're impossible." But she leaned in to kiss him.

The next morning, Chakotay woke up to find the pallet empty. That was hardly unusual—Kate was an early riser, and liked to spend her mornings guzzling coffee and tinkering with *Geronimo*. (Sisko had managed to find a supply of coffee—the real stuff, not that *raktajino* swill the Klingons preferred—and that supply line had survived the captain's death, to Kate's oft-expressed relief.)

After Chakotay splashed some brackish water from the basin onto his face, he flipped aside the tarp that separated his and Kate's private area from the rest of the base. As he exited, he found Seska walking toward him holding a padd.

"Good, you're up. I've put the word out."

Confused, Chakotay asked, "What word?"

"About Kes. I still have some contacts in the Alliance, after all, so I should be able to find her."

Chakotay fixed the Cardassian woman with an irritated glance. "I thought you'd decided Neelix was a spy."

"I was *concerned* that he was a spy, but I'm convinced he isn't now." She started making notes on her padd.

"What convinced you?"

She shrugged. "A number of things. Tuvok and I spoke about it a bit this morning, and he feels the evidence in support of Neelix's story is pretty strong. But mostly that Kes is too valuable a commodity for the Alliance. If we let those Klingon butchers get their hands on a telepath, it'll all be over."

With an effort, Chakotay restrained himself from pointing out that the Cardassians were going to make just as much use of Kes, if they could, but he had long ago realized the futility of challenging that blind spot. Seska always argued whenever they struck a Cardassian target, and felt that the primary sin of the Alliance was that Klingons were involved, and if they could just get rid of *them,* Cardassia would be restored to glory.

The exception was Evek, of course, for whom Seska's animus was frighteningly extreme.

"Also," she added, "Harry talked to him."

Fury started to boil inside Chakotay's gut. "I specifically said—"

Quickly, Seska said, "Harry didn't interrogate him, they just talked, and it was at my request. He has a good sense of when someone's telling the truth, and I wanted to gauge his feelings on it."

Angrily, Chakotay said, "Kim is not yours to order, Seska, understand? If you ever do an end run around me again like that, I'll make you regret you were ever born."

Seska sneered. "Don't pull that on me, Terran—you need me."

"Only as long as you follow my orders. If you can't, then you're useless to me, and I tend to kill things that are useless to me. Understood?"

After staring at him defiantly for several seconds, she finally nodded.

"Good. What did Harry ask him?"

Shrugging, Seska said, "Some simple questions, and some trick ones. Harry thought he was telling the truth. And he also said he'd know for sure if you'd let him loose."

"Right now," Chakotay said in a hard voice, "the only person I'm inclined to let him loose on is you. There are a lot of people who'd be perfectly happy to shoot you on sight, Seska, just because of what you look like. And right now I'm one of them. So don't tempt any of us."

With that, he angrily turned on his heel and walked away. He needed to find a certain Vulcan.

He found Tuvok in the mess hall, opening one of the ration packs they'd stolen from a raid on a derelict *K'Vort*-class ship they'd found in the Badlands. There had been very little that Tuvok would eat in those packs, as he had at least made an effort to conform to the ancient Vulcan tradition of vegetarianism, but practical reality had made that particular stricture a difficult one to maintain of late.

Not that Chakotay gave a damn. He sat across from the Vulcan just as Tuvok dabbed some of the purple paste that was in the pack on his finger. "May I help you, Captain?"

"Yes, actually—you can stop going behind my back."

To his credit, Tuvok did not equivocate. "My apologies, but I felt it was necessary to garner support among the remainder of the *Geronimo* crew before approaching you with the necessity of rescuing Mister Neelix's paramour."

Smiling wryly, Chakotay asked, "So should I expect Annika to be pleading with me next?"

"No. I do not feel that Ms. Hansen possesses enough interest in the particulars of the rebellion to be worth the attempt to gain her support."

Chakotay silently agreed. Annika was all sass and smarts, but didn't question very much. The real surprise was that she was part of the rebellion in the first place.

"Look, I don't disagree with you, Tuvok. But we have one big problem. We—"

"—do not know her current location. Yes, that is true. However, Ms. Seska is currently inquiring among her remaining contacts, and—"

"—and she's found something."

Chakotay turned to see Seska entering the mess hall and making a beeline for their table. "You've found something?" he asked.

She gave Chakotay a dirty look, then regarded Tuvok. "I just got a squib from a friend of mine who runs one of the comm relays in the Chin'toka system. He's picked up comm traffic between the *Bak'rikan* and Ardana."

Tuvok's eyebrow climbed his forehead. "Indeed?"

"I don't get it," Chakotay said with a frown. "Ardana's a barren rock now. They squeezed that place dry of zenite, what, fifty years ago?"

"Fifty-one-point-nine," Tuvok said. "However, in recent times, the Alliance has repurposed the city of Stratos on that world to serve as a base for scientific research."

Still looking only at Tuvok, Seska said, "Last I heard, they had just put some Klingon-Terran halfbreed in charge."

That got Chakotay to sit up on the bench. "That halfbreed wouldn't be named B'Elanna?"

Now, finally, Seska turned back to Chakotay. "I think so, yes. You know her?"

"By reputation, from Harry and Kate. She was the Intendant of Cestus III when those two escaped. They dropped a building on her head, but we've heard rumors that she survived that. I'm amazed she survived the Alliance, though."

Seska snorted. "If she made it as far as an Intendant as a halfbreed, whichever of her parents is the Klingon must be *very* influential for her to even survive to adulthood, so she probably had someone scratching her back with the Regent." She shook her head. "Anyhow, it doesn't matter. That's where Evek went right after he left the Badlands, breaking a rendezvous with Gul Jasad at Elvok Nor."

Chakotay rubbed his chin. "He must know what he has."

Tuvok said, "If the *Bak'rikan* is headed for Ardana, it's possible that Gul Evek wishes to verify the alien woman's telepathy before turning her over to the Alliance. Complete testing for such abilities is beyond the purview of a ship of the *Bak'rikan*'s class."

"Evek and Jasad hate each other," Seska added. "Evek wouldn't want to risk Jasad taking credit."

Nodding, Chakotay said, "All right, I'm convinced. We'll go get her. But we'll need everything you can give us on Ardana."

Seska got up. "Whatever you say, Captain," she said with a sneer, and departed.

Again, Tuvok's eyebrow rose. "I take it that you and Ms. Seska had a disagreement?"

"Something like that." Chakotay rose. "Next time, Vulcan, just tell me what you want. I'm sick of people going behind my back."

"Again, Captain, my apologies. It will not happen again."

7

A *telepath?* You're sure?"
 Evek ground his teeth. He stood across from Supervisor B'Elanna alongside Doctor B'Oraq. The halfbreed's hideous face—a mixture of the worst elements of her Terran and Klingon heritage—was framed by a glorious view of the planet Ardana that Evek would have been in much better condition to appreciate without the dispiriting effect of the supervisor's presence. He had beamed down to Monor Base from the *Bak'rikan* with the doctor because B'Oraq had claimed friendship with the supervisor.

"No," B'Oraq said, tugging on her braid, "we're not. That's why I recommended we come here. The equipment we have on the *Bak'rikan* can only prove that there is the *potential* for telepathy. But I knew you were doing experiments in that regard—and you'd almost *have* to have better diagnostics than we do." The latter was said while leaning forward with an almost conspiratorial tone.

B'Elanna laughed, a sound that made Evek's spine ache. "Understandable. But I'm not sure why you came to me, as opposed to one of the closer bases. There are at least two facilities closer to the Badlands than Ardana."

Evek stepped in. "The doctor told me much of your work here. For so important a matter as this, I thought it prudent to make the most accurate determination possible."

Nodding thoughtfully—though Evek doubted her mind to be all *that* full of thought—B'Elanna said, "I see. Very well, have the specimen beamed to Laboratory 3. That's where Doctor Zimmerman is working."

That didn't sound right to Evek. "Zimmerman sounds like no Klingon or Cardassian name of which I am aware."

"No reason why it should," B'Elanna said with a smile. "Doctor Zimmerman is a Terran—and also is the one who's made the most progress in developing telepaths of anyone in the Alliance."

Glaring at his doctor, Evek started to seriously doubt the efficacy of this plan. "Supervisor," he said, trying to give B'Elanna as bland a look as he could in order to conceal his growing disgust, "I would prefer it if a Klingon or Cardassian performed the examination." That was half a lie—he trusted Klingon scientists even less than Terran ones, since the latter were motivated to perform well by the alternative of the mines being dangled before them. But he felt he should play to his audience, as it were.

"I'm sure you would, Gul Evek. I'm sure you'd also prefer that Glinn Seska was still your first officer instead of gallivanting around the Badlands with the rebellion. Sadly, we live in an imperfect galaxy, so you'll just have to settle for Zimmerman."

Before Evek could respond to that, B'Oraq said, "I'm sure he's the right man for the job, B'Elanna, thank you."

"Of course. And I'm willing to overlook the breach in protocol for your sake, Doctor. You did my mother a great service, and that's not something I forget."

That got Evek's attention. B'Oraq had only said that they were old friends.

B'Oraq offered an inclination of her head. "It was my pleasure, Supervisor. Your mother is a great woman, and so dishonorable a death would have diminished the Alliance."

"Yes." B'Elanna rose. "Very well. Have the specimen transported. Doctor, you will meet me for supper tonight—we'll catch up."

"I would like that very much," B'Oraq said with another inclination.

"You're both dismissed."

Evek ground his teeth some more at that. He was a gul in the Alliance fleet, not some toady to be "dismissed." But he wisely said nothing. For all this woman's bluster, she was still Evek's best shot at redemption—or rather, this Zimmerman person was. *Still, better either of them than Jasad. . . .*

Turning on his heel, Evek departed B'Elanna's office and headed straight for the transporter platform, neither knowing nor caring if B'Oraq followed him or not.

"They think she's a telepath?"

B'Elanna found herself once again torn between admiring Zimmerman's effrontery and wanting to stab him in the eye for it. "They're not sure. Doctor B'Oraq found elevated levels of something or other in her brain that indicated the possibility, but that was as far as her own testing facilities could go."

"Where'd they find this woman, anyhow?"

"In the Badlands, while chasing a rebellion ship."

"What's a telepath doing in the Badlands, of all places?"

"I don't know," B'Elanna said slowly. "Possibly the rebellion found her, in which case it behooves us to learn the truth. Or, rather, behooves *you*. I want a full workup on the alien by this time tomorrow."

"What about—?"

"Nothing else matters," she said emphatically before the Terran could start whining about whichever of his tiresome projects was at a "critical stage." Scientists always said that whenever you interrupted them, and she was well and truly sick of it.

"Very well, Supervisor," Zimmerman said in a put-upon tone.

"Out." B'Elanna closed the communication.

Letting out a long breath, she turned her chair around and looked out over Ardana. Even fewer lived on the surface than in the cloud city. A few small townships, shadows of their former selves, dotted the landscape. The towns somehow managed to sustain themselves and pay their taxes, so the Alliance left them alone. At least one township thrived on gambling and rest facilities that were used by the remaining citizenry of Stratos when they felt the need to have a planet beneath their feet but couldn't afford to travel offworld. B'Elanna had never made use of those facilities herself. Rank had its privileges, after all, and if she wanted to rest or relax, she had levels seven, eight, and nine of Monor Base.

She leaned back and closed her eyes, thinking back on the pleasure her favorite Terran's screams provided her—a pleasure that increased a hundredfold when she felt his sweat-drenched hands on her naked body. He was always best at pleasing her, and she knew that she would keep him forever.

Her fond recollection was interrupted by a communiqué coming in. She prepared to give Vralk a tongue-lashing for interrupting her when she realized that it was on her private line, the one that bypassed operations. Only two people in the galaxy ever used that channel. One was the Regent—or one of his underlings—who had direct access to *any* communications console in the Alliance. The other was her mother.

B'Elanna wasn't sure which option she preferred less.

Activating the comm on her end, she saw the screen on her wall light up with the perpetually scowling face of Miral. *"Greetings, Daughter."*

"Mother," B'Elanna said with a mixture of relief and apprehension. "To what do I owe this honor?"

"Several things, actually. First of all, why have I received notice that you have requested a replacement scientist?"

Sighing, B'Elanna thought sourly, *Bad news travels quickly, it seems.* "Kurak is dead."

"How? What happened?"

"She challenged me; she lost."

Sounding dubious, Miral repeated, *"She* challenged *you?"*

B'Elanna leaned forward. "I am not a liar, Mother."

"Of course you are, Daughter, don't be foolish."

"There were witnesses, Mother," B'Elanna said tightly, "including Moset." B'Elanna knew that Miral would not trust the word of one of B'Elanna's Klingon guards or of a Terran—while she'd accept many a Terran into her bed, she'd not trust one's word, not entirely without reason—but Moset was a respected Cardassian scientist, and his word would carry weight with her.

"Very well. In any event, I also have news: I've been promoted. The Regent has generously granted me the post of Intendant of Earth."

For three seconds, B'Elanna's mouth moved, but words would not form. This was a most unexpected piece of news. "You're leaving Qo'noS?"

Miral nodded. *"Apparently, the Regent feels that B'Etor would be more useful to him on the homeworld."*

"More useful? I wasn't aware the Regent's private life was now fodder for euphemism."

At that, Miral laughed. *"Indeed. In truth, I do not know if Worf is taking B'Etor back to his bed. The relations between the House of Mogh and the House of Duras have always been . . . tumultuous."*

"To say the least." B'Elanna had heard rumors that the Regent himself fancied Miral. But Miral hadn't slept with a Klingon in years, and B'Elanna doubted her mother would start now, even if it was with the Regent. She was simply too much a slave to her passions.

Thinking of the lower levels, she added to herself, *A problem I can sympathize with.*

In any case, it was quite likely that the Regent grew tired of Miral's lack of response, and so re-fired the urge in his loins for the sister of Duras, who had been his bedmate for years before she was "promoted" to Intendant of Earth, a change in position that everyone assumed to be due to B'Etor's inability to provide the Regent with a son.

If Mother is being exiled to Earth, she may be less of an asset than she once was. Now Evek and B'Oraq's stumbling on that alien woman was even more fortuitous. *It is long past time I made my own way.*

Speaking of whom . . . "By the way, Mother, we have guests on Ardana, and one of them is an old friend."

"Oh?"

"The *Bak'rikan* has pulled into orbit with some specimen they want us to examine," she said dismissively. If Miral was no longer on Qo'noS, her usefulness was reduced, and therefore B'Elanna had little to gain by sharing news of Evek's prize with her. Besides, like Evek, she didn't want knowledge of it to spread until they had confirmation that she was everything B'Oraq hoped she was. "That vessel's head doctor is B'Oraq."

At that, Miral's face brightened. *"B'Oraq! How is she faring?"*

"She's assigned to a Cardassian ship, so probably not all that well. Worse, she's assigned to Evek."

"The traitor himself. How ignominious. I should have a word with General Martok, see about having her reassigned. The woman who saved my life deserves better than to serve with that petaQ *Evek."*

B'Elanna said nothing. Seven years earlier, when both Miral and B'Oraq had been on Cestus III, Miral had fallen ill. None of the physicians on Cestus—all Cardassians—could find a cure. It was B'Oraq who had found a treatment, one that boosted Miral's own immune system enough for her to fight off the illness herself.

When she later heard of B'Oraq's assignment to the *Bak'rikan,* B'Elanna often wondered if it was because B'Oraq had embarrassed so many Cardassian doctors, at least one of whom was brother to a legate, that her requests to be posted to a Klingon base or ship were denied, instead being dumped onto the traitor's vessel.

Not that it mattered. B'Oraq had saved Miral's life. That put her in B'Elanna's mother's debt, a debt the physician no doubt was calling in now to help her and her Cardassian master regain some lost prominence.

"Well, I must be off, Daughter," Miral said. *"I will be leaving for Earth on the* Negh'Var *tomorrow morning."*

"Quite an escort," B'Elanna said. The *Negh'Var* was among the cream of the Klingon fleet.

"Indeed. Good-bye, Daughter. Give my regards to Doctor B'Oraq."

With that, Miral's face faded from the screen.

"I will, Mother," B'Elanna said quietly, then rose and headed for the lift, ordering it to level seven. She suddenly found herself full of nervous tension she wanted to work off before supper.

★ ★ ★

"Where is the entrance to the Ocampa city?"

Kabor kneels in front of her, smiling as he uses the metal tool to shatter the bones in her fingers even as Jabin asks the same question he always asks, the one that she never answers.

"Don't worry, my love, I'll get you out of here somehow. Just be patient."

Neelix stealing a moment with her behind the Kazon-Ogla's back, promising a rescue she fears will never come.

"Those are just stories, Kes, legends told of a time that never existed."

The Ocampan elders think that being over eight years old somehow gives them wisdom, yet they refuse to question any of the assumptions about the Ocampa that had accreted over the decades.

"Where is the entrance to the Ocampa city?"

Jabin keeps asking the question.

Kes keeps refusing to answer.

The pain never ceases, agony piling on agony.

"Where is the entrance to the Ocampa city?"

She keeps thinking they have run out of ways to hurt her. They keep proving her wrong.

"Where is the entrance to the Ocampa city?"

Stop hurting me! Stop the pain, please, I'll do anything!

"Where is the entrance to the Ocampa city?"

Kabor applies a piece of metal to her head.

"Where is the entrance to the Ocampa city?"

The pain is blinding.

"Where is the entrance to the Ocampa city?"

Kabor goes to the next highest setting. The pain is worse.

"Where is the entrance to the Ocampa city?"

"You'll never know!"

Kes screamed as she remembered the thoughts of all the Kazon-Ogla as they died. Some plotted revenge or mutiny against Jabin. Some thought about their next meal. One thought about a painting he'd left unfinished back home. Another wondered about the fate of his son.

None of them expected to die. Nor had Kes expected to kill them.

"Interesting."

Opening her eyes, Kes saw a strange alien-looking man standing over her. Only then did she realize that she was lying down, and that she couldn't move. She saw no restraints—she appeared to be lying flat on a bed of some kind—but every attempt to move was met with overwhelming resistance.

The man standing over her could have been Ocampa, if not for the lack of hair on his crown and his peculiar ears. Her experience of aliens was limited to the Kazon and the Talaxians—neither of them looked as much like the Ocampa as this man did.

She tried to speak, but only a croak escaped her lips.

"You must be parched," the man said. He stood between the bed and a console of some kind. Turning, he pressed a control. With a whirr of machinery, something lowered toward Kes. It had a nozzle at the end, and it squirted water into her mouth.

Coughing as the water forced its way down her throat, Kes wondered where she was. She knew that water was at a premium on most worlds in this area of space. *Whoever my captors are, they must be very wealthy.*

After she finished coughing, and swallowed all the water, the nozzle whirred back up to wherever it had come from.

"Where am I? Where's Neelix?" she asked, her voice a croaking shadow of what it should have been.

"You are in Laboratory 3 of Monor Base—the foremost scientific think tank in the Klingon-Cardassian Alliance. At least, that's what they claim." The first sentence had been spoken as if he was reciting a lesson learned by rote. The second had been laced with what Kes interpreted as sarcasm or contempt—or both. "My name," the man continued, "is Lewis Zimmerman, and I'm a Terran. The fact that I can give you my name rather than a number is a testament to my considerable genius, which is being put to use in this think tank. Right now, my job is to find a way to create telepaths. So who should drop on my doorstep but you? You call yourself Kes, correct?"

That brought Kes up short. The last thing she remembered was being in the escape pod from Neelix's ship. She recalled no conversations with this Luisimurman person. "How did you know that?"

Luisimurman started pressing more controls on the console. "I'm a *scientist*—it's my *job* to know things that are hidden to most. I know that this Neelix person you queried me about is the love of your life." He looked back at her. "Such a *charming* notion." Turning back to the console, he went on: "What confuses me is that you claim to be from a world and a species that I do not recognize— and neither does the computer, which pays more attention to the comings and goings of aliens than I. It doesn't know who the Ocampa, the Kazon, the Talaxians, or the Haakonians are, either." He turned to stare down at her, his arms now folded. "Where do you come from, Kes of the Ocampa?"

"You've answered that question," she said. "I'm from Ocampa. I'm afraid that's all I can tell you."

Shaking his head, Luisimurman said, "No, you see, that's just not good enough. Now, I was able to extract this information thanks to this little gadget of mine." He pointed at a piece of machinery that sat on the other side of the bed. Kes hadn't noticed it before, but she had been focused on Luisimurman, noting the differences between him and a typical Ocampa. She wondered where Terrans came from, and if they were perhaps related to the Ocampa in the distant past. The tendency to lose hair and the strange ears could, perhaps, be explained by differences in environment. . . .

She forced herself back to the present. While Luisimurman didn't have the Kazon-Ogla's overt cruelty, he was also holding Kes against her will. She doubted his intentons were any more honorable than Jabin's.

"This is my own variation on a Klingon mind-sifter." Luisimurman shook his head again. "Barbarians, the Klingons. Their version is almost appallingly crude, and generally leaves the subject in a vegetative state. What, I ask, is the point in *that*? A waste of material." The Terran seemed lost in thought for a moment, then shook his head quickly. "Anyhow, that's neither here nor there. I was able to use it to probe your memories. It also was able to penetrate your psionic shields, which alone gives me a very important piece of information, to wit, that you *have* psionic shields. You are, indeed, a telepath."

Suddenly, Kes realized what was missing. For weeks, she had been in the company of the Kazon-Ogla, as well as Neelix, and as time went on, she sensed more and more of their thoughts. When she killed Jabin and his people, she knew what each of them had in their minds at the moment of death.

But I'm not hearing anything now. Is Luisimurman immune somehow?

"Luckily for my own peace of mind, I was able to use a psi-inhibitor on myself." He frowned. "At least, I think I did. The only tests I could run were to make sure there weren't any harmful side effects. Since there *are* no telepaths extant, I have no way of knowing if it truly blocks my thoughts from your ability to read them." He took a breath. "Still, it should keep my head off limits to your prying."

That explains that, then. Kes still knew very little. She was obviously a long way from home. *The Caretaker must have sent us far away to keep us out of Kazon hands.* It made sense—the Caretaker had been looking out for the needs of the Ocampa for many generations. He must have done the same for her when the Kazon was in pursuit.

Aloud, she continued to say nothing. She saw no reason to do anything to help this man—any more than there had been reason to help Jabin.

"Now that we've established for sure that you *are* a telepath," Luisimurman said as he walked over to the console again, "we need to run some tests. Of course, you need to be conscious for those, which is why I woke you up in the first place. First things first—testing your pain response."

"Aaaaaauuuuuuuuuuuuuuuuggggggggggghhhhhhhhhh!" It was Kabor all over again as every nerve ending in Kes's body suddenly felt as if it were on fire. She screamed and screamed and screamed until her throat was raw, and then she screamed some more, wishing it would stop, stop, *stop, STOP!*

And then it did.

"Interesting." Luisimurman hadn't touched any of his controls until after he said that word. Then he did, and a humming that Kes hadn't noticed stopped. "You were able to block the pain when it got to be too much. Also some impressive fortitude—any Terran or Cardassian would have fallen unconscious from that much pain, and some Klingons might've as well."

Kes did not explain that she had quite recently suffered far worse at the hands of the Kazon-Ogla.

"So, we'll have to see how far that goes. Let's try the second level."

Steeling herself, Kes prepared for more pain. *I resisted Kabor, you monster, I can resist you, too. . . .*

"Uh, sir? We've got Monor Base—the supervisor."

The communications officer spoke those words to Evek as soon as he entered the bridge, Doctor B'Oraq alongside him, blathering on about the chief engineer being sick with something. Evek would have been more interested if the engineer in question wasn't an insubordinate *tralk*. As it was, Evek was simply glad that the glinn was suffering.

Evek was equally glad to be hearing from the halfbreed. For one thing, it meant B'Oraq would shut up. More importantly, though, it meant that a determination had been made regarding the alien woman—no other news was likely to prompt her to call him.

"Put her on-screen."

The main viewer shifted from a vista of Ardana from orbital heights to the ugly face of Supervisor B'Elanna. *"Gul Evek, Doctor B'Oraq—I'm afraid I have some bad news."*

A pit opened in Evek's stomach. He turned angrily on B'Oraq. "Damn you, woman, you—"

"The alien woman is a telepath."

For a moment, Evek stood there with his mouth open. Then he turned back to the viewer. "How, precisely, is that bad news, Supervisor?"

"Oh, it's good news for me, Evek. You see, the woman—her name is Kes, by the way—Kes is quite a powerful telepath. Doctor Zimmerman did several comprehensive tests."

Evek turned around so he could sit in his command chair. "I still fail to see how this qualifies as bad news. With this Kes woman, we—"

"We? Oh, you are *presumptuous, Evek. There is no 'we.' There is you—who violated Alliance regulations."*

Evek straightened in his command chair. "Violated? I did no such—"

"Alliance procedure calls for Command to be notified immediately *if a potential telepath is detected. That has been a standing order for as long as the Alliance has been in existence. Do you know what the punishment is for violating Alliance procedure?"*

At sensor control, a glinn whose name Evek had never cared enough to learn said, "Sir, we're being targeted by weapons on the surface of Ardana."

The pit opened wider. "You wouldn't—"

"Wouldn't what?" B'Elanna asked in a sweet voice.

B'Oraq stepped forward. "Supervisor, I can explain this. Perhaps when we dine tonight, we—"

"We won't be dining tonight, Doctor. Don't you know the Klingon code of not drinking with the enemy? I don't eat with one, either."

That caused the doctor to recoil as if she'd been slapped. "I am not your enemy, Supervisor!"

"You cured my mother of a poison that I administered at great personal expense. Years of work undone by your treachery! For that, you deserve to die. As for you, Evek—no one will miss you or your crew. You're a traitor captaining a ship of incompetents."

Evek finally found his voice. "Helm, take us out of orbit, evasive action!"

B'Elanna simply laughed at that.

The glinn at sensor control said, "Sir, energy readings on the surface are consistent with a nadion-pulse cannon. It's firing—impact in ten seconds."

"Go to warp, *now!*"

"Sir, we can't this close to a gravity well," the helm officer said. "The risk—"

Pounding the arm of his chair, Evek cried, "I don't give a *damn* about the risk, we need to get out of here! Deactivate safeties! Go to warp before—"

Evek didn't live long enough to finish the sentence.

B'Elanna smiled as the transmission from the *Bak'rikan* was cut off at the source, along with the *Bak'rikan* itself. The view on her screen switched to that of a vessel exploding in orbit. She imagined the agonized screams of Evek and B'Oraq as they were incinerated, knowing as they died painfully that all their carefully laid plans were for naught.

The nadion-pulse cannons had been even more expensive than the poisoning of Miral had been. Luckily, B'Elanna's *petaQ* of a mother convinced Command to keep her at an Intendant's pay scale even though she was demoted to supervisor, so she was able to accumulate the necessary funds. *It's not as if I have much of anything else to spend them on here. . . .*

She went into the computer and erased all traces of her last transmission to the *Bak'rikan.* If nothing else, she had incriminated herself, and she didn't particularly want evidence of that in the computer. *But I couldn't resist letting that* toDSaH *B'Oraq know just how close our "friendship" really was.*

Opportunities to kill her mother were few and far between, and with Miral now assigned to Earth—assuming she lived that long, and that the Regent's "promotion" wasn't simply a cover for him to do to her what B'Elanna longed to do—it would be even more difficult.

But Miral needed to pay. She had brought B'Elanna into this miserable universe, and then conspired to keep her alive in it, even though she had no place. That required punishment.

For today, though, it was enough that the woman who had saved Miral's life paid for it.

Best of all, she thought with a happy smile, *I have my very own telepath. If Zimmerman can train the little girl, perhaps I can take my revenge on Miral after all—once I've had the alien "convince" the Regent to abdicate and make me ruler of the Alliance. . . .*

8

"What is *taking* so long?"

Chakotay was beginning to regret providing Neelix with access to *Geronimo*'s flight deck. Then again, there weren't too many alternatives. Most of the ship's space was taken up by cargo and engines. The barracks were a corridor with hammocks strung up, the galley was set in one of the corridor walls, and the mess hall was wherever you happened to be sitting or—more likely—standing when you ate. The only places to send Neelix were the engine room—which wasn't going to happen, not if Chakotay ever wanted to have sex again—or the cargo bay, which was currently filled with assorted textiles to facilitate their cover as independent traders.

By way of answering the alien's question, Chakotay said, "We can't very well take a direct route from the Badlands to Ardana, we—"

Neelix, however, was shaking his head contritely. "My apologies, Captain. This entire ordeal has been . . . difficult for me. You must understand, I spent a long time trying to get Kes away from Jabin, and to succeed, only to have *this* happen . . ."

Before Chakotay could muster up something vaguely comforting to say, Seska, of all people, spoke up. "We've all got our reasons for being angry, Neelix. You lost your woman. Chakotay lost his sister. Tuvok lost his wife and children. Harry and Annika both lost their parents. Kate—well, I don't know what she lost, but I'm sure she lost something. And as for me—I lost my people." Seska got a faraway look in her eyes. Then she blinked and turned to Neelix. "The trick is to use that anger against them."

"I was a soldier once, Ms. Seska. Believe me, I know how to fight when it is necessary."

Tuvok was currently in one of the hammocks below, meditating—another old Vulcan tradition he insisted on maintaining. Harry had taken his position on the flight deck, and now he said, "Alliance vessel decloaking ahead! They're hailing us."

Chakotay let out his father's curse, then said, "On audio."

A bored-sounding voice said, *"This is Gul Daro of the Alliance scout ship* Bok'nor. *Please state your reasons for being in this sector."*

Getting up from his seat, Chakotay said, "Get Tuvok up here."

Nodding, Harry opened the intercom and said, "Tuvok, we have company. Get to the flight deck now."

"Acknowledged."

Again nodding, Harry also rose and followed Chakotay.

"What's going on?" Neelix asked as Chakotay pulled him toward the door to the flight deck, which slid open.

"Keeping our cover." The door slid shut behind them.

Chakotay and Harry led Neelix into the narrow corridor. They pressed up against the side to let Tuvok pass.

Once the Vulcan entered the flight deck, Chakotay switched on one of the monitors.

As Tuvok took his seat, Seska said, *"Open a channel."* Once Tuvok did so, she said, "Bok'nor, *this is the trading vessel* Falrak's Pride. *We're bringing textiles to Camp Khitomer."*

Daro still sounded bored. *"And you are?"*

Seska grinned at that. *"I'm Falrak, of course."*

"Hm?" Daro sounded like he was distracted by something. *"Oh, yes. Alliance regulations require visual communication."*

"Of course. Put us on-screen, slave." The latter was said to Tuvok.

Neelix gave Chakotay a quizzical glance. "Slave?"

"Most Vulcans are slaves to Cardassians or Klingons."

"Oh." Neelix nodded.

The viewer activated. Chakotay saw Gul Daro's eyes light up at what he saw. Now sounding less bored, he said, *"That Vulcan— he's yours?"*

Seska gave him a sweet smile. *"Everything on this ship is mine, Glinn—at least until I'm given adequate compensation."*

"I find that hard to believe."

"Excuse me?"

Chakotay didn't like the sound of this.

"Where does someone who drives a dungheap of a boat like yours have the cash to buy a Vulcan? I can't even afford a Vulcan."

Again, Chakotay let out the curse. The last thing they needed was a mid-ranking Cardassian with slave envy.

Rolling her eyes, Seska spoke as if she'd been asked this question a thousand times before. *"I won him in a* tongo *game last year on Terok Nor."*

Daro still looked suspicious. *"From who?"*

Shrugging, Seska said, *"Some gul. I never got his name—I think he captained a freighter. Anyhow, he was the worst* tongo *player I've ever met—never seen anyone confront with so little in his hand. He ran out of money pretty quick, but he kept playing. The guy next to me got his private yacht, the woman next to him got an exemption on her tariffs in the Bajoran sector, and I got his prize slave."*

Daro looked off to the side, then nodded. *"All right, scans show you're only carrying textiles. We're only reading two life signs."*

At that, Chakotay breathed a sigh of relief. Kate kept insisting the life-sign masker Annika had cobbled together wouldn't work; Annika had taken that as a challenge. For once, he was grateful his chief engineer was wrong.

Now Daro smiled. *"I don't suppose I could talk you into letting me take that Vulcan off your hands."*

Seska smiled right back. *"You just said you couldn't afford him. Besides,"* and her face grew serious now, *"I need him to help run the ship. Trust me, this is* not *a one-person craft. It's barely a two-person one."*

"That's certainly true," Daro said with a laugh. *"All right, Falrak, be on your way. I just hope your textiles will make for nicer clothes than Klingons usually wear."*

In a conspiratorial tone, Seska said, *"Don't I wish. No, it's the usual eyesores. But they pay well for them, so who am I to judge?"*

"We're Cardassians—which means we have aesthetics. That's who we are to judge. Don't ever forget that, Falrak."

"I don't. But I don't turn down money, either."

Daro nodded. *"Wise of you. Safe journeys,* Falrak's Pride.*"*

"And to you, Bok'nor.*"*

Neelix started to make for the flight deck as soon as Daro's face faded from the screen, but Chakotay held him back.

"Bok'nor *is going to warp,"* Tuvok said. A few seconds passed, during which Neelix fidgeted. Finally: "Bok'nor *is now out of sensor range."*

Looking down at Neelix, Chakotay said, "Now we can go."

They went back onto the flight deck. "Good work, Seska," Chakotay said as they entered.

Getting up from her chair and approaching Chakotay, Seska said, "Of course it was good work. I'm a Cardassian officer—a professional. Good work is what I do."

Then she punched Chakotay in the stomach so suddenly that he had no time to prepare. His muscles contracted and he couldn't breathe, the wind having been knocked out of him by the strike. He doubled over, trying desperately to get his breath back, clutching his belly and coughing raggedly, his cheeks burning and his stomach hurting. As he was about to try to straighten up, Seska's fist hit his jaw. He fell back against the bulkhead, the salty taste of his own blood filling his mouth along with at least one tooth that she had loosened.

"This rebellion would be *nothing* without me, you hear, Chakotay? *Nothing!* And it's about time the chain of command around here reflected that!" She then whirled around and pulled a disruptor on Tuvok. "Don't even *think* about it, Vulcan! I've had it with all of you. We only got those parts for O'Brien's ship because of me, we only knew about Ardana because of me, and we didn't just get boarded by a Cardassian scout ship *because of me!* So from now on—"

Seska did not get the opportunity to explain what she thought would happen from now on due to the jumping kick from the foot of Harry Kim colliding with her chest. The pair of them landed on the deck in a tangle. Seska tried to get to her feet, but Harry slammed his palm heel into her face. Her nose now bloodied, Seska snarled and punched Harry in the chin, which sent him reeling.

As she scrambled to her feet, Tuvok calmly moved behind her and grabbed her shoulder. Before Tuvok could apply the nerve-pinch, however, Seska elbowed him in the face.

That distracted her long enough for Harry to kick her hard in her left shin. Chakotay heard the snap of bone; so did Neelix, based on the wince and expression of disgust he made upon hearing the sound.

Seska screamed as she fell again to the deck.

Harry, however, wasn't finished. He kicked her in the face again, this time with the heel of his leather boot, then moved behind her, slid his arms under her shoulders, lifted her up, and then levered his arms upward, causing two more sickening snaps.

Now, Seska's screams filled the flight deck. Tuvok, green blood pooling under his nose, reached around Harry and again applied his hand to her shoulder.

The screams stopped a moment later.

Throughout the entire scuffle, Harry's face never changed expression. Indeed, his hair wasn't even mussed. Now, though, he scowled at Tuvok. "I wasn't *finished* with her yet."

"Yes, you were," Chakotay said before Tuvok could reply. "Good job, both of you. Put her in her chair, Harry. Tuvok, find me a hypo with a stimulant."

Tuvok nodded and moved to the first-aid kit that was under one of the consoles.

"Captain," Neelix said slowly, "is this how you usually discipline your crew?"

Angrily whirling on Neelix, Chakotay said, "This is how I deal with *mutiny*, Mister Neelix. We're hanging on by a thread here. Any second, I'm half expecting an Alliance ship to waltz in and blow us to pieces. The only way to keep alive is to keep discipline, which isn't going to happen with my subordinates punching me and pulling disruptors on my crew. If you have a problem, you can walk the rest of the way to Ardana."

Holding up his hands, Neelix said, "No, no, that's all right! I was simply inquiring about the differences in dealing with insubordination on your side of the galaxy. That's all. My apologies, Captain, I am simply anxious about Kes. After all we've been through—"

Turning his back on Neelix, Chakotay said, "Save it."

Tuvok was applying the hypo to Seska's ridged neck. A second later she awoke to find herself facing the barrel of Chakotay's disruptor.

"You don't listen very well, do you, Seska? I told you that you were barely tolerated here, and then only because you have uses. You just proved that usefulness a few minutes ago—and then threw it away when you attacked me. By rights, I should beam you into space, and if we didn't need you to get onto Ardana, I would. Once we've rescued Kes"—*if we rescue Kes,* he thought bitterly— "I may still exercise that option. Understand me?"

Seska just stared at him for several seconds. Then, finally, she nodded.

"She requires medical attention," Tuvok said.

Harry was still staring disapprovingly at the Vulcan. "'Requires' is stating it too strongly, I think."

"Take care of her, Tuvok," Chakotay said as he took his seat. He set *Geronimo* back on course for Ardana.

As Tuvok did so, Harry walked over to Chakotay. "I could've taken care of her permanently."

"We still need her," Chakotay said with a shake of his head. "We won't get on Ardana without her. After that—" He hesitated, then realized he had no choice. Seska would never follow his orders again, if she ever truly did in the first place. *If that speech I just gave Neelix is supposed to mean anything, I have to follow through.* "After that, Harry, she's all yours."

Rarely did Harry Kim smile, which was just as well, as his face wasn't really suited for it. When he did smile, it looked more like a Klingon baring his teeth in combat than an expression of happiness.

He smiled now. "In that case, I can't wait for this mission to be over."

Taking his seat to Chakotay's left, Harry continued smiling. Chakotay decided not to look at him until he was finished.

It was the better part of a day before they arrived at Ardana. As the orange planet came into view on the screen, Chakotay summoned Seska to the flight deck, but it was Tuvok who replied, saying, *"We're on our way."*

Moments after that, Seska hobbled into the cockpit, Tuvok supporting her and leading her to her seat on Chakotay's right. Her left leg and both arms were covered in plaster casts. They had slightly more sophisticated medical equipment back in the Badlands, but it was at a premium, and they couldn't afford to take it on ships that went in the field and could be destroyed. So Seska was stuck with old-fashioned—and cheap to obtain—remedies for the nonce.

At no point during her journey across the flight deck did Seska look at any of them—not even Tuvok, who was supporting her.

"You ready to do your part?" Chakotay asked her.

"For now—because I don't want that halfbreed *tralk* to get her hands on Kes. But after that . . ." She finally turned to look at Chakotay. "We're done. I'll save Cardassia my own way."

"Fine by me." Chakotay didn't bother returning her glance. He was focused on the final approach to Ardana. Once he was sure they were on course, and that they would be able to come in on a standard orbit that would put them over Stratos, he stole a glance at Harry and simply nodded, wordlessly acknowledging Chakotay's earlier order.

When Harry turned back to the console, he frowned. "Picking up a debris cloud in orbit of Ardana."

Tuvok stood over Harry and looked at the sensor data. "Indeed. Based on the composition and size of the debris field, I would hypothesize that it is the remains of a large, spacefaring vessel, one that was destroyed by a high-energy weapon within the last twenty-four hours."

"That's odd," Seska said.

Now Chakotay looked at her. "What's odd?"

"The composition isn't just that of any old ship—the alloys I'm reading are consistent with a *Galor*-class ship. The mass is a little off, but that can be accounted for by the vaporizing."

"She is correct," Tuvok said. The Vulcan was now bent over the console.

After a second, Harry just got up and got out of the way.

Tuvok continued: "The *Galor* class was the first Cardassian ship to use kellinite for its exterior hulls. All previous ship designs primarily used rodinium or duranium, and the only other ships that use kellinite are too small to account for so large a debris field."

Neelix chose that moment to pipe up. "What if it's more than one ship?"

"Unlikely," Tuvok said without sparing the alien a glance. "The trajectory of the debris radiates from a single, very focused source."

Harry said, "If something happened here that caused a *Galor* to be blown up, I'd say it's good for us."

"Let's hope so," Chakotay said as he opened a channel to engineering. "Kate, Annika, is our 'leak' ready?"

"It will be in a minute, Chief," Annika said cheerfully. *"Kate's just gotta make one last adjustment, and we're good to go."*

"Good." Chakotay rose. "Come on, let's let Seska be Falrak again."

Neelix and Harry followed Chakotay off the flight deck. Chakotay switched on the viewer and observed as Tuvok opened a channel. *"Monor Base,"* he said, *"this is the trading vessel* Falrak's Pride, *requesting clearance to land."*

A Klingon face appeared on the screen. *"Falrak's Pride, this is a secure installation. What is your purpose?"*

Seska gave the Klingon a sheepish smile. *"Repairs—both personal and structural. We were on our way to Khitomer when we got a coolant leak. When I tried to fix it, half the engine room fell on me."* She held up her plaster-cast arms. *"I'm in no shape to finish the repair, and we don't have anything like a medical bay here. I can't risk going back to warp until this leak's under control, and I have to be at Khitomer by tomorrow night. My slave is useless when it comes to this kind of thing—computers are no problem, but getting a Vulcan to fix something is like getting a Ferengi to give you a fair deal."*

The Klingon laughed at that, though which ethnic slur in particular amused him was unclear. *"All right, come in to Bay 5. We'll see what we can do for you."*

Letting out a long sigh of relief, Seska said, *"Thank you, Monor Base. In exchange, I might be able to see fit to giving you first shot at our cargo—I have the finest textiles from Cuellar III."*

That got the Klingon's eyes to widen. *"Oh really? Well, we'll have to talk when you arrive, Captain."* He peered down at his console. *"That's odd—I'm not reading a leak in your coolant systems."*

To her credit, Seska spoke without hesitation. *"I took the entire system offline. It wouldn't register on a scan. Trust me, when your engineers get here, they'll know what's happening."*

Neelix looked at Chakotay. "I thought the idea was that they were to *detect* the false leak that Ms. Janeway concocted."

Angrily, Chakotay said, "It *was*." He started striding purposefully down the corridor toward the engine room. He and Kate were going to have words about this. . . .

Before he could turn the corner to the engine room, however, Kate herself came running toward him, her hair disheveled and the right shoulder of her coverall burned and ripped, exposing equally burned flesh underneath. Her right arm hung limply at her side, and she held a disruptor in her left.

"What the hell happened?" Chakotay asked.

"It's Annika," Kate said breathlessly. "She's working with *them!*"

"What?" Chakotay couldn't believe it.

Kate continued. "I was all set to get the fake leak going, when suddenly she whipped out a disruptor. I managed to duck it, but she kept firing, saying that she was relieved that she could finally be extracted."

"'Extracted'?" Neelix said quizzically.

Nodding, Kate said, "Her tone of voice was *completely* different. She said she's been collecting data on us for *months.*"

Shaking his head, Chakotay said, "Dammit." He unholstered his own disruptor as they came to the door to the engine room. It was just yesterday that he was pondering what Annika's motivation was for joining the rebellion. *Now I know.*

"I managed to seal the room off," Kate said, "but she'll be able to get through that pretty quickly."

Chakotay thought for a moment. "Let's not give her the chance. Kate, can you get the door open?"

"Of course."

"Good—you do that. Neelix, hang back—you're unarmed. Harry and I will take care of this."

"I don't suppose," Neelix said, "this is an ideal time to point out that I am quite capable with an energy weapon and—"

Whirling again on the alien, Chakotay said, "Hang *back*— Harry and I will take care of this."

Neelix opened his mouth, closed it, opened it again, then finally said, "As you say, Captain."

"Good." He moved to the left-hand side of the door, and nodded to Harry, who took up position on the right-hand side, his own disruptor charged and ready.

To Kate, he said, "Do it."

Kate had removed one of the panels on the bulkhead behind where Harry was standing, and now pulled three wires out in succession. The door slid open.

Chakotay and Harry both leapt into the now-open doorway with disruptors pointed in front of them—but there was no sign of Annika, nor of anyone else.

Slowly, they moved in, walking cautiously. Despite his booted feet, Chakotay—remembering long-ago lessons learned from Kolopak before the Alliance came—made no sound as he entered. Harry was not so cautious, his leather outfit making squeaking noises, his footfalls echoing in the room. *But then, subtlety has never been Harry's strong suit.*

While there was still no sign of Annika, there were plenty of signs of the firefight Kate had described. In fact, Kate hadn't come close to doing it justice. Conduits, consoles, manifolds—all were scarred black with disruptor fire. Chakotay noted with relief that the warp core was, at least, untouched, but he wondered how much control they were going to have over the ship when they went out again.

He also wondered what was happening on the flight deck. *Geronimo* was moving now, but only with thrusters. So far, the artificial gravity was keeping her steady as she entered the stratosphere. Unfortunately, the screen that would have told him such useful information as position and hull temperature—the latter a big concern when entering atmosphere—was so much shattered plasteel, thanks to either Kate's or Annika's disruptor fire. Still, they weren't being fired on, so he assumed that Seska was working her magic on that Klingon.

Of course, with Annika being a traitor, they may be letting us onto the base on purpose. He didn't see a scientific base as a likely spot for an extraction, but Annika may have wanted to deliver Neelix to the same place that had Kes, thus providing both strange aliens at once.

Chakotay pointed to his left. Harry nodded and moved toward the starboard side of the engine room. Chakotay worked his way along the portside wall. He saw that the shield output indicated the heat from atmospheric entry, but nothing else untoward, which came as a relief.

Turning a corner, he saw Annika hunched over the environmental controls. "Don't move," he said.

She didn't, to her credit. He inched closer to her, never lowering his disruptor.

Then, suddenly, Chakotay realized why she wasn't moving. She wasn't breathing, either.

Harry came up from the other side at the same time that Chakotay reached the body, which had a giant scorch mark in the chest. Now that he was close enough, Chakotay was able to distinguish the burnt-flesh smell from the burnt-console-and-conduit smell that was much more prevalent.

"The hard part was propping her body up on the console so it'd look convincing."

Chakotay whirled around to see Kate pointing two disruptors, one each at him and Harry. He stared at her, open-mouthed.

Then he didn't see anything at all.

9

The last thing Seska remembered was hobbling over to the airlock and watching it start to open.

What might have happened after that, she had no clue. She could not recall who or what was on the other side of the airlock. They had landed safely in Bay 5, as instructed. Chakotay and the others weren't in the corridor, which meant all was going according to plan. Once they landed, Chakotay was to take Neelix and Kim and hide in engineering with Janeway and Hansen until the way was clear.

She tried and failed to shift position, and then realized many things at once.

The first was that she was bound to a marble column. Restraints bit into her wrists, which were pulled behind her on the sides of the column. She tugged on them, which made her realize that her legs and arms didn't hurt. Somehow, they'd been healed. She was able to determine this fairly quickly in part because she didn't feel the numbed pain—the numbing provided by the painkillers Tuvok had administered—and in part because she was no longer wearing the plaster casts and the plain earth-tone coverall. When she'd left Gul Evek's command, she'd been able to grab only a few drab coveralls. Laundry facilities were mediocre in the rebellion, so she tended to get most of a week out of a given coverall, which resulted in a lack of cleanliness that had appalled Seska at first, but to which she found herself growing accustomed.

Now, though, she was not wearing that coverall, nor anything else.

This realization led to the fourth thing she noticed: for the first time since stealing that shuttle from *Bak'rikan,* she was clean. Not the quick splashing of brackish water onto her face or the ruthless wipe-and-run she'd indulged in when they'd found themselves at a place with proper facilities. She'd been thoroughly bathed, which made her wonder how long she'd been unconscious, since it would take quite a while to get all the dirt off her gray skin. She also had to admit to some irritation, as anticipation of a real bath some time in the future was one of the things that kept her able to survive living among filthy Terrans and Vulcans and the like for so long.

In front of her was the fifth thing of which she became aware. It was another marble column, this one curved in a crescent shape, with the inside of the curve facing Seska. Beyond that was a wide-open space that had several corridors feeding into it at odd angles, with hideous abstract art on all the walls. The walls were made of either a dark wood or plastiform of various colors, as was the molding along the floor and ceiling that was carved with bas-relief depictions of various Ardanan animals. Ironically, all those animals were extinct, having long since been wiped out by the Terran Empire during their brutal strip-mining of the planet.

Structurally, the setup was similar to that of the agony booths that the Terran Empire had favored. The Alliance had made use of that disciplinary tool as well. Created by a Denobulan physician centuries earlier, the agony booth was a place Seska herself had sent many a low-ranking fool who disobeyed.

Oddly, there were no emblems of the Alliance here, and the artwork that adorned the walls was Ardanan. Seska wondered why Supervisor B'Elanna kept the natives' artwork when the natives themselves were long gone.

Again, Seska pulled futilely on the restraints. If they were standard Alliance-issue, she wouldn't be able to destroy them without a disruptor set on high, and even then it would take hours.

And obviously, I don't have anything on me, she thought bitterly.

She heard the footfalls of approaching people before she saw them. Two Terran males, as naked as Seska was, came around the corner and took up position on either side of a chair that Seska hadn't noticed until now. One of the Terrans had sandy hair, pale skin, and blue eyes; the other had skin, hair, and eyes that were all much darker. Both were carrying bowls in front of them, though their contents were obscured by Seska's position.

Then B'Elanna came around the corner.

Seska didn't know B'Elanna personally, but the same contact who had given her the information on Ardana had provided the nonclassified portions of the woman's dossier. Her face was hideous, combining the deformed forehead of a Klingon with unformed face of a Terran.

B'Elanna scowled as she walked in. "In retrospect, I should have had the doctors put your clothes back on, little glinn. Cardassians are ugly enough dressed."

As the supervisor came into the chamber, a familiar face became visible behind her.

"You!" Seska couldn't believe it.

Laughing, B'Elanna pointed to the Terran woman who now entered the room with a wary expression. "Ah, yes, I believe you two know each other. Glinn Seska, traitor to the Alliance, meet Kate Janeway, traitor to the rebellion." She tilted her head. "Well, no, that's not entirely fair. In order to *betray* the rebellion, she would have to have been a part of it. And she never was."

Janeway stepped forward. "If you like, Intendant, I can shoot the traitor for you." She spoke the words with a manic grin that Seska had never seen on the engineer.

Staring at Janeway, Seska said, "You were an Alliance operative the whole time?"

"Not exactly," B'Elanna said as she walked closer to the chair. "Dear Katie has been one of my personal aides for years, going back to Cestus III."

Nodding in understanding, Seska said, "That's why she calls you Intendant."

"Yes. True, I'm *technically* a supervisor now, but that will, I'm sure, be changing soon. You see, Katie was able to insinuate herself into the group that overthrew me on Cestus. She was unable to stop them, but she did play along and become part of that idiotic rebellion of yours. I'd been hoping she'd lead me to a method of stopping your foolishness in a way that would improve my own position."

Seska snorted derisively. "You really think capturing one ship will do the trick?"

At that, B'Elanna touched something on the side of the column Seska was bound to. The facing part of the curved column suddenly lit up with bright lights, and Seska screamed even before she truly felt the pain, as if every cell in her body was being sliced into with a Klingon dagger.

Seconds later, the pain stopped, as did the lights.

B'Elanna said, "Continue, and you will experience more of this, little glinn. The Ardanans called this 'the rays,' unimaginatively enough. But it's quite effective." Leaning in to whisper in Seska's ear, she added, "I don't like insolence."

Smiling sweetly, even as she tried to catch her breath, Seska said, "Then you . . . you captured the wrong Cardassian."

That got the rays going again. This time, though the pain was as great, Seska forced herself not to scream. She'd taken a few trips to the agony booth herself in her time. After B'Elanna shut it off again, she sauntered to the chair between the two Terrans and sat down in it in as ostentatious a manner as possible. Seska wasn't sure who she was performing for. Janeway didn't seem to care, the two slaves were loyal to her by right of sale, and Seska sure didn't give a damn.

"It isn't your ship I care about, little glinn. Yes, capturing the Vulcan and those three Terrans—or, rather, two Terrans, since Katie had to kill that blonde—was useful, but they aren't the true prize, nor is that rattletrap you call a ship. No, it's the two aliens that interest me. One I already have, and now I'm told that she has a lover. He's not as useful as she is, since his species apparently isn't telepathic, but it's possible that he can have some influence on her. That, in turn, helps me."

"If you say so," Seska said glumly. *I should've followed my first instinct and spaced that little troll. Or found some way to stop Chakotay from taking him on board in the first place.*

B'Elanna snapped a finger at the pale slave, who immediately reached into his bowl and pulled out a slice of *jorata*. He leaned over and placed the fruit into her mouth. "In any case," she said with her mouth full, "you're probably wondering why I went to all the trouble of healing your wounds and cleaning you up."

"Not at all. My trial will make for much better entertainment if I'm clean and healthy. No one wants to see a dirty, broken woman on their viewers, even if she is Evek's traitor."

"Oh, no, not Evek's traitor," B'Elanna said with a grin. "Mine. Evek will be unable to participate in your trial by virtue of being space dust." At that, she laughed.

Seska quickly divined B'Elanna's meaning. The *Galor*-class debris they had detected in orbit of Ardana was all that remained of *Bak'rikan*.

Regarding the halfbreed, Seska said, "Congratulations, Supervisor—you've managed to accomplish the one goal we both had in common. Evek's death is a loss to no one."

Swallowing the fruit, B'Elanna chuckled. "That's certainly true." She sat up straight in her chair. "Now, though, I must alert Alliance Command that I have retrieved the traitor."

"Not to mention several rebellion operatives," Janeway added.

B'Elanna fixed Janeway with an odd expression that Seska couldn't make out. "Not quite. You see, while having the traitor here is useful, so is having you inside the rebellion. You're to return to the rebellion alone. Tell the others that you were the only one to escape alive."

Seska made a *tch* noise. "They'll *never* accept that."

"Of course they will," Janeway said contemptuously. "They believed it when Sisko just returned from nowhere after his ship was blown up, they'll buy this."

"Don't be so sure of that," Seska said, though she didn't believe it. In truth, Janeway was right. The only Terrans with brains in the rebellion were O'Brien, Sisko's ex-wife, and Tuvok. Tuvok was here, O'Brien was too focused on building that supership of his, and Jennifer Sisko's intelligence was all padd-smarts, not common sense.

Janeway looked to the side, seemingly lost in thought as she worked her way through the problem. Seska was bitterly amused to see that Janeway's thought process was like that of any engineer, a touch of mundanity that made her hate Janeway all the more.

"We can blast a hole in the flight deck bulkhead. I can tell them that the rest of the crew were blown out into space, so this way you can still keep Chakotay, Tuvok, and Kim here for interrogation. The only body I'll have is Hansen—she would've been with me in engineering. I'll say she died when something exploded."

"And they'll believe that?" B'Elanna asked.

"Yes," Janeway said emphatically.

B'Elanna seemed to consider this. She snapped her fingers again, and this time the dark-skinned Terran reached into his bowl of fruit—

—and pulled out a small disruptor.

Before Seska could complete the thought, *That slave has a disruptor!* Janeway had pulled out her own weapon and vaporized the Terran, who screamed in agony before he disintegrated. The screams echoed off the walls of the large room long after the vocal cords that formed them were gone.

Janeway, oddly, looked stricken. "My apologies, Intendant. I should have left him alive so you could question him."

For her part, B'Elanna looked stunned. The pale slave had dropped his bowl and was now kneeling beside her. "You okay, mistress?"

Brushing the slave aside, she said, "I'm fine, Thomas." She stood up. "Katie, *never* apologize for saving my life. You did very well." She let out a long breath. "I will obviously have to have my security personnel replaced. This *petaQ* should never have been able to get in here armed—or with any intentions on my life."

"Let me guess," Seska said snidely, "all your security personnel are Klingons?" She barked a laugh. "It's a wonder all your slaves aren't high-ranking members of the rebellion by now, if that's what you're relying on."

As expected, that comment earned Seska another harsh glare of the rays, though this one lasted much longer than the previous two.

Janeway once again unholstered her disruptor. "I can kill her for you, Intendant. I'll make it slower than it was for that Terran."

B'Elanna held up a hand. "No. She must be returned to Cardassia for a proper trial. Evek was one thing. He was a branch that had contracted a blight—all that needed to be done was cut it off from the rest of the tree. But treachery such as hers must be exposed and punished publicly. Just killing her outright serves nobody's purpose." She looked down at Seska, then, and smiled widely. "Not even her own. After all, if she's dead, she can't cling to some foolish hope of escape."

Uncaring if it meant another bout with the rays, Seska panted. "If . . . if what just happened is any indication . . . escape should be . . . be easily accomplished by the end of the day."

The halfbreed raised her arm as if to activate the rays again, but refrained. "No—she wishes me to make her appear tortured. That won't do. A ship is en route from Elvok Nor to take her to Cardassia Prime." She looked down at Seska with a sneer. "Your people aren't good for much, but you do conduct the most entertaining trials."

"Your approval means *everything* to . . . to me," Seska said with a roll of her eyes.

Pleading, Janeway asked, "May I at least shatter her kneecap, Intendant? You can't begin to understand how incredibly *annoying* this woman is."

"I'm starting to get an idea," B'Elanna muttered.

For the first time, Seska addressed Janeway. "If I was annoying, traitor, it's . . . it's because I was focused on the *goal*. I . . . I was trying to save Cardassia from . . . from creatures like *her*." She indicated B'Elanna with a jerk of her head, still standing in front of her chair behind Seska. "The Terrans are the best chance of that—and of freeing your people."

Janeway spoke contemptuously. "The Terran people aren't worth saving. They were the galaxy's butchers, and then they were entranced by a fool of a Vulcan. They should all die."

No wonder she never got along with Tuvok, Seska thought. "So . . . so that's it?" she said to B'Elanna. "You turn me over to Central Command, and . . . and your star rises. Then you position your new pet telepath to help you do what? Take over the Alliance?"

Sitting back in her chair, B'Elanna said with a shrug, "Something like that. But that's not your concern. You'll be long dead by then—the fate of all traitors to the Alliance."

"Really? And what does blowing up a *Galor*-class ship get you?"

At that, B'Elanna laughed. "Nice try, little glinn, but Alliance Command has already praised me for my actions against Gul Evek, after he failed to report his capture of an unauthorized alien. You see, he had some strange idea that she was a telepath. Of course, my own people proved that assumption wrong, but Evek refused to believe it, and so he trained his weapons on Monor Base." Holding up her arms, she asked, "What choice did I have?"

Well, at least I know what she's planning, Seska thought dolefully, though while she stood naked and bound, the intelligence did her very little good—which B'Elanna knew.

Looking at Janeway, B'Elanna said, "Your plan sounds workable, Katie—but there's only one problem: Hansen."

Janeway frowned. "What about her?"

"You shot her in the chest. I realize that the rebellion is hardly made up of the finest minds of the galaxy, but I doubt any of them will have trouble recognizing a disruptor blast for what it is."

Shrugging, Janeway said, "We can burn the body, make it look like a plasma fire or something."

B'Elanna shook her head. "Too risky. I wouldn't put it past one of them to examine the body, and the big hole in the chest cavity will be a tipoff. So you'll have to pick one of the others to kill in a way that will track with your cover story." She put a finger to her chin. "It means we lose one for interrogation, but I doubt any of them will say anything you don't already know."

That prompted a pulling back of Janeway's lips, forming a rictus on her face that only the most generous of definitions would allow one to classify as a smile. "I know just the person."

Kate Janeway approached the security office with a spring in her step. It was *such* a relief to be back among Klingons—and Cardassians, if one discounted that *tralk* Seska—after spending so much time with Terrans. Kate had never been comfortable with her own kind—she had learned her lessons well from Owen, the kindly old man who was the overseer of the slave population in the palace on Cestus III. Owen's son had become the Intendant's favorite plaything—in fact, he had been in B'Elanna's throne room earlier, along with that traitor Kate had killed—but for whatever reason, Owen had taken a liking to Kate. Kate's parents had talked of rebellion, and been killed for their troubles. Although he'd never said for sure, Kate had always thought that Owen had been the one to turn them in.

Owen had taught her history when she was growing up, after Kate's parents were gone, and she had developed a loathing for the excesses of her own species. The Alliance had been built through cooperation and strength, bringing together the best of two empires. Terrans were too venal for that: they simply stomped through everything in their path. This planet was a perfect testament to their waste: strip-mining a fine world such as this and turning this amazing cloud city into a ghost town. Were it not for Gul Monor, it might have been lost.

No, Terrans had had their chance to rule the stars. Kate would die before she gave them another chance, which was why she had leapt at the chance to help B'Elanna put down the group on Cestus III. The one good thing that had come out of the dissident movement on Cestus—which had resulted in B'Elanna's demotion—was that it had enabled Kate to infiltrate the rebellion.

She wished she could have talked B'Elanna into letting her stay here on Ardana rather than return to that nest of scum, but there was no arguing with the supervisor when she got an idea into her head. Which was a pity, as she'd gone to all the trouble of faking the problem with the injectors so Chakotay couldn't take them into the Badlands, thus greatly increasing their chances of being captured. The fake had fooled Hansen—who was, Kate grudgingly admitted, a decent engineer, but also was a little too trusting of her betters, and so never checked the injectors for herself—but then Chakotay had to go and ignore her.

Of course, if the Alliance had sent someone competent, instead of Evek, the plan might have worked.

That having failed, she did everything she could to convince Chuckles to rescue the alien girl. She didn't give a good goddamn about telepaths or any of the rest of it, she just wanted to be extracted. *If I had to sleep with that idiot one more time . . .*

That onerous duty, at least, would be spared her. And her "mourning" over dear Chuckles would be all the excuse she'd need to rebuff the advances of anyone else in the rebellion. *Thank God for that—sex with one of them was bad enough.*

She turned a corner through one of Monor Base's numerous archways and entered the security office. There, she was greeted by a familiar face. "Kohlar! You old *toDSaH,* what're you doing here? Still riding on the supervisor's ass?" While she still called B'Elanna Intendant to stay in her good graces, Kate knew full well what her current title was. But it served Kate's own purpose to keep B'Elanna pleased, since as long as B'Elanna was happy, Kate was happy.

"Only the left cheek—you take up all the space on the right one," the large Klingon said as he rose from his seat at the security console. They exchanged a warrior's handshake, each grabbing the other's forearm—a gesture common to both Terrans and Klingons as a way of determining that the person one greeted wasn't hiding any weapons, at least according to folklore on both Earth and Qo'noS. All Kate knew was that few Klingons deemed any

Terran worth the gesture, but Kohlar and she went a ways back to the good old days on Cestus III.

"So you followed the supervisor here?" she asked.

He nodded and retook his seat. "Of course. One of the things I like about the supervisor is her distaste for Cardassians." He bared his teeth. "Cuts down on the foul odor. No, all one has to deal with under Supervisor B'Elanna's command is an overabundance of Terrans. And you I can live with—you know your place, unlike our esteemed allies." The last four words were said with supreme distaste.

"Not all of us do," Kate said in a serious tone. "One of them tried to kill the supervisor."

Kohlar winced. "Tall? Dark skin? Beard? Mole on his cheek?"

Kate hadn't noticed a mole, but the rest of it fit. She nodded.

He shook his head. "I *warned* the supervisor about that one. He used to be one of Gowron's slaves, and you *know* how he feels about crossbreeding."

That, at least, explained to Kate why that Terran didn't seem familiar. She knew most of the rebellion agents working in sensitive areas, and she hadn't known of any here on Ardana. But a prominent Klingon who had gone on the record as being against interspecies breeding, as Gowron had, would be just the type to insert a slave into the heart of B'Elanna's command for the express purpose of plunging a *d'k tahg* into it.

Indicating the monitor screens in front of Kohlar, Kate asked, "How are *my* 'esteemed allies' doing?" There were a total of ten monitors in front of Kohlar, each of which could show up to five cells at a time, thus providing the security office with a full-time view of all fifty cells on level six. At the moment, that wasn't necessary, as the facility had only three prisoners, so only three monitors were lit. Each showed the entirety of the prisoner's cell. The cells had a metal bunk, a hole without a drain for waste, and no windows. Air came through microscopic vents located throughout the walls, none of them wide enough to do a prisoner any good. A secure slot provided gruel once a day, which contained enough nutrients and water to keep a prisoner from starving or dehydrating, though not much beyond that.

These were the only spaces in all of Monor Base that had been completely rebuilt by the Alliance, as the colorful walls had been either covered or replaced by duranium. Kate wondered idly what the rooms' original purposes were.

The prisoners were also stripped naked. Kate supposed that made sense from a security standpoint, but she'd seen enough of Chakotay naked to last her a lifetime and didn't really need to be confronted by the sight again. Harry and Tuvok weren't much of an improvement.

Kohlar snorted. "The Vulcan's spent the entire time meditating."

"Typical," Kate muttered. She had even less use for Vulcans than her fellow Terrans. It had taken all her willpower not to strangle Tuvok in his sleep the entire time she was with the rebellion. Sure enough, as Kohlar had indicated, Tuvok was seated on the metal bunk in a butterfly position, his hands dropped to his sides, his eyes shut, his breathing slow. Kate had encountered many Vulcans in her life, most of them servants, but she'd never seen one who clung to arcane Vulcan ritual the way Tuvok did.

"The one with the tattoo's the only one who's been at all entertaining. The other Terran inspected the entire cell, for all the good it did him, then lay down to sleep. He's been like that all day."

"What has—has the one with the tattoo been doing?" Now that they were on an Alliance base, Chakotay no longer deserved the privilege of having his name spoken aloud. Were he to live long enough, he'd get a designation—possibly the same one he'd had on Drema IV, possibly a new one, it hardly mattered—but he'd be dead soon. *At my hands, no less, which is as it should be.* She'd been rehearsing Chaktoay's murder for months now. *First strangle him, then set fire to his corpse so it looks like he died in a plasma fire.*

"He is pacing like a caged *lIngta'*. He also inspected the cell, but was nowhere as thorough as his comrade, nor as skilled." Kohlar chuckled throatily. "His frustration is all but palpable. It is a joy to watch."

"I bet it is," Kate said, returning the chuckle, though with somewhat less bombast. Something was nagging at her. "The other one, you said he's been lying still all day?"

Nodding, Kohlar said, "Yes. Typical Terran—they'd sleep all day if they could."

"Not this one." Kate didn't like it. Harry Kim checking over the entire cell was in character, but giving up and lying down all day most certainly was not. "He may be the most dangerous person on this base right now," she said gravely.

Kohlar laughed. "A Terran?"

"Don't underestimate him. He's one of the reasons the rebellion has succeeded." Kate shuddered at the memory of what Harry did at Cestus III to those Klingons who'd come after them. She hadn't been able to eat meat for a week after that. Harry's parents had been tortured and killed by a Klingon interrogator working for then-Intendant B'Elanna, and Harry had made it his personal mission to take it out on every Klingon he met.

He also doesn't take kindly to traitors. When they'd discovered that a woman he'd taken a fancy to—her name was something Webber—was working for the Alliance, Harry had taken her into the cell on the base in the Badlands and spent hours with her before she died. Her screams seemed to echo throughout the caverns for days.

No, she would not make the mistake of underestimating Harry Kim. Everyone who'd done that was dead now, and none of them went quietly.

"Flood his cell with anesthezine."

"Why?" Kohlar was looking at her as if she'd sprouted wings.

"Just trust me, I know the man. He's not to be trusted."

Shrugging, Kohlar said, "Very well."

Kate watched the monitor, but nothing was happening. "Something's wrong. There's no gas."

Kohlar was furiously operating his console. "The computer says it's flooding the cell. Sensors indicate ten parts per million of the gas." He looked at her. "What madness is this?"

"Dammit, get a team to meet me down there, *now.*"

Nodding, Kohlar slammed a hand on the intercom. Kate didn't hear what he said because she was already running out the door toward the turbolift that would take her down to level six. B'Elanna had claimed the bottom three levels; the cells were on the next level up.

The lift stopped at level three, and four Klingons entered. Like Kate, they were armed; unlike Kate, they had disruptor rifles, which had much more firepower than her simple hand disruptor.

Against Harry, they're gonna need it.

"Be careful—we don't know what this Terran's done yet. But do *not* underestimate him."

One Klingon barked a derisive laugh. "He's just an Earther. What could he possibly do?"

Kate shook her head. "Listen to me, I know what I'm—"

She cut herself off when the lift doors opened. The four Klingons all had their weapons pointed down the wide hallway before the doors slid apart, but there was nothing there. The Ardanans had built their cloud city with wide-open spaces in mind, and even what qualified as a "narrow" corridor here on the cell level was still wide enough for all four Klingons to walk abreast. The random sculpture that was so common throughout the base was absent here, which Kate rather regretted. She found it to be soothing, and she'd miss it when she went back to the Badlands with Chakotay's corpse.

Chakotay, Tuvok, and Harry had been placed in the three cells of the fifty closest to the lift on this level. One of the Klingons walked up to the wall unit in front of the security field and looked into its retinal scanner.

Recognizing his pattern, the wall unit beeped. "Five," the Klingon said simply, and then the security field dropped. Kate knew that once the field registered five bodies walking through, it would reactivate, and only those five people would be allowed to walk through the field in the other direction.

"Our orders were to check cell three," the lead Klingon said. "Kal, Ch'dak, check cells one and two just in case. Krolk, the Terran, and I will take cell three. Move!"

The two whom Kate assumed to be Kal and Ch'dak activated the doors to the first two cells. Their lack of reaction indicated that they saw exactly what Kohlar was seeing upstairs: Chakotay pacing back and forth and Tuvok meditating.

Kate stood behind the lead Klingon and next to Krolk as the leader opened the door.

The miasma of the anesthezine was still in the air, so the gas *had* worked. Kate couldn't see the whole cell, but what she could see showed no sign of Harry Kim. Sitting on the slab was a device that she recognized as an image confuser, one that could project a particular image to a security camera. The device was quite small, and also covered in some kind of viscous substance that Kate decided she didn't want to examine too closely. Certainly, Harry wasn't above smuggling such a device in whatever body cavity might present itself, especially for a mission where capture was a likely possibility; the discomfort would be of no consequence to him.

Suddenly, the squad leader fell backward, and half a second later, Kate realized why: Harry had leapt down from the wall and kicked the Klingon in the stomach. He had been standing balanced on one foot on what looked like one of the bolts that held the slab to the wall. Said bolt was jammed into the food slot to provide Harry with somewhere out of the way to stand so he could surprise his attackers.

Kate shot at Harry, as did Krolk, but the Terran was using the dazed squad leader as a shield. Without missing a beat, Harry ripped the disruptor rifle from the leader's hands and fired it full blast into the leader's chest. Guessing that he might try that, Kate fell to the floor on her stomach. Krolk had less foresight, and the leader's body went flying into him, sending both of them careening across the corridor.

Even as Kate got to her feet, Harry came out into the corridor and shot Kal and Ch'dak in quick succession, then dove to avoid Kate's own disruptor fire. Kate noticed that Harry's hands were bloody and raw, probably from removing the bolt from the metal slab by hand.

Krolk threw the body of his leader off himself and fired his disruptor rifle again, but now Harry had retreated back into the cell. "No, don't—" Kate started, but Krolk followed him in.

Seconds later, Krolk screamed a noise that she'd never heard a Klingon throat make before—and hoped she would never hear again.

Unwilling to subject herself to the same fate, and seeing that the other three Klingons had gaping, smoking holes in their chests—Harry's shots were all right at the heart—Kate turned and ran through the security field, into the turbolift, and back to the upper levels. Only after the door closed, and she knew she was safe, did she sound the alarm.

10

Harry Kim removed the gore-covered *d'k tahg* from the spine of the Klingon who'd been foolish enough to come in after him. *Janeway should've warned him,* he thought. *Then again, maybe she did. It's not like a Klingon would listen to anyone, least of all a Terran.*

Getting up from his kneeling position, Harry padded out to the corridor just in time to see the lift doors close on Janeway. *The only smart one of the bunch,* he thought, though that was hardly saying much when the rest of the bunch were Klingons. Harry took a few deep breaths to keep his blood oxygenated and to expel the excess carbon dioxide he'd built up from holding his breath for so long against the anesthezine.

An alarm sounded. *Dammit.*

Janeway meant nothing to Harry. Sure, she had betrayed them and killed Annika, but she was obviously an Alliance agent. She was just doing her job. Chakotay, he knew, might have a different opinion on the subject, but that was his problem. As for Annika, she was just someone Harry slept with.

It wasn't as if she was Libby.

Harry had enjoyed flensing Libby when she betrayed them. Her screams were wonderful, though a little too high-pitched.

As far as Harry was concerned, it was all a means to an end. Specifically, the Klingons' end.

The truth was, Harry didn't give a damn about the rebellion or the liberation of the Terran people or any of the rest of it. Although he wouldn't object if the Alliance fell, he didn't much care about it, one way or the other.

All Harry wanted to do was eliminate the entire Klingon species, preferably by killing every one of them himself.

Of course, the chances of his actually accomplishing this goal were minuscule—Harry knew that full well. But that didn't mean he couldn't make the effort, and try to take down as many of those filthy despicable smelly arrogant animals as he could before they finally killed him.

He was also happy to kill Cardassians—or maim them, as he had Seska—but only because they were foolish enough to ally with the Klingons.

Every time Harry Kim closed his eyes, he saw his parents, strapped into one of the Klingons' mind-rippers while he watched, screaming in agonizing pain, screaming until their throats were raw, then screaming some more. The sound of their wails felt like it would shatter Harry's spine, and he'd spent the years since trying to recreate that sound in the throats of each of the Klingons he killed.

The one in the cell had come very close, but the pitch was wrong. Certainly closer than Libby had gotten when he peeled the flesh off her left leg.

Reaching down, Harry threw one of the Klingons' corpses over his shoulder and walked it over to the security field. Stopping about a meter in front of it, he tossed the body to the floor—right in the path of the security field. The field dropped, of course, having registered the Klingon's DNA pattern, and would stay down until he passed all the way through.

Figuring that even the Klingons wouldn't be stupid enough to allow someone to block the field indefinitely before some failsafe protocol kicked in, Harry grabbed the Klingon's rifle and ran back toward the cells. He grabbed the wrist of one of the other Klingon corpses and waved the hand over the sensor next to the cell opposite his. (The Klingons weren't completely stupid. The two who had checked Chakotay and Tuvok had had the wherewithal to close the cell doors before they tried to take Harry down.)

The door slid open to reveal an agitated Chakotay. "Harry! Good work."

"We don't have much time," he said. He dragged the corpse over to Tuvok's cell door. "Janeway sounded the alarm."

"*She* was with them?" Chakotay's agitation became outright anger. "And you didn't kill her?"

Harry tossed the disruptor rifle to him. "Tried. She got away." Then he grabbed another rifle and tossed it to Tuvok, who exited his cell much more calmly than Chakotay had his. Finally, Harry picked up the one he'd used to shoot three of the Klingons.

The lift doors opened. Harry whirled around and fired his rifle several times. By the time the doors parted completely, Chakotay was doing the same.

Six Klingon corpses fell to the lift floor. Harry fired several more times for good measure.

Tuvok finally spoke. "I believe our wisest strategy would be to split up."

"I agree," Chakotay said with a nod. "We need to retrieve Kes and Neelix, we need to find out where *Geronimo*'s being stored." He held up his rifle. "And I need to deal with Kate."

"B'Elanna's mine," Harry said. "I've wanted to hear that half-breed bitch scream since Cestus III."

"We do not have the luxury of indulging in vendettas," Tuvok said. "Our paramount goal should be to liberate Kes and escape this base."

"And the best way to do that is to secure a hostage." Chakotay looked at Kim. "That's your job. Find B'Elanna and take her with you to wherever *Geronimo* is located."

Harry grinned at the prospect of what he would do to B'Elanna, though he suspected her screams would be all wrong.

"*Don't* kill her," Chakotay said emphatically, "yet. Once we get her back to the Badlands, you can take your time with her, but we need her as a hostage to get back to *Geronimo*."

"All right," Harry muttered. He understood the logic, intellectually, and Chakotay *was* the captain. But he didn't have to like it.

"Tuvok, you find Kes and Neelix and free them. Kate's mine."

"I repeat," Tuvok said, "we do not have time—"

Shaking his head, Chakotay said, "This *isn't* a vendetta, Tuvok. If Kate's been working for them, she has intelligence on us—intelligence we can't afford to let the Alliance have. I need to capture her or kill her, and honestly, I think killing her is the safer option."

Tuvok stared at Chakotay for two seconds, then nodded. "Agreed. But what of Seska? She does not appear to be in this cell block."

Chakotay considered. "She has intelligence we can't afford to let the Alliance have, either, and I don't trust her to be able to resist torture forever. If she's willing to come with us, then she can, but if not, she dies, too."

Harry jogged over to the wall next to the turbolift, stepping over the Klingon corpse he'd left to keep the security field down. First he kicked the arms and legs of two Klingons whose bodies had fallen across the lift's threshold. As soon as he did that, the doors closed.

"I can rig the turbolift so it will only respond to our voice commands," he said as he ripped the covering off the wall control. He immediately started reprogramming the duotronic circuitry. Harry had always been good with computers. His parents had encouraged this proclivity on the theory that he might attain a better position in the slave class if he had a useful skill. Unfortunately, the plan backfired rather spectacularly when Harry had been summoned to fix a faulty transporter console, only to discover that it wasn't faulty, it had simply been misprogrammed. The Klingon who had done the programming took umbrage at the accusation—never mind that it was true—and ordered Harry's parents killed for their son's effrontery. Harry was spared because he *did* have useful skills, and the assumption was that the object lesson would make him more tractable.

That plan also backfired rather spectacularly.

Harry looked up at Tuvok and Chakotay, who were now standing over him. "Say something," he said, those words providing his own voice for the computer's benefit.

"Like what?" Chakotay asked.

Tuvok raised an eyebrow. "I believe that will suffice."

Nodding, Harry got to his feet. "This will affect all the turbo-lifts—at least until B'Elanna or one of her security people fix it."

Chakotay seemed to grimace, but said, "Good job."

All three of them entered the lift.

Maybe, Harry thought cheerfully as the doors slid shut, *I'll be able to kill a few more Klingons.*

Every time Neelix heard Kes scream, it was like someone tore out a piece of his heart. Given how much she'd been screaming, it was a wonder blood was still being pumped through his veins.

More and more, Neelix was coming to the conclusion that he really didn't like this part of the galaxy. The people here were vicious and depraved. True, the Kazon were often like that, but that was born out of desperation for resources that were hard to come by. But these people had water aplenty, they had the technology to teleport people from place to place, they had ships that were far faster than anything Neelix had seen in Talaxian or Kazon or even Malon territory—and yet they engaged in acts that could charitably be called venial.

As bad as Captain Chakotay and his band of privateers were—and they could call themselves a rebellion all they wanted, Neelix knew pirates when he saw them—they, at least, had *some* decency. Indeed, the captain himself seemed a noble sort, even if his people were either unemotional automatons or lunatics like Seska.

This Alliance they fought against, however, was beyond the pale. He had seen them strip down the captain and his people and throw them into cells—apart from Seska, who'd been taken elsewhere. Then Neelix himself had been taken to a laboratory where he had finally, for the first time since coming to this mad place, lain eyes on his beloved Kes—only to find her secured to a bed, sweat pouring off her face, her eyes bloodshot. She had been cured of whatever physical injuries the Kazon-Ogla had inflicted on her, thankfully, but from the looks of her, her position had hardly improved since Neelix rescued her.

Rescued her, hah! As if I did anything except provide her with a ride off-planet. Still, he had taken on Kes's life as his responsibility from the moment he had first met her, and so it frustrated him to be forced to watch that doctor torture her.

However, his preferred option—leaving the room and taking Kes with him—wasn't available. He'd been brought into this lab at gunpoint, the gun in question wielded by as scary a creature as any Neelix had ever seen. Based on the descriptions provided to him by Captain Chakotay and his people, this was a Klingon. He had always thought the Kazon to have a fearsome mien, but compared to these Klingons, the Kazon were downright cuddly.

That same Klingon was now standing over Neelix as the latter sat in an uncomfortable chair about halfway across the lab from Kes's bed. The Klingon loomed behind Neelix, announcing his presence with an occasional growl.

The doctor—who was called Zimmerman—touched a control, and Kes's screams, mercifully, stopped. Zimmerman had completely ignored the Klingon, and only paid occasional attention to Neelix.

Make it stop, make it stop, make it stop!

Neelix's eyes widened, but he forced himself not to react otherwise. Though she had stopped screaming shortly after Zimmerman switched the machine off, he still heard Kes's voice in his head!

"Interesting," Zimmerman said. "Well, not *that* interesting, since it was a result I predicted. As expected, the higher the pain, the higher the psilosynine count. At least the inhibitor I gave myself appears to be working." He turned to Neelix. "I assume *you* heard her thoughts just then?"

Neelix shook his head. "I'm afraid I haven't the faintest clue what you're talking about, Doctor."

Zimmerman rolled his eyes. "Save me from the noble lover, trying to defend his maiden fair. Mister Neelix, this entire process will go *much* faster if you just answer my questions simply and directly. Your eyes widened two seconds *after* I switched off the machine. There was no obvious external stimulus to prompt such a response, so it had to be an internal stimulus. While I suppose it's possible that you suddenly, at that particular instant, figured out the secret of interdimensional travel or the solution to Selkor's First Equation, it's far more likely that you 'heard' Kes's voice in your head. Am I correct?"

Still Neelix said nothing. Zimmerman may have been correct in everything he said, but Neelix saw no good reason to help him.

Letting out a very long sigh, Zimmerman said, "Very well. We'll do it the hard way." He walked over to the shelf behind the bed Kes was strapped to, removed a hypo, and started preparing it.

Neelix, can you hear me?

This time, Neelix was able to control his reaction more successfully. However, he had no idea how to respond to her.

Just think the words, my love, and I'll hear them.

Neelix thought she made it sound easier than it was. *I can hear you, yes.*

What happened, Neelix? Where are *we? Do you have any idea?*

Unsure how to convey a sigh, Neelix simply thought, *It's a very long story, Kes. I scarcely know where to begin.*

Simply think about it, Kes told him, *and I'll see.*

So Neelix thought back on the events that had led him here, from the destruction of his ship to his rescue by Captain Chakotay, to learning how far they had traveled and what the state of the universe was in this corner of the galaxy, to going to the rebellion base, to learning where Kes had been taken and mounting a rescue mission.

All the while, Zimmerman was preparing his hypo and muttering to himself. "Too much of this will likely grant her an immunity to it. I hate having to rely on drugs so consistently. Certainly, the window of usefulness is shrinking with each passing dose."

Swallowing, Neelix watched as the doctor applied the hypo to Kes's neck. *Kes, what is that?*

It's a drug of some kind. I hate it—it forces me to speak the truth, and it makes my mind all fuzzy . . .

Those last words were barely "audible" to Neelix. *Kes! Kes, can you hear me?*

But, though he could feel that Kes was still present in his mind, he could no longer hear any of her thoughts—nothing coherent, at least. Her eyes shut tighter as Zimmerman administered the shot, then her eyes opened wide. Once, Neelix would have counted that as one of his favorite sights, for Kes's big, beautiful eyes were always probing, always questioning, always wondering. It was one of the many things he adored about her.

Now, though, those eyes were filled with fear.

Be strong, my sweet one, Neelix thought emphatically, hoping that Kes could gain some measure of strength from him.

"All right then, Kes," Zimmerman said in a deceptively gentle voice, "I'd like you to tell me what you're sensing."

"I . . . I feel . . . feel Neelix."

That caused Neelix to wince. He could hear the struggle in her voice, feel that same struggle in her mind, knowing that she desperately didn't want to answer Zimmerman's questions.

"He's . . . he's concerned about . . . about me. He thinks you're going . . . going to k-kill me."

Zimmerman turned to face Neelix, carrying an expression of sincere insincerity that Neelix recognized all too well—he often saw it in the mirror—which served only to make him trust the doctor even less. "You can rest assured, Mister Neelix, that killing Kes is absolutely the *last* thing on my mind."

"And I feel—"

At that, Zimmerman whirled toward Kes. He obviously hadn't been expecting more. "Yes, you feel what?" His questioning was more eager now. Neelix assumed it was due to having encountered something outside the range of what he had been expecting.

"Belq. He's bored and . . . and wants a . . . a bowl of *gagh* to eat, and then wishes . . . wishes to have sex with Prayak, from the galley. He's been—"

The growl behind Neelix grew louder. Neelix looked up to see that the Klingon had unholstered his gun and was pointing it at Kes.

"Be silent, woman!" Apparently, Belq was the name of Neelix's minder.

With a fleetness of foot Neelix hadn't expected from him, Zimmerman dashed forward to stand between Belq's muzzle and Kes. "Put that away, you big oaf! This woman is the most precious commodity on this base, and if you shoot her—"

"You'll what?" Belq asked with a sneer.

"It's not what I'll do," Zimmerman said tightly, "it's what the supervisor will do. This woman is her prize. Do you *really* think she'd take kindly to you shooting her?"

Belq's sneer became a grin. "Do you *really* think I care a whit what that halfbreed *petaQ* thinks?"

Neelix noticed that Belq's attention seemed to be focused entirely on Zimmerman and Kes and somewhat less so on Neelix himself. Deciding that it behooved him to take advantage, he tried a wrist grab that a friend had taught him once, years ago, one that the friend had said would take a Kazon down with consummate ease.

Of course, Neelix hadn't had the chance to test that assertion on a Kazon, and Belq was quite a bit larger than most of the Kazon Neelix had met in his life. Also, Klingons wore gauntlets that made it somewhat more difficult to maintain a crushing grip on their forearms, as Neelix quickly learned the hard way.

The Klingon laughed heartily at the sight of Neelix trying to grab his arm, and then waved that arm to one side, a motion that made Neelix nauseous even as he lost what grip he had on the arm in question and went flying across the room. Whatever minor pain was in his arms from his attempted grab was quickly forgotten in light of the impact of the back of his head with a shelf on the far wall, not to mention the shards of glass. The latter was, he quickly realized, what remained of the jars on that shelf, which his collision had knocked off.

"You clumsy idiot, I *need* those!" That was Zimmerman.

Neelix's vision was swimming, and he set his hand down to steady himself, only to find it hitting something wet and squishy.

Looking down, he saw that he had placed his hand right into what looked like a brain covered in a green fluid.

Yanking his hand out of the cranial matter, Neelix screamed and tried to get up, despite the swimming of his head.

Belq's disruptor was now aimed right at Zimmerman. "I've wanted to do this for months, Terran."

"If you shoot me—" Zimmerman started.

"Spare me," Belq said with another sneer.

Looking around—and regretting moving his head that much—Neelix grabbed one of the jars that hadn't broken upon impact with the floor and threw it at Belq.

The jar collided with the Klingon's wrist, sending the gun flying across the lab.

Neelix was disappointed initially—he'd been aiming for Belq's head—but he'd take what he could get. Snarling, Belq turned on Neelix while removing a large dagger from his belt. With a click, two smaller blades unfurled near the dagger's hilt.

Oh dear, Neelix thought. He now saw two daggers, but also two Belqs, which meant the head trauma he suffered was getting worse. *How do I dodge when I don't know which one is real?*

Then two Zimmermans sneaked up behind the two Belqs, and they each simultaneously jabbed a hypo into the Belqs' necks.

The Belqs reached around and backhanded the Zimmermans so they went flying across the lab.

"I'll kill you all!" the two Belqs roared with only one voice. "I'll—aaaaaaAAAAAAAAAAAAAAAAGGGGGGGGGGGGHHHHHH!"

Both Belqs' bodies started to convulse. Steam, of all things, came trickling out of their noses and ears, along with drops of blood. The scream became louder, then even louder as the Belqs collapsed to the floor, convulsing like mad, arms clawing at an opponent who wasn't there, legs kicking in all directions, with more steam coming out of every orifice.

Neelix closed his eyes tight, not wanting to see this, but found himself compelled to open them when the scream became more strangled.

There was only one Belq now, but that was enough. His screams were more of a *hkkk* noise now, and his eyes—

His eyes were boiling!

Now Neelix again closed his eyes, and also turned his head away, unable to watch any longer. Kes, he knew, was doing the same. Even as Neelix's head started to clear, he noticed that Kes's seemed to be clearing, as well. Zimmerman's concern about her developing resistance to the drug was apparently warranted, a thought that might have cheered Neelix under different circumstances.

Kes was also trying desperately not to see what was happening. Sadly, that did her little good, as she could still *feel* it all, and Neelix felt it through her: the pain, the anguish, as if one had been lit on fire from the inside, lava coursing through one's veins instead of blood.

After Belq's wails of agony finally stopped, leaving only a sound very much like steam escaping a leaky pipe, Neelix heard Zimmerman say, "Well, that was irritating."

"What did you *do* to him?" Kes asked.

Neelix finally opened his eyes and slowly got to his feet, looking everywhere except at the Klingon on the floor.

Zimmerman was applying some kind of device to his cheek where Belq had struck him as he answered Kes's query. "A compound of my own devising. It excites the red blood cells to the point where the blood reaches boiling temperature within seconds. This was my first time trying it on a Klingon. I wasn't sure it would work, as their blood has a different boiling point from that of Terrans and Cardassians, but it seems to have worked even faster—lucky for us."

Neelix stared angrily at the doctor. "I'd hardly consider that kind of murder 'lucky,' Doctor."

Zimmerman regarded Neelix with an arched eyebrow. "I would think you'd be grateful, Mister Neelix. Had I not intervened, he surely would have killed you, and Kes, and me."

"Grateful? What kind of monster *are* you?"

"I'm a *scientist*, Mister Neelix, and one who still has plenty of that compound left. I've already tested your blood, and its boiling point is within the range of the compound's effectiveness, rest assured." Zimmerman walked over to one of the consoles and hit a control. "This is Doctor Zimmerman—can someone please send security down here? I need a new guard for the prisoner, and someone to dispose of a body."

When Zimmerman looked over at the floor next to Neelix, he grimaced. "Oh, no! Those were my only samples!" He strode over toward Neelix, but stopped short of actually stepping in the spreading green fluid. "Ruined! Absolutely *ruined!*"

Three Klingons came in through the wide archway. "What happened?"

"Take that idiot to a cell," Zimmerman snapped, "he's a *menace!*"

One Klingon moved toward Neelix. The others stood still; one asked, "What happened to Belq?"

"An accident. It's none of your concern," Zimmerman said dismissively as he turned his back on the Klingon and prepared another hypo.

"Don't turn your back on me, Terran—Belq was my *cousin!*" The Klingon stomped over to Zimmerman, grabbed his shoulder, and violently yanked him around with his left hand, unsheathing his dagger—which looked just like Belq's; they were obviously issued to all soldiers—with his right.

Before this tableau could continue, an alarm went off. *"General quarters,"* said a disembodied, mechanical voice that Neelix figured belonged to the base's computer. *"All personnel to duty stations. Prisoners escaped. Code nine. Repeat, code nine."*

The Klingon who had been threatening Zimmerman sheathed his dagger and stared at the other two. "You two, stay here, guard the prisoners." He sneered at Zimmerman. "This one, though, can go to the dogs."

The other two Klingons chuckled as the first one left.

Zimmerman shook his head. "Barbarians . . ."

Neelix, however, was hopeful. *Perhaps the prisoners who've escaped are Captain Chakotay and his crew.* Of course, Neelix had no way of knowing if the captain and his people were even still alive, but this base didn't strike him as the kind of place that had a lot of prisoners.

Still, hope was all he had left.

11

C hakotay was beginning to understand why Terrans had taken to wearing footwear. Few things were more painful than having to walk—or run—on unyielding surfaces in one's bare feet. Dirt and grass were one thing—they changed shape to conform to one's footfalls—but running on the metal floors of Monor Base was getting progressively more agonizing.

He felt horribly exposed, and not just because he had no clothing. Three disruptor rifles—one in each hand and the other strapped over his shoulder—would, he thought, be inadequate protection once Supervisor B'Elanna got her act together and sent a real security force after them. Having control of the turbolifts bought them a little time, but the only way this was going to succeed was if they got out of there as fast as they could.

He'd ordered the turbolift to take him to the level with the guest quarters, figuring that was his best bet for finding Kate. Now he was walking down the wide corridor where the turbolift had left him, pain shooting through his shins, going through archways and doorways, and hoping for the best. He stayed close to the wall, but it was difficult to remain stealthy in this damned building with its wide-open spaces.

The first door he saw wouldn't open at his approach, so Chakotay decided to try it later if he needed to. He wasn't sure how he'd go about that—he didn't have Harry's skills for getting doors open—but he'd cross that bridge if he needed to.

Now he was approaching another of those ridiculous open archways. Chakotay knew that neither Klingon nor Cardassian

architecture featured this open style—both species had a prefer-
ence for dark, winding corridors—and right now he rather wished
that the Alliance had gone to the trouble of rebuilding Monor
Base instead of simply keeping the Ardanan facility intact.

From around the corner of the archway, Chakotay could hear
voices that sounded Klingon. He backed against the wall next to a
tall abstract sculpture, the plastiform warm on his backside. *At
least they didn't make their hallways all metal,* Chakotay thought with
some relief.

He aimed one disruptor high and the other low and, without
looking (and thereby exposing himself more) fired, waving the
rifles back and forth to maximize the range of the shots. To his
relief, he heard screams, then nothing.

Risking a look around the corner through the archway, he saw
two Klingons lying on the floor, scorch marks on their armor and,
in one case, half his face missing.

There wasn't much of this corridor left, so he entered the archway, stepped over the corpses, and continued down the way they
had come.

Just as he'd gotten a meter past the corpses, he heard more
footfalls coming from ahead. Doubling back, he jumped over the
corpses and lay on the ground behind them.

The footfalls came to a stop, but Chakotay didn't dare look—at
first.

"This is Katok," a voice said, presumably into a communicator.
"Tirod and Kamless are dead. One of the prisoners is loose on this
level."

A tinny voice sounded over the Klingons' communicators: *"We
still can't get the* khest'n *turbolifts to work, the access tubes have all been
flooded with gas, and half the security personnel aren't reporting. I'll transport someone down there as soon as I can."*

Chakotay smiled at that, once again grateful that Harry Kim
was on *his* side.

"Oh, and Katok? The supervisor doesn't need them alive."

Katok snarled. "She was never going to get them that way. Out."

That was the magic word for Chakotay. As soon as Katok cut off communication, he jumped up and fired both rifles at Katok and his comrade.

Or, rather, where he hoped they were. He nailed one of them in the chest, but the other shot went far wide of its target and the Klingon was able to fire back.

Pain sliced through Chakotay's torso as he fired again, this time hitting the Klingon dead-on.

Wincing in agony, Chakotay looked down to see a terrible black burn in his flesh right above the left hip. He was going to need that treated, and soon.

But first things first. Kate's got to be here somewhere, and I don't care how many Klingons I have to go through first. As long as Kate remained alive and in Alliance custody, the rebellion was in serious jeopardy. O'Brien would never even get the chance to build that warship of his.

Trying and not always succeeding to ignore the white-hot agony that seared through his left side every time he moved, he padded forward. Stepping over the four Klingon corpses was even more painful, and sweat was pouring down his face, his bare wrist doing an inadequate job of wiping it out of his eyes.

Turning the corner Katok and his friend had come around, he saw a very long corridor. At the end stood a Klingon guarding a door.

If Kate's an important enough spy, she may warrant a guard. Chakotay quickly fired a rifle shot at the guard.

How much of Chakotay's blurred eyesight was due to the sweat in his eyes and how much to the blinding agony he was in wasn't clear, but either way, his condition combined with the great distance to ruin his aim. His disruptor fire went clear over the Klingon's head. Luckily for Chakotay, the Klingon's own disruptor was holstered, so he was barely able to duck out of the way before he could take it out and fire. The beam hit Chakotay's right hand, forcing him to drop his weapon.

Undaunted—he still had two more, including the one strapped to his back—Chakotay tried the same trick again, pointing the rifle in his left hand around the corner and firing at the Klingon, who was now running down the long corridor toward him.

Unfortunately, that trick didn't work a second time. Chakotay unstrapped the other rifle with his right hand, unable to completely ignore the shooting pains that caused. Then he leapt out into the field of fire, rolling and intending to come up firing.

That, he realized, would have been a much more efficacious plan without a large, painful hole in his side, so instead of rolling, he cried out in pain and collapsed on the floor.

Laughing between breaths, the Klingon arrived at this end of the long corridor and said, "You're a fool, Terran."

Chakotay shot him in the face.

As the Klingon fell dead to the floor, Chakotay tried to figure out how to get up.

Come on, it's just crippling agony, it's nothing to keep you down. He'd faced far greater pain and exhaustion in the mines on Drema IV, and he'd survived that, he could damn well survive this.

He just had to make his legs work.

Gathering up every inch, every muscle, every iota of strength, using the stock of one of the disruptor rifles to brace himself, he managed to get to his feet. That effort left his breathing labored, his muscles feeling like they were made of wet noodles, and the throbbing in his left side now matching that of a pounding drumbeat.

Bracing himself against the wall—as that was the only way he could in any way guarantee not falling down again—he worked his way to the doorway the Klingon had been guarding.

The door opened before he got in front of it. Kate Janeway walked out, disruptor pistol in hand. At the sight of Chakotay, her eyes widened, and she raised her arm to fire.

Somehow, Chakotay was just a little bit faster, and he managed to shoot her in the leg. It wasn't an ideal place to shoot her, but he lacked the strength to lift his arm any higher.

With a most satisfying scream, Kate collapsed to the floor, gripping her right knee.

Chakotay hobbled past her. She somehow had the wherewithal to grab for his ankle, and he responded by kicking her.

That action, sadly, took most of his remaining strength. He managed to gather enough energy to direct his fall, but fall he did, onto Kate's couch.

Aiming both his weapons at her, he said, "Toss the disruptor, Kate."

She did as instructed, tears pouring down her proud cheekbones, but she wasn't crying out in pain anymore. "You've looked better, Chuckles," she said snidely.

"It's just a flesh wound." He tried to sound nonchalant, and could tell he wasn't really succeeding.

"I was referring to your state of undress. But then, seeing you naked always made me gag."

Chakotay shook his head, which had the unfortunate effect of making it swim, and he forced himself to hold the disruptors steady. In a ragged voice, he said, "So all the time, you were working for them."

"Not for them, for *her*. B'Elanna's been my patron all my life. She's given me a better existence than any I could ever have among the Terrans."

"You're good," Chakotay said with a bitter chuckle. "I never suspected. I just figured you were bitter because of what the Alliance did to you."

"The Alliance *saved* me! They gave me a home! What will you give the people, Chakotay, when your *precious* rebellion takes over? More tyranny? Because let me tell you, as bad as you *think* the Alliance is, it's nothing compared to what our people do when they're put in charge. Terrans are the filth of the galaxy, Chuckles, and I'll do everything I can to make sure they never get the chance to rule again."

As Kate spoke, her grip on her right knee grew tighter, and more tears streamed down her cheeks. She was doing everything she could to avoid showing how much pain she was in. Under other circumstances, Chakotay might have admired her attempt at stoicism. But now he realized that whatever doubts he might have had about killing Kate—and only now did he admit to himself that the doubts were there, as he only had Harry's word that Kate had turned—they were now eliminated. Kate wasn't just a spy, she was a fanatic, and she obviously really believed the nonsense she was spouting.

Then, suddenly, she dove for her disruptor. Chakotay shot at the disruptor, but hit her hand instead. Again, she cried out in pain as the beam cut into her hand, her flesh sizzling.

Anger and outrage lent strength to Chakotay's weakening limbs and he got to his feet as Kate writhed in agony on the floor of . . . whatever this room was. He assumed it was her quarters, but he was focused entirely on her right now and couldn't afford to look around the room. Haltingly, he stumbled over to where she lay. "You betrayed us, Kate. We can't afford to let you live."

"Typical." Somehow, Kate managed to sneer the word, something Chakotay hadn't thought possible. "The Terran solution to everything: kill it."

"Not everything," Chakotay said as he sank to his knees so his face was close to hers—as it had been so many times in the past months in what Chakotay had thought to be argumentative affection—and he imagined he could smell her tears. "Just those who endanger our cause."

He fired one disruptor. The beam struck Kate's pretty face, slicing through it. Bits of blood spurted before the beam could cauterize the wound it caused, and Kate fell backward, dead in an instant.

Chakotay let out a moan of anguish. Fatigue drained what energy was left in his limbs to the point where he could barely feel the tips of his fingers. The disruptors fell to the floor. The darkness he'd been staving off ever since he got shot at last consumed him. He wanted to open his eyes, but he couldn't.

His last thoughts were both regret at how it had ended between him and Kate and relief that he had saved the rebellion.

12

B'Elanna had been in the middle of flogging her favorite when the alarm sounded. Hastily throwing some clothes on, she led him to the turbolift.

It opened at her approach, but when she said, "Level one," nothing happened.

After three more tries, she activated an intercom. "Security, this is Supervisor B'Elanna, why aren't the turbolifts working?"

Kohlar's voice came back: *"The prisoners have escaped, Supervisor, and they have done—something to the turbolifts. They will not accept any voice commands. They have also flooded the crawlways with gas."*

"Fine. Transporter room, this is the supervisor—two to beam to the security office immediately."

"Yes, Supervisor."

Moments later, B'Elanna was standing over Kohlar, her favorite behind her. "How did this happen?"

"One of the prisoners did something to his surveillance. We flooded his cell with gas, but no gas could be seen on the monitor. The Terran Janeway—"

"Katie? Is she all right?" B'Elanna asked, concerned, as Katie was B'Elanna's primary source of intelligence on the rebellion.

Kohlar nodded quickly. "She is well. She led a team to investigate the prisoners—she was the only one to leave alive."

"Which prisoner altered his surveillance?"

"The palest of the three."

B'Elanna cursed. "Dear old Harry. I should have killed him as soon as I saw him in that damned ship. That also explains the turbolifts. Where's Katie now?"

"Under guard in her quarters."

"Good." B'Elanna nodded. "Do a scan for Terrans and Vulcans, and—"

"I've *done* that," Kohlar said snappishly. "Unfortunately, every security force I send after them stops reporting."

"Supervisor, this is Doctor Zimmerman."

"Not now, Doctor," B'Elanna said angrily. "I'm busy."

"I'm sure you are, but this is rather important. Something's wrong with the alien girl, and your security people have all been called away."

B'Elanna didn't like the sound of that. "What's wrong?"

"It's complicated. But you should get down here right now."

"Very well." B'Elanna turned to Kohlar. "*Find* those rebels and *kill* them. They have no value to me alive anymore. The aliens and Katie are all that matter. Gas the whole base if you have to, and we can sort it out later."

"Yes, Supervisor."

Activating the intercom, she said, "Transporter room, two to beam to Laboratory 3."

"Yes, Supervisor."

When they materialized in the lab in question, Zimmerman nearly jumped out of his skin, which gave B'Elanna no small amusement. She noted that a Klingon was on the floor, his corpse looking a bit mangled in the face, and that there were no other soldiers around, as Zimmerman had indicated. The two aliens were both sedated on biobeds with force-field restraints activated.

"My goodness!" Zimmerman said.

"I'm sorry," B'Elanna lied, "but the turbolifts are down. Now what has happened?"

Zimmerman whipped out a disruptor. "Nothing much, Supervisor, I simply needed you as a hostage."

At that, B'Elanna laughed. "Really? To get you where, exactly? That civilian freighter that you've been communicating with for the past day? I'm afraid they're space dust alongside Evek's ship."

The look on Zimmerman's face—eyes widening, mouth open in a rectangle—was priceless. "You're lying."

"She isn't," said a voice from behind her.

Whirling around, B'Elanna saw her favorite standing with a familiar-looking disruptor. Looking quickly down at her hips, she realized that it was hers.

"*You* betrayed me?" B'Elanna asked with a fury that she hadn't felt since Miral survived her poisoning.

"With a disruptor in my hand and a song in my heart," the Terran said with a grin. "What, you thought I *liked* being your boy toy?"

"This is all well and good," Zimmerman said testily, "but what about Volnak's ship?"

"It's not like Volnak was *on* it," her former favorite said with a roll of his blue eyes. "It was just a courier. There's a perfectly good ship in Bay 5."

"What?"

Sighing, the Terran said, "The rebel ship."

Zimmerman nodded. "Ah, of course. We can steal that and deliver these two to Volnak."

"At which point, we get enough money to live somewhere far away from Klingons and Cardassians."

B'Elanna snorted. "I hate to interrupt your grandiose plans, but you'll never get near Bay 5, and even if you do, there's no place in the galaxy far enough for you to hide from me."

"We'll make it fine with you as a hostage," her ex-plaything said with an insincere smile.

"I wouldn't be so sure of that," Zimmerman said archly. "That one was willing to murder our telepathic girl, and was unimpressed when I told him the supervisor wouldn't like it. 'Do you *really* think I care a whit what that halfbreed *petaQ* thinks?' were his exact words."

With his face so mangled, B'Elanna didn't recognize the soldier in question—not that she necessarily would have even if his face wasn't half boiled away—but she couldn't bring herself to be surprised at the disloyalty, either. Her Terran blood meant all too many Klingons would view her with disgust, no matter her position or her mother.

Her former favorite shrugged. "Kohlar's loyal to her, and he's the only one that matters."

Shaking her head, B'Elanna said, "You had everything. You were treated better than any Terran on this station. I gave you more love than any other creature in this galaxy! And this—*this* is how you repay me?"

The Terran smirked. "Life's a bitch, Supervisor."

B'Elanna smirked right back. During her speech, she had slowly moved her right hand to the hilt of her *d'k tahg*.

"So am I."

With one fluid motion, she whipped the dagger out and flung it at her former favorite.

The *d'k tahg* now protruding from the Terran's left eye, he fell to the floor, disruptor fire flying into the ceiling as his finger spasmed. Death was instantaneous—he hadn't even had time to let out one of those joyously erotic screams of his.

"I should thank you for that," Zimmerman said calmly. "It just means I don't have to split Volnak's reward. And I can assure you, that trick won't work on me, especially since your only other weapon is currently lodged in young Thomas's cranium."

B'Elanna regarded the Terran doctor. "It seems we have a standoff, then. Because I will not allow you to take me as a hostage. And I don't think you have the stomach for a fight."

"I don't need the stomach, Supervisor, when I have this." With the hand not holding the pistol, he held up a hypo. "This contains the compound I used on that one over there. It brings the blood to a boil almost instantly. I promise you, it's a much messier death than the one you recently visited on young Thomas."

"You'd have to touch me to inject me, Terran, and that, I promise, you'll never do."

Suddenly, Zimmerman's eyes widened, and he looked past B'Elanna and said, "Who are *you?*"

Rolling her eyes, B'Elanna said, "Really, Doctor, if you expect me to fall for *that* old—"

A hand clamped down on B'Elanna's shoulder, and then the world went dark.

During his years as T'Kar's thrall, Tuvok had learned the fine art of moving without being noticed. It was an art that was crucial for servants to know.

Admittedly, it was one thing not to be noticed on an estate where you were the primary caretaker of the house and therefore expected to be present, if not noticeable, and quite another to attempt such a trick of pseudo-invisibility when you were running naked through an Alliance base full of personnel with instructions to kill you.

Moving silently through the wide corridors of Monor Base, Tuvok eventually found his way to a computer terminal. His years under T'Kar served him well, as the Obsidian Order agent had little skill with machines—an oddity in an intelligence agent who relied on them to do his work, but the Klingon Tuvok had served possessed many eccentricities. It was through the exploitation of them that Tuvok had been able to make his escape and insinuate himself into the Terran Rebellion—and also work his way through the Monor Base system and determine his current whereabouts, the location of Kes, and the fastest route between the two. He also determined the location of *Geronimo,* and mentally filed that away for future use, assuming he was able to effect the rescue.

En route he encountered only two Klingon patrols. The first he was able to avoid, the second he disabled with the nerve pinch. In both cases, random chance favored him, something on which Tuvok knew he could not depend.

When he finally arrived at the laboratory, he saw a tableau he had not been expecting. Supervisor B'Elanna—whom he recognized from the files on Ardana that Seska had managed to obtain—was being held at disruptor point by two Terrans, neither of whom Tuvok recognized.

He did, however, recognize the two aliens on the biobeds: one was Neelix, and the other Tuvok recognized from Neelix's descriptions as Kes.

B'Elanna managed to throw her *d'k tahg* into the head of one of the Terrans before he could do anything, but that still left the other one for the supervisor to deal with.

Remembering an old cliché that he'd heard a few times during the days of the Terran Empire—"the enemy of my enemy is my friend"—Tuvok decided that he would do well to ally himself with the surviving Terran.

Since B'Elanna's back was to him, he could easily approach her from behind, which he did.

The Terran's eyes grew wide, and he exclaimed, "Who are *you*?"

As Tuvok moved to apply the nerve pinch to B'Elanna, the latter said, "Really, Doctor, if you expect me to fall for *that* old—"

Then she collapsed to the floor.

"To answer your question, sir, I am Tuvok of Vulcan, and I am here to take Kes and Neelix back to the Terran Rebellion."

"I'm sorry, Tuvok of Vulcan, but I'm Doctor Lewis Zimmerman, and these two aliens are my meal ticket." Zimmerman had yet to lower his disruptor pistol.

Tuvok had half expected this. He was familiar with all the Terrans involved in the rebellion, so the fact that he did not recognize Zimmerman or his cohort meant they were eighty-two-point-nine percent more likely to be opposing B'Elanna for their own personal gain.

He weighed his options. One was to attempt to overpower Zimmerman. Given that the doctor was armed and in his own territory, as it were, Tuvok doubted very much that his own superior strength would do him much good.

Then a jar went flying across the room between Tuvok and Zimmerman.

The doctor turned his head toward where the jar had come from, as did Tuvok, but no evidence of the method by which the jar had been flung across the room presented itself.

Another jar also flew through the air, this time toward the entryway. Then another. Then a large scanner started shaking on the floor, as did several items on shelves.

Since tectonic stress was an impossibility in a city suspended in the sky, Tuvok deduced that there was a seventy-three percent chance that these actions were due to psychokinesis. *If so, Kes's psionic potential is far greater than that of even the most powerful telepath among the Vulcans,* Tuvok thought soberly as he ducked another piece of equipment that he was too busy dodging to identify. A glance at Kes's prone form showed that, though she was still sedated, her mind was active. She was sweating profusely, and she appeared to be in the throes of rapid-eye movement. Of course, a REM state could mean something completely different for Kes's species, but still, Tuvok thought it to be an indicator of tremendous cranial activity.

Most of the debris currently flying through the room was doing so at roughly one-point-seven-six meters above the floor. Tuvok therefore thought it best to dive to the floor, where his chances of being struck were considerably reduced.

Zimmerman either did not make this deduction or simply was unable to react fast enough to implement any action in response to it, as he was struck on the side of the head by a heart stimulator. Point-nine seconds later, he joined Tuvok on the floor, albeit in a state of unconsciousness, and with a head wound that resulted in copious amounts of blood pooling on the doctor's forehead and the floor beneath him.

Crawling on the floor proved efficacious, especially since the items being thrown about the room were all flying freely until they struck something, usually a wall. Tuvok was far enough away from the walls that, as long as he stayed low, his risk was minimal.

When he reached Kes's bed, he got to his knees and reached out toward Kes's face, the tips of his fingers touching the parts of the face covering the neural pathways to the cerebellum.

Then he started speaking the mantra that was one of the most closely guarded secrets on Vulcan, words that had rarely been spoken in the presence of a non-Vulcan for many centuries:

"My mind to your mind. My thoughts to your thoughts. Our minds are becoming one."

Suddenly, Tuvok found himself flooded with strange images . . .

. . . an underground city full of people like Kes. These were the Ocampa, who lived a contemplative life, one that Kes found dull, though Tuvok thought it rather inviting . . .

. . . a gap in a security field, designed to keep the Ocampa safe, but which Kes used to escape, to explore . . .

. . . capture by the Kazon-Ogla, aliens that Kes found fearsome and strange, but whom Tuvok recognized by type, if not specific species: scavengers, pirates, thugs—and torturers, as they visited horrible pain on Kes . . .

. . . the smiling face of Neelix, the oasis in the desert of her imprisonment by the Kazon-Ogla . . .

. . . striking out at her jailers, killing them all with her thoughts . . .

. . . Neelix coming for her, rescuing her, taking her to this strange place . . .

. . . Zimmerman's experiments, worse even than the Kazon-Ogla. Those scavengers were motivated by hunger, thirst, and a need for resources. Zimmerman, though, was using her for his own selfish purposes, though Tuvok knew that there was both more and less to Zimmerman's experiments . . .

. . . and throughout it all, still the desire to explore, to see, to learn, and to do it with Neelix by her side.

Tuvok saw all this and more, and also tried to convey his own inner calm to Kes, teaching her to relax and not tie her telepathy so closely to her emotions, to control her urges and anger and frustration.

It was not an easy task. Tuvok was horribly out of practice, for one thing, not having actually participated in a mind-meld in fifty-three years, ten months, three days, and that was under controlled conditions with a fellow Vulcan who engaged in the mind-meld willingly.

But he persevered.

Take your mind away from the pain, he urged. *The pain is a river that is flowing away from you.*

I don't want to feel the pain anymore! Kes's voice was plaintive.

Tuvok tried to be reassuring. *You do not have to. You can put the pain aside.*

Neelix! Is he safe? He's—

Naturally, her first thoughts would be of her paramour—and also the only familiar person in her world right now. *Do not be concerned. Neelix is here with you, and Doctor Zimmerman is unconscious.*

For the first time, Kes seemed to realize that there was another presence with her. *Who are you?*

I am Tuvok of Vulcan. I was on the ship that rescued Neelix's escape pod, and I am here to rescue you—both of you, he added, knowing that Kes's feelings for Neelix were strong and not wishing to alienate her.

And then, realizing that it was a huge risk, but seeing no alternative—especially since more of Supervisor B'Elanna's soldiers could enter at any minute, and the sight of four bodies on the floor, one of which was the supervisor's, and Tuvok standing over their prize prisoner was not likely to engender a positive result—Tuvok opened his mind to Kes.

Seventy-six years, eleven months, and three days ago, Tuvok stood in the receiving room of a stately house in ShiKahr on Vulcan. With him were several other Vulcans, all appearing to be approximately as young as Tuvok—who had recently reached the thirtieth anniversary of the year of his birth—and who had all received the same peculiar summons. The house belonged to Sarek, the father of Emperor Spock, and was decorated sparingly but tastefully, with a ryill hanging in the center of one wall and sand sculpture against the opposite.

Tuvok knew few of those present. He recognized Captain Saavik, who had taken command of the Emperor's former ship, the I.S.S. Enterprise. Tuvok, a ten-year veteran of Starfleet, himself served as captain of the I.S.S. Excelsior, having killed Captain Styles when he proved to be working against the Emperor. (Tuvok would have preferred to take Styles alive, which was now Empire policy rather than assassination, but Styles gave him little choice, refusing to disarm.) None of the others in the room, however, were known to him personally.

Sarek himself entered the receiving room, followed quickly by Emperor Spock and Empress Moreau. Tuvok raised an eyebrow in surprise, for as a Starfleet captain, he had been made aware of the Emperor's itinerary. According to the latest reports from Starfleet Command, as reported to Tuvok by Lieutenant Valtane that morning, the Emperor was on Andor and the Empress on Luna. What's more, the royal personages were dressed, not in their traditional robes of office, but in drab civilian garb.

The Emperor spoke without preamble. "All of you have many aspects in common. You are all Vulcans, you have all proven yourselves to be loyal to me and my policies—and each of you has a psionic index of seven-point-nine or higher."

That caused a visible stir throughout the room. Psionic indices had not been spoken of publicly in over three centuries, since first contact with Earth. To speak of them in the presence of an alien such as Empress Moreau was a breach of Vulcan protocol the likes of which Tuvok had never seen.

"The Terran Empire is doomed," Spock continued. "Its fall is inevitable. I, however, can see no reason why the forces of entropy should be allowed to take the Empire when we can all work together to see that change occurs within our expected life spans. However, in order to bring about a truly free nation in this galaxy, we must still, to coin a Terran phrase, stare into the abyss."

From there, the Emperor went on to explain an audacious plan, one that required the elimination of the Terran Empire, conquest by external forces, and the insertion of millions of Vulcans as sleeper agents. He spoke of a project called Memory Omega, and two Terrans, Doctors Carol and David Marcus, a mother-and-son team who would safeguard the full repository of the Empire's scientific knowledge after the inevitable fall, and serve as the caretakers of Spock's plan after his likely execution.

The plan had been conceived, and its first stages executed, more than two decades earlier, at approximately the same time that Spock assassinated Captain James T. Kirk. The Emperor, recognizing the need to recruit younger Vulcans to his cause, had brought Tuvok and the others here now in hopes of convincing them to participate.

At first, Tuvok was skeptical. So were several of the other Vulcans in the room, and the discussion that ensued lasted through the night and into the next dawn. Eventually, Tuvok was swayed by the arguments presented— less so by Spock, Moreau, and Sarek, and more by Saavik, who brought a youthful passion to her defense of the Emperor's plan. He agreed to participate, as did all the others.

Within thirteen-point-four months of this meeting, the Alliance succeeded in conquering the Terran Republic—as Spock had renamed it a scant three-point-seven weeks after the meeting at ShiKahr—and then the plan had truly begun.

While Terrans were mostly sent into slavery, Vulcans were made servants, as Spock had predicted. Tuvok had thought this to be the largest flaw in Spock's plan, as Vulcans' superior strength and stamina might make them more attractive for mining work, but Tuvok had reckoned without the sadistic aspect. Both Klingons and Cardassians preferred to humiliate those they conquered—a trait they shared with the Terrans, truth be told—and Vulcans were not nearly as much "fun" in that regard.

But the efficacy of Spock's plan depended on the secret of Vulcans' telepathy continuing to remain just that: secret. It also depended on the lack of telepaths in this part of the galaxy. The Terran Empire had all but eliminated those species that had psionic abilities out of fear, and that fear served Spock's plan well.

Kes, however, changed everything. She could not be allowed to remain in Alliance hands. . . .

Tuvok opened his eyes, taking his hands away from Kes's face. Her eyes were also open, and staring at him. "That's all I am?" she asked in a ragged whisper. "A commodity to be kept out of one nation's hands or in another's?"

Bluntly, Tuvok said, "Unfortunately, the answer is yes. While telepathy is common among your people—though apparently the levels you have achieved are unusual—it is all but nonexistent here."

"Except for Vulcans."

"A fact we have labored to conceal, and which I revealed to you at great risk."

Nodding quickly, Kes said, "I understand what's at stake, Tuvok."

"Good. Now it is imperative that we depart." He deactivated the force field that restrained Kes to her biobed, then did the same for Neelix. He hefted the unconscious alien—who weighed more than he appeared, to Tuvok's chagrin—over his shoulder.

Kes was staring at Zimmerman and B'Elanna, who were both unconscious, and a Klingon and Terran, who were very obviously dead. "What happened?"

"That is the subject of a protracted discussion that is best postponed to a later date. We must proceed to *Geronimo* and prepare to depart."

With that, Tuvok led Kes out of the laboratory and into the corridor, moving toward Bay 5.

13

Seska stood dolefully, still bound to the marble column, the cold stone pressed against her back, rear end, and legs. The alarms had long since ceased, and the silence was deafening. She had already tried to pull the restraints out of the column seven times since B'Elanna and Janeway left, but they showed not the slightest sign of giving.

A few Klingons had run past, ignoring her completely. She knew that the prisoners had escaped, but she had no idea which prisoners. For all she knew, B'Elanna had others incarcerated here. Even if the prisoners were Harry, Chakotay, Tuvok, Neelix, or Annika, Seska wasn't entirely sure she wanted to be rescued by them.

No, not Annika. B'Elanna said that Janeway killed her. That was a pity, as Annika was the only person besides Tuvok in the entire rebellion that Seska actually *liked.*

And, she realized, her thoughts were ridiculous. Yes, she'd told Chakotay that she was done with the rebellion, and she probably was—but she also preferred being rescued by them to being lashed to this damned column where B'Elanna could hit her with the blinding, painful rays until she was remanded to Cardassia for trial.

The sound of footfalls got her attention, even though she was fairly sure it was another few Klingons running about trying to locate the prisoners. That they were having so much difficulty bespoke the likelihood that Harry Kim was one of those who had escaped.

That hypothesis was proven correct when Harry himself came around the corner—though Seska almost didn't recognize him. He was wearing a pair of pants from a Klingon soldier's uniform, stained in spots with blood. Harry's bare torso was likewise smeared in blood—all of it, she realized, Klingon—underneath two bandoliers strapped over each shoulder covered with *d'k tahg*s, disruptor pistols, and one *mek'leth*. His face was also bloody, again all of it Klingon, and his hair was mussed and caked with more blood. There wasn't, however, a single scratch on him—aside from his scar, of course.

In each hand, he held a disruptor pistol. Upon seeing Seska lashed to the marble column, he stopped short, looked her up and down, and said, "Well well well, what have we here?"

Of course, given a choice, Seska would have preferred that Tuvok do the rescuing, or that alien Neelix—certainly not the one who had broken three of her limbs.

"There's a button on the side that'll let you finish the job you started on *Geronimo*," Seska said with a sneer.

"Tempting—very, very tempting." Harry walked over to the side of the column, and Seska braced herself for the onslaught of the rays.

However, instead of pushing the button, Harry instead put both disruptors in his left hand, grabbed the *mek'leth* from the bandolier with his right, and then raised that arm. He swung down—

—just at the right angle to slice through the left restraint without cutting into her flesh.

Not wanting to look a gift *vrok* in the nose, she quickly undid the right restraint with her now-freed left hand. Her wrists had gone yellow from the days of being bound. To her relief, there were no foot restraints. Almost leaping down off the column, she put as much distance between it and her as she could.

Speaking honestly, she said, "I wasn't expecting that."

"You're lucky on two fronts. One is that I need you for something—something no one else can do."

"What happened to the others?"

"We all escaped. Tuvok's going after Neelix and his woman. I've been trying to find B'Elanna—no luck so far—but I do have a plan, and, like I said, I need your help to make it work."

Seska asked, "What about Chakotay?"

Harry shook his head. "That's the other front you're lucky on. I found him and Janeway, both dead. They probably killed each other."

"Good," Seska said emphatically. She wouldn't cry any tears for either of them. Chakotay wasn't fit to run a race, much less a rebellion cell, and Janeway was the lapdog of that halfbreed *tralk* and deserved to die at the hands of the man she betrayed most directly.

"Chakotay's orders," Harry said, "were to kill you if you weren't willing to come back with us."

Stunned that Chakotay had been willing to give her that chance, Seska asked, "Then I'll come back with you. What's the plan?"

It was rare for Harry Kim to smile, so when he did so now, Seska got a cold feeling in her gut. "Oh, it's a good one, trust me. Here," he added, handing over one of his disruptors, "you'll need this."

When Neelix came to, he found himself bouncing on his stomach and looking down at the dark feet of someone running down a corridor. He was also nauseous.

After a second, he realized that he was being carried over someone's shoulder. "Er, excuse me?"

The feet stopped running, and he felt himself being tossed gently forward. Landing on his feet, he found himself facing the naked form of the Vulcan from Captain Chakotay's group, whose name he couldn't for the life of him recall. "Thank you very much, Mister Vulcan," he said cheerfully.

"His name's Tuvok," said the most beautiful voice he'd ever heard, "and he saved our lives."

Whirling around, Neelix saw Kes, upright, alive, and looking . . . not well, truly, but better than she had in some time. Grabbing her shoulders, he cried, "Kes, my love! You're all right!"

"Getting there," she said with a small but difficult smile.

"We will have time for reunions at a later date," Tuvok said. "We must make haste to Bay 5."

Kes nodded, started to walk forward, then stopped. "Someone's coming."

Sure enough, two Klingons turned the corner. Upon sighting the three of them, they raised their disruptors.

Then those same disruptors flew into the air toward the ceiling.

Snarling, the two Klingons unsheathed their *d'k tahg*s and charged—

—for about three steps. Then they stopped in their tracks, grabbed their heads, and howled with agony before collapsing to the floor, blood trickling out of every orifice in their heads.

Just like the Kazon-Ogla, Neelix realized as the nausea threatened to grow worse. He put his hand over his mouth.

"Impressive." Tuvok's declaration struck Neelix as the greatest understatement in the galaxy.

Kes, however, stumbled forward. Neelix grabbed her arm. "Are you all right, dearest?"

Nodding quickly, Kes said, "I'm fine. I'm afraid Doctor Zimmerman's experiments were more . . . draining than I thought."

Turning to Tuvok, Neelix asked, "What happened to him?"

"He suffered cranial trauma. If he receives medical treatment, he will recover. Whether he receives that treatment is not within our control." He started walking forward, stepping over the two Klingons. "We must proceed with all due haste."

"You should have made sure he was dead," Neelix muttered as he fell into step behind Tuvok.

"Doctor Zimmerman is the least of our concerns, Mister Neelix."

"That's easy for you to say," Neelix said angrily, "you didn't see what he did!"

"If you are referring to the experimentation he visited upon Kes, I can assure you, I am more aware of that than you."

Turning to Kes, Neelix asked, "What is he talking about?"

Kes started to say something, then stopped. "It's difficult to explain."

"Mister Neelix," Tuvok said before Neelix could ask another question, "while I understand your emotional need to have everything explained, I suggest that we table our discussion until such a time as we are a safe distance from Ardana."

Letting out a long breath, Neelix said, "Of course, my apologies."

They continued through several curving and angled corridors, taking so many turns that Neelix had completely lost his bearings—not that he ever really had them in the first place. Tuvok seemed to know where he was going, though.

Neelix wondered what would happen next. Assuming they were able to escape this wretched place, what would he and Kes do? Would they return to Captain Chakotay's base? Work with their ragtag group of rebels? Find their own way? How could they do that, if Kes was such a valued commodity in the Alliance?

He put the thought in the back of his mind. Since his family had been killed, Neelix had lived most of his life from day to day, and it didn't look like he'd have any reason to change that, now that he was halfway across the galaxy.

Perhaps Kes and I can find a ship and try to get home.

That, however, was an issue for later. They turned another corridor and found themselves at a small marble staircase that occupied the right half of that corridor and led up to a massive doorway. It was labeled in a language that Neelix didn't recognize.

Tuvok said, "That is our destination." He had also stopped walking.

"What are we waiting for?" Neelix asked as he pushed past the Vulcan. This was no time to be hesitant.

Neelix's forward motion was arrested by Tuvok's arm on his shoulder. The Vulcan was deceptively strong. "Ow!"

"To answer your question, Mister Neelix," Tuvok said, without losing his grip on Neelix's shoulder, "we are waiting for a proper explanation as to why there are no guards." With his other hand, he raised an energy weapon and fired it toward the staircase.

The energy beam came to a sharp stop right in front of the staircase, an effect accompanied by a sparkle of lights.

"A force field," Tuvok said.

"What do we do now?"

"I can bring it down," Kes said.

One of Tuvok's eyebrows rose without the other one moving, a trick Neelix rather envied. "Are you sure, Kes?"

Smiling, Kes said, "No—but I'd like to try."

"Our options are limited," Tuvok said. "Proceed."

Kes stared at the staircase, focusing all her attention on it. Neelix stood by, thinking the most encouraging thoughts he could, hoping it would help.

It does.

Neelix smiled at the whispered thought his love sent him as she concentrated.

Suddenly, sparks shot out from the wall to the left of the staircase.

Again, Tuvok's eyebrow rose. He fired his weapon once again, and this time the beam went straight through to the staircase, which smoked from the beam's impact.

"Well done, Kes!" Neelix said, once again grabbing her shoulders.

This was fortuitous, as she started to collapse. Gripping her more tightly, he said again, "Kes?"

She managed to stabilize herself. "I'm fine." Her pale, sweaty face and whispered voice belied her words.

"I think it would be best," Neelix said slowly, "if you let Mister Tuvok and myself handle things from here on out."

"Agreed," Tuvok said. "You are new to these abilities, and the strain may prove more than you can bear."

"I'll bear the strain if it means getting out of this place," Kes said with more fervor than she'd spoken with a moment ago.

Neelix smiled. "We'll get out of here, my love, of that you can rest assured." He turned to Tuvok. "Shall we?"

"Indeed we shall," Tuvok said.

Still smiling, Neelix walked forward and stepped on the first of the stairs—

—which was when the beam sliced through his stomach.

Clutching his belly, Neelix fell onto the stairs headfirst. He tried to keep his eyes open, and only partially succeeded. Tears welled up, forcing him to blink.

He heard someone scream. It was Kes, but he wasn't sure if he heard her voice in his mind or in his ears. Perhaps it was both. . . .

Then the pain hit his mind, worse even than the pain in his body. But behind it wasn't simply the agony of a wound, but the bright light of Kes. Neelix felt her presence in his mind even more than he had when she communicated with him on his now-destroyed ship or in Zimmerman's lab. Then, she had been a voice in his head; now she was a beacon that was inside his very soul.

He had always found her beautiful, but now he truly appreciated her magnificence. She was an incandescence that he felt in every part of his body—and that burned at her touch if she so desired, a fact the Klingons who had shot Neelix learned to their regret.

Through her thoughts, Neelix was able to feel the moment when the Klingons' brains exploded, and hear their final thoughts before expiring. He was able to feel Tuvok's shock at Kes's latest demonstration of her psionic abilities, and the pain he felt as a piece of sculpture sliced through his arm.

When that happened, Neelix realized that Kes was moving many objects in the area with her mind. The large door shattered into millions of shards of metal; the sculptures were ripped from the walls and sent flying across the room, the furniture likewise; the bodies of the four Klingons who had been approaching from the other direction exploded into a pulpy mess of blood and muscle and bones.

Kes's light shone even brighter, then.

It was the last thing Neelix saw before he gave in to the pain at last. . . .

Harry had killed seven Klingons by the time he and Seska reached the turbolift. Four he had killed with continuous disruptor fire that had started as soon as they came within Harry's sight and didn't end until fifteen seconds after they were quite dead, their bodies a sizzling mess of burnt flesh and destroyed nerves. One he had killed by sneaking up behind her, slicing her throat with a *mek'leth,* then cutting open her crest. The remaining two were the ones on duty in the security office. He had killed them by throwing two *d'k tahg*s, the first of which lodged in one Klingon's throat, the second in the side of the other guard's head; he had then used the *mek'leth* to cut off their heads and toss them into two separate corners of the office.

The turbolift that was taking them down to the Monor Base's sub-basement responded to Harry's voice commands, which surprised Seska. Harry shrugged and said that he had reprogrammed them. "I'm surprised the Klingons haven't gotten control back."

Seska wasn't at all surprised.

As soon as the turbolift doors opened, Harry and Seska both fired repeatedly, he high, she low. When the resultant screams finally stopped, they stopped firing. She looked down the corridor to see two Klingons on the floor, in front of a secure doorway painted with the emblem of the Alliance. Seska realized that it was the first instance of the emblem she'd seen on Monor Base. *B'Elanna isn't just scum, she's disloyal scum.*

Then again, she thought with a wry smile, *so am I.*

They walked toward the large door. "Here's why I needed your help. I was hoping to reprogram the computer so that it would accept my DNA signature to open the door."

"You couldn't do it?" That shocked Seska, as such a feat was within the expected range of Harry's capabilities.

Harry knelt down at the door control and pried off the panel cover. "The problem is the system's hardwired to only accept the DNA of a Cardassian or a Klingon. Presumably, it'll accept the supervisor's patterns, so halfbreeds can get in, but a full-blooded Terran won't work."

Seska nodded. "But I will."

"That's right."

"I'm missing something, Harry—what's on the other side of this door? It's not part of the base, is it?"

"No, it's the control room for the entire city. On the other side of this door are the antigravity generators that keep Stratos afloat. They've got to be *very* finely honed and carefully tuned. I'm willing to bet the reason *why* the electronic security here is so strict is because it wouldn't take a lot to sabotage those generators." For the second time, Harry smiled. "This base is full of Klingons and the finest scientific minds in the Alliance."

Seska's eyes widened. "You want to crash Stratos?"

"It'll be a great victory for the rebellion, and hundreds of Klingons, a few Cardassians, and that halfbreed bitch will all die horribly." Harry said the words with a frightening calm.

Finding herself unable to muster up a good argument against the notion—since she knew Harry wasn't suicidal, and therefore knew that their being off Ardana before the crash happened was part of the plan—Seska said, "Let's do it."

14

The first thing B'Elanna did when she woke up was look around Laboratory 3. As she feared, the prisoners were gone. However, she was surprised to see that Zimmerman was lying on the floor near her, blood pooling from a head wound, and that the lab looked as if it had been hit by a cyclone.

The first thing she did was walk over to her former favorite's corpse and yank her *d'k tahg* out of his eye. Wiping the blood and ocular fluid off the blade with her sleeve, she then walked over to Zimmerman and thrust the weapon into the back of his neck. Ripping it out, she then jammed it into the side of his head, near the wound, then yanked it out again and stabbed him in the back. Then she just stabbed him randomly over and over again, his blood spurting everywhere, his body convulsing in its death throes, a scream forming in the back of her throat, eventually becoming a death-yell that echoed in the wide-open spaces of this thrice-damned base. Over and over again she plunged her family dagger into the body of this mewling, irritating, obnoxious, foul, contemptible *Terran.*

She hated them. Every single one of them, from whichever smooth-faced *petaQ* caught Miral's eye and Miral's eggs to impregnate her with B'Elanna, all the way to this bald, smirking irritant of a scientist who conspired with Thomas to betray *her* . . .

Thomas . . .

She stopped in mid-thrust and turned to look at Thomas's corpse, his beautiful, smooth, loving face forever marred by the wound made by her *d'k tahg.*

The sad part was, she had enjoyed him. Perhaps she hadn't actually loved him—B'Elanna wasn't even sure what that emotion *was*—but she had loved being with him, loved feeling him, loved everything they did together. Ultimately, the time she spent with him was the only occasion in her miserable halfbreed existence that she was ever truly happy.

Raising her gore-covered *d'k tahg* again, she made as if to thrust it into Thomas's scarred body, but hesitated before she could bring her arm down.

Damn you, Thomas. She couldn't do it. Killing him in the first place, that was an act of self-defense, but in the cool light of premeditation, she found she couldn't even bring herself to defile his corpse.

Damn you, Miral.

She needed to be away from this place. If nothing else, Kes, the alien woman, was gone, and B'Elanna needed her found. She activated an intercom. "Kohlar, this is the supervisor, what's happening?"

There was no response.

"Transporter room, beam me directly to the security office."

"Yes, Supervisor."

At least someone's answering, she thought angrily as the transporter beam took her from the devastated lab to the more pristine security office.

Mildly more pristine, in any case—there was blood all over the place, and two corpses on the floor, both Klingons. She could not immediately identify them, due to their being decapitated. Looking around the room, she saw Kohlar's head in one corner. In the opposite corner was another head, but the face was turned away from her, and B'Elanna found herself unwilling to walk over and turn it so she could see who else had been killed.

The important thing wasn't who was dead, but who had killed them. "Harry," she said with a growl.

She walked over to the computer console, which was almost as stained with blood as B'Elanna herself, and called up the surveillance camera in Katie's quarters. There was still one Terran she didn't despise, and that was dear Katie Janeway, who'd been so unswervingly loyal to B'Elanna throughout everything. *As long as Katie's okay, everything will be—*

Her face fell. Katie wasn't remotely okay. Katie's body was on the floor of her quarters, her face marred by the telltale scarring of a disruptor blast. The culprit was probably the naked Terran on her couch, whose eyes were closed and who wasn't moving. The tattoo over his eye identified him as Chakotay, their leader.

She checked the sensors and saw that there was a minimal life sign. It must have been Chakotay, clinging to life despite the gaping wound in his side.

Her lips curling into something that was half snarl, half smile, B'Elanna instructed the computer to flood Katie's quarters with nerve gas. It wouldn't hurt Katie at this point, and it would guarantee that her murderer paid the price for ruining B'Elanna's plans.

As she fed the instructions, she noticed that her hands were covered in blood. Putting one hand to her face, she felt the blood and gore that was caking on her cheeks and realized that she probably looked a mess.

No, she thought, *I look like a Klingon who has gone into battle. And I will not rest until all my enemies are dead.*

She started examining other parts of the base. First, she checked on Seska; true to the way this day had been going for B'Elanna, the traitor had been freed. The security feeds to the entire hangar bay were nonfunctional for some reason—B'Elanna assumed that Harry was responsible—so B'Elanna checked the other part of Monor Base where she least wanted Terran rebels to be wandering around free: the hallway that provided access to the city's control room.

Sure enough, she saw two dead guards and Harry Kim and Seska kneeling in front of a control panel.

Just as B'Elanna was debating whether or not it was worth flooding the hallway with nerve gas—her hesitation arising mainly from the loss of Seska's trial, which was an important part of her plan to regain status with Alliance Command—Harry and Seska managed to get the door open.

Damn them! The security measures weren't active in the control room itself, as both the anesthezine and the nerve gas were too risky to let loose around the sensitive antigravity equipment that kept Stratos in the air.

Not nearly as risky as letting two rebels in there, though. "Transporter room, beam me to the corridor outside the control room, *now!*"

"*Yes, Supervisor.*"

She wished she could have beamed directly in, but transporters didn't operate within the room, either, for the same reason the gases didn't.

It wasn't until she materialized that she realized that she had forgotten to retrieve her disruptor from Thomas's corpse. *Well, it's not like I would've used an energy weapon in there anyhow.*

It still put her at a disadvantage, however. Harry and Seska would have no qualms about firing their weapons, as their likely goal was to sabotage the antigrav generators that kept Stratos aloft.

The phrase *control room* didn't do the space justice, since the word *room* implied a relatively small, enclosed area, even on Ardana where spaciousness was the order of the day. The control room took up the entire length and breadth of the city, save for that one corridor that led to the turbolift into which B'Elanna had materialized. The four corners of the space were taken up with huge cylindrical generators, protected by duranium sheaths, and each half a *qell'qam* in diameter. Throughout the massive space were various control consoles. B'Elanna moved toward the nearest of the generators.

Sure enough, she saw Harry and Seska operating one of the consoles—B'Elanna didn't know which one, as the minutiae of engineering bored her to tears. Besides, unlike the equipment in the security office and operations, these generators hadn't been replaced with Alliance models, as it was deemed too risky to take the existing Ardanan equipment offline in order to replace it.

To B'Elanna's relief, that very feature was vexing Harry and Seska right now, as they appeared to be having difficulties with the interfaces.

Quickly, she reviewed her options. She doubted she could sneak up on them—certainly not on Harry. Only the room's sheer size had allowed her to remain unnoticed so far. She had no energy weapons, and couldn't risk firing them in any case. As for Harry and Seska, they'd be more than happy to risk it and, she could see now, they were both quite well armed (though not well dressed; Harry was as covered in gore as B'Elanna, and was wearing only some stolen Klingon uniform pants, and Seska had yet to put on any clothes).

Then she broke into a smile. She didn't need to confront them at all.

Slowly, she backed out of the control room, then ran down the corridor toward the turbolift. Activating an intercom, she said, "Transporter room, beam me back to the security office."

"Yes, Supervisor."

As soon as she materialized, she immediately went to the computer and implemented a biohazard protocol, which meant quarantine procedures had to be undertaken. That meant that bulkheads would close over any access points to level ten. *They may sabotage the generator, but they'll be trapped here.*

There was a part of B'Elanna that was quite willing to die along with Stratos. She had lost Kes, lost her favorite Terran plaything, lost two of her three best scientists, and lost her informant on the Terran Rebellion. A quick computer check revealed that Katie had begun her report on the rebellion's activities, but she hadn't gotten very far when Chakotay shot her. The supervisor had nothing left.

But no—I'm still alive.

Just then, Crell Moset ran into the office. "Supervisor, what's happening? Security won't respond to my— Oh, dear." That last was added when Moset caught sight of the decapitated bodies.

Looking up at B'Elanna, he asked snidely, "Has Zimmerman taken more brains for his experiments?"

"Zimmerman's dead." She whirled around, startling Moset, who likely hadn't expected to see his supervisor covered in Terran blood. "You have a ship in Bay 9, yes?"

"Of course." Moset was a very wealthy scientist, after all, and had several private ships. Most were at his home on Chin'toka II, but the one he originally came to Ardana in was docked here.

"Good." She turned back to the computer. "Give me the access codes to your ship's computer."

"What?"

Turning back around, she snarled, "Now!"

Recoiling as if slapped, Moset quickly dashed over to stand next to B'Elanna and input an access code. B'Elanna then core-dumped Monor Base's entire memory to the ship.

Just as the computer finished, the floor tilted under her feet, and she and Moset both fell to the floor and slid toward the back wall.

"What's happening?"

"The end of Stratos." The base started shaking uncontrollably, making B'Elanna's teeth rattle as she struggled toward the intercom—now an uphill climb up the angled floor—and said, "Transporter room, this is the supervisor—two to beam to Doctor Moset's ship."

There was no answer.

I suppose I should be grateful they stayed at their posts this long. She allowed herself to slide down the floor toward the exit, grabbing Moset along the way. "Come on, Doctor. We're leaving."

Tuvok sat in the pilot's seat of *Geronimo,* the unconscious Neelix next to him in Seska's chair. Once Kes had completed her rather impressive display, the way was clear for Tuvok to retrieve *Geronimo,* start it up, and pilot it away from Stratos. After taking care of one last piece of business—also putting on a coverall, treating Neelix's wound, and treating his own lesser one—he was ready to proceed back to the Badlands.

However, it behooved him to attempt to rescue as many of his cohorts as he could. He scanned the base—

—and was rather shocked to discover that the city was now listing a bit. Further scans revealed a catastrophic failure in one of the antigravity generators. Tuvok would have thought that the generators were designed to withstand the failure of one of them, but either the Ardanans hadn't programmed such redundancy, or the generator had been sabotaged in such a way as to bypass that safety feature. A life-sign scan of that particular area revealed a Terran and a Cardassian, at which point Tuvok suspected he knew who was responsible for the sabotage.

Unwilling to take any chances, he activated the security field around the two-person transporter pad at the back of the flight deck and then beamed the two life-forms aboard.

Harry Kim and Seska materialized a moment later, at which point Tuvok lowered the force field. Harry was quite disheveled, and also quite armed, and dressed in Klingon uniform pants. Seska, despite her nakedness, looked better than she had when Tuvok had last laid eyes on her.

"Good timing," Seska said. "Someone locked us into the bottom level."

"It is fortuitous that my assumption that you were in the generator room proved correct." Tuvok turned back to the console. "I have, however, been unable to determine the precise location of Captain Chakotay among the Terran life-sign readings I am detecting."

"Don't bother," Harry said, taking Tuvok's usual seat. "Chakotay's dead—he and Janeway killed each other."

Tuvok raised an eyebrow. "Indeed?"

"No loss, on either front," Seska said. "I see you rescued the annoying one. What about the telepath?"

"She is no longer a concern," Tuvok said. "Her psionic potential has turned out to be far greater than any of us anticipated. Her final blow against the Alliance officers on Stratos—that which allowed Mister Neelix and me to board *Geronimo* and depart without interference—was a psychokinetic display of such magnitude that it left Kes—" Tuvok hesitated. "I am afraid I have no words that can properly convey precisely what happened to Kes after that, except that it was most . . . fascinating." He turned to look at his comrades. "I can say that Kes is no longer corporeal. For many centuries, scientists have theorized that the next stage in humanoid evolution would be to become beings of energy. I believe that Kes has, in that sense, evolved."

"So she's out of Alliance hands?" Seska asked.

"Yes."

"That's all I care about. I'm gonna put some clothes on." She turned on her bare heels and left.

"I assume," Tuvok said to Harry, "that you wish to bathe and change your clothing as well?"

"Not yet," Harry said, his eyes fixed on the viewscreen. "I want to see this first. I didn't get to kill B'Elanna, so this is the next best thing."

Following Harry's gaze, Tuvok saw Stratos City start to sink into its cloud.

The antigravity generators on Stratos kept it at the top of one of Ardana's clouds, which was artifically kept in place and intact in order to create the illusion that the city sat atop it at all times. In reality that was, of course, impossible without artificial means— but so was keeping an entire city afloat. Tuvok appreciated that the visual impact of a city on a cloud was greater than a city simply floating, and so understood why the ancient Ardanans had constructed the city thus.

With Harry and Seska's sabotage, however, that was undone. Stratos was now listing at a forty-nine-degree angle and seemed to be falling *into* the cloud. Within three-point-nine seconds, the entire base was invisible, but only for point-seven seconds, as the lower portion that had first sunk into the cloud was now emerging beneath it.

A flash of light suddenly appeared within the cloud, which Tuvok's sensors indicated were chemical explosions. He hypothesized that the sudden change in pitch had a deleterious effect on some of the experiments that were no doubt being conducted on Monor Base. In addition, several small vessels were flying out of the cloud, each on an orbital course. One was an atmospheric craft with a wing that was on fire. It could not achieve escape velocity; the flames spread to the rest of the ship, and it plummeted toward Ardana in a plume of fire.

Stratos itself was picking up speed. A section of the base that was becoming visible under the cloud was aflame, probably from one of the generators malfunctioning.

Tuvok kept the image translation of the sensor images trained with the base at the center of the viewscreen for Harry's benefit. The curve of the base's descent increased as it fell. The fire in the section where the chemical explosion had been continued to blaze, though it blew upward as the base accelerated.

Two of the city's buildings were ripped from their foundations. Tuvok saw several bodies plummeting into the sky out the buildings' windows. The two structures were soon torn apart by wind shear. Only some of the bodies made it as far as the ground—many were pulverized in midair. From this distance, Tuvok could not determine individual characteristics or species, but as each life was snuffed out, Harry Kim's smile grew wider.

More explosions racked the lower portions as the generators failed. Within nine-point-one seconds, the entire base was sheathed in flames. Tuvok projected the descent of the base and saw that it was going to make planetfall in a lake—one that, if his calculations were correct, would become much larger from the impact crater, and also much shallower, at least for a time, as the flaming base would boil away a large percentage of the lake's water.

"I'm picking up a ship scanning us," Harry said. He looked up. "It's a Cardassian civilian ship, but I've got an anomalous life-sign reading that I'm willing to bet is the supervisor."

Tuvok immediately started the warp engines. "We must depart immediately."

Harry nodded. Tuvok was grateful that the Terran's blood-thirsty need to see the complete destruction of Stratos was not overwhelming his common sense.

Geronimo went to warp, and began the journey back to base.

B'Elanna couldn't figure out which ship was which in the dozens of warp signatures that were fleeing Ardana like rats departing a sinking windboat. She had hoped to find Kes on one of them, but that appeared to be a forlorn hope.

Instead, she resigned herself to the inevitable and set a course for Archanis. She had a friend there who would take her in, at least until she figured out her next move.

And that would take a considerable amount of figuring. She didn't have her alien telepath, she didn't have her rebellion mole, and she didn't have her state-of-the-art facility and brilliant scientists.

"Excuse me, Supervisor?"

Well, she had one brilliant scientist, at least. Turning to Moset, she said, "Yes?"

The doctor was holding a padd. "I've been reviewing the notes Zimmerman made when he was working with that alien girl, and—" He smiled. "It's *most* fascinating. I believe that his work points in some very promising directions."

Again, B'Elanna found herself growing impatient with the scientist's equivocation. "What 'directions' might that be?"

"I believe it's quite possible that, using this and other information Zimmerman gathered, I might be able to genetically engineer telepaths."

B'Elanna's eyes grew wide. "Is that so?" She leaned back in her chair. "Tell me more, Doctor."

15

The flitter was a one-person craft, considerably smaller than *Geronimo*. Tuvok took it, explaining that he needed to go meditate, as was traditionally done on Vulcan on the fifth of Tasmeen.

It was a lie, of course, one that was readily believed thanks to Tuvok's carefully crafted persona as someone who observed antiquated Vulcan ritual. It was the fifth of Tasmeen, true, but the only ritual associated with that day involved lighting a candle.

It did, however, provide excellent cover for his trip to Regula.

The asteroid served as one of the bases for Emperor Spock's plan, which had the code name of Memory Omega. Several scientists, and their descendants, were sequestered here awaiting the day the final stages of the late Emperor's plan would be put into effect.

When Tuvok brought the flitter in to land, he saw another small craft docked there, one he had last encountered four days, three hours earlier in orbit of Ardana.

After disembarking, he walked across the landing bay to the duranium door that provided ingress to the rest of the Memory Omega base. Tuvok placed his right hand on the plate and said, "Tuvok of Vulcan."

The door slid aside. He walked through a long corridor, then came to another door, which slid aside at his approach.

On the other side of the door were T'Pel and Kes.

Back on Monor Base, it had been extremely difficult for Tuvok to carry both the wounded Neelix—whom he had rendered insensate with a nerve pinch—and Kes—who had collapsed from the effort of mind-blasting every

Klingon within a half a qell'qam *and also damaging much of the equipment in that same radius—onto* Geronimo *by himself, but the lack of resistance from Alliance security, either personnel or devices, eased Tuvok's burden considerably. He placed Kes on the transporter pad, after determining that her breathing was regular, if shallow, and Neelix in Seska's usual chair. Then he started the preflight sequence.*

After a quick trip to his footlocker to retrieve a coverall, he returned to the flight deck just as the preflight concluded. As he guided Geronimo *out of Monor Base's Bay 5, he sent out an encoded subspace signal.*

That signal reached a ship that was hidden in the Oort cloud of the Ardana system, a ship that now moved out of the relative protection of the cloud and set course for Ardana. Within seven-point-eight minutes, it was within visual communications and transporter range. The face of T'Pel appeared on the screen.

"Are you ready for transfer, husband?" *she asked.*

"Yes," *Tuvok said.* "Please treat her carefully, my wife, as she has been badly abused by the Alliance."

"That is not surprising," *T'Pel said.*

"Transporting now." *With those words, Tuvok beamed Kes to his mate's ship, which then left the system at warp eight, headed for Memory Omega.*

"Tuvok!" Kes said now as he entered. "What happened? Where am I? This woman won't tell me *anything,* and I—"

"My apologies, Kes. This is T'Pel, she who is my wife."

Kes frowned. "Your wife?"

"Yes. She, and this base, are a part of the plan I revealed to you. And you, Kes, can be a very important part of that plan."

"I don't understand— Where's Neelix? I want to—"

"Mister Neelix is in the Badlands. He believes that you have . . . have evolved to a higher plane of existence."

"I don't even know what that means."

Tuvok inclined his head. "It was misdirection in order to convince the others that you were out of the picture, as it were."

T'Pel added, "It was necessary. If you were alive and known to be part of the Terran Rebellion, it would become a much greater target for the Alliance's ire. Your existence must remain a secret, even from the other members of the rebellion—even from Mister Neelix."

"At least," Tuvok added in the hope it might mollify her, "for the time being."

At that, Kes stood up. "Tuvok, this isn't fair! I didn't ask for this, and I certainly didn't ask to be taken from Neelix! You have to take me back to him!"

"I am afraid that I cannot. The risk is too great."

"What, the risk to your rebellion? You think I care about that?"

Calmly, Tuvok said, "The risk to the rebellion is of considerably less consequence than the risk to you, Kes. Do you recall what happened on Monor Base before you fell unconscious?"

"I—" Kes hesitated, looking down. "I don't remember. We were heading for that staircase, and then I saw Neelix struck down, and then—" Again, she hesitated, then looked helplessly at Tuvok.

Suddenly, her eyes widened, and she sat back down again, whispering, "No . . ."

Tuvok saw no reason not to be blunt. "Yes. You killed dozens of Klingons, as well as damaging a considerable amount of equipment. What's more, you were able to protect myself and Mister Neelix, as well as the ships in the bay from your psionic assault."

"I don't know how I did that," she said in a small voice.

T'Pel nodded. "*That* is the risk. Your power is too great, and too uncontrolled. You must be trained, and that must be done in seclusion."

"I—I suppose." She looked up. "But I don't like it."

"In truth, none of us do," Tuvok said gently. "But if your training goes as planned, then you will be in a position to right that wrong."

Kes looked up at Tuvok. Her jaw was set and her eyes showed a deep determination. "In that case, Tuvok, I'd like to start that training as soon as possible."

* * *

"I'm sorry, Neelix."

The Talaxian was sure that Seska meant the words she said, but it was inadequate. "How could this have happened?" he asked, tears streaking down his cheeks.

"I honestly don't know. Tuvok couldn't even explain it, and he can explain anything. And unlike the rest of us, he was *there*. But it seems that Kes—I don't know, transcended the flesh, maybe."

Neelix shook his head. "It's that Zimmerman person. He did . . . did *something* to her. *He* caused this."

"I wouldn't be surprised if his experiments had something to do with it," Seska said with an agreeing nod. "But he probably died when Stratos was destroyed."

"Yes, I'm sorry I missed that."

Seska grinned. "Harry made a recording."

"Good." Neelix wanted to see that hateful place crash to the ground in a fiery conflagration, if for no other reason than to see if the reality matched the dream of it happening that he'd been having since he was first imprisoned there.

They were sitting now in the mess hall of the rebellion base in the Badlands. They had stitched up Neelix's wound, and now he was eating some kind of soup. Seska wasn't eating, but sipping some kind of yellow drink.

"Where is Tuvok, anyhow?" Neelix asked. "I wanted to thank him for rescuing us."

"He's away from the base for a bit—some kind of meditative retreat. He does this every once in a while, some kind of Vulcan thing." She shook her head. "I've known plenty of Vulcans over the years, and I've never seen one who obsessed over their old traditions the way Tuvok does. I suppose it's his way of clinging to the way things used to be."

"Understandable." Neelix sipped his soup and wondered how much of that he would be doing in the future.

"So what's next for you?" Seska asked.

Remembering the last confrontation Seska and Chakotay had before they arrived at Ardana, Neelix smiled. "That was going to be my question for you."

"I was going to abandon the rebellion, but with Chakotay dead, I'm not sure a problem exists. I saw how far O'Brien's gotten with that warship of his, and I'm starting to think this rebellion might stand a decent chance of making some headway." She sighed. "Besides, I don't have anywhere else to go."

"Neither do I. If you'll have me, I'll willingly be part of your rebellion."

"You sure? Most of the people here are fighting oppression. Me, I'm trying to restore Cardassia to what it was before the Klingons subverted it. But this isn't your fight, Neelix. Don't you want to try to get home?"

"It is very much my fight," Neelix said in a quiet voice. "It was the moment they imprisoned me and tortured the woman I love into something that took her away from me." He set down his spoon. "It has been many years since I encountered a cause that was worth fighting for, Seska. I believe, in this rebellion, I've found one. The Alliance stole the creature I've loved more than anything in the universe, and I won't rest until they pay for that. As for home—" He hesitated. "The Haakonians took my home from me. I was cast adrift, wandering the stars. I believe this rebellion can put me back on course."

Seska smiled. "Then welcome aboard, Mister Neelix. There's a lot of work ahead of us, and we'll need all the help we can get."

With a grim determination he hadn't felt since his family was killed, Neelix said, "You can count on me, Seska."

Cutting Ties

Peter David

Historian's Note

This story unfolds concurrent with the events chronicled over the course of the first four *New Frontier* novels, concluding during the period between *Fire on High* and *Martyr*, and roughly around the end of *Deep Space Nine*'s fourth season.

1

The sun hung heavily in the blistering Xenexian sky on the day that Gr'zy of Calhoun reluctantly said farewell to one of his sons and gratefully bid good-bye to the other.

Gr'zy didn't acknowledge the intensity of the heat, and probably wasn't even aware of it. Part of that stemmed from the fact that the huge, grizzled warrior had become inured to the most daunting aspects of his homeworld's inhospitable climate. He had used to complain about it in his youth until his father had beaten his whining out of him. Gr'zy had resented the hell out of his old man for it at the time, but as an adult he'd come to appreciate his father's actions. It had toughened him, and made it possible for him to endure not only the harshness of his world, but the tragedies that were thrust upon him by his world's enemies.

Those enemies were surrounding him now.

The rebellion had failed.

His greatest son, the foremost leader of the rebels, now lay before him. More precisely, his remains lay before him, and they were not going to be around for much longer.

Gr'zy wanted to avert his eyes, but he forced himself to keep watching as the body of his mighty son lay upon its funeral pyre. Flames licked the body hungrily, and the air was filled with the smell of burning meat. The aroma itself, and the knowledge of what was causing it, made him want to retch. But what sort of message would that have sent to his fellow tribesmen, if they'd seen their leader down on his knees and vomiting like a pregnant woman? So he contained himself behind a stoic mask and watched his son's remains crackle, burn, and flake away, spiraling skyward amid the twisting smoke.

Other Xenexians were grouped around in a loose configuration, murmuring prayers or rocking back and forth in mute sorrow. There had been more Xenexians mere months ago, far more of them. But they had died in pitched battle with their oppressors and conquerors, the Danteri. With their conquerors . . . and their conquerors' allies, damn them. Gr'zy kept telling himself that, had it been only the Xenexians against the Danteri, the people of Xenex might have stood a chance. They might have managed to make their battle for freedom succeed, despite the overwhelming odds they had faced. But when the Danteri's allies had made their presence known, the Xenexians had no prayer.

He had said as much to his son, but his son had refused to believe it. Now his son's body was finishing its journey from flesh and blood to ash, and Gr'zy felt his hardened heart cracking in his chest.

There was a soft footfall near him. He didn't bother to turn and see who it was. He knew.

"It didn't have to be this way, Gr'zy of Calhoun," the soft voice of Falkar of Danter purred to him. That was Falkar's way. He always spoke very, very quietly, forcing listeners to have to strain to hear him. It was obviously a game he liked to play, to exert control over those to whom he was speaking. They had to come to him. Gr'zy didn't even glance at him. If he had, he would have seen an assortment of Falkar's personal guards nearby, as well as Danteri mixed in with the mourners. They were there to put across the message that the Xenexians would never again remain unobserved or on their own. Plus, Gr'zy thought privately, they probably wanted to make sure that Gr'zy's son was truly dead. Considering the number of Danteri his son had killed single-handedly, they would want to see for themselves that their greatest enemy was never again going to be a threat.

"Had you reined in your son . . . had you heeded our warnings . . . none of this would have been necessary," Falkar continued. "He would never have been in opposition to my forces, and my soldiers would never have had to defeat him."

"Defeat him," Gr'zy echoed hollowly, his voice rumbling. "You call what you did 'defeating' him?" Now he turned to face Falkar, and the air crackled with something other than flame. "There was no honor in your triumph. There was no opposition by the best man who triumphed over him. Your people managed to target him and drop a bomb on him from thousands of feet in the air. How do you take any pride in killing an enemy that way?"

"That may well be the difference between you and me," replied Falkar, appearing to take no offense at the anger and challenge in Gr'zy's voice. "I don't take pride in killing any enemy. It's simply a part of war. Your son's death was necessary, as were the deaths of any of the Xenexians who stood against us. If I was able to accomplish those necessary deaths with minimal risk to my own people, and with maximum efficiency, then so be it."

Gr'zy did not reply. He merely made a disdainful snorting sound and turned back to his son's pyre.

Falkar took a step closer to him and continued, "This business isn't quite over, you know."

"Isn't it?" demanded Gr'zy.

"No, it isn't. You cooperated with the criminals who rebelled against us, Gr'zy. Your son's punishment is due to the vagaries of war. But all you've done is extend a formal surrender. What of *your* punishment?"

"Mine?" Gr'zy looked back at him, and there was deep sorrow in his eyes that contrasted sharply with the quiet fury in his voice. "My son is dead. What punishments do you think you can dole out that would begin to match that?"

"Not very much, admittedly. Still," and he appeared to think, although Gr'zy was certain that that was merely a ruse and that Falkar had already determined exactly what he was going to say. "Still, that was truly something that your son brought upon himself. It was not inflicted upon you, nor administered by—"

"What is your point?" Gr'zy cut him off.

Falkar's calm demeanor never wavered. Why should it? He had all the advantages. "My point is, even though you have surrendered . . . even though you acknowledge our supremacy as rulers of this world . . . how do we know it will last?" He nodded in the direction of Gr'zy's burning son. "A martyr can be a very powerful cause around which to rally support. Now you may be in mourning. But sooner or later, the veil of mourning will flutter away, uncovering deep anger and a thirst for vengeance. We could be looking at yet another revolt."

"What will you, then?" demanded Gr'zy. He stared unflinchingly into Falkar's eyes. "Do you wish to strike me down? Is my life forfeit to help secure your dominance, is that what you're saying? If you think I'm going to beg for mercy . . . if you think I have any care for living after this . . . then you are sadly mistaken. Kill me, don't kill me. It makes no difference to me."

To Gr'zy's annoyance, Falkar actually laughed as if he were sharing a joke with an old, beloved friend. "Oh, that would most certainly be about the worst thing we could do, old chief. Not only would we provide your people with a second martyr, but we would also deprive them of your leadership. And as long as that leadership doesn't bring Xenex into further conflict with our soldiers, I would just as soon leave you in charge. They are going to need your wisdom and skill in the months and years to come. No, no . . . you think far too much in extremes. I was merely trying to decide how best to secure your . . . future cooperation. To secure, if not your loyalty, at least your bond that there will be no further mischief."

"What would you have of me?"

"A hostage."

Gr'zy looked at him sidelong. "Hostage? What sort of hostage?"

"Any highly placed Xenexian, other than yourself, will do. Someone of sufficient rank, and sufficient meaning, to ensure your goodwill. The hostage will be removed from this world and kept in a secure location. As long as you cooperate, as long as there is no uprising, he or she will live, unharmed. If, on the other hand,

Xenex should once again rise in revolt," and Falkar allowed to slip, ever so slightly, the veneer of courtesy, "then the very first Xenexian blood to be spilled will be that of the hostage. Do we understand each other?"

Gr'zy nodded slowly. "Yes. Yes, we do."

"I will give you time to decide who—"

"No need. I've already decided."

A look of surprise passed over Falkar's face. It was the first genuine emotion he had displayed in the entire encounter. "Have you now."

"Yes. My eldest son gave in to the forces that made him become a leader of a rebellion. Gave in to the pressures of expectation. I would make certain that my other son—my younger offspring— does not succumb to the same temptations."

Falkar nodded slowly. "That is very wise, Gr'zy. I see our faith in your decision-making was not misplaced. Perhaps, in a strange sort of way, this turn of events will benefit everyone."

Gr'zy turned and scanned the crowd of onlookers. His gaze caught that of a boy, not quite thirteen summers old. He made a curt gesture for the boy to advance. The stupid youngster turned and looked over his shoulder to see to whom his father was gesturing, then turned back and touched himself quizzically on the chest, his eyes widened in obvious surprise. Gr'zy, trying not to let his impatience show, repeated the gesture in an even more commanding manner. The boy separated from the crowd and approached his father. The boy's hair was a mop of unruly black hair and his eyes were colored a deep purple.

The boy stopped respectfully several feet away and bowed his head.

Without preamble, Gr'zy pointed in Falkar's direction and said to the boy, "You are to go with him."

The boy looked up, clearly startled, and Falkar immediately said, "Actually, no, Gr'zy. My apologies: I didn't make that quite clear. He will not be going with me. I've no need of a Xenexian youth running around in my court. Plus there is sufficient anti-Xenexian feeling among my people thanks to the long years of fighting that I fear I could not guarantee the boy's safety. No, he'll be residing with someone of far greater importance than I." Without waiting for Gr'zy to inquire who was being referred to, Falkar raised his wrist and spoke into a communications device. "All is ready," he said. Then he lowered his arm and smiled at Gr'zy. There was nothing remotely pleasant in the smile.

There was a pause. Gr'zy felt as if he was waiting for something to happen, but couldn't figure out what it might be. Suddenly the air was filled with a loud hum, then slowly a figure began to materialize out of thin air.

Gr'zy knew exactly what it was, of course. He wasn't ignorant, nor were his fellow Xenexians. All of them knew very well of matter transportation technology—one of the many small miracles that were so much a part of everyday life in the great, vast galaxy beyond the land borders of Xenex. Nevertheless, they rarely saw displays of such things, and so the many Xenexians who were watching the proceedings gasped as one. Many stepped back, even though they were nowhere near the figure that was coming into existence. A number even looked away, as if fearful that staring straight at it would cause their eyes to be burned right out of their sockets.

Slowly the air coalesced into a most impressive-looking individual who was neither Xenexian nor Danteri.

He was dressed in glittering armor, with a helmet that had been fashioned to resemble the head of a fierce, predatory bird. Slowly he reached up and removed the helmet. There was much muttering upon seeing the elegant, pointed ears that made clear to what race he belonged.

"Gr'zy," Falkar said with that unctuous graciousness that Gr'zy had quickly grown to despise, "may I present his high lordship, Hiren, the Praetor of our esteemed allies, the Romulan Empire. Hiren, this is Gr'zy, High Chieftain of Calhoun, the oldest and largest settlement in all of Xenex."

"And the most belligerent, from what I've heard," said Hiren.

Decades earlier, following the fall of the Terran Empire and the short-lived republic that had supplanted it, most of the worlds under the Terran yoke were absorbed by the Klingon-Cardassian Alliance. Faced with an enormous and dangerously aggressive rival on their doorstep, the Romulans had sought to deter the Alliance from further expansion by seeking allies of its own. The Danteri had proven useful in restoring balance to the scales of galactic power.

Although it had been widely known that the Danteri were allied with the Romulans, the Romulans had not had much of a presence on Xenex itself. Instead they had supplied weapons and ships that had helped pound the Xenexians into submission. They had not dirtied their hands with ground fighting.

Hiren's arms were draped behind his back, covered by a fluttering cape. He strode toward Gr'zy, his pointed chin outthrust as if he were daring someone to take a swing at him. It was a dare that Gr'zy would happily have accepted, but that would hardly have accomplished anything except perhaps getting Gr'zy—and gods knew how many others of his people—killed.

"The chieftain," Falkar continued as if he were serving as host at a convivial party, "has agreed to turn his son over as a hostage in exchange for his good offices."

"For how long?" Gr'zy added, almost as if it were an afterthought.

The Praetor fixed a level gaze on him and said, "Until we decide we are satisfied. There's no timetable here."

The boy looked from one to the other. "I . . . I don't understand. What's happening?"

"You're going with him," Gr'zy said brusquely, and he pointed at the Praetor.

"But . . ." The boy's chin began to tremble, and his round eyes started watering. "But I don't want to—"

It was everything Gr'zy could do not to cuff the boy. If his enemies had not been standing there, he would have hit the boy so hard it would have spun his head around. "Stop it. Stop sniveling," he ordered, and the boy did the best he could. He steadied his chin, but his eyes were still large in his head. "No one asked you if you wanted to. This is what's to be done. It's the price to be paid for," and he looked briefly in the direction of the now-smoldering remains of his eldest son's corpse, "for your brother's failure. You'll do what you're told, and you won't complain about it. Is that clear?"

It was with a visible effort that the boy forced a nod. He turned and looked up at the Praetor. The Praetor stared down at him impassively.

"What's your name?" he demanded.

The boy replied. It was a mind-numbing agglomeration of syllables and vowels that the Praetor couldn't even begin to understand. It sounded like "Muh-uh-kuh-uh-en-zuh-hy." He looked to the father for help, his face a question.

Gr'zy repeated slowly, "M'k'n'zy."

"Well . . . I'm not even going to try and say that," said the Praetor. He studied the boy for a moment and then said, "I'm simply going to call you Muck."

"But my name isn't—"

Whereas Gr'zy had restrained himself from striking the lad, the Praetor felt no such urge. His mailed hand swung around and slapped M'k'n'zy across the face. The boy cried out, grabbing at his face and dropping to his knees. Blood welled up between his fingers. "Let me see," ordered the Praetor.

M'k'n'zy forced himself to lower his hands. A long, thin wound ran diagonally across his face, blood seeping onto the lower half of his face.

"Let that be a reminder," Hiren informed him, "that expressing your opinion to me, when unasked for, is never a wise move. Instead, when I make a statement, you will simply say, 'Yes, Praetor.' Is that understood?"

The boy appeared ready to make a different response, but he caught himself and instead simply responded with a timid, "Yes, Praetor."

Hiren nodded approvingly and said to Gr'zy, "He learns quickly."

Gr'zy stared at his son, his face inscrutable. He had hoped, just for a moment, that M'k'n'zy would have the nerve to stand up to this oppressive bastard. Instead his younger son had remained what he had always been: Timid. Afraid. Easily beaten down. M'k'n'zy of Calhoun had never had any taste for war or fighting or standing up for himself. His older brother, D'ndai . . . ah, now there had been a fighter. A warrior. Brilliant in his schemes, daring in their execution. As chieftain, Gr'zy had walked a fine line. He could not fully commit to publicly supporting the actions of "those rebels," for he'd had the safety of his people to consider. But privately he had extended what support he could to his notorious renegade son, and cheered D'ndai's successes while in the privacy of his tent. Gr'zy would sometimes imagine his people freed from the yoke of Danteri oppression, and if the newly freed Xenexians called for D'ndai to take over as chieftain in reward for his exploits, Gr'zy would not have said no. The father had come to realize that the son was destined to be a far greater leader than he.

But destiny had fallen short. D'ndai was dead, the last of his remains fluttering away on the winds.

What, then, was Gr'zy left with?

His mewling puke of a younger son, who had trembled and whined with fear whenever news of D'ndai's exploits, out there in the savage badlands where the war of resistance had mostly been waged, had reached them. M'k'n'zy, who couldn't hold a sword properly, who uncontrollably flinched away even during the most rudimentary of training exercises.

It should have been you, Gr'zy thought furiously. He knew he should be ashamed of even contemplating such a thing, and yet he did. *It should be you, you little waste of flesh and blood, who lie dead, and my magnificent D'ndai should be leading our people toward glory.*

M'k'n'zy the beggar, they called him. The beggar brat, and Gr'zy knew all too well why. He and this useless little nothing, bound forever due to a single act that displayed M'k'n'zy's craven nature for all to see.

As Gr'zy offered up his youngest son to the Danteri, not a single one of his people questioned why. Trust the Danteri to be so stupid that they didn't see it.

Let them take him, then. Let him be brought to Romulus. Let him live there, let him stew there, let him die there, and good riddance to him.

Gr'zy barely heard his son's muted farewell, and only chanced to glance in his direction at the last moment before the boy vanished in a haze of transported molecules. Hurt and rejection were plastered on the boy's face, so much so that a lesser man would have been cut to the quick by them. Gr'zy, however, was not.

Instead, registering and then forgetting about the departure of his youngest son, now renamed Muck and aptly so, Gr'zy watched the last of the black smoke representing his incomparable D'ndai drift lazily toward heaven, and one thought was uppermost in his mind:

He will not have died in vain.

2

Hiren, the Praetor of the Romulan Empire, waited for Muck to make some sort of comment.

He watched the boy stand in the middle of the quarters that had been assigned to him at the palace. They were not ostentatious by any means. The Romulans, by nature, tended to be somewhat spare in their furnishings. But it was nevertheless far better than anything the boy could have experienced in that rough agglomeration of huts and tents the Praetor had spied when he'd spend his brief sojourn on the surface of Xenex.

Muck said nothing.

This wasn't entirely unexpected. The boy had been mostly silent the entire journey from Xenex to Romulus, save for when the Praetor had addressed him directly about something. At those times, the response had been a terse, "Yes, Praetor," and that was all. The Praetor had almost been disappointed. He'd seen the savage mien of the Xenexians, seen the quiet hatred that burned in the eyes of the boy's father. So naturally he had expected to experience some of the same in Muck himself. But there seemed to be absolutely nothing. *He's the son of a chieftain. How could I have broken him that easily?*

It made Hiren think that either the boy had been broken by the father long ago, or else that he simply had never possessed any strength of character in the first place. Either way, it was of no consequence to Hiren beyond academic interest.

The boy's fascination with space, however, had been a sight to see. After all, he had never been off the surface of his homeworld.

Hiren, like any Romulan worth his salt, was thoroughly accustomed to traveling through the void in vessels. For Muck, it was an entirely new experience. He had pressed his hand repeatedly against various bulkheads, as if uncertain that they would be able to stand up to the rigors of space travel. He had stared through a viewing port in utter astonishment at his world as it turned far, far below him. When they had turned away from it, the vista of stars that lay before him nearly caused him to choke, and he had uttered one of the only sentences that was not, "Yes, Praetor." He had said, *"The stars are broken,"* and at first the Praetor had not understood what in the world the boy was referring to. But then he did, and explained patiently, if brusquely, why stars didn't scintillate when one was out in space. Later, when they had leaped into warp space, and Muck had watched space itself twist and bend around them, the Praetor had thought the boy's head was going to explode.

Experiencing space travel through the eyes of a child had been privately amusing to the Praetor.

"Are these quarters satisfactory to you?" he asked Muck as the boy glanced around. He waited for the boy to respond with his typical "Yes, Praetor." Instead Muck didn't reply. Keeping the impatience out of his voice, he said, "A Praetor is not accustomed to repeating himself. Are these satisfactory to you, yes or no?"

Slowly the boy turned his deep purple eyes upon the Praetor. His voice utterly flat, he asked, "Does it matter?"

The question caught the Praetor off guard, but he didn't let it show. Instead he paused, giving it due consideration, and then shrugged. "I suppose it does not, no."

Muck nodded as if that confirmed what he'd already thought. He walked slowly around the room like a caged animal.

"You will be treated as a guest, for as long as your status warrants it," said the Praetor.

The phrasing of the statement caught Muck's interest. He stared at the Praetor with an upraised eyebrow. "Warrants it?"

"Your father," the Praetor told him, "gave you over all too easily. I tend to be suspicious, more often than not, of anything that transpires too easily. Falkar of the Danteri is under the impression that your father was simply in shock due to your brother's death, but I believe otherwise. I think that your father will betray his agreement with us. That he will betray you." He tilted his head slightly, like a curious dog. "Do you think that possible? Or likely?"

"I don't know."

"You don't know. You must have some opinion on it."

Muck shook his head. "No, Praetor."

"What do you think your father will do?"

"I don't know."

"I'm not asking what you know. I'm asking what you *think*."

Muck licked his lips, looking nervous, as if he wished he could be anywhere except where he was at that moment. "My father doesn't like it when I think. He says I think too much. He says that's bad."

"Bad?" The Praetor didn't quite know what to make of that. "How is that bad?"

"He says a man who sits around and spends too much time thinking is a man who doesn't spend enough time doing."

"I see. One of the great philosophers of our time, your father is." He saw the confusion on Muck's face. "What is it?" When the boy hesitated, the Praetor said impatiently, "Spit it out. What is it?"

"What is philosophers?"

The question made the Praetor laugh. It was a sharp, unpleasant sound, and Muck winced at it. "A philosopher," he explained, when he realized that Muck was serious, "is someone who sits around and does nothing but think." He saw a flash of interest in the boy's eyes, just enough to make him wonder whether the child—worthless as his father clearly thought he was—might have some potential after all. "There are great Romulan philosophers. Would you care to read some of their works?"

Muck shook his head.

"Why not?"

Shrugging, the boy said, "I cannot read. My father said it was a waste of time."

"Yes, he would. And even if you could read, you certainly wouldn't be able to read Romulan. No matter, then. There are teaching vids available, if you're interested. Would you like to see them?"

"I suppose."

The Praetor's brow darkened. "That is not an answer. To 'suppose' something is not an answer. It's mealymouthed. It's indecisive. I never want to hear those two words in conjunction with each other coming out of your mouth. Am I clear?" The boy nodded quickly. "Now . . . would you like to see them?"

"Yes, Praetor." Then he added, "Very much."

The Praetor nodded once in satisfaction and started to head for the door. He was brought up short when Muck said, "Praetor?"

The Praetor turned, hiding his surprise that the boy had actually dared to launch a query. "Yes?"

"Are you going to kill me?"

The words might have indicated fear from someone else. A dread of the unknown. But the way that Muck had asked it, it came across as a simple query. A distant, even clinical interest in his fate, as if it involved someone other than himself.

"I don't know," the Praetor said in all honesty. "Quite possibly. We'll have to see how events unfold."

"I sup—" He caught himself and instead nodded and said, "Yes, Praetor."

The Praetor glanced behind as he exited the room, and saw that the boy was simply standing there, watching him go. "Odd one," he muttered to himself as the door slid shut behind him.

Although he could have dispatched an aide to attend to it, the Praetor decided to bring the vids to the boy himself. He held the assortment of data disks in his hand and entered the room without bothering to knock.

The boy was asleep.

He was not sleeping on the bed, however. Instead he was on the floor next to it. The Praetor felt an odd sensation in the lower half of his face and realized that it was a smile. He couldn't remember the last time he'd done that.

Hiren walked over to the sleeping Muck and lifted him. He was surprised; he had expected that the slender boy would weigh next to nothing. Instead he was much heavier than anticipated. There was muscle on his frame that his build didn't even hint at. Muck didn't stir as Hiren lay him on his bed. He didn't pull the boy's boots off or change him out of his desert rags; he wasn't Muck's mother, after all. But he did take the time to drape a thin blanket over him. He stepped back and watched the boy breathe steadily in deep sleep.

He hoped he wouldn't have to kill the boy. It struck Hiren that it might well be a tragic waste of material.

3

Muck had become accustomed to the Praetor entering his room without any announcement of his intentions. Sometimes he thought that the Praetor was trying to catch him at something. Making some seditious plans, perhaps. The Praetor studied Muck's face very carefully each time he showed up, scrutinizing him for some hint of guilty reaction or conscience. Every time that occurred, the Praetor looked disappointed.

And for good reason. Muck wasn't planning anything. He had little interest in scheming against the Praetor or anyone in the Romulan Empire.

The simple fact was that, in the year that he'd been there, Muck had been treated better on Romulus than he had been on his homeworld.

First of all, they left him alone for the most part, except for the occasional surprise visits from the Praetor. It was a solitary life. But back on Xenex, any time that Muck (he had stopped referring to himself by any other name) had any sort of interaction with other Xenexians, they had treated him with scorn. No doubt they had picked up on their chieftain's view of his youngest son and acted accordingly. So it wasn't as if he'd had any friends back there.

Second, he had employed his time well. He had not only become absorbed by the many vids that had been made available to him, but he had taken it upon himself to learn how to read Romulan. This had opened up his horizons to various publications and documents, for he found that he could absorb the material far more quickly by reading it than by hearing it. He had mowed through assorted Romulan philosophers, and had moved from there to the writings of various warriors. Although he still had no stomach for actual fighting, he considered the theories and strategies of warfare to be endlessly fascinating. He was reasonably certain he would never find himself thrust into some sort of battle situation. But in the unlikely event that he was, he had found enough precedent to draw on that he believed he could outthink an opponent.

This belief was lent additional weight when he discovered a computer program that contained chess games from several different worlds. Chess, he discovered, was a fundamental strategy game. The specifics and pieces varied from one culture to the next, but the theory was much the same, and he became quite adept at it. He played the computer, and although he never beat it, he had managed to play it to a stalemate on a number of occasions. He had taken great pride in those draw victories, and only wished that he'd had someone with whom he could share his achievements.

He decided that the next time the Praetor came by to try and catch him out or simply visit with him or whatever, he would tell the Praetor of his accomplishments and perhaps even challenge him to a game.

But when that day finally arrived and the Praetor burst into his quarters, Muck could tell instantly that this was not the time to speak of games. There was burning anger in Hiren's face. Muck wondered for a heartbeat what he could possibly have done to draw such ire from the Praetor.

Almost immediately he realized that there wasn't a single thing he could have done. He had done nothing this day or this week that he had not done every single week since his arrival there a year ago. If none of those activities had angered the Praetor before, they certainly wouldn't have done so now.

Which meant that something else had transpired to incur the Praetor's wrath, and the Praetor was associating it with him for some reason.

There seemed to be only one real possibility as to what that might be.

All of that went through the boy's head in a matter of seconds, and so it was that before the Praetor could speak, Muck spoke first and asked, "What did my father do?"

The matter-of-fact tone of the boy's voice brought Hiren to a halt in mid-step. His eyes narrowed in suspicion after a moment and he snarled, "How did you know?"

Muck shrugged. He had no real means of breaking down the thought process that had come so easily to him.

"Did he tell you somehow?" demanded the Praetor.

Muck looked puzzled. "You monitor any messages I receive . . . except I never receive any. So how would he?"

"That's not an answer," the Praetor reminded him stubbornly.

"Very well. No, sir. He did not."

The Praetor hesitated, and then nodded to indicate that he found the response acceptable. Then he growled angrily, "Your father has landed you in a world of trouble, is what he's done."

"Are you going to kill me?"

Once again the Praetor was clearly surprised by the dispassionate tone of Muck's voice. "Do you feel you should die?"

"If that was the arrangement," Muck said distantly, "then that's the way it must be."

Even though he had seen the boy, spoken to the boy, repeatedly over the past months, he studied Muck as if seeing him for the very first time.

"We leave for Xenex immediately," the Praetor told him, "and that visit shall determine whether you live or die."

"All right," said Muck, who didn't appear to have much stake in the subject no matter which way it went.

4

M uck did not recognize his father.

Some of that had to do with time. It had, after all, been a year. A year can be a lifetime to a child.

In this case, though, a mere day could have passed and Muck would still have had difficulty realizing that the man in front of him was the man he'd grown up knowing and fearing.

They had returned to Xenex, but they had not descended to the surface. Instead they were in the Praetor's personal ship. The Praetor had despised Xenex during his extremely brief stay, and had no desire to lower himself to going there unless it was absolutely necessary. He had the savage bastard named Gr'zy brought to him. The Danteri had been more than happy to cooperate.

It was obvious from Gr'zy's appearance that the Danteri had not simply been sitting around waiting for the Romulan Praetor to make his triumphant return. They had brutalized him, beaten his face into a twisted mass of meat. The only things remotely recognizable were the eyes that glared at the Praetor with unbridled hatred. Muck knew that glare all too well. He had been subjected to it any number of times. Seeing it now, for the first time in a year, reminded him of how much he had hated it.

Gr'zy's hands were bound behind his back with gleaming metal cuffs. He had materialized on the platform in the transporter room, and he was on his knees. Even in this completely humbled position, he didn't act as if he were someone whose life would likely be coming to an end. He looked as if everyone in the room—the

Praetor, Muck, the guards who had weapons leveled upon him—
were dirt beneath his feet.

Muck didn't know whether to admire him for it or feel sickened.

"Well, well," the Praetor said, moving toward the Xenexian
chieftain. He walked with a sort of swagger that Muck had come
to know quite well. "It seems, good sir, that you have not exactly
behaved yourself since last we met, have you?" When Gr'zy did not
respond immediately, the Praetor took a swift step forward and
drove his foot into Gr'zy's stomach. Gr'zy gasped, but otherwise
did not acknowledge the impact. "Have you?" repeated the Praetor.

Gr'zy glared at him once more.

"You tried to lead a rebellion," the Praetor continued. "You
tried to take the place of your late son. Apparently you have a
desire to share his fate."

Still Gr'zy made no reply.

The Praetor suddenly pulled a dagger from his belt, stepped
behind Muck, and put it to the boy's throat. He noticed that Muck
made no sound at all. He wondered what was going through the
boy's mind at that moment and then decided he didn't actually
care all that much. "And what of him?" he demanded. "What of
your son who lives? Did you consider the impact your decision
would have on him? Did you care that his life would be forfeit for
your going back on our agreement?"

"Agreement?" Gr'zy growled. He spit on the floor. The puddle
it left was dark red. It was entirely possible the man was bleeding
inside. "That makes it sound like I had a choice."

"You had a choice in your subsequent actions." The knife didn't
waver from Muck's throat. "You had a choice as to whether to risk
your son's life or not. Don't you care if he lives or dies?"

Gr'zy appeared to consider the question, as if it had never occurred to him before. When the answer came, as harsh as it sounded,
it was one that Muck was already more than prepared for.

"No," he said.

Slowly the Praetor lowered his knife. In wonderment, he said,

"And I thought my father was a cold-hearted bastard. You and he would have gotten on well."

"Why should I care about the boy?" demanded Gr'zy. "He humiliated me!"

In spite of himself, the charge caught Hiren's interest. "In agreeing to come with me?"

"No," Gr'zy said impatiently as if the Praetor was a cosmic fool. "Several years ago. When D'ndai first launched his rebellion against the Danteri." He shifted slightly on his knees. "The Danteri came. They arrested me. They demanded to know where he was. I told them I didn't know. They tied me to a stake, started to beat me. They would have beaten me to death. They would have made a martyr of me. And then," and his hate-filled gaze shifted from the Praetor to his son, "this little fool stepped in."

"You mean he saved you?"

"I mean he ran from the crowd, ran up to the Danteri, and begged them to spare me. *Begged them.* A son of mine . . ." His voice trailed off in anger and incredulity. "On his knees, he wept. Blubbered for the entire populace to see. Told them I didn't know anything. Told them that D'ndai was acting entirely on his own. Told them killing me would solve nothing except to leave him an orphan. He . . ." His voice became so choked with fury that he couldn't even speak.

The Praetor looked toward Muck. "Does he speak true?" he said. "Did it happen as he says?"

Muck simply nodded.

"And they spared him?"

Muck nodded again.

"Yes . . . spared me," Gr'zy grunted. "They claimed they were convinced. The boy convinced them I was no threat."

"I didn't . . ." Muck had spoken, his voice barely above a whisper. "I just . . . didn't want them to kill you. I was trying to help—"

"*Help!*" bellowed Gr'zy. "I would have had a death that meant something! Instead, thanks to you, I had a life that meant nothing! You useless coward! You sack of—"

The Praetor lashed out again, this time kicking Gr'zy in the head. The chieftain was knocked over, landing heavily on his side. This time no sound escaped his lips.

Muck said nothing, did nothing. He just watched, his eyes wide. The Praetor looked from Gr'zy to the boy and back, and then said, "Muck. Do you understand that this man does not care whether you live or die?"

Muck began to nod, but then somehow sensed that the moment called for more than a mere gesture. "Yes, Praetor. I understand."

"In fact, he went ahead with his actions, knowing that they would very likely lead to your death. You understand that as well."

"Yes, Praetor. I understand."

The Praetor walked slowly around the chieftain and continued, "In his thoughts and in his actions, this man has abandoned you. He has abandoned all paternal feelings for you, and as such, you should in turn have no fealty to him. He has betrayed your loyalty. He is not worthy of it. Would you say that's a fair assessment?"

"Yes, Praetor."

Gr'zy made a contemptuous snarl. "The boy is weak-minded. Always has been. He'll say whatever you want him to, do whatever you want him to."

"Really. Funny you should say that. I'm interested in putting that to the test." He was still holding his dagger, and now handed it to Muck. Muck took it automatically in his hand, but now that he was holding it, he stared at it in confusion. "Muck," continued the Praetor, "you owe this man nothing. But you owe it to yourself to solidify your status with me. Your father does not respect weakness. Neither do I. He thinks you are weak. I . . . am willing to remain open-minded on that score. And since your fate is now in my hands, it would behoove you to do whatever you could to earn my respect."

"You want me to kill him."

The Praetor had to admit to himself that the boy certainly grasped situations with impressive speed. "Yes. That is exactly right."

Muck was holding the dagger straight out, but he was staring at the blade as if he had never seen such a weapon before. "You . . . you want me to . . ." He made a forward stabbing motion with the blade.

"Correct. If you do that, then your future with the Romulan Empire will be assured . . . and it will be a most impressive one at that."

Gr'zy gave a contemptuous laugh. It was clear what he thought his son would do, or not do.

"And . . . if I don't?" asked Muck.

Considering the man's attitude toward his son, and expecting some degree of reciprocation from Muck, the Praetor was surprised he even had to ask. "Then it will not go well for you."

"You'll kill me?"

"Quite possibly."

"He won't do it," Gr'zy informed the Praetor. "Even with his own life at stake. He won't have the nerve, will you, boy."

The Praetor watched, not the boy's face, but the knife. Sure enough, the blade was trembling slightly. The boy's hand was shaking.

"This should be an easy decision for you to make, boy. The easiest of your life," said the Praetor.

"But . . ."

"But what?"

"He's my father. How can I kill my own father?"

"You have the knife," the Praetor said bluntly. "He's helpless. To the chest or just under his throat, either way. All effective."

"I . . . I mean . . ."

"Do you see?" demanded Gr'zy. "Do you see what I am up against?"

"Kill him," the Praetor challenged Muck, "or I'll do it myself, just to shut him up."

"Come on, boy," Gr'zy said. "Come on, weakling. I dare you to do it. They'll kill me anyway. You'd just be saving me some time and them the satisfaction of taking my life. Go on. Kill me."

Muck's face seemed a study in conflict. He was trying his best, and the Praetor could even see him make a few half-hearted endeavors to thrust forward with the knife. It was soon clear, though, that half-hearted was as far as he was going to get.

"I . . . I . . ." he stammered.

Suddenly Gr'zy was on his feet. How he had had the upper body strength to pull himself to his feet, bound as he was, the Praetor would never know. Gr'zy lunged forward as hard and as fast as he could.

He didn't have to travel far. The sharpened knife in Muck's hand slid into his chest, easy as anything, and pierced his heart.

Muck let out a cry like the damned, and Gr'zy tumbled over. "At least," he grunted, "I don't have to listen . . . to the boy's excuses . . . anymore . . ." His body trembled, shuddered once, and then a deep breath rattled from his throat in a manner the Praetor knew all too well.

Ashen, the boy stared at the blood on the knife and then dropped it as if it were going to contaminate him.

"That," the Praetor told Muck, "was the most pathetic display I have ever witnessed." His hand swung around quickly, catching Muck in the side of the face. Muck went down, landing atop his father's corpse. The boy let out a loud, mewling cry that was exactly the type that must have driven his father to distraction. The Praetor had little regard for the creature that had called itself Gr'zy, but at least he could understand somewhat what had been going through the man's mind.

"Mourn his passing as you see fit," said the Praetor, and he turned and walked out of the transporter room, leaving Muck to sob piteously into the stilled chest of the man who hadn't given a damn about him.

Muck continued to sob all the way back to Romulus, and in his room for several more days. The Praetor had wanted to show patience, had thought that the boy presented some promise. But the boy's incessant caterwauling played havoc with the Praetor's dwindling patience, and finally he had had enough. He consigned the boy to the mines of Remus on the assumption that they would kill him, and gave Muck no more thought. It would be hard to blame him for that. He had a great many things on his mind, and certainly had no time to waste dwelling upon some sobbing, worthless orphan savage who didn't even have the nerve to dispatch a father who hated him.

No. No sympathy for Muck at all.

5

Labec of the House of Ta couldn't take his eyes off the comely Romulan lass.

She had invited him to her home for the stated intention of "getting to know him." She had encountered him at a social function that had been staggeringly dull, sidled up to him, and said softly, "My understanding is that your House has formed an alliance with that of my father. I must say, I find that . . . excellent news. I have always considered you a rather handsome specimen of Romulan manhood, and would not mind taking some time to become better acquainted."

Labec knew that the lass had something of a reputation as "enjoying the company of men." Particularly men who were doing business with her father. It would have been unfair to say that her well-known preferences were a factor in deciding whether or not to do business with her father, but, Labec thought as he smiled lasciviously, it certainly was not a disincentive.

Now she leaned forward on the couch, her eyes so focused upon him that he felt as if he were drowning in her gaze. Labec wasn't an especially handsome Romulan, but he had power and prestige and consequently had no difficulty in finding female companionship. But there was something different about this one. She seemed far more hot-blooded than any Romulan woman he'd ever met. Not just that: Her stare was so penetrating that he couldn't take his eyes off her.

She reached up and stroked his cheek. In contrast to the intensity of her bearing, her breathing was slow and relaxed. "It is difficult to believe, Labec, that no woman has managed to claim you as her own."

"Well, I . . . I prefer to keep my options open," he said casually. "I'm very . . . judicious . . . in whom I ally myself with in all areas."

"I can appreciate that. You appear tense, though."

"Not at all," he assured her, but nevertheless she moved her fingers to his temples and began to knead them gently. He gasped and relaxed. Apparently she'd been right. Labec hadn't *thought* he was tense, but clearly he'd been wrong. He started to drift, losing track of time. Then the world coalesced around him and he refocused. She was still staring at him with that same probing gaze, and he reached over and started to slide his hand under her tunic.

"Apparently my timing could not be worse."

In his confused haze, Labec thought for an insane moment that the rough male voice had emerged from the woman's mouth. Then he abruptly realized that it was, in fact, her father, standing in the doorway with his hands firmly on his hips and a look of dark amusement on his face.

Labec was on his feet immediately, and he coughed slightly as he tried to pull himself together. "Rojan!" he said, his voice going up an octave. He felt ridiculous, as if he were some adolescent caught out while making his first explorations of a woman's anatomy, rather than an experienced captain of Romulan industry. "I . . . was under the impression you were . . ."

"Away on business? My business concluded," he said with a small, almost apologetic shrug. "Apparently, however, your business was just beginning."

"I . . . I . . ."

Rojan waved it off as if it were of no consequence. "My daughter is a grown Romulan female, Labec, and keeps her own counsel on who interests her. Who am I to gainsay her? If you wish, Soleta, I can depart . . ." and he gestured toward the door.

Soleta had gotten to her feet and was demurely smoothing down her tunic. "That will not be necessary, Father. The, eh . . ." and she glanced in mild embarrassment at Labec, ". . . mood . . .

has been somewhat disturbed. No one is to be blamed. These things happen."

"Yes, well . . . yes," Labec said, striving to collect his thoughts. He harrumphed deeply, as if that gave him some gravitas, and then announced as if declaiming to an audience in the upper balcony, "It has been a lovely evening, Soleta."

She extended two fingers and very quickly he touched them with his own. Then, bobbing his head in acknowledgment of Rojan, said, "I look forward to a long and healthy business association, Rojan," and exited as quickly as he could.

Rojan and Soleta stared at each other in silence for a long moment, until both were satisfied that Labec was gone. "Well?" Rojan asked finally.

"He does not intend to betray you at this time," Soleta said briskly. Her tone and attitude were light-years from the almost seductive manner she had adopted earlier. "He has genuine interest in business dealings with you. His greatest weakness is in his holdings in the Remus mines. Their value has taken something of a dip in the past few months, due to a downturn in worker productivity. He is intending to present his holdings as being far stronger than they are to encourage you to buy in with him, in order to minimize his exposure. Oh," she added almost as an afterthought, "he does know of one man, Prenan, who feels you are ripe for conquest through assassination."

"A man wants me dead and you thought to make that the last thing you told me?"

"You need not concern yourself," Soleta told him easily. "Labec is very concerned about Prenan's intentions toward Labec himself, and is arranging to have him disposed of even as we speak."

"I see. And Labec's concerns first occurred to him . . . ?"

"Very recently. Within the last few minutes, in fact," Soleta said.

He touched his hand to her chin. "Why dirty your own paw . . ."

". . . when you can use another animal's paw," Soleta finished, knowing the credo quite well.

"You are a wonder, Soleta," said her father. "Whatever fluke of genetics endowed you with your telepathic talents has served our family well, and will take us far."

"Provided that we continue to keep my abilities our little secret," she reminded him. Thanks to the paranoia and shortsightedness of the long-dead and accursed Terran Empire, true telepaths were an exceedingly rare commodity these days. Soleta wondered at times if her mother, a Vulcan Rojan had "acquired" in his youth, had shared those talents. Rojan claimed otherwise. But still Soleta imagined that the woman who had died giving birth to her, and whose true identity Rojan had kept hidden from other Romulans, must have known something that would explain Soleta's seemingly miraculous and exceedingly useful powers.

Rojan glanced automatically in the direction that Labec had gone. "You do not think he suspects, do you?"

The edges of her mouth turned upward. "You always do this, Father. After I obtain information for you in my usual method, you always start to worry that my subject might figure out what has transpired, that he might realize he'd been the subject of a mind-probe. It has never happened. It never will. No one suspects that I am a telepath, nor that I am not of pure Romulan blood. No one is going to. I will continue to be your secret weapon, and our small but powerful family will build power and prestige beyond anyone short of the Praetor himself."

"Why stop there?" asked Rojan.

Soleta hesitated slightly, and then her smile broadened. She had such a lovely smile, particularly when she bared the lower part of her teeth in wolfish anticipation.

"Why indeed?" she said.

6

Soleta had never been anywhere so oppressively hot in her life. If she'd given a damn about the poor wretches who worked in the mines of Remus, she would have wondered how they managed to tolerate it for whatever brief periods of time they managed to survive there.

She and her father were looking down at the miners like angels regarding damned souls from the safety of paradise. Labec was with them, dabbing sweat from his forehead with studied intensity. He kept casting glances in Soleta's direction, which she considered amusing, although she displayed no sign of her amusement.

The ramps were designed in such a way that there were passages for overseers and visitors, and passages that were for the use of workers. The two were separate so as to avoid any "ugliness," as Labec put it. There were guards posted at all the entrances to the overseer ramps. Any worker who approached them was shot on sight.

Soleta watched the workers trudging along the rampways. There seemed to be nothing going on behind their eyes. It was as if they had already died inwardly and were only going through the motions of existence. The fact didn't touch her emotionally—nothing really did—but she found it intriguing from the point of view of a student of the mind.

In the vast mining pit that yawned beneath them, she could see the slaves—or miners; "miners" was a far more polite word—clambering around on ropes affixed to the walls through a series of hooks. They would climb to a particular point and proceed to dig the dilithium out of the walls with various cutting tools. She even noticed that the miners walking around on the suspended catwalks nearby were carrying the ropes and grappling hooks over their shoulders or around their chests. She nodded in their direction and asked, "Why such primitive equipment? Would not gravity boots be far more efficient in enabling them to scale the walls?"

"Efficient, yes, but also usable in escape attempts," Labec replied. "We've found it's inadvisable to provide our workers with too much mobility."

"Ah."

"As you can see," Labec continued, speaking with authority, "the mine is a highly organized endeavor. Designed for maximum output in exchange for minimal expenditure."

"Most impressive," said Rojan. He looked to Soleta, who nodded her agreement. "And how much dilithium does this particular mine turn out?"

"We meet our quotas," Labec said. Rojan didn't need Soleta's intuition to sense that Labec was being slightly defensive. But he didn't feel the need to press it. Soleta had already told him exactly how the mine was doing; he was just curious to see whether or not Labec was willing to own up to it or not. If Labec wanted to be coy, well, that was fine.

"Now if you'll come this way," Labec said, gesturing ahead of them, "I think you'll find the cracking process to be particularly intriguing."

Soleta walked on ahead of him. She found that she was still looking down at the dizzying depths below them. She fancied that she could hear distant screams from the workers, or moans of pain. There was a heated glowing of flame far below from one of the processing engines. *It truly is perdition,* she thought, and wondered about a universe that would condemn people to such a fate simply because they were luckless enough to be born in the wrong place at the wrong time.

That was when the ramp collapsed directly beneath her feet.

The ramp was built in sections, so the piece where Rojan

and Labec were standing fortunately remained intact. But the support struts on the section where Soleta had stood gave out seconds after she stepped onto it. The ramp tore away, sending Soleta plummeting.

Blind luck saved her. Her hands flailing, she barely managed to snag one of the lower support struts that was projecting from the wall. The piece of ramp that had given way beneath her tumbled down, down into the pit below. Cries of alarm sounded from beneath as slaves scrambled to get out of the way.

Soleta's legs pumped frantically as she dangled above the drop. The metal strut, now ending in a jagged edge, was about ten feet long and anchored to the wall. Rojan and Labec were twenty feet above her, looking down desperately, shouting words of encouragement and assuring her that they were going to get help down to her within seconds.

Suddenly there was a groaning of metal, and an abrupt jolt. Soleta momentarily lost her grip and skidded further down the pipe. She almost fell completely off one end, but managed to clutch on. Then she saw the source of the groaning and realized that it was coming from the point where the strut was anchored to the wall. Apparently it wasn't anchored as well as she would have hoped.

Shoddy workmanship, she thought at first, and then she decided this simply couldn't be an accident; this had happened through malice.

And just as the far end of the strut began to tear completely away from the wall, everything happened very quickly. She heard a voice shout, *"Hang on!,"* echoing above the bellowing for help that was coming from Rojan and Labec, and she heard a distant clank of metal on metal, and the anchor point gave way entirely. With a final groan the strut tore away from the wall, Soleta was in free fall, and then she wasn't. Something slammed into her from the side, moving remarkably fast. She was being carried in an arc toward the section of the ramp where her father and Labec were standing. Rojan, on his knees and gripping the railing, reached out and snagged her by the forearm.

"I've got you!" he cried out unnecessarily.

"So do I," said another voice from right at her ear.

Her head snapped around, and she found herself looking into a distinctly un-Romulan face.

It was a slave, with long, shaggy black hair that hung wild around his face. He was older than Soleta, or at least she thought he was. She suspected that life in the mines tended to age people quickly. He had a scar that stretched diagonally across his face, and the most remarkable eyes she had ever seen: They were deep purple.

He was holding on to a rope. She risked a glance upward and saw that it was attached to a grappling hook that was, in turn, hanging from one of the railings overhead. Her savior was gripping the rope with one hand while his other arm was around her waist. She was stunned at the strength in it. She could see the muscles playing along the surface of his arm.

"Hold on," he said, and thrust her upward so that her father could get a better grip on her. He did so and, moments later, Rojan had pulled Soleta to safety. He gasped in relief and embraced her, and she returned it.

"Come," said Labec briskly, "we must report this at once. Someone will be dealt with harshly over his lack of attention to safety."

"That is good to hear," replied Rojan. "This type of sloppiness cannot be tolerated."

They started to walk away, Rojan having one arm draped around Soleta's shoulder. But she pulled away and said, her eyebrow arched, "Father . . . don't you think you're *forgetting* something?"

"What am I . . . ?"

There was a soft grunt and Soleta's rescuer pulled himself, hand over hand, up the rope. He grasped the bottom section of the railing and started to haul himself up onto the rampway. Soleta started to move toward him, but he waved her off. She stepped back and watched with fascination as he pulled himself to safety.

For the first time, Soleta had a sense of what it was like for others when she stared into their eyes with the intention to mindmeld, albeit without their knowledge. His gaze seemed to bore into the innermost recesses of her brain. She felt naked under his scrutiny and cleared her throat loudly. He wasn't breathing hard; it didn't seem as if he'd exerted himself in the slightest. If it had not been for the strength he'd displayed in rescuing her, she never would have thought he was especially strong. He was not broad in the shoulders, nor did his upper body—which she could see quite well through his tattered shirt—appear sculpted or particularly muscular. But she knew appearances, in his case, were not reflective of reality.

"Did you . . . ?" She glanced over at the hook, and then at the slave ramp some distance away. "Did you see me in trouble from over there . . . throw the hook and rope . . . and swing over here to catch me just as I was falling?"

"Yes," he said. His voice was strangely accented. She couldn't place it. It sounded Romulan, but he could simply have picked that up from prolonged exposure to them.

"Where are you from?" she asked.

"Sector 11A."

"No, I mean . . . before this?"

He stared at her fixedly, clearly not knowing why she was asking.

She was about to speak again when Rojan stepped in, putting an arm around her shoulders. "Thank you," he said, "for coming to my daughter's aid."

"Why did you?" demanded Labec. When he saw Soleta's surprised look, he shrugged. "I'm merely curious. The workers have no love for us. One dead Romulan is as good as another. This creature risked his life in order to save yours, and I would like to know why."

The man studied Labec, and there was something in the look

he gave Labec that caused the Romulan—puffed up with his own importance—to deflate visibly.

"I saved her life," said the man, "because it needed saving. If I'd had time to think, like as not, I'd have let her drop. Does that answer your question?"

Labec's mouth moved but nothing emerged. The man nodded as if satisfied and started to bring his hook up into his hand. Soleta realized that he meant to throw it back to the other walkway and swing back to where he'd come from. It was obvious why: If he endeavored to depart the walkway he was on now via a normal exit, the guards would shoot him down.

"Wait!" she said with more urgency than she'd expected. He paused and looked at her with quiet impatience. "What's your name? At least tell me that."

"Muck."

Soleta made a face. "Muck? That's a name?"

He made no effort to reply; he just stared at her.

"Come, Soleta," Rojan said briskly. "We must—"

She shook her father's hand clear of her arm and then said to Muck, "Do you wish to stay here?"

He clearly had no idea what she was talking about. "Wish?" he finally echoed. "My wishes mean nothing. I mean nothing. That's been made clear to me over the years."

His voice was low and flat, but she couldn't look away from his eyes. They burned with an inner fury. So much anger, so much hatred, bottled up. He was like a star on the edge of going nova.

"He is a slave, Soleta," Labec reminded her. "He is correct: His desires are of no relevance. His status cannot be changed."

"Perhaps," she said. "But it can be relocated. Father," and she turned to Rojan, "I desire to bring him back to Romulus. Make him a personal servant."

Rojan didn't reply at first. He always wanted to maintain a united front with his daughter, at least when he was in public and certainly in front of a newly acquired business associate. He forced a smile and said to Labec, "A moment, please." Labec, who looked as surprised by Soleta's pronouncement as anyone, simply nodded. As for Muck, he just stood there with an expression of careful indifference. There would have been no way of determining what he was thinking simply by looking at him.

Rojan pulled Soleta a short distance away and then said so softly that no one, even with those unnaturally sharp Romulan ears, could have overheard them, "Are you out of your mind? Did you strike your head as you were falling?"

"No to both."

"He's a slave!"

"So? We have slaves serving us already at home. What's one more?"

"Did you ever consider that this is, perhaps, exactly what he wanted? That he saved you in order to gain your gratitude so that he could get out of here?"

"I doubt that, but even if that is the case . . . so what? Who would *not* want to get out of here? And by the way, I suspect that Labec did a poor job of plotting to kill Prenan. I've no doubt that Prenan learned of the plan and this was a preemptive strike. Labec was supposed to be the one to fall to his death, not I."

"Yes, I've already figured that out," said Rojan impatiently. "And you're trying to distract me. What if he runs away?"

"Then we'll bring him back. How far could he get? He's clearly not Romulan. It's not as if he can blend in."

"Soleta . . ."

"Father," she said, her voice firm and unyielding. "I have done everything you've ever asked of me. I've asked for very little in return. Find a way to make this happen for me."

"Why?"

"Because . . ." She paused, trying to answer the question for herself as well as her father. Finally she shrugged and said, "I like his eyes."

"I can have them removed and put in a jar for you."

She did not look impressed.

Rojan sighed heavily, then forced a jovial expression upon his face, turned to his new partner, and said, "My dear Labec . . . I was hoping you might be able to attend to a change in ownership of a slave . . ."

Soleta looked to Muck to see his reaction, and all she saw from him was more smoldering hatred.

This should be interesting, she thought.

7

Muck grabbed her from behind and began to squeeze.

Soleta struggled furiously, staggering, trying to pry his arm off. She couldn't believe that he was managing to keep her immobilized. Her strength was far superior to his; there was no way that he should have been able to do this. And yet he was, his own strength amplified by what she had come to think of as his boundless capacity for hatred.

One arm was wrapped tightly around her waist, and the other was in a choke hold around her throat. It was getting hard for her to breathe. He hadn't choked off all her air, but it was clear that he could have. It was as if he was toying with her.

He brought his mouth close to her ear, as if she couldn't have heard him without the intimacy, and snarled, "I'm going to kill you, and you can't stop me."

She brought her heel fiercely down on his foot once, twice. He didn't appear to notice. Her strength was starting to give out and then, in a desperate burst of determination that might well have been the last efforts she had to give, she leaned as far forward as she could. Her strength was such that she was actually able to haul Muck off the ground a few inches. It was just enough for her purposes, and she backpedaled as quickly as she could. For a heartbeat she thought she was going to fall over, which would have destroyed whatever hope of leverage she had. But she managed to remain upright, and in seconds she was slamming Muck against the far wall. The impact caused him to grunt, which brought her some brief satisfaction. She threw him back against the wall again, two, three times, as hard as she could. The impact was bone-jarring. He grunted each time, and then, just for a moment, she felt his hands slip.

It was all she needed. Bracing herself with one foot against the wall, she gripped his arms and snapped her body forward almost in half at the waist. He flew over her head and hit the floor.

In an instant he had rolled forward and was on his feet, facing her. She came in fast with a rapid series of leg sweeps and hand stabs. He deftly blocked each one, then caught one of her forward thrusts by the wrist and snapped it around. Instantly Soleta was twisted around on her foot with her back to him, held once more in that iron grip.

"What in all the hells is going on?"

When her father had walked in on Soleta and Labec that time, he had made a great and controlled show of indignation. But a show was all it was, carefully planned and rehearsed between father and daughter. Since Rojan was in fact not all that brilliant an actor, anyone who wasn't flustered should have been able to see right through his performance. Fortunately, no one ever did.

There was no performance this time. Rojan was genuinely outraged.

Muck seemed to consider keeping Soleta immobilized, but then he released her and stepped back. He did not smile. Instead he lowered his head slightly, his long hair thick with sweat and dangling in front of his eyes. Soleta backed away from him. She was breathing hard and, likewise sweating, wiped the droplets from her face. She noticed that, unlike hers, Muck's breathing wasn't labored at all. In fact, she suspected his heart rate hadn't even increased.

"It's just a workout, Father." She pointed to the loose-fitting clothes they were wearing. "Just sparring."

"Sparring! I thought he was going to tear your head off! Where does sparring end and murder begin?"

"When someone dies. Which," she added hurriedly, "wasn't going to happen."

Muck, as was typical for him, said nothing. Rojan glared at him for a moment, then indicated that Soleta should join him in the hallway outside the recreation room. All of the other exercise equipment in the room had been pushed back and to the side in order to provide maximum room for grappling. With a shrug, Soleta headed toward Rojan. "Stay here, Muck," she ordered. It was merely a formality. It wasn't as if Muck was going anywhere. Nevertheless he bowed slightly at the waist in acknowledgment.

The moment they were outside, Rojan rounded on her. "You must be out of your mind. There's no other explanation for it. Out of your mind."

"I know what I'm doing, Father."

"Do you?" He pointed toward the room they'd just left. "He's supposed to be your slave! That was the agreement. Your servant! That means he . . . he brings you things! Waits on you! Does what you tell him to!"

"And he does," said Soleta.

"He just tried to kill you!"

"I told him to." She sounded so reasonable about it that Rojan felt as if he were losing his mind. "But it's not as if he was really going to be able to do it. And if he were to come close, I'd just order him to stop."

"How exactly would you accomplish that," he demanded, "if he had crushed your windpipe?"

Soleta started to respond, but then closed her mouth. She didn't have a ready answer to that one.

Rojan composed himself and forced a smile, trying to sound reasonable. "Soleta . . . I know you appreciate challenges. That's what you told me when you brought Muck here a month ago. That he represented a challenge. But you have yet to tell me what that challenge is, aside from seeing how close you can come to having that fool slave be the death of you."

"He has anger, Father. Passion. A burning hatred like nothing I've ever seen. I wanted the opportunity to study it up close."

"And you've had that opportunity. For a month now. I'm sending him back to the mines—"

"No, Father."

"My decision is final."

"Fine. Then I'm going with him."

He uttered a dismissive laugh as if this were a mere jest, but then he saw the look in her eyes and the amusement faded. "You're not serious."

"I'm perfectly serious."

"You wouldn't!"

"I would."

Rojan stared at her with open astonishment. "Gods, I think you would. Just to spite me?"

"No. To make clear to you that I feel strongly about this. I am a student of the mind, Father, in all things. I want to understand how his mind works. I want to understand the forces that shaped him. It's not my fault that there are no records of him."

It was true. The standard procedure was that, when someone became a slave to the mines, their entire background was literally deleted from all records. Thus did they become nonpeople, with no existence save what they had in the mines. So she had been utterly unable to learn anything of the circumstances that had landed Muck, a Xenexian (she'd been able to determine that much at least, through a bioscan) in the Reman mines.

She had even tried her meld on several occasions, but had had no luck. There had to be a calmness, a serenity for the involved mind to be able to blend with hers. There had been none such for Soleta and Muck. The only time he permitted himself to come into physical contact with her was when they were sparring, and a furious battle was hardly the time to do a mind-probe. Even so, despite the difficulty of it, she had endeavored to at least brush against his thoughts, but she had been soundly rebuffed. She didn't think that he was doing it consciously. It was just that his thoughts—his very personality—were so forceful that they pushed her away mentally.

Rojan placed his hands on her shoulders. "Listen to me, Soleta. Listen carefully. That day at the mines, that terrible day, I almost lost you. That was quite possibly the worst moment of my life. I don't wish to take any chance of such a thing happening in actuality. And this . . . this Muck . . . I believe he could be the death of you."

"I am asking you to trust me, Father. Do you?"

"Of course. Just—" He glanced at the closed door that led into the room where Muck was waiting, perhaps prepared to ambush her. "Just be careful, please."

"I will, Father."

He walked away, and Soleta reentered the workout room. Muck was standing right where she had left him.

They said nothing for a moment. Finally she informed him, "My father is concerned you're going to kill me. Are you?"

"I am your slave."

"So?"

"Killing you is not an option."

She strode toward him, eyebrow cocked. "What if you were not my slave? Would that be an option then?" When she saw his uncomprehending stare, she continued, "I don't think you would kill for no reason. And you have no reason to kill me."

"Don't underestimate yourself."

If he was trying to say something that would shock her, he wasn't successful. All she did was laugh.

In a rare instance of initiating a question, Muck said, "Do you find that so difficult to believe? That I would have reason to kill you?"

She stopped laughing then. Her father's warnings rang in her head, and it was becoming increasingly difficult to ignore them. "What possible reason could you have? I've treated you well since bringing you here. If not for me, you'd still be in the mines."

"Of what importance is that to you?"

"It's not important. It's simply a fact."

His lack of response seemed to indicate it was not a fact that especially interested him.

"Could you do it?" she demanded. "In your opinion. I'm asking you. Could you kill me? Would you?"

"I would find someone else to do it," said Muck. "Why dirty your own paws when you can use someone else's paws."

Soleta's eyes widened, and she rocked back on her heels. "You quote Landar the Elder?"

"Yes." He seemed oblivious to her sparked interest.

"Did someone tell you that quote?"

"I read it. I've read all his works."

"They have those works in the mines?" She was finding that very difficult to believe.

"No. I read them before I went there."

"And that was when?"

He drew himself straight, formal in his bearing and tone. "If you have no further need of my services, Mistress . . ."

Soleta walked toward him, keeping a pleasant smile on her face. "Now, Muck," she said coyly, and placed a hand gently on his forearm, "there are certain services that you could pro— *owwwww!*"

He had snapped his forearm around and snagged her hand. He was squeezing it incredibly tightly at the wrist. For a moment she thought her hand was going to pop right out like a cork from a bottle. He yanked her close and snarled in her face, "Don't try your mind-probe tricks on me." Then he pushed her away so hard that she thudded against the wall. But it was the surprise of his words that caused her to slide to the ground, looking stunned.

"How . . ." She glanced left and right, as if concerned that they were being listened to despite the fact that they were in the basement of Soleta's own home that she shared with her father. Her voice dropped to a whisper. "How do you know about that?"

"Because I'm not stupid. I can feel you, trying to root around. Most people don't know their own minds. I know mine. Stay out of it."

He released her with a slight push to speed her along, and then stepped back. Once again, his voice completely flat, he said, "If you have no further need of my services, Mistress . . ."

Rubbing her wrist, she shook her head. He turned and walked out, heading back to the tiny, Spartan room that served as his quarters.

Her head was swimming with the emotional intensity of the encounter. Although Romulans were an offshoot of the Vulcan race, and not mired in the demands of repressed emotion, nevertheless they were still not an especially demonstrative people. This came more from political reasons than any deep philosophy. It was generally considered wise to keep one's feelings to oneself so that potential opponents would not be able to utilize them against one.

So the emotional intensity displayed by Muck had been a new experience for her, one that she was finding overwhelming. And most significant of all was that, as quickly as Muck had shut her down . . .

. . . she had still picked up something. Just a hint of it, the faintest whisper, but still something.

The hate was there, oh yes. The burning hatred that she had found so compelling, so fascinating. But what she had not considered was that flame was always fed by something, and in the instant when she had launched the beginnings of a meld, she had obtained the briefest glimpse of what was fanning that fire.

It was sorrow. Sorrow and a sense of almost infinite loss.

Whoever this Muck was, he had lost everything that ever had meaning to him.

Soleta sat there, unmoving, for a long time, giving the matter more thought than she had ever given anything, before she finally resolved what to do.

Later that evening, there was a soft knock at Muck's door. He answered it to find Soleta standing there, her shoulders squared with a very formal attitude about her. There was no surprise on his face, as if he'd been expecting her. "What do you require, Mistress?" he asked.

She held out a blue chip. He stared at it uncomprehending. "Take it," she said. He did as he was bidden. "It's your freedom."

"What?"

"It's your freedom," she repeated calmly. "I've given you your freedom. You're not a slave anymore. You can go anywhere on Romulus you want. You can go to Xenex. You can go to hell for all I care." She paused, looking at him fixedly, and then in a gesture that was totally unplanned, she reached out and extended two fingers. She brushed them against Muck's cheek ever so gently. He didn't flinch away. "Have a good life, Muck."

"Why?" he said angrily. "Why would you do this? You paid good money for me. What do you get out of this?"

"Do people only do things because they 'get something' out of it?"

"Yes," he told her without hesitation. "In my experience, yes."

"Well, then . . . you have something new to add to your experiences."

She started to walk away from him, but he grabbed her by the elbow and turned her to face him. "Why?" he asked again. There was no anger in his voice this time, just curiosity. "I . . . would really like to know."

"Because . . ." Her jaw was set. She was angry at herself over the depth of emotion she was feeling for this random slave, welling up from somewhere she couldn't begin to understand, as if the two of them were somehow connected at a level so deep she couldn't see its bottom. "Because you've had so much pain in your life, and I don't feel like being a cause for any more. That's why. Are you satisfied? You've discovered what's in it for me." She pointed at the chip. "There's also a link to an account with a thousand credits in it. Enough to get you wherever you need to go. Good luck."

She tugged slightly and it was only at that point he realized that he was still holding her arm. He released it, and Soleta walked away from him as quickly as she could.

Soleta returned to his quarters the next morning. He was gone. She wasn't certain what she had expected, but in retrospect she supposed that she shouldn't have been all that surprised.

A week passed. Two.

The beginning of the third week, she lay asleep in bed, and something—some inner sense of warning—awoke her. She sat up, peering in the darkness, and saw the outline of a figure standing there.

She was nude, as she always was when she slept. The blanket had fallen away to expose her breasts. She started to reach for the blanket to cover up, but then defiantly left the blanket where it was.

She said nothing, although she was suddenly aware of the beating of her heart. Instead she waited.

"When I first arrived in the pits," came Muck's voice from the darkness, "I wanted to die. That's all. Simply die. They wouldn't let me. Amusement doesn't come easily in the mines of Remus, and I was seen as an opportunity for . . . entertainment. They delighted in tormenting me. All of them. I would have killed myself, but I lacked the . . . nerve . . . to try it. Because I knew my father would be waiting for me in the afterlife, and suicides are tortured for eternity. I didn't want to give my father the satisfaction of inflicting that upon me. So, against all my hopes, I continued to live. Had they left me alone, the brutal conditions in the mines would have killed me, given time. But then they would have been robbed of their fun. Whenever I was ill, or the conditions became such that I nearly died, they would nurse me back to health, so that they could continue to have their . . . favorite plaything.

"And it continued for years. Years."

He fell silent.

"Until . . . ?" Soleta prompted him.

"Until I killed a man. I ripped his throat apart with my teeth. Then they feared me. Feared me so much that five of them came to me in my sleep with the intention of smashing my head open with a rock. I woke up. I killed them all. Six corpses in one day."

"What did the overseers in the mine do?"

"Dumped the bodies. Life is cheap in the mines. They didn't care. If we all killed each other, they wouldn't care. They'd just get more slaves. There are always more slaves. Anyway, from then on, I was left alone." He paused and then added, "Again."

At that point, she didn't need her telepathy. The hurt, the frustration, the isolation that this poor creature had endured year after miserable year radiated from him so fiercely that she thought she was going to drown in it.

Slowly she slid her legs out from under the covers and stood, naked in the darkness. He didn't move. She felt as if the world had vanished, and they were the only two beings left in existence.

Soleta walked very slowly toward him, as if concerned that the slightest move on her part was going to cause him to vanish, popping like a soap bubble with sunlight directed toward it. She reached out tentatively, hesitantly, and rested her hand on his chest. His breathing continued slow and steady, but she detected the slightest catch in it when she first made contact.

Slowly she pulled his shirt up over his head. Her eyes had adjusted to the darkness by that point. She had never seen him fully stripped from the waist up. Running her fingers over his skin, she gasped as she found what seemed to be dozens of scars. "So many . . ." she whispered. Then she looked up at him, up into his eyes. They still blazed with hatred. Seized with impulses she had never experienced before, she wanted to thrust herself into that blaze. "But I suppose the worst scars we carry . . . aren't on the outside."

"No. They're not," he said, his voice deep in his chest. Then he hesitated.

"What?" she asked.

He actually sounded charmingly embarrassed. "I've . . . never done this before. It's . . . not as if the opportunity presents itself in the pits. I think . . ."

"That's your first mistake. Don't think."

She pressed herself against him and was rewarded, finally, with a change in his breathing rate. It sped up. She could feel his heart thudding against hers. He lowered his lips to hers and kissed her, and reached down and touched her and she gasped into his mouth.

At that moment, all the reasons she'd had for her interest in Muck went away. All the notions about plumbing the depths of his hatred, or using him as a weapon if she could master those emotions of his and point him in the right direction. Every self-serving motivation she'd ever had concerning him was washed away.

They never made it to the bed. They had to make do with the floor.

8

Hiren, the Romulan Praetor, stood in his private reception room and spread his arms wide. "It is good to see you, my friend. You have not aged a day."

"The same could be said of you, Praetor," replied Si Cwan of the Thallonian coalition. The red-skinned member of Thallonian royalty had to bend over slightly in order to embrace the Praetor, who was a head shorter than Cwan. "It has been too long."

"Indeed it has," agreed the Praetor, gesturing for Cwan to take a seat.

Si Cwan did so, and then leaned back, looking extremely casual. His legs were extended and crossed at the ankles.

"So," said the Praetor, "I have read the specifics of your ship's escapades. Impressive endeavors, Cwan. Most impressive."

"Thank you. The *Stinger* is a quality vessel."

"You undersell yourself," the Praetor told him, his voice slightly scolding in tone. "From everything I've seen and heard, the *Stinger* is the flagship of the Thallonian fleet. Faster, stronger, more ma-neuverable. Some who have seen it in battle claim the ship has a mind of its own."

Si Cwan laughed at that. "Only my mind, Praetor, I assure you. Well, mine and my command crew. The simple truth—which others have no desire to admit—is that we're able to anticipate what others are going to do and react before they have a chance to take action. There's nothing mystical or wildly advanced about that. That's just good, old-fashioned skill."

"I suppose you're right." Hiren leaned forward, his voice dropping to a conspiratorial whisper. "But the power source. You can tell me *that,* at least. It's not dilithium crystals."

"And you know that how?" Si Cwan studied the Praetor suspiciously. "You haven't been spying on us, have you, Praetor? That's certainly no way to earn the good will of an ally."

"Spying? Of course we haven't been spying. However," the Praetor continued in a casual manner, "when your vessel is in orbit around our world, certainly we're going to take as many sensor scans as possible. That should be obvious. Go ahead and tell me that you wouldn't be doing scans of vessels incautious enough to orbit *your* homeworld."

"Fair enough," Si Cwan admitted. "I suppose we would."

"There you are. And our scans detect nothing of the normal particle trails that would accompany the standard means of propulsion. So I ask again: What is your power source?"

"Our ship is powered by the support and good feelings of the Romulan Empire."

The Praetor stared at him for a long moment, and then threw his head back and laughed. He laughed so hard and so long that Si Cwan began to be concerned about Hiren's health. Who would believe it, Si Cwan wondered, if he wound up having to tell everyone that the Praetor had laughed himself to death.

Fortunately enough, Hiren was able to pull himself together before his amusement proved terminal. He sighed deep in his chest and said, "You're really not going to tell me the *Stinger*'s power source."

"It is a state secret," Si Cwan assured him, with a clear bit of chagrin over having to keep it from the Praetor. "It is not for you to know nor me to tell. I am truly sorry, my friend."

Hiren waved off Cwan's concern. "I was merely curious, that's all. As long as your vessel functions, and as long as it serves the interests of the Romulan Empire when we have need, what care I how the vessel does the job?"

"And as long as the interests of the Romulan Empire coincide with ours, then we should continue to have a healthy relationship. May I safely assume that you have new business?" asked Cwan. "I would think that you would not have asked me to come were that not the case."

"How do you know?" the Praetor demanded. "Has it never occurred to you that I might simply desire to bask in the pleasure of your company?"

Si Cwan smiled thinly. "Never."

Again the Praetor laughed, although this time it was more controlled and lasted a far briefer time. "Well, the fact is, there are times I do desire to bask in the pleasure of your company, but this is not one of them. There is, in fact, a matter that I'm hoping you and your formidable crew could attend to for me."

"You have but to speak and it will be attended to."

"Very well then. Do you know of the Danteri?"

"Of course," Si Cwan replied. "A formidable but not especially threatening race, considering their weapons capabilities are satisfactorily behind our own. Allies of yours, if I'm not mistaken."

"Yes. Allies of mine," said Hiren, and there was a distinct sound of sourness in his voice. "If you must know, I 'inherited' them, in a manner of speaking. They would not be my first choice for allies, and all too often, their concerns are not remotely our concerns. But I was disinclined to sever the partnership or, even simpler, just have every last one of them annihilated. It seemed . . ." He paused, contemplating the best way to put it. "It seemed a waste of material."

"And now?"

"Ahhhh, now," Hiren said slowly, his brow furrowing. "Now, my friend, would seem to present the problem. I believe they are plotting against me."

"Against you? Why would they be doing that?"

"Because I have power, Lord Cwan. There are always those who desire to take that power. We have been working closely with the Danteri, and I believe they are not quite as technologically backward as we thought. Indeed, they have scientists who have built upon what we showed them and have made some considerable leaps. From what I understand, they are developing meta-weapons. In order to make certain they do not employ them, I feel it imperative to make a first strike. But it cannot be unprovoked. So I need you to . . . provoke it."

"May I ask the source of your information?"

"A trusted adviser named Prenan, who had been an inspector to that world."

"I would like to speak to him," said Si Cwan.

"Tragically, that is not possible. He was assassinated last month." He lowered his voice and continued, "It is my belief that Danteri agents learned that Prenan was on to them, and had him killed. Further proof of the inroads they've made into the very heart of Romulan society."

Si Cwan's face was carefully neutral. "If you believe the Danteri present that much of a threat, then why not simply send Romulan vessels? Why do you require us?"

"Because we are dealing with subtleties. With politics," said the Praetor. "Not everyone agrees with my assessment of the situation, nor are they convinced that the Danteri are the threat that I believe them to be."

"Is it possible that they are not?"

"Yes, it is possible," Hiren readily admitted. "By the same token, it is possible that they are. For all I know, others in the ruling council are in league with them and are also plotting against me." He sighed heavily. "When one is in my position, it is difficult to know whom to trust."

"Obviously. And yet you trust me."

He leveled his gaze on Si Cwan and said quietly, "So far. Should I have reason not to?"

"No," replied Si Cwan. "Then again, if you did have a reason not to trust me . . . I would hardly be the best person to ask, would I?"

"That's very true."

Si Cwan forced a smile. "Your trust is well placed. I will be happy to demonstrate that by attending to this matter. None will know that you are, in any way, connected to the strike order. And in return for my 'provoking' the Danteri into showing their hand, I am to receive . . . ?"

"My sincere thanks."

Si Cwan waited.

"Plus the usual amount of gold-pressed latinum."

The Thallonian tilted his head slightly in acknowledgment. "A pleasure doing business with you, as always."

"There's more."

Si Cwan had started to rise from his seat, but now he sat once more. "Is there?"

"Yes. You're going to be taking a passenger along with you on the *Stinger*."

"A passenger."

"An observer. We must have some ties in this business to the Romulan Empire, to give it some emotional weight."

"I see. And is there any particular criteria as to why this particular passenger is being taken along, may I ask?"

"That," said the Praetor, "is a very good question. I believe—"

"Wait," and Si Cwan put up a hand. "Let me guess: You believe he or she is plotting against you."

"You see, Lord Cwan?" the Praetor said with obvious satisfaction. "This is why we make such excellent allies. We practically read each other's thoughts."

9

Zak Kebron, the massively built Brikar who not only served as the first officer of the *Stinger* but was one of Si Cwan's oldest and most fiercely devoted friends, listened with his customary lack of visible emotion until Si Cwan finished recounting the details of his meeting with the Praetor.

"Well?" asked Cwan, leaning against one of the several ornate chairs that decorated his private quarters on the *Stinger*. "What do you think?"

"He's paranoid."

"That's what occurred to me as well," Si Cwan admitted, folding his arms across his chest. "But perhaps he has reason to be."

"They're *all* against him?" rumbled Kebron. Whenever he spoke, it sounded like rocks sliding down the side of a mountain.

"Unlikely."

"Yes."

"But not impossible, considering his society. Romulans eat their own young if their children even look at them wrong. Even you have to admit that, Kebron."

"Not impossible, then. But still unlikely. And . . ." He paused, putting forth an aura of deep thought, and then finally added, ". . . stupid."

"Again, I agree. But I see little problem for us. We are being well compensated for our time, the Danteri mean nothing to us, and it serves to maintain our alliance with Hiren. A valuable alliance, I might add. . . ."

"Until we kill him ourselves."

"Well," smiled Si Cwan, "since he believes so many people are plotting against him, it would be a shame for his worries to be utterly groundless. It wouldn't speak well of him, would it?"

"No. It would not."

"I'm glad we're in accord on this, old friend. Oh," he added, almost as an afterthought, "we'll be bringing someone with us as well. A Romulan named Rojan. His job is to report back to the Praetor."

"And our job?"

"To make certain that he does not."

10

No."

Rojan, in the midst of having a servant pack clothing for him, sighed in exasperation and ordered the servant to depart the room. He turned to his fiercely determined daughter and said, "You know, it doesn't help matters when you snap orders at me in front of the help."

Soleta ignored the gentle remonstration. "No. I refuse to let you go," she told him.

He knew he should be angry with her, but all he could do was be amused and even a little flattered by her intensity. "You refuse? The last I checked, I was an adult, capable of making my own decisions."

"Apparently that's not the case if you're agreeing to this."

"Soleta . . ."

"I absolutely refuse to—"

"*Soleta!*" His tone was harsher and far sharper than it had been before, so much so that she couldn't help but be silenced by it. He waited a moment to make certain that she was attending to his words, and then continued in a more normal and calmer tone, "The Praetor has asked me to do this for him. I cannot refuse."

"I don't trust him."

"Nor do I. But I refuse to live my life in fear."

"It's not the way you live your life, Father," she said. "It's the prospect that your life may end. There is something about this that simply doesn't smell right. Give me time."

"Time?" He looked quizzical. "Time for what?"

"Time to determine what it is that he's up to."

"What are you saying? Do you plan to try and seduce Hiren so that you can employ your meld with him? Is that your plan?"

"I'm not certain what my plan is," she admitted. "I've only just learned of this. I need a little time to put a good plan together."

"That, my dear, is not something we have in abundance. I am to depart within the hour."

"The hour!" she almost shouted, and when she saw the annoyed look from him, she repeated, albeit more softly, "The hour? Father, it's incredibly obvious that he's doing this to give you no time to think, to plan. He is suspicious of you. He thinks you plot against him."

"How do you know that?"

"It's what everyone says. He sits there, isolated, stewing, contemplating every possibility and how all those possibilities lead back to him. Some say he's partially unhinged. Others say . . ."

"Others say what?"

"That he's totally unhinged."

"That's as may be . . . but Soleta, if I refuse this directive of his, then I've signed my death warrant."

"And if you obey it, it's a death sentence."

"We don't know that for sure," he reminded her, "and besides, I can take care of myself."

"You can, yes. But in this instance, you won't have to."

"What does that mean?"

"It means," she said, drawing herself up and squaring her shoulders, with an attitude that practically dared Rojan to disagree with her, "that I'm coming with you."

"No."

"Then *you've* signed *my* death warrant."

Rojan did nothing to hide his total sense of confusion. "How will I have done that?"

"Because if you leave me behind, I'm going to confront the Praetor with as many people around as possible and tell him exactly what I think of him. And how well do you think that is going to go down with him?"

He was about to say in horror, *"You wouldn't!"* but he contained himself because he knew perfectly well that she was more than capable of it. Instead, switching approaches instantly, he said, "I would . . . far prefer that you not do that."

"And I would far prefer that you not embark on this suicidal mission at the behest of a Praetor who may well have less than your best interests at heart. But since you appear determined to commit to this lunacy, then I'm going to be there watching your back for you."

"Really."

"Yes," she said firmly, and, in a gesture of tenderness, touched his face. "We're a team, you and I."

"If that's the case," said Rojan, taking her hand from his face and enfolding it within his far larger one, "then allow me to ask the following: If you're going to be busy watching my back for me . . . who is going to watch your back for you?"

"Actually," replied Soleta without hesitation, "I have just the person in mind."

11

M uck had never actually seen the outside of a large space vessel before. He had only voyaged into space a few times: on the sojourn to and from his homeworld, and when he'd been brought to and from the mines of Remus. In the former case he'd been beamed; in the latter two instances, he'd been loaded into a cramped and unimpressive shuttle.

This time out, he was actually riding in some comfort. The private shuttle that was escorting Rojan, Soleta, and himself from the surface of Romulus to the Thallonian vessel that they were to board was roomy enough. The three of them were seated in the rear section, a good distance from the pilot. Muck watched in fascination as they slowly approached the ship that was in orbit around Romulus.

Every so often he would glance in Soleta's direction. His feelings for her were still incredibly complicated, so much so that he wasn't entirely sure what to make of them. The fact that he had any feelings at all irritated the hell out of him. The deep fury that burned within him had enabled him to survive all these years. When he was with Soleta—when they were sneaking moments together, and he was burying himself in her—the anger still burned within him, yes. But it was after those times, when he would lie next to her and their bodies would slowly cool from their ardor, those were the times that he actually felt a sense of peace for the first time in his life.

It frightened him.

All those years in the pit, he had not known fear. When he had instinctively leaped to her rescue, risking a terrible death from a long plummet, he had not known fear. But this slip of a woman and her feelings for him . . .

What feelings? Who knew if she had any feelings for him at all?

It was not as if she had spoken words of love to him. She had given him his freedom, and yet he remained, and not much was changed in their status. Rojan had not been happy that Soleta had freed him in the first place, but had been openly astounded when Muck had returned. He had installed Muck as a freeman, which essentially meant that his duties were unchanged, but he could come and go as he pleased. It had pleased him to remain where he was.

Muck's emotions were in turmoil when it came to Soleta. The fact that he was feeling anything besides hatred was—he hated to admit—of interest to him. Something in his long-buried intellect made him want to explore that further. But it had been more than that.

When it came down to it . . . where was he going to go?

He had no family, no place on Xenex. He could have wandered other worlds, friendless and alone. The problem was that friendless and alone was exactly how he had spent his exile in Remus. What point was there in escaping from a prison if you then carried that prison with you wherever you went? The only other individual on Romulus he really knew was the Praetor. Muck was concerned that if he presented himself to Hiren, the Praetor would simply turn around and have him shipped back to Remus once more. He was impossible to predict in that regard.

So he had returned, and he and Soleta had become . . .

Well . . . he didn't really know what they were.

He wondered if her father knew about their assignations. He suspected that, if Rojan did, he wasn't particularly happy about it. Rojan also knew, however, that his daughter had a mind of her own and so would be more than likely to leave her to conduct herself as she saw fit. Still, from time to time he would encounter

Rojan in the corridors of the house, and Rojan would look at him silently in such a way that made Muck think that, oh yes, Rojan knew.

Now Rojan and Soleta continued in deep conversation while Muck looked in wonderment at the ship they were approaching.

It was an impressive-looking ship, and that wasn't merely guesswork on Muck's part. Other vessels, Romulan vessels, were in evidence around the planet, and the *Stinger* stood out from those others. Romulan ships were all harsh angles and straight lines. The *Stinger* flowed, its lines curved and fluid. They were coming up from underneath and he could see what he believed to be powerful armaments in place. According to Soleta, it had stealth capability and enough firepower to lay waste to the surface of an entire world.

Muck felt a deep-seated tinge of envy, and he couldn't for the life of him figure out why.

Meanwhile, Soleta and Rojan continued their discussion in low voices.

"If you are so certain they mean me harm," Rojan said, "then why don't they simply blow us out of space during the approach?"

"Because Hiren is going to assume that people know we're coming up here," Soleta said reasonably. "He's not going to want us destroyed in sight of all these ships. Plus, he has no idea what sort of communications mechanisms we might have for staying in touch with ground allies while we're still in orbit. There's absolutely no point in having anything happen to us while we're still in proximity to Romulus. Time is on their side, not ours." She paused and then said, "It's not too late, you know, for us to commandeer this vessel."

"And do what? Go where?"

"Anywhere that's not here."

"That is not going to happen," Rojan said firmly. "Whatever happens, I will live or die as a Romulan, and face my enemies head-on. And since you've insisted on joining in this endeavor, you have no choice but to do the same."

"I know," she said. She glanced out her own viewing port at the approaching vessel.

"If things don't go right," Rojan continued, sounding philosophical, "we'll make sure to take as many of the bastards with us. Blow up the whole damned ship if we have to."

"Blow it up?" She snorted derisively as if the very thought was absurd.

"Why? What's your plan?"

"My plan," she replied, "is that if things don't go right . . . I wind up in command of the whole damned ship."

Rojan grinned at his daughter. "I have to say, I like the way you think."

"You should. You taught me how."

The shuttlecraft drew closer and closer, and eventually maneuvered itself into the docking bay. The craft's outer hatch cycled through and, moments later, Rojan, Soleta, and Muck were standing in the opening. Soleta braced herself. Despite what she had told her father, she wouldn't have been the least bit surprised if they'd been greeted by a firing squad ready to blast them to pieces and toss their remains into space.

Instead there was only one individual standing there. Soleta wasn't entirely sure of the person's gender. He or she was tall, slender, with white-blonde hair that was cut short and framed the face. He or she also wasn't simply upright; the person was in a semi-crouch, as if waiting and ready to pounce. There was no tension in the posture, though. It seemed to be the preferred method of standing.

"Greetings," said the person briskly. "I am Burgoyne 182, head of security. Welcome to the *Stinger*." He or she smiled, and there were small fangs on either side of the mouth.

That was when Soleta figured it out. The feral demeanor, the fangs, the indeterminate gender—it all added up. "You're a Hermat," she said aloud before realizing that she was actually speaking, and then she quickly added, "I'm sorry. I didn't mean to—"

Burgoyne's expression didn't change, although something in hir eyes did. Soleta couldn't tell whether s/he was offended or amused or what. Since Soleta was, by nature, generally rather attuned to people's emotions even without melding with them, she found that inability to read below the surface somewhat disconcerting. "No need to apologize," Burogyne said, hir voice soft. "I'm actually impressed you knew; my people aren't renowned for getting out into the great, wide galaxy all that much." Then hir attention became riveted to Soleta's right, and she realized why: Muck was standing there.

Burgoyne moved across the distance between hirself and Muck, and Soleta was amazed by the silence with which s/he moved. S/he continued that animalistic crouch, every so often touching the floor with hir knuckles for balance. S/he came to within a foot of Muck and hir nostrils flared as if getting Muck's scent. Muck simply stared at hir, not making a move.

"You weren't on the passenger manifest," Burgoyne said. It almost sounded like a purr.

"This is my servant," Soleta told hir. "Why? His accompanying me doesn't present a problem, does it? I find it hard to believe that the presence of one servant could be a hardship for you."

"No hardship at all," Burgoyne assured her. S/he didn't take hir eyes from Muck, however. "You're obviously not Romulan, sir. Whence do you hail?"

Muck said nothing at first. The silence was palpable, and Soleta stepped in. "He's from—"

"With respect, I did not ask you," Burgoyne said sharply. "I asked him. And I am accustomed to having people answer questions when I ask them. Unless they are too afraid to." S/he looked challengingly at Muck. "Do you require the woman to do your talking for you?"

Soleta, angry, moved to intercede, but Rojan put a hand on her shoulder and, almost imperceptibly, shook his head. Against her better judgment, Soleta did nothing.

Muck allowed the silence to build a moment more, and then said, so softly that Burgoyne had to strain to hear him, "I consider myself a man without a planet."

"Indeed. Not quite an answer, though."

"Perhaps you would care to try to beat a better one out of me."

The words had been spoken in that same soft, noncommittal manner, but the challenge was implicit just the same.

Burgoyne took it in, and then replied, "Perhaps. Now, though, is certainly not the time. Welcome to you too, then, servant." S/he turned to Rojan and Soleta. "One of my men is waiting outside to escort you to your quarters. Enjoy your stay."

"Thank you," Rojan said, bowing slightly. The three of them crossed the shuttlebay toward the exit door.

In a low voice, Soleta said, "What the blazes was that about?"

Muck made no reply, but Rojan did. "When someone who is in charge of protecting territory encounters new individuals, it is instinctual for them to challenge whoever they think is the most powerful warrior." He glanced sidelong at Muck and said, with a touch of envy, "Obviously the head of security here seems to feel that would be you. You should be flattered."

Muck said nothing, but merely stared straight ahead, unable to escape the feeling that something was wrong. Something beyond the suspicions as to their safety, or the ulterior motives for having them brought aboard the ship, or whatever challenges Burgoyne felt s/he had to issue in order to show who was in charge.

It was the ship itself. Something about the ship itself felt completely and utterly wrong. The ship felt . . .

. . . he tried to think of the word, the emotion . . .

. . . the very atmosphere felt . . .

. . . despairing.

That was it.

A sense of despair hung over the ship like a shroud, and he didn't know what was causing it or where it was coming from. He could sense it just the same, though. He looked over at Soleta, and his intimacy with her enabled him to read her in a way that others couldn't. As the promised guide brought them to their quarters, Soleta was looking around, her eyebrows knit, as if she too was sensing it. Her gaze met Muck's at one point, and the question was there in her face even though it remained unspoken: *Do you feel that? Do you sense it?*

He nodded, almost feeling relieved that he was not alone in his concern.

There was something wrong in the very air of the *Stinger,* and he was going to figure out exactly what it was.

12

The spread of food on Si Cwan's table was extremely impressive. Soleta wasn't all that familiar with Thallonian delicacies, but she had to admit that they were quite palatable—much more flavorful than most Romulan food, which was relatively plain.

Naturally she was also concerned about possibly being poisoned, but it wasn't as if she, her father, and Muck were the only ones at the table. Joining them for the welcoming dinner that Si Cwan had arranged in the senior dining hall were his first officer, Zak Kebron, Burgoyne, whom they'd met earlier, and Cwan's sister, Kalinda, a young female Thallonian with an ethereal air who was in charge of the ship's engines. This fact had been of particular interest to Soleta, for she was curious as to what sort of fuel source powered the *Stinger,* and Kalinda seemed to be the right person to ask. But Kalinda was evasive, and it quickly became apparent that it was a topic Si Cwan preferred not be broached.

Si Cwan, for his part, found it fascinating that Muck had joined them at the table. "As your host, I am happy to accept those things that make you happy," he said politely, "but I find it curious that you would desire to have your servant seated with you at the table. Are you quite certain that's all he is?"

"Quite certain," Soleta said firmly, taking care not to look in Muck's direction.

"Curious. And a potentially dangerous attitude to have," Si Cwan said, leaning back in his chair and scratching his chin thoughtfully. "You would not want to risk giving your servants a false sense of equality."

"With respect, Lord Cwan, there's no danger of that," said Rojan. "Muck knows his place."

"With respect to you, Rojan, I generally find the best way to make certain a servant knows his place is to keep him in that place. Case in point . . ."

He clapped his hands sharply. There were two serving girls in charge of making certain that the glasses of wine remained filled and the dirty plates were promptly removed from the table and replaced by clean ones. Their hair was unkempt and dirty, and they looked as if they desperately needed to take a long shower. They came immediately to Si Cwan's side at his summons, standing on either side of him. They hung their heads quietly. "When I first saw your servant," Si Cwan continued, "I thought he was Terran, like these two specimens. I was even slightly concerned that, seeing the way you treat him, it might prompt our own 'less fortunate' individuals"—the others at the table laughed at his phrasing—"to want better treatment for themselves. Not that it would have happened, mind you, nor do they have the fortitude to make such a thing happen. But it's always preferable to crush dreams before they take root. Elizabeth, Robin, this individual"— and he pointed at Muck—"is not a Terran. I'm telling you that so you don't get the wrong idea. He is a Xenexian." Muck did not allow himself to look surprised at being identified, but Si Cwan seemed to intuit it. "Burgoyne was canny enough to run a biocheck on you while you were settling into your quarters," he said in a conversational aside.

Then he turned back to the women. "Not that a Xenexian is all that much higher in the grand scale of things than you . . . but he is higher, make no mistake. So don't be getting any ideas, all right?" He paused and then repeated, *"All right?"* And he reached up toward the woman he'd called Elizabeth and cuffed her fiercely in the side of the head. Elizabeth went down like a bag of rocks.

Robin automatically took a few steps back, trying to distance herself so as to avoid similar treatment. Si Cwan noticed it but did nothing except smirk and chuckle aloud.

Robin made no move to help Elizabeth to her feet. Elizabeth finally managed to stand on her own, although she wavered slightly and touched the side of her head. There was a welt already rising from where she'd been struck.

Hit him back, Muck thought unreasonably, furious at the casual brutality he'd just witnessed. The problem was that he knew if she did such a thing, it would likely be a death sentence. That didn't need to stop him, though.

As if anticipating what was going through his mind, Soleta—under the table—slid her hand over and placed it on top of Muck's. *Don't,* her mind seemed to echo faintly in his. He knew she was right. It was even patently obvious what Si Cwan was up to: He was trying to provoke a reaction from Muck.

But why?

Muck didn't know, but it certainly wasn't for any reason that was going to be of benefit to him. He forced the tension to ebb from his body.

"I'm still waiting for an answer, Elizabeth," Si Cwan was saying.

"Yes, all right, Lord Cwan," Elizabeth said quickly. A trickle of blood had seeped from the wound and stained her strawberry blond hair. She brushed it away casually, as if such abrasions were nothing new for her. Muck suspected that was very much the case.

"Good. Clean these dishes away, the both of you."

Elizabeth and Robin quickly went to work. Muck watched Elizabeth as she drew near him, and as she moved to take away his plate, their eyes met briefly.

Very subtly, he mouthed the words, *I'm sorry.*

She appeared to be looking right through him, and then, ever so slightly, she nodded her head in mute acknowledgment of his sentiment. And then she was gone.

Muck slowly shifted his attention back to Si Cwan, who was laughing over some joke that Burgoyne had just made. Muck suddenly wondered what Si Cwan would look like with a dagger buried squarely between his eyes.

He decided that, if the opportunity arose, he might seize it so that he could satisfy his curiosity.

13

Robin Lefler was crying in her sleep.

Deep in the bowels of the *Stinger,* where the grinding of the ship's mechanisms could be deafening at times, and hot mist discharged from the air filtration system could leave them bathed in sweat, Robin Lefler and Elizabeth Shelby lay on their threadbare mats and tried to get some modicum of sleep. The only time Elizabeth managed it was when she was sleeping so deeply that she didn't hear the outcries from Robin's usual spate of nightmares.

This was not one of those times. Robin's cries in the night awakened Elizabeth, who had just managed to fall asleep. Elizabeth was so exhausted from her day's activities that she sorely wanted to smother Robin with her own sleeping mat, but she contained herself. It just wasn't fair to hold the poor woman responsible for things that she was doing while she was unconscious, but this was too much.

She reached over and shook Lefler fiercely, ignoring the old superstitions that one should never awaken a dreamer. She knew that superstition stemmed from the notion that, when one was dreaming, the soul was off and about, exploring different realms, and waking the dreamer could result in the soul's being stranded elsewhere. This idea held no fear for Elizabeth for two reasons: One, it was nonsense. And two, if it were true and Robin Lefler's soul were trapped somewhere else . . . well, anywhere else had to be better than where it was now.

"Robin!" she whispered sharply, and shook Lefler yet again. Robin's arms flailed about in response, almost clipping Shelby in the face, before she snapped awake, gasping. "Robin, are you okay?"

Robin put a hand to her chest, steadying herself, and then slumped back onto the floor. "Oh God," she moaned. "Oh God . . ."

"Another nightmare?" Elizabeth asked with a weariness that she couldn't quite keep out of her voice.

"I'm not sure what it was."

"Not sure . . . ?"

"It was . . ." She turned to Elizabeth, and even in the darkness, Shelby could see that Robin's eyes were glittering with tears. "I was dreaming of a world where Terrans weren't . . . weren't . . . what we are. Where we had respect . . . from others. For ourselves. Where you could wake up each morning and go to sleep each night feeling good about yourself."

"And *that* made you cry out in your sleep?"

"Of course. Because we couldn't have it."

"Oh," said Elizabeth sadly, realizing. "Yes. That would be enough to—"

Suddenly they heard an unusual noise from one of the nearby service ducts. In their time they had come to know every sound that the *Stinger* might make in its day-to-day operations, and this one was nothing like any of those.

The women were immediately on their feet, tense and uncertain. Something was coming their way, and it wasn't as if they could summon help. Even if they tried—even if they had the capacity to do so—no one would come. Who would give a damn about a couple of Terran females in difficulty?

Elizabeth looked around, saw a stray piece of piping, and grabbed it. The metal felt cold and comforting in her hand. She stood in front of Robin, waiting, and now she could see a shadow stretching from the service duct. She thought of shouting out a warning in hopes of keeping the intruder or intruders away, but then tossed aside the notion. Why willingly sacrifice the element of surprise?

Every second seemed to stretch into eternity, and then there was someone crouched there, right in the mouth of the duct, surrounded by shadow. Elizabeth, without hesitation, charged forward, swinging the pipe.

She never even saw the shadowed hand move. All she knew was that one moment she was holding the makeshift weapon, and the next it was clattering across the room and landing on the floor. She stared dumbly at her empty hand and then back at the newcomer.

He lowered his head, and there was surprise on his face. "You're the slaves," he said. "From the meal."

"Who are . . . ?"

Elizabeth's words caught in her throat as he fully emerged from the duct and stood straight. "You! You're the . . . what was it? Xenexian?"

He nodded. "Muck. They call me Muck."

"We've been called worse," Lefler said ruefully.

"What are you doing down here?" demanded Elizabeth, even as she stepped back to allow him room into their cramped area. "Did you . . . come looking for us?"

"No," he said, looking around. "I was just exploring. Finding ways to get around the ship that might not attract attention."

"Why would you be doing that?"

"Because," he told Elizabeth, "I wanted to see the parts of the ship they didn't want us to see. Also, if things go wrong, I want to know where we might be able to find escape."

"If things go wrong, you're dead," Robin assured him.

"Well, let's hope you're not right about that." He paused, and then said apologetically to Elizabeth, "I'm sorry I didn't do anything at the dinner."

She honestly had no idea what he was talking about at first. When she looked at him blankly, he reached up and touched the abrasion on her face, and then she comprehended. "Oh," she said. "That. I . . . wasn't even thinking about it. You get used to it." Then, without quite understanding why, she reached up and pressed his hand against her face, holding it there. She stared into his eyes and asked, "Have we met? I mean," she added hastily, "I've never been to Xenex . . . or Romulus . . . so I know it's not likely . . . but you look . . . you look familiar to me, and I don't know why. . . ."

"Maybe you met in a previous life."

They both stared at Robin. She shrugged. "Well . . . some people say we all live multiple lives and we keep running into the same lovers and enemies, except in different bodies."

"Some people are stupid," Muck told her.

Elizabeth slowly lowered his hand away from her face. "Yes. Some people really are." She held his hand a moment longer than she really needed to and then released it.

"How came you here?" he asked. "The both of you."

Elizabeth looked down. It was clear she had no desire to discuss it. Robin, however, spoke up and said, "We were taken from slave labor camps. My parents . . . and Elizabeth's parents . . . they actually used what shreds of influence they had left to get us out of there. To 'sell' us to the Thallonians. They thought it would be a better life than being under the yoke of the Alliance."

"Were they right?"

This time Robin said nothing. It was Elizabeth who said quietly, "My parents are dead by this point, most likely. It was years ago. I would have given anything to die with them. They hoped for better for me."

Robin laughed with a bleak lack of amusement. "As if 'better' exists in this galaxy."

"There are rebels fighting for better," Elizabeth reminded her.

"Idiots, the lot of them. They'd do just as well to chop off their own heads and be done with it."

"So you've given up," said Muck.

His tone of voice caused her temper to flare, more than Elizabeth thought Robin was still capable of. "Don't you judge me. Don't you dare."

"Fine," said Muck, who apparently didn't consider her worth expending all that much energy upon.

His lack of interest in pursuing the matter seemed to take some of the edge off Robin's anger. There was an uncomfortable silence for a time, and then Elizabeth said, trying to sound casual, "So . . . you're looking around? Just . . . exploring?"

"He's lying."

He looked over at Robin and said in a flat voice, "I can't say I appreciate being called a liar by—"

"A Terran woman?"

"—anyone."

"I just don't believe you," she said with a shrug. "You strike me as someone who's goal-oriented. Nothing you've said sounds remotely like a goal, that's all. So unless you've got something else to say that's at all interesting or maybe even, you know, honest . . ."

"Robin," Elizabeth scolded her, "that's enough—"

"She's right," Muck admitted. "Except . . . I don't know what I'm looking for, exactly. The source of . . . a feeling."

Elizabeth and Robin exchanged glances. As if she already knew the answer to her own question, Elizabeth said, "What sort of . . . feeling?"

He described to her what he had felt when he had first boarded the ship. That free-floating sense of longing, of hopelessness and despair. "I don't know what it is, or who it is, or where it's coming from. But I want to find out. I feel as if it may be . . . important somehow." He studied the way that the women were looking at each other. "And you know something about it, don't you."

"Something. Yes." She gestured vaguely toward the upper reaches of the vessel. "They probably don't hear it or feel it. They're not Terran. Kalinda does, though."

"Kalinda . . . ?"

"The chief engineer." Elizabeth snorted disdainfully. "Engineer. That's a laugh. She knows nothing about how engines work. Then again, the engines and power source of the *Stinger* aren't like any other. She's probably the only person in the house of Cwan who's able to . . ."

"Able to what?"

"Understand it. Siphon it. Control it, presuming it can be controlled."

"But we can sense it. We're Terrans. We're more closely connected," said Robin. "It's always there in the backs of our heads, like . . . like machinery. Maybe Xenexians have that same kind of . . . sensitivity."

"Not particularly," said Muck. "I've just always had a knack for knowing when there's trouble. A feeling for danger. So it might be related to that."

"You're a very interesting person, Muck," Elizabeth said. "Would you mind telling us how in the world you wound up associated with Romulans?"

"No," he said flatly.

"No, you wouldn't mind?"

"Just no."

"Ah."

There was a short silence, and then Muck leaned in close toward Elizabeth. She felt as if he were undressing her down to her soul with his eyes. "Tell me what it is I'm sensing," he said.

"I'll do better." She glanced nervously at Robin, as if looking for moral support, and Robin nodded. "I'll show you."

14

Muck had not known what to make of these women. He had felt immediate sympathy for them when Si Cwan was making a point of humiliating them. Some of that certainly stemmed from his own experiences, his own hardships and heartbreak.

But it wasn't in his nature to sustain such concerns for long. Whatever softer emotions he felt for anyone, be it those women or Soleta or whomever, usually gave way to a sense of anger at the world so ingrained that he had literally forgotten what it was like not to be angry all the time.

So when he had encountered them in his wanderings and snooping around the vessel, his first reaction had been deep disgust. They lived in a slovenly state and they never had any hope or ambition for more than this. Granted, his own living conditions had been no better when he'd been condemned to the pit. But at least he had enough personality to hate all those who had done it to him, and contemplate what it would be like to avenge himself upon them. These women just seemed to have given up. On that basis, whatever sympathy he might have had for them, however minimal, had burned away.

Still, he did find the slightly conspiratorial attitude they were now displaying to be interesting. And if anyone was going to know the secrets of the *Stinger*, it was going to be these women who knew it inside and out. They were leading him now through more of the service ducts, these far narrower than the ones he had traversed to get there.

"Why don't you destroy it?" he asked at one point.

"It? What 'it'?" asked Elizabeth, who was crawling ahead of him. Robin was behind.

"The ship. You likely know the weak points. You could exploit them. This life is no life for you. End it and take them with you."

She stopped and twisted around so she could see him over her shoulder. "You're serious."

"Yes. Why not?"

"Because we dream of something better," Robin spoke up. "And we're not ready—or at least, I'm not ready—to give up my dreams."

"Then you're wasting your time and your life."

"It's ours to waste."

He shook his head in disgust at their lack of strength. "You feel the same, Elizabeth?"

"No."

Robin gasped slightly, clearly startled by Shelby's reply. "Then why not?" demanded Muck.

"Because of what you're about to see," she said.

She started moving again without another word, and Muck followed her. He did not offer more questions, for he sensed that she was not going to answer them. So behind her he went in silence, although he found himself mutely admiring the shape of her rear. That was odd, and yet it shouldn't have been *that* odd. His involvement with Soleta, the sex they'd shared, had awakened something deep and hungry within him, and he was looking at women differently than he had in the past.

He started to feel something beneath his hands before he heard it. It was a deep, regular, thrumming vibration, as if he were crawling toward a gigantic heart pumping blood through a system. It caused the duct to vibrate steadily, and then he began to hear it as well. The sound matched up perfectly with the trembling of the shaft under his hands. "What is that?" he asked, dropping his voice to a whisper even though no one had told him to do so.

"You'll see," she told him.

Whereas before they'd been climbing at an angle, now they were moving in a horizontal manner. Furthermore, the sound was changing, sounding deeper and more hollow. It appeared to be originating from some sort of vast chamber ahead of them.

And there was more to it than even that. That vague sense of despair that Muck had been feeling was becoming even more focused. Whatever its origin, it was directly ahead of him.

There was some grillwork up ahead, and Elizabeth, straightening her legs and arching her back, crawled over it without once touching it. She gestured for Muck to follow her and indicated that he should look through the grillwork. At first he couldn't quite make out anything, because the room he was staring down into was dim. Then, as his eyes adjusted, he wasn't certain he understood what it was that he was looking at.

Seeing the confusion in his face, Elizabeth said, in a hushed voice, "That's the null sphere. It's the source of the ship's abilities."

"Abilities? I don't understand."

"It's the *Stinger*'s power source. It's what causes the ship to move . . . to think. It thinks for the ship."

"But ships don't think."

"This one does, because he does."

"He?"

That was when Muck finally spotted it. Spotted *him*.

The null sphere was little more than a gigantic ball, filled with some type of liquid. There were tubes and circuitry connected to all sides of it, running off in all directions. The distant pulsing that the chamber had been generating sounded like a heart for good reason; it was not dissimilar from that organ at all.

It was the contents of the chamber, beyond the fluid, that was the most shocking to Muck. There was a man within, naked and bald, curled up in a fetal position, his eyes closed.

"The fluid in the null sphere—they call it a positron flow—taps into and conducts the bioenergy he creates, amplifies it, and feeds it through to the ship's generators. The vessel runs on that bioenergy."

"But . . . who is that in there? How can it be that a whole ship runs on energy generated by one person?"

"His name's McHenry," Robin told him. "He's a Terran. When he was just a child, he got scooped up into a scientific experimentation program. He was a guinea pig."

"A what?"

"A lab animal. He was found to have almost godlike powers. They never knew why, or where the powers came from. But they spent years filling him with drugs, stripping him of a personality, until they reduced him to . . . to this. Turned him into raw fuel."

"How do you know all this?"

"Because," Elizabeth said with grim amusement, "it's easy to hear things when people are accustomed to acting like you're not there."

He nodded, finding that easy to believe. He went back to staring at the pathetic creature called McHenry, floating in his own little world. "So he powers the ship?"

"He *is* the ship," Robin told him. "He just floats there with no sense of his own identity and outputting enough energy to light up Vulcan."

"So the ship couldn't function without him."

"It's designed around him."

"What if he dies?"

"From what I've heard," Elizabeth said grimly, "he's functionally immortal. The ship will wear out before he does . . . at which point they'll probably just build another one around him."

"How does he survive?"

"I'm not sure. I think they introduce nutrients into that . . . that concoction they have him floating in."

Muck studied it, drumming his fingers thoughtfully, and then he pulled experimentally on the grating. It lifted up with no effort.

He saw the panicked look in Shelby's eyes. "No. You can't," she said urgently.

"I have to see him closer."

"And what? Talk to him? You can't. It's impossible."

"Have you tried?"

"No."

"Then you don't know."

"I . . ." She looked to Robin for help in trying to convince this madman of the folly of his notion. Robin just looked at her helplessly, shaking her head.

Muck didn't bother to wait for Robin to come up with something to say. He pulled open the grating and insinuated himself through the hole.

Elizabeth was desperately trying not to panic. The drop from the duct to the floor below was too far, much too far. There was no doubt in her mind that Muck was going to break his damned legs and lie there, writhing in pain until someone came along, found the fool, and blew his brains out in order to put him out of his misery.

"Stop!" she hissed at him, but it was too late. Muck released his hold and dropped to the floor. She closed her eyes, unable to watch, even as she waited for the inevitable loud thud.

There was nothing. The only thing she heard, after a couple of seconds, was Robin's startled gasp. She opened her eyes and looked at Robin questioningly. "He must have hollow bones or something," Robin said. "He landed like he weighed nothing. He fell into a crouch, rolled forward, came right up onto his feet. Unbelievable."

Elizabeth now peered down and, to her amazement, Muck was walking with perfect ease toward the null sphere. She wasn't sure how it was at all possible. Robin was still incredulous, and she'd actually witnessed it.

Meantime, unaware and uncaring of the astonishment with which the women above were watching him, Muck approached the source of that despairing sensation he'd experienced when he first stepped aboard the ship. It was amazing to him that the others on the vessel couldn't sense it. Moreover, it put the lie to what

Elizabeth and Robin had said to him earlier: that this McHenry had been stripped of all claim to personality. No one who was without a sense of himself would be able to feel or project the sort of things that Muck was perceiving. They must have known that. Perhaps they simply chose to ignore these contradictory pieces of information so that they were spared having to deal with the hopeless cruelty of what was going on.

It wasn't just the brutality of what Muck was witnessing that compelled him to draw closer, to connect with this poor bastard. Instead his thoughts were driven to what the women had been saying to him earlier, about encountering people again and again in various lives. He didn't believe a word of it, and yet . . .

And yet he felt connected to this McHenry somehow, in some way that he couldn't begin to articulate. Every fiber of his being told him that what he was witnessing not only was wrong, but flew in the face of what should have been or at least could have been.

He knew it wasn't within his power to fix things, but he could still do something. *Something.* He just didn't know what.

Slowly Muck placed his hands on the curved surface of the vast container. He wished that he had the capability to project thoughts and perceive them the way Soleta did. In his time with her, he had experienced the true strength of his own mind, in that he was still capable of keeping her out of his thoughts through the sheer ferocity of his own personality. He also had that uncanny ability to perceive danger. So he wondered if it wasn't possible that he had the vaguest rudiments of the ability to go the other way and project his thoughts. Not to anyone who was "normal," certainly, but who knew the capabilities of this McHenry creature? It was Muck's hope that, through sheer force of will, he might somehow be able to connect with McHenry and stir him to . . .

To what?

Muck wasn't sure. He was still working out much of what he was doing even as he went ahead and did it.

He focused his thoughts on McHenry. *Can you hear me? Are you in there? I want to help you.* He paused, uncertain of what he was waiting for in terms of response. *My name is Mu . . .* He stopped, and then corrected himself. *My name is M'k'n'zy. I'm Xenexian. What they've done to you is barbaric, and I want to help. But I don't know how. You need to help me in aiding you.*

Long minutes passed as he kept at it. He mentally repeated much the same thing, over and over, and the longer he went without perceiving any sort of reply, the more frustrated and dispirited he became.

They say you have no personality. They say that there's nothing left to you. I don't believe it. I think you're there, all right, but you're hidden. Hidden so deep that no one can hurt you. I can understand that, better than probably anyone here. But you have to reach into yourself now. Reach in and find the real you, and bring it out to me where—

He thought he felt something. He couldn't be sure; it might have been self-delusion, a mental response to wishful thinking. It wasn't words or coherent thoughts. It was a sort of tickling in the back of his head, the most preliminary of contacts. Or maybe it was nothing. Nothing at—

Down!

It might have been McHenry who had "said" that to him, or else it might well have been his own finely honed inner early warning system. Either way, it prompted Muck to drop to the ground just as something passed with vicious speed over his head. Instinctively he thrust upward with his legs. His feet slammed into something and he sent a body flying.

Instantly Muck was on his feet, just in time to see the object of his two-footed offensive strike roll onto its back and then up onto its feet. He recognized Burgoyne instantly.

Burgoyne's lips were drawn back in a snarl and hir long fingers were fully extended with fearsome claws. S/he didn't ask what Muck was doing down there; instead s/he came straight at him with such terrible speed that Muck barely got out of the way. As it was, s/he brought one of hir clawed hands sweeping around and shredded the front of Muck's shirt. Muck wasn't certain whether he'd just barely managed to get out of the way, or if Burgoyne was toying with him.

He slammed a foot upward toward Burgoyne's midsection as s/he flashed past, but this time the Hermat was ready for him. S/he caught the foot by the ankle, twisted hard, and sent Muck slamming to the ground. Muck started to get up immediately, but Burgoyne was atop him cat-quick, and hir claws were suddenly an inch from Muck's face. Muck sharply drew a breath and remained bolt still.

"Try it!" Burgoyne dared him with breathless ferocity. "Make a move! Struggle! Try to get away! Give me an excuse!"

Realizing that it was his only chance for survival, Muck didn't make the slightest move.

"Come on! You know you want to!" Burgoyne urged him.

The hell of it was that Burgoyne was right. Every instinct in Muck's being was telling him to fight back. But he was resisting it because he wasn't certain he could win, and even if he did, the long-term results would be disastrous, particularly when they had ramifications upon Soleta and Rojan. As it was, any fallout from this could be attributed to Muck's being out and about and acting like an idiot. Even if he were able to kill Burgoyne—which he wasn't entirely certain was the case—the impact it would have for the Romulans would be gargantuan. He couldn't allow that to happen. Not yet, at any rate.

So, overcoming his instinct, he remained exactly where he was.

Burgoyne stayed atop him, hir claws poised and ready to rake down, hir breathing harsh and ragged in hir throat. Then, very slowly, s/he managed to compose hirself. Hir face twisted in disappointment over Muck's refusal to provoke hir further. Finally s/he said, "I thought you had more nerve than that," and stepped back and off him.

Slowly, never taking his gaze from hir, Muck got to his feet. They stood there, face-to-face, although Burgoyne was still in the ready-to-spring pose that might better have suited a wild animal.

Finally, hir voice husky in hir throat, s/he said, "What did you think you were doing? How did you get here?"

Muck said nothing. He saw no advantage in answering any questions that Burgoyne might have to pose. Not at this point, at least. If later on it became necessary to explain himself, then he would. But he'd be damned if he'd knuckle under to the demands of this . . . this creature.

Burgoyne seemed to sense that Muck wasn't about to answer hir questions. "I could just tear you apart until you tell me what I want to know," s/he pointed out.

"You could try," replied Muck.

"Ah. So finally he speaks."

Burgoyne looked as if s/he was weighing the advantages and disadvantages of pressing the matter: the effectiveness and practicality of attacking Muck as opposed to it simply not being worth hir time. Certainly the prospect of a prolonged battle didn't seem to weigh into hir decision; s/he wasn't the least bit intimidated by Muck. And Muck supposed there wasn't really any reason s/he should be. Muck didn't look particularly imposing, and certainly didn't have fangs and claws with which to rend an opponent.

Yet Muck found himself hoping that Burgoyne *would* make the move. He didn't know if he could beat hir, but he was extremely interested in finding out.

Finally Burgoyne sheathed hir claws and took a deep breath, composing hirself. Then s/he glanced upward. Muck did as well.

The metal grating which he had set aside when he dropped through had been put back into place. There was no sound from overhead. The likelihood was that Elizabeth and Robin were still there, but completely immobilized—afraid to make the slightest move lest Burgoyne detect them.

Apparently satisfied that the sheer drop would have been too much for the unimpressive-looking Muck to have survived, Burgoyne turned back to him and said, as if it were a matter of only passing interest, "How did you get in here? How did you find it?"

"You asked me that."

Burgoyne's lips thinned to an almost imperceptible line, and then s/he said, "Get out of here and don't come back. If you do, I'll kill you where you stand."

Good luck with that, thought Muck, but—just as Burgoyne apparently had—decided that now would not be the best time to press the matter.

Instead Muck turned and headed out the door, pausing only to glance over his shoulder in a challenging manner.

Burgoyne laughed.

It was at that moment that Muck decided, sooner or later, he was going to wind up shoving that laugh down Burgoyne's throat.

15

"You were insane. That's all. Simply insane."

It was the next morning, and Soleta had come to Muck's quarters with something other than sex on her mind. Muck simply sat there as Soleta tried, and failed, to contain her anger over his previous night's activities.

Stabbing a finger at him, she said, "You are supposed to be here to watch out for my father and me, not to embark on late-night exploratory expeditions that could get you killed."

"Does the prospect of my getting killed concern you because you don't want me to die? Or because then you won't have me watching out for you?"

There was no trace of bitterness in his tone. He actually sounded genuinely interested.

Despite her ire, she paused and considered. "Equal parts both, I suppose."

Muck nodded. If he took any offense, it didn't show.

She stormed around the quarters, venting her annoyance, although it seemed to Muck that she was more upset over being confronted about Muck's "indiscretions" by Burgoyne first thing in the morning than the actual acts themselves. Muck said nothing more to interrupt her until she finally ran out of steam, at which point she slumped into a chair. She glanced around as if concerned they were being watched and then said in a soft voice, "So . . . what did you find?"

He told her. He left out Elizabeth's and Robin's involvement since he wasn't at all convinced that there weren't eavesdropping devices in his quarters, and he decided it was best to limit the conversation to things that any potential listeners already knew for themselves. As a result he wasn't able to go into what he knew about McHenry's past, restricting his description purely to what he had seen with his own eyes.

Even so, it was enough to cause Soleta's eyebrows to rise so high that they practically touched the top of her scalp.

She leaned back in the chair, thinking about what he'd told her. He knew what she was musing over: Whether, with her far more advanced skill, she could somehow make contact with McHenry— reach whatever personality was left and . . . do what? Accomplish what? Free him? Take over the vessel somehow? For what purpose? Soleta said nothing of what she was pondering aloud, though. She was every bit as savvy as Muck and was equally capable of displaying caution over possible eavesdroppers.

"We should tell my father," she said at last, which was the least inflammatory thing she could think of to say.

He nodded and the two of them left Muck's quarters to head for Rojan's. But when they got there, there was no sign of him. They exchanged confused looks. Uncertain of where to go or whom to ask, Soleta went to a wall communications device and tapped it tentatively.

"Yes," came a brusque voice. Muck recognized it instantly. It was the Brikar. She must have connected to the bridge automatically.

"This is Soleta. I'm looking for my father. . . ."

"Meeting with the Danteri."

Soleta and Muck exchanged startled looks. "We've arrived at Danter?"

There was a pause on the other end, as if Zak Kebron were contemplating the blinding stupidity of the question, or even savoring it. Finally he simply said "Yes" in a tone dripping with contempt.

"Please inform him I'm coming up. . . ."

"Not allowed."

"But I—"

"Not. Allowed." The communication clicked off without any further comment.

Muck saw the obvious worry reflected in Soleta's face. He fully understood why it was there. She was concerned that her father was in over his head . . . and Muck couldn't say that she was wrong.

16

Rojan entered the conference room that was adjacent to the ship's bridge—or what Si Cwan referred to as the Nerve Center—and saw that Lord Cwan and a member of the Danteri race were already waiting for him. "Falkar, this is Rojan, a representative of your allies," said Cwan. "Rojan, Falkar."

Falkar inclined his head slightly in acknowledgment of Rojan's presence, and Rojan did the same. They sat down opposite each other, Si Cwan in the middle. "How is the Praetor?" Falkar asked politely. "It has been some time since I've seen him."

"He is well," lied Rojan, feeling that discretion was going to be more advisable than honestly stating he thought the Praetor was out of his mind with fear and seeing enemies everywhere.

"That is good to hear. Good to hear. May I ask why he did not come for this visit himself?"

"He has many concerns on his mind. He sends his regrets."

Falkar nodded as if that satisfied him, although Rojan suspected it did not. He drummed his knuckles on the table for a moment and then said, "So. May I ask what all this is about? Your arrival here was unannounced, and your reason for showing up remains murky."

"Truthfully, I am uncertain as well," Rojan admitted, seeing no reason to cover up on the Praetor's behalf. "The Praetor has explained the full details of our mission here to Lord Cwan. I am merely an observer to the proceedings. I believe the Praetor wanted me here in order to have an impartial point of view. . . . Am I right, Lord Cwan?"

"Something like that," said Cwan. He leaned forward, squaring his shoulders. "Honorable Falkar, it is the Praetor's belief that the Danteri are creating metaweapons, and that these weapons are designed to be employed against the Romulan Empire, or in some other way pose a threat to Romulan interests and other Romulan allies."

"Metaweapons . . . ?" Falkar looked completely blank. "What . . . ?" He stared uncomprehendingly at Rojan, who shrugged. Falkar paused and then forced a smile, as if the very suggestion was too absurd to contemplate. "Lord Cwan . . . honorable Rojan . . . I give you my personal assurance, on behalf of my people . . . we have no such programs in place. We have no reason to. Our alliance with the Romulans has satisfied whatever needs we have for defensive capabilities."

"I wish I could say that the Praetor believes you," replied Cwan. "But he has information—highly reliable information, I should add—that indicates your researchers have been obtaining certain materials from unsavory sources."

"What sort of materials?"

"The dangerous sort. The sort that can be utilized to create matter/antimatter bombs of far greater potency than any that currently exist."

"Really." Falkar seemed more amused than anything else. "At the risk of sounding repetitive, what type of potency are we talking about?"

"A dozen of these devices could lay waste to an entire planet's surface."

At that, Falkar threw back his head and laughed loudly. It took him a few moments to compose himself. Rojan saw that Si Cwan's face remained unchanged. Apparently he did not see the humor of it.

"Lord Cwan," Falkar finally said when he had managed to stop laughing, "I am afraid that someone has been having some fun at your expense. We do not have any such weapons. We do not have either reason or need to create them. Even if, for some insane reason, we did create them, there is no planet we find so offensive in its existence that we would feel the need to drop a dozen or so bombs upon them to annihilate them. This entire business is an exercise in futility."

Si Cwan steepled his fingers and spoke sadly, as if he very much regretted the next words he was to speak. "Tragically, Falkar, the Praetor was concerned that you might adopt this line of denial."

"Line of d—?"

"And he wishes for me to convey to you the following," Si Cwan continued as if Falkar hadn't even tried to speak. "You must promise to disarm immediately. You must turn over all your—"

"*Disarm!?*"

"Turn over all your weapons and the various substances and sources you are using in the production of them, or the Praetor will be forced to use our resources to disarm you himself."

Now there wasn't the slightest hint in Falkar's bearing that he thought any of this was remotely amusing. He considered Cwan's words for a moment, and then slowly turned his attention to Rojan as if Si Cwan were not even in the room. "You realize this is madness, do you not?"

"I am merely the impartial observer."

Falkar shook his head. "No. You are part of some sort of carefully orchestrated nonsense. Either you are here to add a veneer of respectability, or you are simply another victim in whatever the mad purpose of this scheme might be. Either way, unless you can provide me with a single good reason to do so, I am not going to remain here and endure these insinuations and calumnies one moment longer." He rose, turned back to Si Cwan, and said, "Lord Cwan, I am officially requesting that you return me to my government. I will convey your concerns to them, but in point of fact, there is absolutely no way that they will see this as anything other than groundless accusations. Unless you have anything else with which to approach us, this discussion is at an end."

The disruptor was in Si Cwan's hand so quickly that Falkar didn't even have time to register that Cwan was holding it. Si

Cwan fired off a quick blast, and Falkar's chest exploded. He fell back, dead before he hit the chair, his eyes wide in confusion that quickly faded along with the life light in his eyes.

Rojan jumped back in his chair, startled. "Have you completely lost your mind?" he demanded just before he saw the barrel of the weapon swing in his direction.

That was when he understood.

He'd known that he was in trouble no matter which way he approached the situation presented him by the Praetor. It had seemed to him there was no way out.

He now realized, beyond any question, that he'd been right in that assessment.

At that moment he focused every fiber of his being into one single word:

Vengeance.

It was the last thought that ever entered his mind. Seconds later his mind was decorating the wall.

17

Soleta had remained in Muck's room, venting her frustration over the situation that they had found themselves in. Finally she stood up, bristling with determination, and said, "Enough of this. I'm going to find my father and, if necessary, force my way into the meeting. I need to know if you're going to support me on that."

"Will I have to hurt someone?"

"Very likely."

"Let's go."

She started to head for the door, and suddenly she stumbled back. Soleta would have fallen if Muck hadn't caught her. Her face had gone slack with shock, and all the green had gone out of her skin. Her eyes widened and she moaned low in her throat. "Soleta!" he cried out, concerned that she had had some sort of stroke. "Soleta, what's wrong?"

"My father," she whispered.

He knew, with a terrible certainty, what had happened. "He's dead," Muck said.

She wasn't even able to nod. All she could manage to do was turn and look at him, and there was mute confirmation and sorrow in her eyes. But the sorrow didn't remain there for long. It gave way to seething fury. Muck saw it in her and recognized it and welcomed it. Even though they had been lovers—if "lover" was a word that could be applied to such as they—this was actually the first time he truly felt close to her. For in some small measure, she had become more like him.

"What happened?"

"I don't know," she said tightly. "I don't know. We have to find him. We have to—"

"We have to survive," Muck cut her off. "That's what he would want."

"I know what he would want," she replied. "He would want all the bastards killed."

"Then that's what we'll do," said Muck. "But we're not going to be able to do it from here."

They headed for the doors. They slid open.

Two security guards were, at that very moment, moving toward the doors, their weapons drawn.

Burgoyne, with a detachment of several other guards, showed up seconds later to discover the advance guards down and their weapons gone. The Hermat snarled in rage, cursing hirself for not having been down there for the arrest. Instead s/he had remained on duty just outside the conference room until Lord Cwan had been able to confirm that both Falkar and Rojan were dead. S/he hadn't wanted to take any chances that either or both of them somehow might have, against all odds, managed to smuggle aboard some sort of weapon and thus posed a threat.

Now, though, it was clearly the daughter and her servant who posed the threat. And Burgoyne wasn't about to let that threat go unattended to.

At that moment, Si Cwan's voice came through the ship's loudspeaker.

"My friends," he said, "I have distressing news to tell you." Indeed, he certainly sounded as if he were reluctant to pass it on lest there be full-on rending of garments and mourning. "Falkar of the Danteri, when confronted with the evidence of Danteri duplicity, attempted to kill both myself and the noble representative of the Romulans, the honorable Rojan. Why he embarked on such a foolish—nay, suicidal—course, I could not begin to tell you. I can assure you, though, that I am safe. My reflexes and facility with weapons enabled me to cut Falkar down before he could accomplish the entirety of his deadly intent. However, tragically, I was unable to intercede before he murdered the honorable Rojan. Yes, my crew . . . Rojan, the affable, well-spoken ambassador from Romulus was killed. Murdered in a manner most dishonorable and foul. He was, truly, the most noble Romulan of them all. I know the Praetor will want to give him a hero's funeral once he is returned home from what was, in the end, his final mission.

"But it cannot end there, my friends. Oh, no. No, not at all. If for no other reason than for the attempt on my life, the Danteri must be made to pay. And they will be made to pay. I have sent a message to the Praetor informing him of this most terrible turn of events. It is my firm belief that he will ask us to wreak a horrible vengeance upon the Danteri. They took the life of a Romulan. Is not one Romulan worth a thousand, a hundred thousand—nay, a hundred *million* Danteri? Rojan's soul, only a little way parted from us now, can still be heard demanding justice for his untimely demise. Justice. And as soon as we hear back from the Praetor as to exactly how he wants that justice administered, then by all the gods of the house of Cwan, we will administer it."

A cheer arose from everywhere in the ship. Or, at least, almost everywhere.

From deep within the service tunnels that Muck had recently explored, there was no cheering. Instead there was only a growl of disgust that came from the throat of Soleta as if she were a boar. Si Cwan's words had echoed distantly through the ducts, and Soleta's acute hearing had ensured that not one single lying word had been missed.

Muck said nothing. He felt no need to. This was not the time for words; that time had ended when Rojan's life had likewise ended. This was the time for action, and he knew precisely where to go and what to do. More accurately, he knew where to go and what to do, but without the slightest idea of whether he'd be able to go there and accomplish his intentions.

It was at that point he realized that he had no choice. If he didn't manage to do what he was setting out to do, then he and Soleta were as good as dead, and Rojan would have died for nothing.

For Muck, this was simply unacceptable.

18

Elizabeth Shelby and Robin Lefler, after engaging in their dead-end and depressing duties of general scullery work and various degrading tasks for another day, returned to their grubby "homes" as exhausted as any other day. But on this particular day, Elizabeth's mind was racing with concern over what was going to happen to Muck. She didn't especially give a damn about either Romulan. If they'd been blown out the airlock, it would have been no problem for Elizabeth. Muck, however, fascinated her and worried her. She felt as if he had tremendous potential—so much so, in fact, that he was blind to his own leadership skills. She didn't want anything bad to happen to him.

"Maybe we should help them," she said.

Robin appeared confused. That was understandable: Elizabeth had been contemplating the situation and had only spoken at the tail end of her thoughts. "Help who? About what?"

"Muck and the Romulan woman."

"Help them with what?" Robin repeated, having come no closer to comprehension.

Elizabeth shook her head, amazed that she had to spell it out. "Burgoyne and hir people are going to come after Muck and the Romulan next. It's obvious."

"What the hell are you talking about? The Danteri shot the Romulan ambassador. How are—?"

"Don't be naïve! Cwan shot them both."

"What?"

"You know Burgoyne. You know what s/he's capable of. Do you seriously think s/he allows some visitor to the ship to smuggle in a weapon of any kind and present a danger to Cwan? Of course not!" she continued, not waiting for Robin to reply. "Cwan shot the Danteri, and he shot the Romulan man."

"But why?"

"Who knows? Who cares? The moment he did that, Muck and the woman—"

"Soleta. Her name's Soleta."

"The moment he did that, Muck and Soleta had targets on their backs."

"Then they could be dead already."

Elizabeth shook her head fiercely. "No. I don't believe that. Because if I could figure it out, so could those two. They probably fled into hiding the moment they heard."

"Maybe they didn't have the time."

"Maybe," she admitted. "But I'd bet everything that they did."

"Easy for you to say. We don't have anything."

"Face it, Robin: Burgoyne's people and Burgoyne hirself are out looking for Muck and Soleta right now. They can last for a while, but it's a spaceship, for God's sake. There's only so many places they can go."

Robin was aware that there was something being left unsaid hanging in the air.

"So?"

"What if they came to us?" she muttered to Robin.

"If Burgoyne comes to us, we just say we haven't seen them since the night of the dinner. S/he can't prove—"

"No, no." She shook her head. "I mean, what if Muck and—"

"No."

"Robin—"

"Uh uh."

"Robin!"

"Are you insane?" Robin demanded. "Yeah. Yeah, I think you are." She was raising her voice and she caught herself, concerned that somehow what she was saying would echo and carry to un-sympathetic ears. "Look, it was one thing when it was bending rules, sneaking around in the ducts, showing him McHenry. Even then we came damned near to getting into serious trouble. If you're right about what you're saying, then they're fugitives. We help fugitives, we get blown out the airlock, presuming that Burgoyne lets us live that long."

"But we have to do something—"

"No. We don't."

And then, to Robin's utter shock, Elizabeth grabbed her by the front of her shirt and yanked her forward so that they were almost nose to nose.

"I am so sick of your whining. Of your defeatism. Of your saying that you dream of a better place, of a better life, where Terrans have rights and freedom, but you don't do a damn thing to make it come about."

"I dream of one place. I have to live in this one."

"What about making it better? What about us making it better?"

"We're just two people, for God's sake!"

"Sometimes that's all it takes!"

She released Robin then, albeit with a slight shove so that she fell back onto her buttocks. They sat there, a distance between them that was far greater than the few feet of floor that separated them.

That was how they were when Muck and Soleta found them.

At first they said nothing. They all just stared at each other. Soleta, crouched, looked around, and then said laconically, "I love what you've done with the place."

Ignoring her, Robin said, "You could get us killed, you know. Showing up here."

"The hell with you," Soleta shot back. "I just lost my father."

"I barely remember mine," retorted Robin. "Be grateful for what you had."

At first Elizabeth thought Soleta was going to reach across to Robin and strangle her. Instead, much to her surprise, Soleta lowered her head and said, very softly, "That is . . . a valid point."

The change was so marked that Robin, obviously feeling guilty, said, "I'm sorry for your loss."

Soleta waved it off as if it were of no relevance. "There will be time to mourn him later . . ." and then she added ruefully, ". . . maybe. 'Later' may see me dead, though, so it's difficult to be certain."

"You want me to bring you back to McHenry, don't you," Elizabeth said without waiting for him to tell her.

"Yes," he replied. "The ducts are a maze. I was lucky enough to find my way back to you. There's no way I'd be able to retrace the path you took me on earlier."

"You went out through the main door," Robin reminded him. "You must remember where that was."

"The main door will be guarded."

"How do you know?"

"Because I would guard it. So I have to assume that Burgoyne will do the same."

Elizabeth nodded. "Seems reasonable. But what do you think will happen differently if you seek out McHenry now? You weren't able to get to him. You'll still be on the outside looking in."

Muck looked significantly at Soleta. "I think it will work out differently this time."

"Why?" Now she shifted her attention to Soleta. "What are you not telling us?"

"I have . . ." Soleta paused, and then said simply, ". . . certain talents. Muck thinks this McHenry creature might be of aid. And, frankly, I don't have any better ideas."

"Will you help us?" asked Muck.

Elizabeth looked from Muck to Robin and back to Muck. "Yes, all right."

"Elizabeth . . ." Robin moaned.

"Don't start."

"Fine. But then you're doing it on your own. You don't need me along anyway."

"And you'll do what?" demanded Muck. "Stay here and hide?"

"I'll stay here and live, if that's okay with you."

"That's fine," Elizabeth said sharply. "I'm going to go and get things done. You just stay here and dare to dream." Then she nodded to Soleta and Muck and said, "This way."

Moments later, Robin Lefler was alone. Alone with her dreams. She sat with her legs curled up and her arms wrapped around them. Then she felt a stinging sensation in the corners of her eyes and wetness running down her cheeks. She was truly astounded, for she had thought that she had long ago cried out all the tears she had to cry. Annoyed, she drew her hand across her face and wiped them away, cursing Elizabeth Shelby. Cursing Muck. And cursing Soleta. Nowhere in her excoriation did she reserve any harshness for herself, which was ironic considering she was truly the only one with whom she was really angry.

19

Once again Elizabeth Shelby led the way. Muck watched the confidence with which she moved, the determination. Here was a woman who had been beaten down all of her life, much like him. And now she was risking her life for someone who was still, relatively speaking, a stranger. Which, he remembered, he had done for Soleta when they first met. It gave him a sense of kinship with Elizabeth that he didn't fully understand.

Soleta followed without a word. Her breathing was a bit labored from the exertion, but otherwise she was silent.

They all tried to be as quiet as possible. Every so often, from a distance, they could hear the echoes of running feet, or orders being shouted. They were able to hear enough to tell them what Soleta and Muck had already suspected: The ship was about to attack Danter. *An excuse. All of this an excuse, just to satisfy the Praetor's paranoia,* Soleta thought grimly. She found herself hoping to survive this experience so that she herself could return to Romulus, find the Praetor, and strangle him with her bare hands.

Elizabeth stopped where she was and then pointed a few feet ahead. Muck recognized the grating that he had previously dropped through to get to McHenry. He nodded and began to slide toward it.

As he reached for the grating, Elizabeth leaned forward unexpectedly and planted her lips against his.

The movement caught him off guard. Soleta gave a disapproving grunt from behind, but Muck didn't hear her. Instead he was, just for a moment, swept away in the warmth of the kiss.

Then Elizabeth pulled away. She gazed into his eyes, and he into hers, and there was something there, a connection that called to him in a way that he had never experienced with Soleta or with anyone else.

Elizabeth didn't speak but instead mouthed the words, *You can do this. I believe in you.*

And suddenly his preternatural sense of danger warned him.

He yanked back, clearing the grate, just as the utility duct seemed to explode with noise. Something was pounding in through the bottom of the duct, repeated blasts, and he realized that they were finely honed blaster shots—far more effective over distance than disruptors.

He twisted his upper body, but one of the blasts ripped a wound across his right bicep. He heard a moan behind him. Soleta was clutching at her right shoulder, green blood spreading from a vicious wound.

Elizabeth said nothing. He looked to her. She stared at him with lifeless eyes, the top of her head blown off from a shot that had entered right below her chin.

In that instant, Muck went insane.

He smashed through the grating, sending it crashing to the floor, and dropped to the ground directly after it. Burgoyne was there, holding the smoking blaster, and three of hir men were backing hir up.

"I'm going to have your blood for breakfast, fool," Burgoyne said. "Impressive how you handled that fall, though. I would have thought—"

Muck didn't hesitate. He grabbed up the fallen grating, drew his arm back, and flung it forward with all his strength. Burgoyne, eyes widening, dropped to the floor. It sailed over hir head, spinning end over end, and lodged squarely in the skull of one of hir men, nearly bisecting his brain into its separate hemispheres. The guard went down without uttering a word.

Muck yanked out the disruptor that he had removed from the guard who had earlier tried to stop him. Soleta still had the other one, and Muck had no idea if she was alive or had bled to death overhead. Barely a second had passed since Burgoyne had witnessed the brutal death of one of hir people, and in that moment of stunned lack of reaction, Muck was already moving. He threw himself to the left, dodging a blaster shot from one of the guards, and returned fire. He missed the guard he was aiming at completely. Luckily he struck the one he hadn't been aiming at, who was blown backward and slammed against the null sphere. The guard he'd missed fired back, and the rapidly moving Muck barely avoided having his head blown off. The shot came so close that he could feel his hair sizzle. He returned fire and blew out the man's legs. The man went down screaming, and Muck got off one more fast shot that silenced him.

He whipped the disruptor around just as Burgoyne got a bead on him.

They stood there, frozen, both of them, a moment etched in time, both with their weapons aimed. Neither of them would miss.

"This," said Burgoyne, "would be the ideal situation for us both to throw down our weapons and have it out hand-to-hand."

Muck said nothing.

Burgoyne fired at point-blank range. There was no way for Muck to avoid it.

He avoided it just the same.

Burgoyne's surprised expression lasted just long enough for Muck to bring the butt of his disruptor around and smash it into hir face. Burgoyne let out a startled, angry howl even as the weapon slipped out of hir fingers. They tumbled to the ground in a tangle of arms and legs, and Muck tossed aside his disruptor.

Burgoyne released an outraged roar and clawed at Muck. Hir claws raked into his torso, shredding his shirt. Muck didn't feel it. His fists were flying as if they had minds of their own.

He wasn't even seeing his opponent. He was seeing Elizabeth lying there, dead, staring at him with eyes that he imagined to be darkly accusing him of causing her demise. He saw Soleta lying there, grabbing at her shoulder. He saw the image of his father sneering, of the Praetor exiling him, and he saw the face of every bastard in the pit who had tormented him or abused him. All of them were circling him, and he had already gone insane with grief and fury, reckless in his moves, uncaring of what happened to him. Now his mind simply departed his body, and his muscles continued to function without guidance of any part of his brain except the deepest, fiercest, most primal instincts.

And his heart rate still never sped up, nor did his breathing increase. He was a bizarre combination of berserk and methodical.

It look him long moments to realize that Burgoyne had stopped clawing at him, stopped moving, stopped breathing. The world was a haze of red, and when that haze began to dissipate, he slowly held up his hands and looked at the blood and gore that covered them.

He raised the hands and put them to either side of his face, like a perverse lover's embrace. Then he smeared them back and forth, creating a mask of blood on his face. He looked like something that had once crouched behind a primitive fire, staring balefully toward the edge of the woods where glowing eyes would look back from the forest depths . . . and be afraid to approach him for fear of what he would do. When he was satisfied that his face was sufficiently adorned, he licked the rest of the blood from Burgoyne's hands, and then allowed them to drop lifelessly to the floor.

Then he stood and looked at the null sphere that still held McHenry. Without hesitation he reached down, picked up the disruptor, aimed, and fired.

It had no effect at all. The blast just bounced off harmlessly. Firing with the blaster he picked up from Burgoyne's dead hands had the same lack of result. Whatever the hell this stuff was made of, it was certainly constructed to withstand assault from standard weapons.

"Muck . . ."

He almost didn't hear the voice calling to him. He looked up.

Soleta was peering down at him through the hole that the grating had left behind. She was clearly in agony, but just as clearly she was still alive.

He waited to feel some sort of reaction to that development.

He felt nothing. He registered that she had survived, at least for the time being. Beyond that, there wasn't any sort of response. A distant part of him wondered why that was, but not with any concern. Rather it was more of a *"Hmmm. That's interesting"* passing thought, considered for half a heartbeat and then tossed aside as irrelevant.

Soleta frowned when she finally managed to make Muck out down there in the darkness. She wasn't able to discern at first what was wrong with his face. When she finally realized, she gasped and managed to say, "Are . . . are you all right? Are you bleeding?"

"No."

"But . . . your face . . ."

"I'm fine," he said. It wasn't said in a reassuring manner so that she wouldn't be concerned. He simply stated fact, his voice flat and disconnected. "Come down here."

"How? I—"

"Fall."

She hesitated, but then gritted her teeth and—in an impressive show of faith—hauled herself forward, insinuating her head and torso through the hole. Seconds later, she tumbled down toward him like a dead weight.

Muck watched her fall, took a few steps over, and caught her effortlessly. Even so, she instinctively threw her arms around his neck until she was certain that she was safe in his arms. She stared into his bloodied face as if she didn't recognize him.

"Can you stand?" he asked, and without waiting for her to respond, put her on her feet. Soleta wobbled and put out a hand to him to steady herself. He didn't take it. She almost fell over because of it. Finally she forced herself into proper balance and stared at him in confusion, unable to understand what in the world had happened to him. Nor did she understand why he didn't ask after her health other than to inquire if she could stand. She had a gaping wound in her shoulder, her right arm was hanging limp at her side like a piece of detritus, and the entire upper half of her tunic was soaked with green. Yet he didn't seem to care.

They were startled by the sound of the doors to the chamber opening. There, in the doorway, was the chief engineer, Kalinda. She took a couple of steps in, clearly concerned about something, and then she froze in place when she saw Muck and Soleta, not to mention the bodies that were scattered on the floor.

Muck didn't hesitate. He raised his gun and shot her before Soleta could even get out the words, "Muck, no!"

The blast from the disruptor struck Kalinda in the chest, lifting her clear off her feet and sending her slamming into the far wall. She made an awful thud when she hit it and then slowly sank to the floor, her head lolling to one side.

"We could have used her!" shouted Soleta.

"We didn't need her."

"You don't know that! She could have given us information! Or served as a hostage! Anything!"

He looked at her coldly and said, "Her brother killed your father. She deserved what she got. They all do. No mercy."

"Muck—"

"No mercy," he repeated coldly. "The sooner you understand that, the better chance you'll have of surviving."

Frightened and exasperated, Soleta suddenly noticed that Kalinda was still breathing. Apparently Thallonians were made of fairly sturdy stuff; the disruptor shot would have killed most others. She chose not to draw Muck's attention to that fact; he might well have walked over and broken her neck.

Muck, meantime, seemed to have forgotten about Kalinda entirely. Instead his attention was completely focused on the floating McHenry. "Can you reach him?" he asked.

"I'll try."

He didn't appear satisfied with that answer, but he simply nodded.

Soleta tentatively placed one hand against the smooth surface of the null sphere and reached deeply, deeply into herself. That was the key to a proper meld: to get a solid sense of herself, of all that she was, and then send that self outward into the mind of another. The problem was that she was accustomed to being in physical contact with her subject. From a distance, her abilities were stretched or even useless. Nevertheless she did everything she could to reach out and get some sort of sensation or connection with McHenry.

At first there was nothing. The slightest, faintest stirrings, but beyond that, she couldn't perceive a thing. She continued to probe. She had a mental image of herself, of her essence, floating through the liquid toward McHenry, but she couldn't get close to him. She wasn't sure if it was simply the distance, or perhaps there was even some sort of barrier that was preventing her from reaching him.

She had to fight down her sense of frustration. Such emotions would impair her ability to accomplish what she had set out to do. She refocused herself, but still she couldn't seem to get through to him.

She withdrew, lifting her hand from the sphere, and turned to Muck. His face was a mask of disapproval. She ignored it and instead said, "You said you felt as if you were making a connection with him before?"

"Distant. Vague. Nothing useful."

"Come here." He paused. "Come here," she repeated more forcefully.

He stood closer to her. She extended her other hand and placed it against Muck's temple. Automatically he started to pull away. "Don't," she said sharply, and Muck overcame his instinct and remained where he was.

She slid into his mind with ease, and the moment she was there, wanted to run screaming from it.

His body might well have left the mines of Remus behind, but his mind was still in the pit. His mind itself *was* a pit, bottomless and devoid of hope or joy or love or anything except that same burning hatred she had seen in his eyes when she'd first encountered him. She had thought their time together had allayed some of that, and perhaps, in some surface way, it had. But if one tossed a blanket over the top of a pit, that didn't mean the pit had gone away. It was just obscured from sight for a little while.

With effort, she buried the revulsion that she felt upon making that contact. Instead she tapped into the sheer, burning fury that fueled the blackened personality that had once been M'k'n'zy of Calhoun and now belonged to the being called Muck. It provided her own efforts with additional intensity, as if she were feeding off the mental energy she was generating.

Once again her hand went against the smooth exterior of the sphere, but this time she didn't place it gently. Instead, as if she'd lost control over it, she slammed it flat against the barrier with unexpected force, so hard that she felt the jarring sensation down to her elbow.

Now. Now. McHenry, speak to me now hammered through her mind, and she had no idea whether it was Muck's thoughts, her own, or some combination of the two that was inseparable. All she knew for certain was that, as opposed to the cautious probing she had utilized before, this was a force that was ripping through her consciousness like a spear.

They say you're not in there, McHenry. They say you've no personality. That you're nothing. They think they've broken you completely, washed away everything that made you human, so they could turn you into this . . . this thing. This creature. Not a life or even a half life do you have, but just an existence. They did this to you. Do something to them. Cry vengeance. Stab back at them. **McHenry! Let vengeance fill you! Fill up your mind, your spirit, every cell of your body! Vengeance on those who did this to you! Vengeance on their allies! Vengeance! <u>Vengeance!</u>**

Soleta thought she was going to scream. She felt as if her brain were being ripped in two, and she was a microsecond from pulling completely away when suddenly she felt something coming at her from the other direction. She "saw" it as a surge of energy, waves undulating through the ether, overwhelming the mental projection of herself that existed only for her own consciousness.

And then it seemed as if white light was exploding behind her eyes. For one second she could see nothing and everything, all at the same time, and even though she was still on the ground, she felt as if she was hovering high above it. She saw herself, she saw Muck, Si Cwan, the crew, the Danteri—everyone all around her including herself, frozen there as if locked into amber. Time had stopped. She walked casually around them, looking at them in amazement. She reached out to "touch" one of them and her hand passed right through them. She didn't know whether they weren't there or she wasn't there or even where "there" was.

Suddenly she was floating, weightless, and she knew with abrupt, crystal clarity that she was in the null sphere. There was an instant of panic because she knew she couldn't breathe in that environment, and then she realized she wasn't breathing.

McHenry was floating there opposite her. Hairless, browless, and he couldn't possibly see her because he didn't appear to have any pupils. His eyes were simply balls of white, unable to focus on anything. And yet he appeared to be looking right at her, even without the proper ocular mechanism.

And then words appeared in her head.

She didn't know how to express what she was experiencing. It was more than simple telepathy. It was as if she could actually see the words floating before her.

It took you long enough, McHenry thought to her.

And then he shut down the *Stinger.*

20

S i Cwan had been busy locking coordinates of the main weapons onto key planetary targets when the entire tactical array went down. Seconds later, so did the lights.

"Of all the—" Si Cwan began.

Then the gravity went out.

The entire crew of the nerve center suddenly found itself floating. Si Cwan shouted a particularly obscene Thallonian curse. Everyone else was floating and cursing as well, with the exception of Zak Kebron. Kebron wore a gravity compensator to make up the difference between his environment and what his body was accustomed to from his homeworld, so all he needed to do was make a quick adjustment and he thudded back to the floor within seconds after the gravity ceased to function.

"Zak!" shouted Si Cwan. "Call down to Kalinda! Find out what the hell is going on!"

Kebron, anchored firmly to the floor, tapped the comm unit and started to speak into it. But before he got more than a word out, Si Cwan—kicking off the ceiling—angled down toward the comm unit so that he could speak himself. Kebron obligingly grabbed Si Cwan by the arm to keep him stable so that he wouldn't float off.

"Kalinda!" shouted Cwan. "Report! Why is the gravity out all over the ship?!"

"Not all over. It's not out down here."

It had been a female voice over the comm unit, but it wasn't Kalinda's. It took Si Cwan a moment to identify it, and then his face twisted in rage. "You Romulan bitch!" he snarled. "What do you think you're doing?"

"I think I'm taking control of your ship," her voice came back.

Si Cwan twisted around to look at Kebron and snapped, "Where's Burgoyne!? Get hir down there! Make sure s/he brings a squad with hir. I want that damned Romulan's head on a—"

"My head is staying on my shoulders, and Burgoyne is dead. Hir squad is dead. And if you don't shut up, your sister will join them in short order."

Instantly the mood in the nerve center changed. Kebron's face showed no surprise; it never did. But Si Cwan was thunderstruck, his face becoming very pale red. "You're lying," he managed to say.

There was deathly silence, and for a moment Si Cwan was heartened by it, for it convinced him that he was correct and Soleta was bluffing. That lasted for as long as it took Kalinda's voice to come through the speaker. It sounded much deeper and raspier than usual. She was clearly in pain, and it seemed to Cwan that she could barely catch her breath.

"It's true," she said.

Once again silence reigned in the nerve center. Si Cwan, still floating, licked his lips nervously and said, "Kally . . . have they hurt you?"

"They shot me. He did. The Xenexian."

"He did it to threaten me," Si Cwan assured her. "He wouldn't dare to kill you."

"Actually," Soleta's voice now cut in, *"Muck thought he had killed her. He'd like to kill her right now. He'd like to kill all of you. But I'm going to give you and your crew a chance to live. Because you're no longer in control of this vessel, so there's really no reason for you not to leave."*

"So . . ." Si Cwan tried to rally his confidence, although it was difficult for him to do so, considering that he was floating. "So you managed to overcome some circuitry. Figure out a few things about the ship's mechanisms. That doesn't mean you can stay in control. We'll regain it, mark my words, and when we do . . . and when we find you . . . if my sister is not still alive—"

"You still don't quite seem to understand. I do control this ship. I control McHenry. Or rather . . . we're of one mind, you might say. And it appears that he's rather sympathetic to my cause. Watch . . ."

The gravity suddenly came back on. Si Cwan and the others thudded to the floor. But before they could stand or pull themselves together, the gravity cut out again, sending them tumbling upward with great velocity to bang against the ceiling. There were cries and grunts of frustration, and then the gravity returned . . . and vanished . . . and returned . . . and vanished. They bounded up and down like so many rubber balls until Si Cwan literally didn't know which way was up.

"Having fun? I am," came Soleta's voice, and she allowed the gravity to come back on again. The nerve center crew crashed to the ground, as did all of the other people populating the vessel. This time, though, the gravity did not disappear again. Si Cwan and the crew lay there, gasping for breath, trying to pull themselves together. Soleta said nothing for a time, perhaps allowing them the time to compose themselves. When she spoke again, her voice sounded lower and fraught with warning. *"And that's just the gravity. McHenry informs me you have some impressive internal defensive weapons on this vessel. They were designed to protect you against intruders."*

A pencil-thin beam of concentrated light sizzled out from an overhead nozzle and sliced into the floor directly between Si Cwan's legs. He froze for a second and then scrambled backward. The beam was designed in such a way that it could have tracked him, but it didn't. Instead it held its target for a few moments and then shut off.

"But how," continued Soleta, *"are you going to protect yourselves from your protection?"*

Once again she lapsed into silence. Si Cwan was breathing heavily, and he felt the gaze of his command crew upon him. His mind raced desperately, trying to come up with some sort of alternative, some sort of plan. The only thing he could think of was to blow up the ship—except he was positive that the occupant of the null sphere was never going to allow that to happen. He had never expected them to get to McHenry. How the hell had they managed it? Romulans weren't telepaths. It should have been impossible. What sort of freak—or freaks—had he allowed onto his vessel?

At that moment he wanted nothing more than to get his hands on the Praetor and throttle him for getting him into this fix.

"Do you wish to get out of this alive, oh killer of my father?"

The challenging tone got his attention. He hadn't come up with any way out of this damnable situation on his own; there was no harm in listening to what the bitch had to say. "What do you suggest?" He saw the startled expressions of his people, but he just glared at them. It wasn't as if he had a lot of options.

"You can't be especially happy with the Praetor right now."

"You read my mind," he said, and then added suspiciously, "*Can* you actually do that?"

"Oh, I'd rather leave you wondering that. Here's the offer: You and your people depart this vessel in the various shuttles you have available to you. You make your way back to the Praetor. You make clear to him how upset you are about the situation."

"I 'make clear to him.' Meaning . . ."

"You assassinate him."

"I suspected as much," said Cwan. "And just out of curiosity, once I've accomplished that little feat, how do you suggest I get off Romulus alive?"

"That's not my concern," replied Soleta. *"That shouldn't even be your concern. Your concern should be how you're going to get off this ship alive."*

"True. And if I do not kill the Praetor?"

"Oh, I have every confidence that you will."

Slowly Si Cwan got his feet under him. Inwardly he was seething over the situation. That slip of a Romulan girl, and her idiot servant, had somehow outmaneuvered him. Him! Si Cwan of the House of Cwan, lord of Thallon.

Si Cwan was ever a practical individual. He had to acknowledge that, yes indeed, she had outmaneuvered him. He could resent the hell out of her for it. However, that wasn't going to change the reality of it. Kalinda was being held hostage, the ship itself had been turned against them. If he refused to cooperate, he was dead. If he cooperated . . .

. . . if he cooperated, he would live to fight another day. And Kalinda would be safe.

"Very well," he said. His jaw was so tight that the words were almost incomprehensible. "Bring Kalinda to the docking bay—"

"Ohhh no. No, she stays here."

"If she stays here, you have no deal."

"If you stay here, you have no life. Your choice. It's my way of making sure that you do as you promised regarding the Praetor."

"I thought you had 'every confidence' that I would."

"That's correct. It's because I'm going to hold on to your sister until you do."

"How do I know that you won't kill her as soon as I leave?"

"Because, Lord Cwan," she said, the anger surfacing in her voice, *"if I did that, it would make me a cold-blooded murderer . . . like you."*

Zak Kebron made a noise that sounded like an avalanche deep in his chest. "Let me kill them," he growled.

"I heard that," came Soleta's voice.

Kebron replied, "I don't care."

"Cwan," came Kalinda's voice, *"do as she says. I beg you. I'll be all right. But if she uses the ship's self-defense weaponry against you . . . if she kills you because you didn't want to leave me . . . I can't live with that."*

Si Cwan was standing by that point. He leaned forward on the nearest console and stared at Kebron. He had never felt more helpless. Kebron mouthed the same words: *Let me kill them.*

It was so very, very tempting. But it was a temptation to which he dared not yield.

He clicked another switch, putting the internal communications unit on throughout the entire ship. "Attention all hands," he said, his voice flat. "Assemble in the shuttlebay. We are abandoning ship. Repeat, we are abandoning ship."

There was an outburst of protest and shouts from the command crew, but Cwan silenced them with a look.

"Very wise, Lord Cwan," came Soleta's voice. *"And I have every confidence that we will meet again at some future date."*

"As so I," he assured her. He pulled out his weapon and fired off a shot at the communications device. The speaker exploded in a shower of sparks. Then he turned to his crew and said, "This isn't over. I swear by all my ancestors, I will kill her slowly and painfully. Now let's go." There was some hesitation and he said sharply, "That's an order."

Suddenly one of his men stepped forward, his own disruptor in his hand, and he snapped, "This for your orders, you coward!" and he fired.

Kebron, moving with a speed that belied his size, had enough warning to step between them. The disruptor blast struck him squarely in the chest.

It made no impression at all.

Before the offending crewman could do anything, Kebron reached out, grabbed him by the head, and squeezed. There was a muffled crack like an egg shattering, and what was left of the mutineer slumped to the floor.

"Anyone else?" asked Kebron calmly.

There was rapid shaking of heads, and moments later the nerve center of the *Stinger* had cleared out. Si Cwan was the last one out. He cast a frustrated glance behind him and then whispered a silent prayer to the gods of his people that Soleta and her servant would die a slow and lingering death.

The minute that Si Cwan and his people were out in space in shuttlecrafts, the big guns of the *Stinger* opened fire and blew them to atoms.

21

*W*hat did you do? What the hell did you do?"

Soleta was standing in the nerve center, staring in horror at the viewscreen where pieces of Si Cwan's ships and Si Cwan's crew were floating past. Her shoulder was numb from the pain medications she had self-administered, and the wound she had sustained was cleaned and dressed. She was still a little unsteady on her feet, but she suspected that would pass before too long.

"What you didn't have the nerve to do," Muck replied coolly. "Your father's death cried out for vengeance. You wouldn't do it. So I did."

"I wanted to use him to kill the Praetor!" She advanced on Muck, waving her hands around in frustration. "The Praetor is the one who is *truly* responsible for my father's death! Cwan was just a means to that end!"

"You wanted him dead. Don't deny it."

"I don't, but—!"

She tried to compose herself, covering her face with her hands and slowing her breathing to compose herself.

You're upset.

McHenry's voice sounded in her head. She glanced up at Muck, but he didn't react at all. Apparently McHenry was speaking solely to her.

"Stay here," she said sharply. "Don't kill anyone while I'm gone." She stalked out of the nerve center before Muck could say anything else.

She strode a short way down the hall and then stopped at a door. At first she wasn't sure what had compelled her to halt there, and then she realized.

Your father is in there, yes.

Her eyes narrowed in annoyance. "For someone who was basically comatose for as long as anyone can remember, it's amazingly difficult to shut you up."

Blame yourselves. When you and M'k'n'zy made contact with me, I imprinted on your personalities. I managed to absorb a lot . . . especially from M'k'n'zy. His personality is quite powerful.

"I know."

She hesitated a moment more and then decided that hesitating wasn't going to do any good. So she took a deep breath and strode forward. The door hissed open and there was the body of her father, slumped back in his chair. Sprawled forward on the table was the Danteri ambassador. The red blood of the Danteri had mixed with Rojan's green blood, creating a murky puddle on the tabletop.

She went to her father and gently touched his face. His eyes were still open in shock. She put a hand on them and gently closed them. "I'm sorry, Father," she whispered, wiping a tear away. "I should have done better for you. I should have talked you out of coming. I should have . . . done more."

M'k'n'zy was correct. You wanted to kill them as well.

"Yes."

But you decided to pursue another path . . . or at least you did before M'k'n'zy did what he did.

"Before you did it," she corrected sharply. "He couldn't have done it without you. You're in his head the same way you're in mine now, right?"

That's right.

"And he wanted them dead and you helped him do it."

That's also right.

"Why?"

Because it's what he wanted. And because he wanted it, I wanted it. That's not terribly complicated, is it?

"It's incredibly complicated," she sighed.

But I don't understand the problem. If you wanted them dead, why were you offering them a way out?

"If you're in my head so much, you tell me."

There was a slight pause. Then the voice said, *Because you had a glimpse into the depths of M'k'n'zy's soul, and you felt that pursuing cold-blooded vengeance would make your own soul much the same. And you were daunted by that. You feared for what you would become. So you decided that doing something other than simply killing them would be preferable.*

"That's more or less correct," she said wearily. She felt much, much older than she'd been the previous day.

Then I don't see what the problem is. You wanted them dead. But you were reluctant to because of what you felt it would make you. Instead M'k'n'zy killed them. So your goal was accomplished and your conscience remains clear. It seems a win all around for you.

"You don't understand."

Please explain.

"I can't."

I said please. He sounded almost petulant about it, like a small boy who was irritated because he'd asked nicely and still hadn't been given whatever he desired.

"It's involved," she said, "and it's confusing. And I haven't worked it out yet." Gently she traced the tip of her father's right ear with her finger.

What are you going to do with his body?

"Bring it back to Romulus for a proper burial."

What about the Danteri?

"That I will leave to his people. In fact, thank you for reminding me."

Reminding you of what?

"To contact the Danteri, tell them that their beloved allies, the Romulans, have turned against them, and that, if it weren't for us, this ship would have laid waste to their planet. That they're safe."

Are they? McHenry inquired.

There was something in the way he said it that Soleta really, really didn't like.

22

Kalinda lay alone in the sick lab.

The healing instrumentation was positioned over her and making soft, pulsing noises. For safety, she'd been strapped in place so that she couldn't start wandering around the ship, looking for a way to sabotage it. Not that either Muck or Soleta thought there was a serious chance of that, but it didn't hurt to be cautious.

Although the disruptor blast had not killed her, the impact had been severe enough to injure her to the point of being life threatening. But as long as she was receiving treatment, she would survive what she had endured.

She floated in and out of consciousness, her body numb from the neck down thanks to the medications being administered by the healing devices.

Kalinda heard a soft footfall near the door. She didn't open her eyes at first; she found she didn't especially care who it was. So much had happened so quickly that she was, to some degree, still in shock over it and having a difficult time processing it all. Eventually, though, she sensed that there was someone standing near her. Slowly she opened her eyes, very narrowly, to see who was there.

"Oh," she said.

Robin Lefler was standing there, staring at her. "Oh? That's all you have to say to me? 'Oh?'"

"What else—" She stopped. The pain was starting to overcome the meds. Her chest throbbing, she took as deep a breath as she could, and then began again. "What else would you have me say?

You won. You and your allies. You won. You got the ship. You got it because you . . ." Another pause for pain, and another start. "You got it because you used me as a club against my brother. And now he's dead."

"Dead?" Robin was surprised and didn't make any effort to hide it. "Si Cwan is dead? I thought they agreed to leave. I heard—"

"What you heard doesn't matter," said Kalinda. "I know he is dead."

"How do you know that?"

Kalinda stared glumly at the ghost of her brother, at the ghosts of the other members of the crew, drifting through the sick lab. "I just know." Then she fixed her attention back on Robin. "Does that matter to you? Aren't you happy about it?"

"I'm not like you," Robin replied, clenching her fists as if trying to contain herself. "I don't enjoy killing people for no good reason."

"Nor do I."

"You enjoyed treating Elizabeth and me like we were trash. Like we were garbage. You never gave a damn about us."

Regarding her as if she had started speaking in tongues, Kalinda winced her way through another wave of pain and then asked, with no trace of irony, "Was I supposed to? I mean," she added, "you and the other . . . Elizabeth . . . you're Terrans. Am I supposed to give a damn about you? I'm sorry if I sound callous, but . . . nothing in Si Cwan's attitude . . . or even yours . . . indicated to me that I was supposed to give you even the slightest thought. Was I wrong?"

"Were you . . . ?"

Robin didn't know what to say.

She had just come from the chamber where the null sphere was contained. She had not descended into the chamber, however. Instead, once all the fighting and shouting had died down, she had finally summoned enough nerve to make her way toward the chamber. She wanted to catch up with Elizabeth, to find out what was going on, and perhaps even—if she could summon her courage—help.

Instead she had discovered Elizabeth's corpse lying in the duct.

She had screamed upon making the discovery, but no one had heard her. Or, if they had, they simply hadn't given a damn. With tremendous effort, she had taken hold of Shelby's body and dragged her, foot by agonizing foot, back to the shabby place they had shared for so long that Robin was unclear how much time had passed. Elizabeth had left a trail of red behind her that had progressively thinned out as her body had run out of blood.

Once they had returned "home," Robin had propped Elizabeth up into a semi-seated position and just sat across from her for a time, staring at her as if wondering whether somehow, miraculously, her body was going to return to life—destroyed skull and all. Unsurprisingly, that did not happen.

All the time she sat there, she berated herself for not coming along with Elizabeth, for not being there to guard her back. Although the truth was that there wouldn't have been a single thing that Robin could have done to save Elizabeth Shelby, that didn't prevent her from second-guessing herself and blaming herself. As she did that, she listened with one ear to all the noises of the angry crew being forced to depart the ship. When all had lapsed into silence, she had dared to climb out of her hovel, certain that Soleta's declaration that all of Cwan's people had to leave the ship couldn't possibly have applied to her.

She had then walked around the ship aimlessly. She wasn't sure why she was doing it or what she expected to find. She just wanted to experience what it was like to be in a ship without worry over being cuffed, beaten, or dispatched to do menial tasks.

All the time she did that, she wondered why she hadn't listened to Elizabeth. There were indeed Terrans who dreamt of more than just this half-life they were living. They were fighting to make the world the sort of place that Robin only imagined. And the fact was, she realized, that Elizabeth had been right. Dreams are all well and good, but sitting around dreaming them only went so far. Sometimes one had to seize the opportunity to make those dreams become reality.

It was at that point that she heard the steady droning of medical equipment and wondered if anyone had been left behind in the rush to vacate the ship. Her jaw had dropped almost to her knees when she'd opened the door and discovered Kalinda, sister of Lord Cwan himself, lying there helplessly.

Her first impulse had been to bash in her brains, but she decided against that as being too premature. First she wanted to talk to her. Then she'd bash her brains in.

So now she had spoken with her.

And the young woman—hell, the girl—had been so naïve, so incapable of being disingenuous, that she had asked a simple question to which Robin had no answer. Except that wasn't quite true. She did have an answer; it was just one she wasn't fond of.

"You were wrong," she said, feeling exhausted, "that we didn't matter. But I can . . . I can see how you would have thought that. That none of us matter. That I don't matter. I can see, if that's all you know . . ." Her voice trailed off.

Kalinda glanced around the sick lab. "Where is the other woman? The one you're usually with? Elizabeth? Where is she?"

Lowering her head, Robin was about to tell her, and suddenly Kalinda said, "Oh. Never mind."

"Never mind?" Robin felt a flare of temper. "What do you mean, never mind?"

"I mean I know. And I am very sorry for your loss. Very sorry."

The words stunned Robin, cut her to the very fiber of her being. Without even realizing she was saying it, Robin replied, "And I am sorry for your loss as well."

"No, you're not," Kalinda told her. There was actually a hint of slyness around the edges of her mouth.

"Well then . . . I suppose you're right."

"Odd how I derive no satisfaction from that." She had lifted her head slightly to get a better look at Robin, but now lay her head back on the bed. Staring up at the ceiling, she said, "You were thinking of killing me, weren't you."

Robin was taken aback at the statement. Not that it was without foundation; it was, in fact, true. But hearing Kalinda say it aloud the way she had made the . . . the immorality of it more stark somehow. "No," she said quickly.

Kalinda chuckled, and then coughed and gasped because the laugh had pained her. "Are all Terrans as terrible liars as you?"

"Most aren't, actually," she admitted.

"I suppose that's good to know. If you . . ." She looked back to Robin, and there was sadness but also understanding in her eyes. "If you think that killing me will make things better somehow . . . go ahead. Death holds no fear for me, and life holds very little of interest. Do what you will."

"I don't need your permission to kill you if I'm of a mind to," Robin said.

"That's very true. Very well: Please don't kill me. I don't want to die," she said in what sounded vaguely like a plea. Then her voice returned to normal. "Is that better?"

"Oh, just . . . just stay here and heal," Robin snapped at her, and she stormed out of the medical facility.

Kalinda watched her go, then slumped her head back once more, shook it, and sighed, "What an odd species."

23

Bragonier was a member of the royal house of Danter. His face was on the viewscreen of the *Stinger*, and he could not have looked more shocked as Soleta laid out for him, as clearly and succinctly as she could, all that had transpired.

"And you owe it all," she concluded, "to him. To this man. A Xenexian," she added, making sure to underscore the last words. She gestured for Muck to step in next to her. He said nothing, but did as she bade, and gazed balefully at Bragonier.

The older man was shaking his head in astonishment. *"This . . . this is quite extraordinary. And you're now in command of the ship, you say? What of this . . . this McHenry?"*

"He remains in the null sphere for the time being."

I've no desire to leave. It's far more peaceful here.

"He is . . . content there," Soleta continued, giving no indication that McHenry had said anything to her. Once again she cast a sidelong glance at Muck, but he remained inscrutable. It would have been easier to get readings off a black hole.

"I see. And . . . a Xenexian. What is your name?"

"Muck," he said.

Bragonier looked skeptical. *"That doesn't sound like a Xenexian name to me."*

"I was . . ." Muck hesitated, and then said slowly, carefully, as if he was out of practice and had trouble remembering, "M'k'n'zy. Of Calhoun."

The name clearly resonated with Bragonier. Possibly without

even knowing that he was doing so, he got to his feet. *"M'k'n'zy. Son of Gr'zy, brother of D'ndai."*

Now it was Soleta's turn to be surprised. "You know him?" She turned to Muck. "He knows you?"

"Listen to me, M'k'n'zy," Bragonier said quickly. *"What happened to your brother and your father was not my fault. What happened to you was not my fault. No one told your brother to rebel. No one told your father to do the same, thus condemning you to whatever hell the Romulans put you through."*

"I know," Muck said very quietly.

Bragonier looked incredibly relieved to hear Muck say that. So was Soleta, who said, "So . . . now that you know your allies are—"

"However," Muck continued, interrupting Soleta as if she hadn't been speaking, "I'm going to kill you anyway."

Soleta's head snapped back around. *"What?"*

"Me?" said Bragonier. *"But I told you, I had no direct hand—"*

"Not just you," said Muck in a voice that was deathly cold and devoid of anything even resembling pity. "All of you. McHenry . . . take them. Take them all."

The *Stinger* shuddered as the great cannons beneath her opened fire on the planet surface.

"Muck!" screamed Soleta, and then she cried out, *"McHenry!"*

Yes, Soleta?

"Stop it! Stop it this instant!"

I can't. It's really important to M'k'n'zy that all the Danteri die, and I have no desire to disappoint him.

"Oh my God!"

She ran straight at Muck, shouting, "You have to stop! You have to stop this, now!"

"They don't deserve to live. They destroyed my life. They destroyed my people's lives. They deserve to die."

"All of them?" She grabbed at his shirt. "Men, women, children who know nothing or contribute nothing to any of their policies? People who want nothing but to live their lives in peace? What have they done to deserve to die?"

"They were born."

"Muck—!"

"What did *I* do to deserve it?" There was cold anger in his voice. She almost would have felt better if he had lost control and screamed at her.

"Nothing. But that doesn't excuse you if you kill everyone down there."

"I don't care."

"Muck, this is wrong! This is—!"

He grabbed her hands, holding them immobilized. "It's not wrong," he said, and Soleta knew that if she could ever hear a dead man speak, this is what he would sound like. "It's the beginning."

"The beginning of what?"

"Of the mission."

"*What* mission? What are you *talking* about?"

He took Soleta firmly by the shoulders and pointed her toward the screen. She watched helplessly as the *Stinger*'s weapons continued to pound relentlessly upon the planet's surface. "We're going to destroy all life upon Danter. All of it. They all deserve to die because of what they did to me and to Xenex. And after that, when we're done . . . we go to Xenex . . . and we destroy all life there as well."

"What? But they're your own people!"

"My people? How are they my people? None of them spoke up on my behalf. No one interceded. My father despised me the entire time that I lived there, and they all followed his lead. I had year upon year of torment. They knew I was powerless. They called me coward. They said I lived in fear. Now they will get to live in fear, for the short time they have left to live, as the sky rips open and death rains from above. And then . . . then, Soleta, once we've accomplished that, we will go to Romulus and destroy all life there as well."

Not for a moment did Soleta believe they would be able to

accomplish that. Annihilating all life on helpless worlds was one thing. Slaughtering the inhabitants of the Romulan homeworld, which would be protected by Romulan war vessels, was impossible. "Why?" she whispered. "Why would you possibly want to commit to this . . . this insanity?"

"Because it's not insanity," he told her with conviction. "It's the only way that we can possibly be free. I know it's a tremendous risk. But if we can accomplish it, we'll be free from everything that bound us to our old lives. The people who wronged us, the situations that frustrated us. All gone, all ties severed. We will travel the galaxy as angels of death, bringing pain and destruction to every living thing . . . because they all deserve to die. All of them."

"You're dead," she whispered.

He looked at her in amusement. "Is that a threat? You think to kill me?"

"No, I . . . I mean that inside, you're dead. All the rage, all the anger you feel . . . it's burned away everything else. And you're determined to carve out a reality where the outside matches your inside."

"Maybe. Or maybe . . . I'm simply right. About all of it. Maybe this entire universe deserves to die. Maybe we all do."

She looked deeply into his face, seeking some hint of the man she had known, or at least thought she had known. If she could have seen behind his eyes, she would have realized he wasn't looking at her at all. There was the memory of a dead woman, Elizabeth Shelby, occupying that space. But she couldn't know that, and one final time, she said, "Muck . . . stop the attack now."

There was clearly so much he wanted to say to her.

But all he said was, "No."

She rested a hand on his shoulder and squeezed.

Muck's head snapped to the right, his eyes widening. His body trembled and he did everything he could to pull her hand away from him. Everything, in this case, amounted to nothing, and Muck went over like a felled tree.

She stepped back and stared down at the unmoving Xenexian.

No other Romulan knew or understood or would have been able to apply the Vulcan nerve pinch. But she was like no other Romulan.

"McHenry," she called out.

Yes, Soleta?

"Stop the attack. Now."

Unfortunately, I promised M'k'n'zy that I would only cease the attack if he requested. Not anyone else.

"If he . . ." She stopped and looked down with a growing sense of helplessness at his prone form. "McHenry, he can't tell you to stop! I just dropped him with a nerve pinch! He'll be out for an hour!"

All right. Ask him to speak with me in an hour.

The guns of the *Stinger* continued to hammer at the targets far below.

At that moment, Robin Lefler walked in. She started in surprise as she found Soleta standing there, staring at her. Neither said anything for a short time.

Then Soleta said, "Do you wish to be of use?"

The answer clearly caught Robin off guard. "I . . . I suppose."

"Good. Watch him. Make sure he doesn't go anywhere."

Confused but game, Robin eased herself into a nearby chair and stared at the unconscious Muck. Meantime Soleta headed for the nerve center's exit. As she did, she paused to look at the blossoming explosions decorating the surface of the planet like lethal flower buds.

"Shit," muttered Soleta, and walked out.

24

She had no idea what it was that brought her to the sick lab to speak to Kalinda. Perhaps it was something as simple as feeling the need to talk to someone, and Kalinda was just about the only one left outside of Robin—and Robin had looked at her with accusation and a deep sense of guilt in her eyes, so Soleta didn't think she was going to be of much help.

She entered the sick lab and, as she did so, overheard Kalinda talking with someone. The problem was that there was nobody there.

Kalinda stopped talking at that point and turned her attention to Soleta. "Yes?"

"Who were you talking to?"

"No one," she said, and then added with what sounded like a rueful afterthought, "Literally." She tilted her head slightly. "What do you want?"

Deciding to get right to it, she said, "Well, McHenry is in the process of destroying every single Danteri."

"Nonsense," was Kalinda's flat response. "It's impossible. To destroy the crew of this ship, the people who exploited him, kept him helpless—yes, I can see. But millions—billions—of people who have done nothing to him? He wouldn't do that. I know him."

"You know him? How can you say that? He's been a blank slate for however long you've been the chief engineer here."

Kalinda laughed softly. "Don't believe everything you hear or everything you're told."

"Then why should I believe you?"

"Good point," she admitted. "I suppose the answer is that *you've* come to *me,* so if you don't believe me, then you're just wasting your time. If you don't want this to be a waste of time, then you're going to have to start taking some things on faith. And I'm telling you, McHenry wouldn't do that. He's too . . . too wise."

"Wise?" Kalinda nodded. Soleta came over to the edge of the bed, staring at her. "How did you . . . do you . . . communicate with him? Are you telepathic?"

"No. It's nothing like that."

"Then what is it like?"

Kalinda looked as if she was trying to find a way to describe it and was not being terribly successful at it. "Do you—I'm sorry if this seems intrusive—do you believe in the concept of the soul?"

Soleta didn't answer at first. She was conflicted over the response. "My own . . . abilities . . . cause me to accept the concept of an inner essence. I'm able to project mine into others, to . . . meld . . . with them. But that essence is so powerful that it exists beyond the body when it ceases to function? I don't know that such a thing is possible."

"It's possible," Kalinda told her firmly. "And it is. I am able to . . . how to put it? I am able to perceive what some cultures would call spirits."

"But how does that relate to McHenry? He wasn't dead. He was never dead."

"No. But his essence—to use your word—was visible to me outside his body. He was, in a sense, perpetually dreaming. Astral projecting. And I was able to perceive that."

"There are some who think that dreaming actually consists of walking among other realms, rather than a simple discharge of electrical impulses in the brain," said Soleta, unaware that she was describing the beliefs of the deceased Elizabeth Shelby.

"They're correct."

"Oh, please," sighed Soleta, becoming totally convinced that she had been wasting her time. She started to step away from the bed. Even though Kalinda's arms were restrained, she was still able to get her hand out enough to grab Soleta's wrist. Her arm was slender, but her hold on Soleta was remarkably strong. She seemed to be pulling strength from some endless reserve, despite her injuries.

"They," she said intently, "are correct. And McHenry was dreaming for years. For years. There are worlds other than what you see before you, Soleta. Possibilities other than what you perceive. McHenry has spent a lifetime walking among them, and even he has only scratched the surface of them."

"McHenry said he 'imprinted' on us."

"He did, in a way. To put it in the simplest terms, you woke him up. His reentry into this world was through the perceptions of you and Muck, and now he shares those. Your priorities— particularly Muck's—are his priorities, the way that a child's are those of its parents."

"But he's a child with incredible knowledge of all creation," Soleta said with a tone of unmistakable sarcasm.

Kalinda ignored her tone. In fact, she smiled. "All children have that. It's called imagination. Why not? They spent months in their mother's womb, doing exactly what McHenry did. But their minds aren't developed enough to retain it, and adults do whatever they can to burn it out of them. 'Grow up.' That's what we say to them. To grow up is to lose touch with the other realms. With any luck, that will never happen to McHenry."

"You can let go of my arm now."

"Oh. Sorry." Kalinda released her grasp on Soleta's arm.

Soleta shook it to restore the circulation, and she regarded Kalinda thoughtfully. The entire thing seemed ridiculous. But the way Kalinda spoke, the tone in her voice, the quiet conviction . . .

The same as you would see in any religious fanatic, she thought, but at the same time, even though it was woefully unscientific, it also made a marginal degree of sense. And it also was consistent with things that she had heard, had read, that there were indeed other realities. Other possibilities. There was even a Vulcan philosophy steeped in that, and if there was any race not prone to flights of fancy, it was Vulcans. If the Vulcans were going to philosophize about anything, it had to have some basis in scientific fact.

"Other worlds," she said slowly. "Other realms. I . . ." Her voice trailed off.

"You what?"

"I . . ." She looked down. "I've always felt that Muck has incredible potential. Initially I found his . . . his endless well of rage to be fascinating. I was drawn to it."

"Understandable," said Kalinda. "Many types of creatures are drawn to physical flames. It makes sense that you might be drawn to an emotional one."

"But now, I . . . I think it may be too all-consuming. That he has potential for so much more . . . and it's being incinerated by the anger he's carrying in him. That it's burning out of control. And that if he were able to direct it, there's so much he could accomplish."

"I don't know him as well as you," said Kalinda. "I don't know him at all, really. But if that's what you believe, then I'm willing to accept that."

"Which is fine. But in accepting that—in knowing that—what am I supposed to do with that knowledge?"

"You want to turn him around."

"I want to pull him up from the pit."

"And you want to know if McHenry can help. If I can help."

Soleta hadn't been aware that was the case until Kalinda said it. Once she heard the words, though, she knew the truth of them. "Yes," she said. "Yes . . . that's right."

"I believe we can," said Kalinda.

"And . . ." Soleta wasn't sure how to say it. "And you would do this . . . even though he killed your brother? Your friends? Even though he tried to kill you?"

To her surprise, Kalinda laughed. "Would you resent someone for changing water into steam?"

"Water isn't alive."

"Really? Stand at a shore sometime and watch the waves crashing in the surf and tell me it's not pulsing with life. The point is, Soleta . . . nothing ever dies. Not really. Nothing ever dies and nothing ever ends. We just lose track of it."

In spite of herself, Soleta actually smiled. "Then let's see about putting things back on track."

25

Slowly, rubbing the juncture where his neck met his shoulder, Muck sat up. Then he realized that he wasn't actually in any pain; the response was just a reflex to his having been dropped by Soleta.

That was when he realized he was no longer in the nerve center of the *Stinger.* Then someone walked through him.

He gasped, grabbing at himself, and leaped to his feet. When he did so, it was a dizzying experience. He had no weight, no mass, no nothing. He spun in place and looked around in complete confusion.

He was on the bridge of a space vessel, he knew that much. But it was unlike anything he had ever seen. As opposed to the darkness and gloom that had pervaded every other ship he'd been on, this one was brightly lit and alive and filled with . . .

. . . with hope.

He didn't know how he could possibly apply such an abstract concept to what he was seeing, but he sensed it in the air nevertheless.

Someone walked back through him. It was a female, and she was taking her position at a station in front of him. She looked familiar, but he couldn't quite—

Lefler. It was Robin Lefler. But she was cool, confident, smiling, and she sighed heavily as she said, "Captain, McHenry's out again." She nodded her head to her right, and Muck turned to see what she was indicating.

It was McHenry. He was wearing a uniform, black and gray, the same as Robin's. He was seated at a station that was similar to Robin's, but with what appeared to be different controls. He was slumped in his chair, his head tilted back. His eyes were closed, and his chest was rising and falling slowly.

"It's all right," came a voice from behind Muck. "We know he'll come to when we need him."

It was a male voice, and another voice—a female—responded sharply, "Mac, I can't believe you let him get away with it."

"He's a better conn officer asleep than most in the fleet are awake."

Unable to believe what he was hearing, Muck turned and saw Elizabeth Shelby. Not a mark on her. Alive and confident and looking with a combination of annoyance and amusement at the man seated in the center chair.

It was Muck.

He had a scar, as Muck did, but it was in a different place on his face. His hair was neatly trimmed.

Behind him was Zak Kebron. Off to the side was Soleta, studying what appeared to be some sort of science array. Coming in through the far door, reading a report of some kind, was Burgoyne, who walked down to the man called "Mac," except s/he addressed him as Captain Calhoun, and gave him an update on engineering.

Muck stood there, astounded, no longer noticing as people walked to and fro, passing through him as if he wasn't there—which, it appeared, he truly wasn't. He lost track of how long he was there just . . . just taking it all in. This Captain Calhoun was strong, confident, and these people—his people—respected him. Took his orders. Talked to him and listened to him with great regard for everything he had to say.

And Elizabeth . . . Muck could see it in her eyes. Even if she sounded slightly impatient with him at times, there was deep affection for the man there.

Slowly Muck walked toward Calhoun, crouching, staring straight into his eyes.

For a heartbeat, Calhoun appeared to be aware of him, looking right back at him.

"Mac? What's wrong?" It was Elizabeth, and she was placing a hand lightly on Calhoun's shoulder.

"I'm not sure," he said. "Did you ever have a feeling you're being watched?"

"Yes, but I'm not about to take chances," replied Elizabeth. All business, she said, "Lefler, run an interior scan. Make certain we're not under surveillance. Kebron, sensors on full sweep. Perhaps there's a cloaked Romulan vessel out there; see if you can detect an anomalous ion trail."

"Eppy, you're overreacting," Calhoun said.

"No, I'm reacting, and don't call me that. I hate when you call me that."

Interesting, isn't it?

Muck jumped and turned to his right. McHenry—the one he knew—was standing there, with a small smile.

"What is this?" demanded Muck. "What are you . . . ? Are you in my head? Is this a dream?"

No. It's real. As real as you are. Just different. I can take you away from it if you wish. Or you can stay as long as you want.

"Get me away from here. Why would I want to stay to see this . . . this—"

Well, because . . . McHenry was looking over Soleta's shoulder. Soleta was frowning, clearly disturbed about something. *There's a star about to go nova, a science research vessel is stranded there, and I believe this ship—called the* Excalibur, *and commanded by a man who calls himself Mackenzie Calhoun, but was once M'k'n'zy of Calhoun—is going to try and rescue them, at great risk to himself and his ship. And I thought you might like to see how it all comes out.*

And Muck was certain he did not. He was certain he wanted nothing but to look away from this . . . this shadow dance, this absurdity, this ridiculous game. He was about to say all that and more.

Instead, what he said was, "Yes. I would."

And he stayed. He stayed for a very, very long time, one day rolling over into another.

He watched what could have been, or perhaps was, and every step of the way he measured himself against it.

And he was ashamed.

And from his shame came great fury that he was being made to feel that way. And when he could take it no longer, he cried out in rage, and the world before him was shredded like tissue paper.

26

Muck sat up, howling in rage, and lashed out. His fist connected with something, knocking it flat, and when his vision cleared he realized that it was Soleta.

He staggered to his feet, looking around in confusion, and discovered that he was outside the null sphere. Soleta was on her back, rubbing her jaw in pain. Robin Lefler was there, standing behind a large life-support chair, and in the chair was Kalinda. They were all looking at him with varying degrees of interest.

He stabbed a finger at Soleta and shouted, "You did that! You did that to me!"

"Yes."

"Why?"

"To show you what you could be!"

"It was lies! All lies—!"

No. It wasn't.

Muck whirled and faced the tank and slammed a fist into it, accomplishing nothing beyond hurting his hand. "Shut up, McHenry! That couldn't be me! It couldn't!"

It wasn't. It was Mackenzie Calhoun. And so is this . . .

And Muck's head exploded with another image. This time he was still awake, but it imprinted on his mind the same way that a sudden intense, brilliant light would sear itself into one's retina. He saw another version of himself, younger, on Xenex, his hair long, his face newly scarred, his arms spread wide as he was shouting to his people, and they were gathered by the thousands, all shouting his name, hailing him as a great hero, and even D'ndai was there crying his praises, they all loved him, they all needed him, they all—

"Stop it! Stop it!" Muck fell to the floor, his hands over his ears, and he started to sob, feeling the last vestiges of his self-control slipping away. "That's not me! It's not!"

No. And it never can be. You are you. You are what you are now. What you wish to become . . . only you can determine.

He pounded the floor in frustration, his fury blasting in all directions, unfocused, like a wildfire, and suddenly there was a pair of arms around him. It was Soleta, holding him as tightly as she could. He struggled in her grasp, tried to pull away, but her strength was considerable.

"What do you want from me!" he howled. *"What do you want!?"*

"For you to be free of your rage. Of your hatred."

"And without those, what am I?"

"Whatever you want to be."

He had stopped struggling. Soleta braced herself for the likelihood that this was a trick. Instead, he said slowly, "I killed all those people on Danter. I can't be 'whatever I want to be.' I'm a mass murderer."

You didn't kill them, said McHenry's voice in his head.

"I know I didn't. You did. But—"

No one did. I fired on the planet's surface. I destroyed their military might. Their ships, their weaponry, the factories that they use to build them. And I annihilated entire surface areas that were largely uninhabited. I scared the hell out of them, true enough, and rendered them powerless. They'll probably spend the rest of their lives living in fear of the wrath of Xenex, which isn't a terrible thing. But they'll live. He paused. *But now that you know—if you want me to—I will indeed kill them. You tell me.*

Muck hesitated a long moment. Then, slowly, he said, "Those images . . . all lies . . . ?"

"They represent other realized possibilities. The multiverse is full of them. Infinite diversities," Soleta told him, "in infinite combinations. And you get to choose what combination you want."

"I don't know what I want."

"Well," she said, "that's a start."

27

The Xenexians of Calhoun fled in fear as the massive ship descended from overhead like a vehicle of the gods. There was a cacophony of babbling and fear and praying and great certainty that they were all going to die. There were cries of "Spare us!" and "We brought it on ourselves!" and much else.

For a brief time, they had thought something positive was transpiring. The Danteri overseers, with no warning and no explanation whatsoever, had fled the planet. This had been widely perceived as a good thing. But now, with the arrival of this vast and potentially lethal vessel, it seemed the Danteri had departed not to free the lives of the Xenexians, but to save their own lives in the face of an even more destructive force.

And in all that time, as they wailed and made ready for the end, the ship did nothing. It came close to the ground, but otherwise took no retaliatory action. Slowly the realization crept through them that they were still alive and the ship hadn't blown them to hell and gone. A silence started to creep through the air, and soon the vast crowd was waiting in wordless anticipation of what was to happen next.

Then the air in front of them shimmered, accompanied by a shrill whining sound. Seconds later, several forms had materialized. A man—a Xenexian, like themselves—accompanied by a Romulan and a human woman. The unlikely trio stared at the Xenexians, and then the man spoke.

"I am M'k'n'zy of Calhoun," he said. "Son of Gr'zy, brother of D'ndai." There were startled gasps as older Xenexians remembered him all too well, and were clearly having trouble squaring the man they were seeing now with the trembling, cowardly boy that had departed the planet so many years ago.

"I have been to the pits of hell and back. I have seen many things. I have done many things. I have laid low our oppressors. The Danteri will trouble you no longer. They are in fear of my power. Their allies have deserted them. You are free."

They stood there for a moment, clearly unable to believe it.

"You are free," he continued. "But others are not."

And he spoke to them. Spoke to his people, and for the first time in his life, they listened. He spoke to them of the Terrans, of the lives they were leading of subjugation and misery. He spoke to them of all that could be accomplished by the Terrans, and by those living in a galaxy that was not being made to buckle under fear and oppression. He spoke to them of a reality that could be, and of realities that were, and how the former could be reshaped into the latter.

The rage was still there, as strong as before, but now it was focused and harnessed, like a forest fire being transformed into the fires of a forge.

His people took in his words, and his spirit, and his vision that involved joining with the Terran resistance that was already in place, and freeing all living beings who were currently bending under the yoke of tyranny.

In the future, when Xenexian historians would write of it— and they would, at length—it would simply be referred to as the Day of Enlightenment.

"I will not lie to you, my people," Muck cried out to them, his voice almost hoarse because he had been speaking for so long. "It will be a long and dangerous endeavor. There is every possibility that all who join me in it could die. *But any who do want to come with me—those who want to embark on a new frontier of greatness—can do so now, and let future generations sing of them and hail them as a band of brothers!"*

He watched and smiled as his people started lining up to join him.

"Well done, Muck," Soleta said softly.

And with a sidelong glance and a small smile, he said, "Call me Mac."

Saturn's Children

Sarah Shaw

Historian's Note

Saturn's Children takes place in late 2375 (Old Calendar), beginning after the seventh-season *Star Trek: Deep Space Nine* episode "The Emperor's New Cloak," and ending concurrent with the events of the series finale, "What You Leave Behind."

Il a été permis de craindre que la Révolution, comme Saturne, dévorât successivement tous ses enfants.

There is reason to fear that the Revolution may, like Saturn, devour each of her children one by one.

—Pierre Victurnien Vergniaud,
French revolutionary politician,
at his trial, October 1793

1

Flung naked from Martok's bed, Kira struck the cold stone floor on her side and curled defensively in upon herself. Sweaty, bruised, and bloody from rough treatment, she fought to ignore the rank odor of the Klingon regent's lust; the smell clung to her, an insult heaped upon her injuries. Martok chortled, smug and malicious. She reached for her rumpled mound of clothes.

"Leave those where they are," he said. "Fetch me a *warnog.*"

The master had spoken. Slowly, Kira tried to stand, one hand pushing against the floor while she used the other to try to cover her breasts, a tiny concession to her illusion of dignity. Martok hurled his empty metal stein at her. It struck between her shoulder blades, a heavy battering impact that forced her back onto her torn-up kneecaps.

"I didn't tell you to stand," Martok taunted. "Pick up my stein and fetch my drink."

Careful to suppress the hatred from her eyes, she scuttled around on all fours and retrieved his stein, which had rolled beneath the bed. On hands and knees she crossed the room to the table, where the bottle of *warnog* stood. Grit collected between her dirty fingers and beneath her brittle, cracked nails. She had to stretch to reach the bottle without standing up. At last her fingers closed around the narrow, dark glass of the bottle's neck. Her hands trembled as she poured a slow trickle of the pungent libation into the large iron mug, whose outer surface was intricately detailed with carvings from Klingon mythology. The only one that she recognized was *Fek'lhr,* the monstrous guardian of *Gre'thor,* in whose likeness she decided Martok had been cast.

Kira stole a glance through the narrow gap in the window's shutters. Outside, a sultry afternoon lay heavily upon the First City of Qo'noS. The musky heat of the hot, rainy summer day filled this sparsely furnished bedroom in Martok's getaway abode, away from the commotion of the Great Hall and safely removed from his family's modest estate in the mountain provinces.

Another difficult stretch and she placed the bottle back upon the table. She had filled the stein almost to its rim, and the liquid sloshed inside it as she crawled on one hand and two knees to deliver it to Martok, who sat on the bed and leered at her, his jagged teeth revealed in a lascivious grin. Vile hatred swelled in her heart when she looked at him. Thoughts of murder, of poisons and garrotes, of sleeping draughts and him in his bed set aflame, a bonfire of Tholian silk and Klingon ego. Not a flicker of her true intentions did she dare let show in her gaze, which she had learned through painful correction to maintain in a delicate equilibrium between adoration and submission. To darken her countenance in the presence of the man who had spared her from the executioner's art would be a grave insult, an invitation to violence, possibly even a death sentence.

She bowed her head and with both hands offered up the drink to him who had spared her life. "My lord."

A rough swipe of his hand tore the stein from her grasp, and he drank half of it in one long guzzle, wet trails of *warnog* sliding through his whiskers, down his throat, and across his chest. Kira had thought the liquor foul-smelling before; mingled with Klingon sweat, its odor was positively disgusting.

Her downcast face remained serene and untroubled. *This is the price of my life,* she reminded herself. Her escape from Regent Worf's flagship had been made in haste, and she had found herself alone and adrift following Worf's capture by the rebels. After what had felt like weeks, but in fact had been only four days, a Klingon cruiser had recovered her escape pod. Though the loss of Worf and his ship had been no fault of the Intendant's, many in the Alliance had found it convenient to lay the blame at her feet. With one grand failure, she had become expendable. And if not for the perverse appetites of the new ruler, Regent Martok, she would surely have been put to death.

Martok, however, had made other plans for Kira. The favors and services that she had bestowed upon him for the past several months had revulsed her. It was an irony of the darkest degree, she knew. For years she had used men and women with equal callousness, treated them as slaves or toys, then discarded them like soiled rags when they had ceased to be useful or amusing. It had been decades since she had played the part of the submissive, since she had been the one on the bottom. Many of her masters and mistresses of years past had harbored streaks of cruelty or sadism, but none had been so savage to her as Martok. His barbarism was not a charade, no pantomime mockery of the illusions underlying power and powerlessness. He was an overlord, a warrior, a brute. When he held Kira facedown on a bed, one massive hand clamped on the back of her neck as he violated her, it was not a game.

He reached down and cupped his hand under her chin, lifted her face to look at him. "You've always been a strong woman, Intendant," he said. Despite all his debasements of her, he had let her keep the honorific before her name—as if she had left office willingly. He turned her face to one side, then the other, his leathery fingers warm on her skin. "I've had Bajoran women before. You're the first who didn't weep."

I never do, she fumed behind placid eyes.

"You remind me of someone," he continued. "Another powerful woman. No one's ever seen her cry, either."

She hoped that he didn't compare her to his raptor of a wife, Sirella. *Bad enough to be his concubine,* she brooded. *I don't need to be thinking of his wife when he's inside me.*

The regent took a sip of his *warnog.* "The one who took your place as Intendant," he said finally. "I see the same hardness in both of you. But it's not exactly the same. Your edge was forged in fire.

Hers, I think, must have been tempered in ice." His fingers stroked a path through her short, red hair. "I've always preferred fire."

Part of her wanted to thank him, but she knew not to speak out of turn. Among the many conditions of her bondage, one of the most strictly enforced was that she was to speak only in response to direct inquiries, and then she was to keep her answers brief, direct, and truthful.

He withdrew his hand. "You're impressive," he said, his breath thick with the bitterly medicinal vapors of the *warnog.* "And you might yet be useful to me." An ugly sneer. "In *other* ways." As he studied her from behind his craggy, weather-worn mask of a face, she leaned back on her heels. It was slightly more comfortable than having all her weight forward on her knees, but mostly she did it to appease Martok, who enjoyed having a full frontal view of her nude torso. "At the request of the Bajoran Parliament, I'm releasing you to their custody. To be more specific, I'm turning you over to Intendant Ro."

The name sent a fearful shiver up Kira's spine. One of the drawbacks of holding the intendancy was the need to always be on one's guard for ambitious underlings. Few members of the Bajoran Parliament had fit that description so well as Ro Laren. Cold and calculating, Ro was a schemer. Worse, she was well known to be sympathetic to the Cardassians' desire to wield greater influence over Alliance politics and strategy, and highly critical of the Klingons' governance. Only a long campaign of deceit and treachery had enabled Kira to keep Ro at bay for as long as she had. Confined to the committees of the Parliament, there had been little Ro could do to interfere with Kira's reign. Apparently, however, Ro had saved her political capital for a moment conducive to ascension—and hadn't hesitated when news of Kira's fall from grace had reached Bajor.

Kira snapped out of her reminiscence as Martok leaned forward, wrinkled his nose at her, and sniffed loudly. "You can't go to the new Intendant like that," he said. "You stink like a whore." A jerk of his wrist hurled the remaining half-stein of *warnog* into Kira's face and chest. Its stench was both nauseating and bracing.

The air in the room, which moments ago had felt so warm, now carried a chill as it breezed over Kira's wet body, raising gooseflesh as it traveled past. "Guards," he called out, and moments later the double doors opened and a pair of Klingon warriors entered. He pointed at Kira. "Take her to her new mistress." One guard scooped up Kira's black body suit from the floor, and the other took hold of her arms and lifted her until only the tips of her toes dragged across the floor while she was carried out.

Watching his men haul Kira away, Martok grinned at her. "You've impressed me, my dear. Let us see if you can impress Ro."

The Cardassian patrol ship was as soft a target as Miles O'Brien had ever seen. One, maybe two, quantum torpedoes and a close strafing of the *Defiant*'s phasers would be more than enough to turn the rust-hued vessel into a cloud of superheated dust. Vulnerable by itself far from the main shipping lanes, it appeared all but stationary on the bridge's main viewer, surrounded by the slow drag of warp-stretched starlight.

A few months earlier, O'Brien would not have hesitated to order the patrol ship destroyed. It was almost certainly on the hunt for the *Defiant* and any other ship aligned with the rebellion against the Alliance. It was a military vessel, a perfectly valid target, and yet, O'Brien found himself wondering about the lives he would be snuffing out. Did they have families at home? Children? Was one of its crew the last member of a family line? For that matter, would destroying this one little ship really make any difference in the overall war effort? Or would he just be killing these men because he could?

Soft computer tones and hushed voices surrounded him on the dimly lit bridge. The illumination was always reduced when the ship traveled under cloak, as if to reinforce the sense of lurking unseen in the darkness between the stars. Like its counterpart in the other universe, upon which this *Defiant* was based, O'Brien's ship had been equipped with a Romulan-made cloaking device, one that Alliance ships hadn't yet learned how to detect or penetrate.

O'Brien had noticed that his bridge crew tended to speak in whispers when the ship was cloaked, even though it made no difference in the vacuum of space. Looking around at them while they worked, he became conscious of how young they all seemed to him. The oldest was Enrique Muniz, his operations officer, a Terran in his thirties. Combat and hardship had weathered Muniz's boyish mien, but even after seeing the worst horrors war had to offer, some spark of youthful vigor continued to show in his eyes.

Slightly younger than Muniz was O'Brien's first officer, Leeta. Even though she was Bajoran, the slender but buxom redhead had committed herself to the rebellion—and not just for the sake of her ongoing romance with Ezri Tigan, a waifish, dark-haired Trill woman who served as O'Brien's tactical officer. The youngest member of O'Brien's crew on the *Defiant,* but no less dedicated, was another idealistic young Bajoran woman by the name of Sito Jaxa. The wide-eyed, twenty-something blonde piloted the powerful warship with grace and aplomb.

Leeta was leaning over beside Muniz at the ops panel. She glanced over her shoulder at O'Brien, who noticed her stare from the corner of his eye. Her look had an accusatory quality, as if to rebuke him for not yet having ordered the attack. He looked away from her, his expression dour. She let him stew in silence for another minute before she prowled over, never shy about flaunting her feminine charms. Bending at the waist, she hovered over his right shoulder, close enough for him to smell faint traces of her perfume and feel the warmth of her breath on the back of his ear as she murmured, "What are you waiting for?"

His reply was low and rasping. "I'll give the order when I'm damn good and ready."

Apparently, she had understood from his tone of voice that she was dismissed, because she walked back to rejoin Muniz at the ops panel. Seating herself on the edge of the console next to his station, she reached into her pocket, pulled out a few strips of latinum, and handed them to Muniz. "You win," she said loudly enough for the entire bridge to hear. "He's lost his nerve."

O'Brien twisted his chair to face her. "The hell I have!"

Leeta's face brightened with mock surprise. "Oh, really?" Her expression darkened. "Then why haven't we fired yet?"

"Because I haven't given the order yet," was O'Brien's sharp retort. "And before you say another bloody word, I don't have to explain myself to you, or anyone else. I'm the captain of this ship and the leader of the rebellion, and I won't be second-guessed. . . . Do you have a problem with that?"

Like a petulant adolescent, Leeta rolled her eyes and heaved a weary sigh. "Whatever you say." For a moment, O'Brien wished that he could order her thrown in the brig, but there was some doubt in his mind whether the rest of the crew would obey such an order. The chain of command in the rebellion was far from strictly enforced—a fact that had become an ongoing source of conflict within the ranks and concern among the leadership.

Everyone was watching him as he swiveled his chair to face forward once again, a slow turn in which he kept his challenging glare fixed upon Leeta until the last possible moment. Then he was looking once more at the Cardassian patrol ship, cruising alone through the cold void, far from home, posing no imminent threat to the *Defiant.* If he chose not to attack, the crew would see him as weak and begin to turn against him; he would be sowing the seeds of mutiny on his own ship. Destroying the enemy vessel was the only reasonable course of action.

He wondered what Keiko would say. *She'd call it a waste of munitions,* he thought. *An ambush for no good reason. A battle that doesn't need to be fought. And she might be right. . . . Or she might not.*

Resigning himself to the inevitable, he gave the order, without once taking his attention off the ship pictured on the forward viewscreen. "Leeta," he said. When he had her undivided attention, he continued, "Destroy that ship."

In the space of a breath Leeta transformed into a soldier, snapping orders quickly around the bridge, executing the protocol exactly as O'Brien had trained her to do. "Quique, get ready to drop the cloak. Ezri, stand by on torpedoes for a snap-shot. Sito, take us to z-plus-eighty meters, nudge our nose down to give Ezri a better shot at their engines."

Overlapping calls of "Ready" came back to Leeta in reply. She turned smartly on her heel to watch the action on the main viewer. "Drop the cloak!" A hum of power coursed through the bridge as the lights brightened. "Fire!"

A volley of three quantum torpedoes streaked ahead of the *Defiant* and slammed through the Cardassian ship's hull, which blistered and burst with gouts of flame, gas, and dusty debris. "Again," Leeta commanded, and three more luminous flashes sped forward, this time devastating the forward hull, where its command center would be located. As the Cardassian vessel lurched out of warp, Sito matched its deceleration almost perfectly, bringing the *Defiant* out of warp at full impulse and maneuvering back into firing position within seconds. "Stand by, phasers and torpedoes," Leeta said to Ezri, who answered, "Target locked."

On the command panel to the left of O'Brien's chair, a flashing icon alerted him to an incoming subspace message from the crippled Cardassian vessel. In the moment between his seeing the message and realizing what it said, Leeta said simply, "Fire."

Furious pulses of phaser energy surged from the *Defiant* and pierced the other ship's hull. A flare of light filled the main viewer for a few seconds, then it faded. Tiny bits of debris tumbled away, scattered into the eternal void. The *Defiant* cruised at full impulse through the dust cloud, dispersing it.

All around O'Brien, the members of his crew congratulated one another on a job well done, a clean kill, another notch on the corner of the tactical console. Leeta gave the order to raise the cloak, and the bridge dimmed once more as the ship vanished into its protective veil of invisibility.

Beaming with pride, Leeta looked at the sullen-faced O'Brien. "Orders, Captain?"

"Back to Terok Nor," O'Brien said. "Warp eight."

Sito plotted the course and jumped the ship back to warp speed. A hush again fell over the bridge, and the mundane tasks of running a starship kept everyone occupied—everyone except O'Brien. His attention remained focused on the subspace message still logged on his command console as unacknowledged. It had been the Cardassian ship's declaration of surrender.

We might as well have shot a bunch of unarmed men in the street, he brooded. When he'd taken a chance on helping a pair of strangers escape from Terok Nor years earlier, he had hoped that he might be charting a path to a better life. A safer life. To freedom. He certainly hadn't set out to become a murderer, but, to his disgust, that's what he'd just become.

The worst part, he realized, was that by the rebellion's standards this had been one of the good days.

2

A circular pressure door rolled open, and O'Brien stepped through it to a hero's welcome. Cheers and applause, no doubt for his most recent victory, washed over him. *It wouldn't be good for morale to tell them I don't deserve it,* he decided. Waving half-heartedly at the well-wishers who thronged around him and those who looked down from the upper level, he pushed through the wall of bodies, eager to reach a turbolift to ops.

It took some effort to reach an open stretch where he could quicken his pace. No sooner had he broken free of the crowd than he found himself walking toward the one person he was in no mood to see tonight. Smiling sardonically at O'Brien was General Julian Bashir, an irritable, impetuous man who had wrangled his way into the top echelon of the rebellion with a potent combination of charisma and cruelty; to O'Brien's dismay, many among the rebellion's rank and file mistook such qualities for leadership.

"Well, well—if it isn't General Miles Edward O'Brien, the architect of the rebellion," Bashir said with his usual snideness. O'Brien continued past him without bothering even to think of a reply. Not so easily brushed aside, Bashir turned and fell into step on O'Brien's left, matching his slightly hurried pace toward the turbolift. "As usual, news of your latest triumph precedes you," he continued. "Though I hear you nearly had a change of heart. Second thoughts, as it were. I certainly hope you're not reconsidering your allegiance." O'Brien confined his reply to a single scathing glower delivered sidelong.

They arrived at the nearest turbolift. An OUT OF SERVICE notice had been posted on its sealed portal. "What a shame," Bashir said, clearly enjoying O'Brien's mounting irritation. *Bloody hell,* O'Brien fumed as he turned and moved on.

Bashir continued to follow him, talking nonstop. "I suppose it's possible that you've been a double agent the entire time," he said. "It would certainly explain why you let the cloaking device from the other universe slip through your fingers."

"It didn't *slip through my fingers,* Julian. I gave it back to the Ferengi so they wouldn't be shot for treason when they went home." They split up and weaved around a cluster of people walking in the opposite direction. Once clear of the group, O'Brien continued, "Besides, we've got a new cloaking device."

"Thanks to Zek," Bashir said. "And no thanks to you."

The pair reached a working turbolift. O'Brien jabbed at the call button with his thumb. "Just because the Romulans were willing to sell us a cloaking device doesn't mean we should trust them." He tried to peek through the portal to see if the lift was coming anytime soon. There was no sign of it. *Damn. So much for a quick getaway.*

"What bothers you more, Smiley? That you were wrong about the Romulans? Or that Zek was right?" Bashir seemed to enjoy gloating more than just about anything else in the world. There was no point arguing with him, though. The Romulan-made cloaking device had given the *Defiant* a decisive tactical advantage over the Alliance ships it encountered, and now that O'Brien and the other top engineers in the rebellion had reverse-engineered its internal workings, they were well on their way to building more.

And it all had been thanks to Zek, a doddering old Ferengi whom O'Brien had harshly dismissed after their first meeting last year as a "worthless whining prune." Zek was a general now, and he had never forgiven O'Brien's hasty insult; he also had formed a solid alliance with Bashir. Together, the pair had begun to sway opinions within the rebellion. They had been cagey about voicing their true intentions, of course, but O'Brien knew well enough what their agenda was: they wanted him out of the way so they could run the war against the Alliance.

A falling whine announced the arrival of the turbolift, which shuddered to a stop. The doors scraped open and O'Brien stepped inside. Bashir smirked, a sure sign that one more verbal grenade was coming O'Brien's way. "Maybe the real reason you hesitated to fire yesterday is that love's made you soft."

As the doors closed with a dry grinding sound, O'Brien got the last word for a change. "Bugger off."

Intendant Ro Laren stood with her back to the panoramic viewport in her stateroom aboard the *I.K.S. Negh'Var*. The massive Klingon dreadnought had just returned to warp speed after a deep-space rendezvous with a transport from Qo'noS. They had taken aboard a notorious passenger—Ro's predecessor, Intendant Kira Nerys. This was a moment to which Ro had long looked forward. She intended to savor it.

The door signal sounded. "Enter," Ro said.

First through the door was the ship's commanding officer, General Duras. Following him at a respectful distance of a few steps, with her chin appropriately lowered, was Kira. The red-haired woman looked broken, exhausted. Her hair was slightly tousled, and the shine was gone from her trademark black body suit, which now was deeply creased and scuffed. Minor rends in its synthetic fabric appeared to have been crudely patched.

Ro regarded Kira's disheveled state with icy disdain. "Qo'noS doesn't seem to have agreed with you, Nerys," she said, choosing to deny Kira the dignity of any degree of formal address. "Fortunately for you, the only services of yours that I require are professional in nature."

Kira marshaled a feeble attempt at an ingratiating smile. "I'm just happy to be of service, Intendant," she said, and sounded almost sincere. "Anything I can do for the good of Bajor—"

"Spare me," Ro said. "The only reason you're still alive is that Martok strong-armed the Chamber of Ministers into making you one of my adjutants. And before you send him a thank-you note scented with your perfume, you ought to know he didn't do it as a favor to you. He did it to undermine me."

Rather than cowing Kira, the verbal assault emboldened her. She straightened her posture and regained some small measure of her former bearing. "I see you've remained true to yourself, Intendant," Kira said. "You never did care for games."

"And you never tire of them," Ro said. "Did you expect to flatter your way into my graces?"

This time Kira looked taken aback. Ro wondered if it was because she was unaccustomed to having her bluffs called so promptly—or at all. The former Intendant recovered her wits quickly. "You think Martok is still looking to take revenge for the Bynaus censure."

"Of course he is," Ro said. "It nearly cost him the command of the Ninth Fleet. And if I'd had my way, it would have."

The accusation forced Kira back into a defensive posture. Ro's confrontation with Martok was fresh in her memory; he had responded to a limited civilian uprising on Bynaus by slaughtering most of the planet's subjugated population. Rather than control his fury and limit himself to a proportional response, he had impetuously all but destroyed one of the Alliance's greatest computer-science resources.

As a senior member of the Bajoran Chamber of Ministers, Ro had authored Bajor's official censure of Martok. The measure passed the Chamber with overwhelming support, and she had expected it to signal an end to Martok's military career and political fortunes. It was a duty and a privilege that she had treated with the utmost seriousness.

Though technically Bajor was a member world of the Alliance, its unique status as a power broker between empires had enabled it for centuries to stand apart and serve as a neutral, impartial mediator. It had forged pacts of nonaggression between such long-standing rivals as the Breen Confederacy and the Tholian Assembly, and the now-defunct Terran Empire and the Talarian

Republic. Furthermore, Bajor's success in defusing tensions between the Cardassian Union and the Tzenkethi Coalition had been a major factor in why Cardassia had asked Bajor to help it unite with the Klingon Empire to destroy the Terran Empire— a goal that Bajor had been more than willing to facilitate.

Aware that her actions would be weighed against her people's long and distinguished history of leadership, Ro had taken pride in wielding Bajor's power to eliminate such a brutal and irrational political actor as Martok. To her lasting shock and outrage, however, her resolution for censure had been arbitrarily suppressed by Intendant Kira Nerys before it reached the Alliance Council for ratification and enforcement.

In many respects a coequal of the First Minister, the office of Intendant of Bajor served as the intermediary between the Chamber of Ministers and the Alliance Council; though intendants were appointed—and could be removed—by majority votes of the Alliance Council, once in place they often acted with de facto autonomy and impunity. While the intendants of other Alliance worlds also enjoyed a measure of mastery over their assigned domains, none had the status or influence of their Bajoran counterpart, which historically had presided over Terok Nor with autocratic authority and enjoyed a broad range of plenary executive privileges.

In Kira's case, that power had been used consistently to punish her political opponents, such as Ro, and to reward her allies, such as the Klingons.

Quietly, Kira said, "I wanted to keep Bajor insulated from that aspect of Alliance politics."

"No," Ro said, "you wanted to keep the Klingons happy because they were your chief political sponsors."

Speaking now with more resolve, Kira said, "If the Klingons and the Cardassians dissolve the Alliance and go to war, I don't want Bajor to get caught in the middle."

"A war?" Ro rolled her eyes. "Between the Klingons and the Cardassians? That's ridiculous." She stopped talking as she realized that Kira had lured her into debating politics as if they were equals. That would not do—not at all. She changed the topic. "Have you been made aware of the nature of your duties, Nerys?"

"I was briefed by General Duras," Kira said. "Though there seems to have been some mistake."

This was the part that Ro expected to enjoy. "Why do you say that?"

"My responsibilities seem . . . *unequal* to my abilities, Intendant. Certainly, someone with my experience could serve you in a more—"

"Your responsibilities are exactly as I desire them, Nerys." She savored the stunned, stupid look on Kira's face. "I might have been coerced into placing you on my staff, but now that you're here, you'll serve as I dictate, and at my pleasure. Is that clear? Or do I need to transfer you to Klingon authority?"

The moment of revenge was even better than Ro had hoped it would be. Kira appeared both mortified and indignant. She seemed at once on the verge of apoplectic rage and hysterical crying. Through a trembling jaw, Kira choked out the words, "I understand, Intendant."

"Good," Ro said. "I'm glad that we understand each other, Nerys." Ro raised one hand and beckoned Duras to approach. "General, take Nerys to her new workstation and get her started on today's assignments." As the hulking Klingon led Kira toward the door, Ro added one final, caustic touch. "And General? Find her some attire of a more appropriate nature. Her new life is going to be horribly mundane; I want her to look the part."

Keiko Ishikawa's hands were warm on Miles O'Brien's tired shoulders, and her voice was sweet to his ears. ". . . and that was how Spock deposed Hoshi Sato the Third to become the first Vulcan Emperor of the Terran Empire," she said, kneading and rolling his aching muscles in her slender but powerful fingers.

"He just *looked* at her and she *vanished?*" The story she had told him sounded absurd. "You're kidding, right?"

She laughed, and the sound of her mirth was brighter than anything O'Brien had ever heard. "No," she insisted. "I've seen holovids of it. It really happened."

O'Brien half-turned to look over the back of the sofa at her. "Holovids? How?" Then he guessed, "The Vulcan woman?"

"Yes, T'Lara showed them to me," Keiko confirmed as she forced O'Brien once more to face forward and sit still. "She had a lot of memory cards from that era." Her hands continued to work at the tight coils of tension between his neck and arms. "Anyway, that was when the Terran Empire started changing for the better."

"Too bad it didn't last," O'Brien said, his cynicism too powerful to be easily overcome. "Nothing good ever does."

"Not true," Keiko said. Her hands let go of his shoulders and clasped around his chest as she leaned down and kissed the side of his neck. Her lips were soft and gentle on his skin, which responded to even her slightest touch as though she were a creature of pure electricity. He twisted and reached back, grabbed her around the waist, and pulled her over the back of the sofa onto his lap. Years of darkness fled from his weathered face in that moment, and he felt a smile take hold of his features. Keiko laughed again, and this time he was able to laugh with her. He pulled her to him and kissed her as he had never kissed any other woman in his life. Kissing her was about more than satisfying a physical need or succumbing to an animal passion. Until he had met Keiko, no one had ever kissed him like this, either. Silently rejoicing in the warmth of her body against his, the pliant softness of her lips, the vital warmth of her breath, he knew without a doubt that he was kissing her because he loved her.

Terok Nor during the rebellion was, of course, the worst possible time and place that O'Brien could think of for two people to fall in love. The rebellion was maintaining control over the station only by holding Bajor itself hostage. If the Alliance attempted to retake the station, the rebellion had vowed that it would unleash the station's arsenal on the planet's surface, inflicting billions of casualties and ruining its environment for centuries to come. Bajor had responded by declaring itself neutral; it was a difficult bit of political triangulation. On the one hand, the Bajoran Parliament could not endorse the rebellion whose stronghold orbited their planet, but on the other they were obliged not to antagonize the rebellion. The reverse, of course, was also true. The rebellion dared not attack the Bajorans, because the moment it did so there would be nothing to stop the Alliance from obliterating the station. Consequently, Bajor and the rebellion forces on Terok Nor lived in a state of mutual distrust and détente.

And yet here he and Keiko were, passionately and profoundly in love while huddled in the orbital equivalent of a walled city under perpetual threat of siege and calamity.

She nestled her head against his chest and smiled as she pressed her ear flat. He chuckled softly at her. "Is it still beating?"

"Mm-hm," she replied. "Still there."

"Well, thank God for that," he said. "Something's finally gone right today."

Looking up at him, she inquired, "Bashir again?"

"Who else?" He stroked his fingers through her soft, raven hair. "He frightens me, y'know? It's all just one big revenge fantasy to him. He talks like the only thing that matters is how many kills we make, how many of their ships we destroy. I don't think he cares *what* we're fighting for, as long he gets to fight."

"The more things change . . ." Keiko said, letting him fill in the other half of the ancient axiom: *the more they stay the same.* She had been regaling him with stories of the old Terran Empire since her first day aboard the station. To his dismay, the most horrifying tales of Terran cruelty and genocide that had been repeated to him by Cardassians, Klingons, and Bajorans throughout his lifetime had turned out, for the most part, to be true. In a few cases, the truth was sometimes even more disturbing than the rumors had been. Terran history was a rich legacy of savagery and barbarism easily on a par with the worst atrocities of the Klingons and the Cardassians combined. Its only recent era of redeeming value was the one that had been initiated by the reforms of Emperor Spock—and brought to a premature end by the brutality of the Alliance.

He and Keiko lay together on the sofa for a while, cuddling in the warm and shadowy main room of O'Brien's quarters. Though she hadn't stirred and he couldn't see her eyes, he was certain that she was still awake. As they rested against one another, their breathing became synchronized; inhaling and exhaling together, it felt almost as if they were one body harboring two minds. It was the closest that O'Brien had ever felt to anyone, and he found the sensation deeply comforting and reassuring. It was a cure for the loneliness that had plagued his life before she'd arrived; she was his panacea, his salvation.

O'Brien's contentment was fleeting, dispelled by a legion of concerns. "The real problem isn't just Bashir," he said. "It's him and Zek together."

"I know," Keiko said. "Zek's shrewd and knows how to get things. Bashir knows how to rile people up. Zek gets them guns, and Bashir tells them who to shoot. It's a dangerous combination."

He nodded. "You're telling me."

She pushed herself up to a sitting position. "Miles, listen to me. You have to find some way to keep the two of them in check, or they're going to end up pushing you aside."

Slipping out from under her, O'Brien sat up and leaned forward, resting his forearms on his knees. "I'm not sure I can, Keiko. I mean, it's not like I was elected leader. It just sort of worked out that way. If they start leading in a different direction and everybody else wants to follow, who am I to tell them any different?"

Disbelief pitched her voice. "*Who are you?* You're *Miles O'Brien.* You're the man who *started* this rebellion."

"That doesn't make it my property, Keiko." He got up, paced a few steps away from the sofa, then turned back. "These people are free to follow me or not. I didn't force anyone to join up, and I didn't make anyone follow my orders. But after we lost Ben Sisko, everyone started lookin' to me for answers. I don't know why, but they did. So I did my best not to get 'em killed. But if they'd rather follow Bashir . . ." His voice trailed off and he turned away from her, unsure how to proceed. Part of him had grown weary of being in command, but at the same time he was also accustomed now to having his orders obeyed. Feeling that control beginning to slip away filled him with a fear he hadn't felt since before the rebellion. It was a state of being he was loath to re-embrace.

She pressed herself gently against his back and coiled her arms around his thick and rounded waist. "People followed you because they could sense that you're a good man, Miles." Her face was next to his, leaning over his shoulder. "They knew you'd help them go forward to something better. But men like Zek and Bashir will take them backward, to the way the Terrans used to be."

Keiko's warning summoned a memory from O'Brien's past, from one of his encounters with the Captain Sisko from the alternate universe. He remembered the disgust and anger that the other Sisko had shown when he'd realized that this universe's Bashir had been torturing the captured Intendant Kira. Despite all the times that O'Brien himself had felt such revulsion at Bashir's behavior, he had never possessed the courage to intervene until after the other Sisko had shown him how. It was a moment that had cast into sharp relief for O'Brien the fundamental difference in human nature as it existed in their two universes, and it had given him something to which he could aspire. He had enforced a ban against torture on Terok Nor since that day—much to Bashir's and Zek's chagrin. The pair had often mocked O'Brien for showing mercy to the enemy, but the truth was that it wasn't the enemy O'Brien had meant to spare but his own people. He would defend the rebellion from becoming the monsters it fought against. It was an agenda that he knew Bashir and Zek did not share, and he feared for the future of all who followed them on their dark road of vengeance.

"You're right," he whispered finally. "They'll destroy everything if I let them take command. But there's nothing I can do to stop them short of betraying them—and I won't do that."

Keiko sighed heavily. "I know."

O'Brien reflected on the man he'd once been. Younger and hotheaded, the engineer who Sisko had nicknamed "Smiley" would have been quick to anger, ready to eliminate a dangerous rival like Zek or Bashir without remorse. That was the way things were done. Life was cheap and death easy; mercy was a fault and cruelty a virtue. Then, by degrees, everything had changed.

Years of battle had worn O'Brien down, chewed him up in its maw of terrors. At first he'd watched fellow Terrans die in battle; later he found that he was losing comrades; and lately he caught himself thinking of the dead as fallen friends. The stronger his bonds of affection for these people became, the less eager he was to put them in harm's way. War demanded sacrifices, however, and so he had continued to order his people into combat. The only thing that had made it bearable for him was that, at every opportunity, he had gone with them, putting his own life in jeopardy, sharing the risks.

Then he'd met Keiko. She had arrived on Terok Nor a few months ago, aboard a stolen transport ship with more than a hundred liberated slaves of various Terran-subject species: Andorians, Tellarites, Bolians, Denobulans, Vulcans, Terrans. All of the refugees had followed her as their leader because, in addition to having once been their supervisor in an Alliance mine, she also had been the one who had organized and led their uprising and escape to Terok Nor. The more O'Brien had learned about Keiko's organizational abilities and tactical skills, the more impressed he had been. Within a few weeks of her arrival, he had made her his executive officer on Terok Nor.

At the same time, she had also become his lover.

Now every kiss, every embrace, every moment alone with her made him savor the taste of life a little bit more, and made him all the more reluctant to go back out to battle. Leeta and Bashir had been more right about him than they had known, or even than he himself had been able to realize until tonight: love *had* made him soft—it had given him a reason to live.

★ ★ ★

Kira's new quarters aboard the *I.K.S. Negh'Var* were little more than a single gray bunk in a crowded berthing compartment. Hers was the top bunk in a stack of four, on a narrow aisle four stacks deep on either side. Thirty-two other slaves, both male and female, and of various species, resided in the tiny space and shared a common lavatory and a single shower stall, both of which were filthy and reeked.

The surface of her unpadded bunk had lifted from a hinge on its far side to reveal a shallow storage space underneath. Inside she had found two identical uniforms, drab gray coveralls. Duras had ordered his guards to strip Kira's black body suit, and they had done so with undisguised amusement. "Put one uniform on now," he had commanded her. "Wear the other while the first is being washed. The Intendant commands you to remain clean and presentable while you remain in her service."

After she had dressed, the Klingons had escorted her to her new workspace, in an anteroom not far from Ro's command suite. Compared to her quarters, her workspace was an oasis of privacy and comfort. Little more than a closet, it was less than two meters wide, with barely enough room for her to slip past the edge of her desk to her narrow, metal seat. The light over her head flickered constantly, throwing annoying shadows and flares across the display of her workstation. Like the rest of the ship's extremely utilitarian interior, the walls of the tiny compartment were featureless, greenish-gray metal. And when the door closed, Kira found herself alarmingly, painfully alone.

It was so hard not to reminisce about the life she had lost. Gone now were the scores of retainers and slaves, the trusted corps of fawning subordinates. Her every move was observed on the *Negh'Var*. Other people decided when she was allowed to eat, when she could sleep, what she was allowed to keep stored under her bunk. Ro called her an "adjutant," but the truth was that Kira had been attired, quartered, and spoken to like a slave in every respect except for her official duties. Those, she was coming to realize, were the labors of a minor bureaucrat. A very boring, ineffectual, and obscure bureaucrat.

The parade of mindless tasks was ceaseless. Administrative formalities complicated even the simplest items of business. Triply redundant layers of review and approval made swift action impossible even on items of minimal consequence. There were dozens of requests pending for Ro's approval of changes to minor ordinances for outlying colony settlements on Bajor VIII, a petition for subsidized duranium refining on Bajor VII, a bill to levy a new tax on uridium producers in Rakantha province, applications for mining licenses to explore the bedrock under Mount Kola—and legal injunctions trying to block those licenses because excavating Mount Kola would mean destroying the ruins of Parek Tonn. It was all the sort of mind-numbing toil with which Kira had never bothered; even during her early years in Parliament, she had made a point of delegating tasks like these to petty, softly middle-aged career civil servants who were not qualified for anything more challenging.

Hours passed in a slow, excruciating march of tedium that was punctuated only by the arrival of new busywork on her monitor. Endless drudgery piled over upon itself, all of it bleeding together and driving Kira deeper into a state of indolent misery, which was the only acceptable camouflage for her rage. This was a subtle form of torture, and she was certain that was exactly as Ro had intended it. *This is her idea of a joke at my expense,* Kira thought, her temper simmering behind weary eyes. *Making me answer to cretins. Wasting my talent on pointless chores unworthy of my gifts. Not because it's necessary, but just because she can.*

The sheer pettiness of it was enough to make her want to scream. Realizing that her workspace likely was soundproof, she threw back her head and let her anger explode. Her shriek of rage was hoarse and colored with bitterness and despair. It didn't help.

When the last echoes of her fury ceased to repeat themselves in her lonely thoughts, she planted her face in her hands. The darkness of her own palms was her last bastion of sanity, her last refuge against the small-minded tyrant who, for now, she was forced to serve. Plumbing the depths of her own memory, she found little reason to hope that her fortunes would improve. The system was rigged, and everyone knew it. Accumulating power was difficult, slow, and costly. It could be lost without warning. Recovering from a reversal such as the one Kira had recently suffered was unheard of. In all likelihood she was going to live out the rest of her days as a slave to her inferiors, and unless she found a way to harness and defuse her rage, it would be her final undoing.

There's nothing else for you to do but go back to work, she told herself. *This is the hand you've been dealt. At least you aren't working under a whip in a uridium mine . . . or back on Qo'noS, being violated by Martok. Be grateful for small mercies.*

A deep breath quieted her thoughts. She forced herself to relax and slow her breathing. When she opened her eyes, she checked the chronometer. The shift would end in less than two hours; her first day in thrall to Ro was almost over.

On the edge of her table stood a small pile of unevenly stacked padds from the Bajoran government. Each one was jammed with a different kind of data. All were marked "urgent."

Kira shoved the padds into the corner behind her chair, then turned back to review the information displayed on her monitor. Working her way quickly through several overlapping screens of data, she found something at least marginally interesting: reports from Bajoran and Alliance criminal investigations that had been flagged for Intendant Ro's review.

Reasoning that any kind of true crime had to be more interesting than reading another briefing on quadrotriticale production in Dahkur province, she loaded up all the current investigation files. The first few were disappointments to her—a few risible requests for clemency from captured Terran rebels sentenced to be executed on Bajor. A quick skim of another read like a textbook example of the brewing conflict between the Klingons and the Cardassians: a Klingon transport leaving Bajor had been hijacked by its onboard domestic slaves—a smattering of Terrans and Andorians, a Tella-rite, and a Vulcan—who had taken the vessel's crew and its fifty-six Alliance passengers hostage. A nearby Cardassian cruiser had intervened and resolved the matter by simply destroying the transport, killing everyone aboard, friend and foe alike. Such tactics were frequently employed by the Cardassians, which was one of the reasons Kira had known never to trust them: they had no honor. Unfortunately, despite the political uproar the incident had caused on Bajor, it was becoming increasingly clear that Ro supported the Cardassians.

After filing away the hijacking report, she skimmed through several more, none of which seemed particularly interesting at first. Most of them appeared to be routine thefts and piracies, or, in some cases, poorly disguised war profiteering.

As she neared the end of the reports, however, she felt a sense of foreboding. Something felt amiss, as if there was an invisible thread of motive running through several of the items she had read. She went back and read them again, consciously looking this time for links, commonalities, themes.

Soon, four reports had found their way to the top of the stack and now were arranged side by side on her display. Ninety-one days earlier, two industrial-sized loads of kelbonite had been heisted from a supply depot on Bardeezi Prime. Sixty-three days earlier, a fully loaded dilithium freighter vanished en route to Ajilon after shipping out from the refinery on Korma II. Fifty-nine days earlier, a freighter carrying a full shipment of antimatter from the refinery on Loval exploded in deep space en route to Goralis—allegedly an accident, blamed on a faulty containment module. And eighteen days earlier, the Cardassian garrison on Amleth IV came up short of nearly two hundred heavy combat rifles during its latest small-arms inventory.

Kira stared at the data, almost shocked that no one in Klingon Imperial Intelligence or the Cardassian Obsidian Order had seized upon these reports. Fuel for a matter-antimatter reactor, combat weapons, and enough shielding material to block something huge from even a close-range sensor sweep. These four ostensibly disparate incidents, viewed together, had the mark of the Terran Rebellion all over them.

Her shift would be over in a few minutes. She wondered how she ought to proceed. If action wasn't taken quickly, there might not be time to stop whatever the rebels were planning. For all Kira knew, it might already be too late. Something clearly had to be done immediately. A spark of self-interest kindled then in her imagination. This was the sort of opportunity that, if parlayed to maximum advantage, could elevate her standing with the Alliance considerably.

The chain of command dictated that Kira report her findings directly to Intendant Ro. Given the circumstances, however, she decided not to do her successor any favors.

3

T his is exactly what I said not to do," O'Brien protested.

Walking as slowly as Zek wasn't easy for O'Brien; not strangling the elderly Ferengi was even more difficult. O'Brien, Bashir, and a small group of high-level rebellion leaders shuffled along the lower level of Empok Nor's dark, abandoned Promenade, making their way in agonizing half-steps behind Zek as he moved like congealing sap toward a flight of stairs.

"You're always too cautious, O'Brien," Zek whined, his nasal bleat of a voice as sharp as a weapon. "We need to act now, before the Alliance gets reorganized."

"That's no excuse for getting careless," O'Brien said. "Doing everything at once, in the same place, is bound to draw attention—and that's the last bloody thing we need."

Lifting one arthritic foot and his gnarled walking stick onto the lowest stair, Zek dismissed O'Brien's concerns with a wave of his hand. "You say careless, I say bold. Setting up one facility takes less time." Another arduous step up left Zek winded. "Doing it here means we can trade spare parts with Terok Nor. And the sooner we finish, the sooner we can start fighting this war on our own terms."

O'Brien knew that there was some truth in what the Ferengi was saying. Zek's aged feet might be slow, but his mind remained quick and razor-sharp; his reputation as one of the rebellion's best strategists had been well earned. Lately, however, O'Brien had begun to notice a disturbing trend in Zek's pronouncements and mission plans: overconfidence.

"Let's say you're right," O'Brien began.

"Of course I am," Zek interrupted.

O'Brien continued, "It would only take one mistake to compromise our security on this station. For instance, hijacking all its supplies from systems in the same sector."

Zek forced his left foot up another step. His breathing was a bit more labored now, and his temper was beginning to show. "It's been months, O'Brien! If the Alliance was going to notice anything, they'd have done it by now." He grunted as he advanced upward another step. "You'd be afraid of your own shadow if the lights in this place worked." Profound wheezing followed Zek's next climbing step. Seconds later, when his breathing calmed a bit, he added, "It's not like I didn't cover my tracks. For the love of money, I made it look like the antimatter tanker *blew up*. Deep-space hijackings don't get much cleaner than that."

"You still should have consulted me first," O'Brien said.

Turning back to face him, Zek blurted, "What for? So you could tell me a hundred reasons why it wouldn't work? Well, it did."

Glowering at Zek's back while they climbed the last few steps to the upper level of the Promenade, O'Brien felt as if he had made the mistake of coming alone to a gang fight; Zek was clearly taking the lead in planning the rebellion's next steps, and Bashir was drumming up all the support Zek would need to overrule any dissent or challenge. Even though they were all supposed to be on the same side, being part of a coalition led by Zek and Bashir filled O'Brien with dread. The Ferengi's motives might be superficially benign, but his tactics, though they were undeniably bold, were foolhardy. This latest stunt of his only confirmed it.

O'Brien stepped onto the upper level as soon as Zek was out of the way. Bashir and the others followed them up, and the group spread out along the row of sloped windows facing out toward the docking ring of Terok Nor's twin-sister station, abandoned years ago by the Cardassians near the cometary debris ring of the Trivas system. Unlike Terok Nor's majestic view of the surface of Bajor,

Empok Nor looked out only on the vast, star-flecked sphere of infinity.

Spreading his arms wide, Zek declared, "Ladies and gentlemen, I give you . . . the future of the rebellion." At each major docking point along the perimeter of the central docking ring, a rectangular cocoon of metal scaffolding had been erected, twelve altogether, of which one was vacant. Inside eleven of the duranium frames, new *Defiant*-class starships were taking shape. It had been evident from the outset why Zek's plan could not be carried out at Terok Nor: an effort on this scale would have been easily detectable from the surface of Bajor, and the Alliance would have had no choice but to risk the planet's annihilation in order to prevent the rebellion from building an entire fleet of ships like the *Defiant*.

O'Brien had insisted that the wisest course was to set up twelve separate, hidden construction shells throughout the Badlands and in unoccupied star systems spread across the adjoining sectors. When he had asked Bashir and Zek for updates, they had insisted that they had "moved the starship-construction project off-site," as he had requested. Until today, he'd had no idea that they'd moved it all here. It was quite possibly one of the worst tactical decisions he had ever seen, but the scope of its engineering achievement impressed him. "How are you building them all so fast?" he asked.

"Each frame has its own industrial replicator," Zek crowed. "Complete with templates for the ship—and its new Romulan cloaking device."

"Hang on," O'Brien said. "You've already got a working template for the cloaking device?"

Zek flashed a sinister grin. "You're not the only one around here who's good with tools, you know."

Chortles rolled through the group. It felt to O'Brien like an undertow beneath his feet in the ocean. Staring at the huge hulks of machinery that festooned the central ring of Empok Nor, he did some quick power-consumption calculations in his head. "Where are you getting enough juice to run twelve industrial replicators?"

"We brought the station's primary fusion reactors back online," Bashir said. "They're all running at 105 percent, around the clock."

O'Brien frowned and shook his head. "You've gone insane," O'Brien said. "Running 'em that hot, you'll light up the sensors of any ship within two light-years."

"Not likely," Bashir countered. "We've shielded the entire core with refined kelbonite. Unless you're within half an A.U., this just looks like another piece of cold metal in deep space."

Zek chimed in, "We're not morons, O'Brien. We took precautions."

"Uh-huh." More skeptical than before, O'Brien inquired, "And where'd you get the kelbonite?" After a few seconds it became obvious that no one wanted to provide the answer. "You stole it, right?" Bashir rolled his eyes like a chastised teenager and looked away. "Of course you did," O'Brien continued. "And to hide a fusion core, you must've stolen a lot of it. A material with no other tactical application except to hide things from sensors. You don't think the Alliance is going to notice *that* sooner or later?"

"And what if they did?" Zek shot back. "What're they going to do?"

"They'll start asking themselves what we'd need it for. And they might wonder what else we needed. That'll lead them to the fuel you stole, and the weapons." O'Brien paced away from the group and eyed the stripped-down frame of the station, both inside and outside. "And what if the evidence leads them here? Have you thought of that? You built your shipyard on a station with no defense screens and no weapons arrays. Most of the power-distribution system was stripped for parts—one good overload and most of your onboard systems are done for. And with your main reactor running over its red line, it won't take much to turn it to slag."

His rant seemed like it was starting to sway some opinion back to the side of reason when Bashir stepped forward, between O'Brien and the rest of the group, and turned back to face the others. "What did I tell you, everyone? Isn't it just what I said he'd do? Take our greatest achievement yet and try to make it sound like a failure!" The younger, thinner man turned and glared at O'Brien as if he were a prosecutor facing a defendant. "It makes me wonder whether he wants to win this war, or if he actually prefers being a victim. Instead of seeing our advantages, he sees only our weaknesses. Zek writes a plan for victory, but all O'Brien can see is a blueprint for failure."

The only thing O'Brien could think about was using his fists to smash Bashir's face to a bloody pulp. It would feel so good . . . and would solve absolutely nothing. Reining in his temper, O'Brien glanced out the window again, and this time he noticed the empty twelfth construction frame. "I see twelve frames but I only count eleven ships," he said. "Something go wrong on number twelve?"

"Far from it," Bashir said with a smug grin, then he turned and looked back at Zek.

The decrepit Ferengi flipped open the jeweled headpiece of his walking stick and spoke into it. "Zek to Demrik—decloak." A few seconds later, a shimmer rippled the starfield outside the observation windows, then the specter of a *Defiant*-class ship resolved into the concrete reality of one. "The first one off our new assembly line," he declared. "My ship: the *Capital Gain*."

Structurally, the ship was all but identical to the *Defiant*. Its only major difference was its color scheme, which featured a large number of dark red panels and black accents. It gave O'Brien a chill as he recognized its cultural heritage—it was an homage to the last generation of ships produced by the Terran Empire. "In less than a week," Zek continued, "the rebellion will have more than a dozen of these battle frigates, each one with a Romulan cloaking device. When all thirteen ships are operational, we'll start building twelve more—and show the Alliance what a real war looks like."

If you don't get caught stealing any more supplies, groused O'Brien's inner pessimist. *If no Alliance ships make a close flyby during a routine patrol. If no one looks for a pattern in your heists. If you installed your kelbonite shielding properly.* Those were a lot more *if*'s than O'Brien was comfortable entrusting with the future of the rebellion.

One of the other rebel leaders, a brown-skinned Terran named Calvin Hudson, spoke up from within the huddle. "If we're going to escalate this war, do we need to talk about the security on Terok Nor?"

"Terok Nor can handle whatever the Alliance can dish out," O'Brien snapped, perhaps too defensively. "You want to worry about a station, start with this one. Bloody house of cards you've got here."

"I wasn't talking about weapons and shields," Hudson said. "I was thinking more in terms of personnel."

The glib insinuation raised O'Brien's ire. "Just what the hell is that supposed to mean?"

Hudson shrugged. "You haven't exactly been careful about screening your top people. What if you've been letting in spies? An infiltrator could just walk in; how would you know?"

"I'd know," O'Brien said. "Don't tell me I don't know my own people."

Apprehensive glances worked their way around the group. A worried look passed between Hudson and Bashir, then Hudson looked back at O'Brien. "In the last two months, four of our camps in the Badlands have been hit by the Alliance."

This was old news to O'Brien, who grumbled, "I know."

"You know it happened," Hudson said, "but do you know why?"

"Could be lots of reasons," O'Brien said. "Maybe the camps' sensor screens weren't good enough. Maybe the Alliance intercepted some of our comm traffic."

Nodding, Hudson replied, "Or maybe one of our people told the Alliance where to find the camps." He added quickly, "All four camps were ones set up by your crew on the *Defiant*."

O'Brien felt the noose tightening. "We set up plenty of other camps, too," he said. "And we weren't the last ship at any of the ones we lost."

"No," Hudson said, "you weren't. But you and your crew are the common denominator. We can't risk trusting anyone too much, not now."

Zek pounced on O'Brien's momentary hesitation. "I've been warning him about this for months," he squawked. "But did he listen? Of course not. He just doled out ranks and racks like it was a clearance sale. He even made some woman he barely knows the X.O. just so he could get her in his bunk!"

"You shut your mouth!" O'Brien roared, lunging forward at the wizened Zek, who flinched. Hudson and Bashir caught the rebel leader and held him back.

"Back off," Bashir said.

Hudson added, "Calm down."

"The hell I will," O'Brien said, twisting in their grasp. "I won't let him stand there and call Keiko a whore!"

Zek responded with a broad, snaggle-toothed grin. "Actually, I was insulting *you*. I don't know her well enough to call her a whore . . . yet."

O'Brien almost broke free this time. Two more men stepped between him and Zek. Hudson tried to referee the situation. "Zek, do us all a favor and be quiet for a moment. Miles, stand down. We all know Zek's over the line here, but there's a reasonable point behind what he's saying."

Still firmly in Hudson and Bashir's grip, O'Brien replied, "Yeah? I'd like to hear it."

"We did some checking, Smiley," Bashir said. "I talked to some of the people Keiko allegedly helped 'liberate' from the mining colony on Korvat. They say the Cardassians made her a supervisor because she was a collaborator. She helped them choose which workers were beaten, which ones got put into solitary—and which ones got put to death."

Shaking his head, O'Brien said, "That's a bloody lie."

"You can't know that for a fact," Hudson said.

"Yes, I can, Cal."

Looks passed between Hudson, Bashir, and several others. Hudson did his best to sound nonjudgmental. "Miles, try to see this from the other side. There are witnesses who're telling us she might be a threat, an Alliance collaborator. Maybe they're wrong—I hope they are. But if they're right, then you've made an enemy agent the first officer of our best stronghold. Is that really a chance you're willing to take? Is that a risk you'll stake your reputation on?"

O'Brien relaxed enough that the men around him let go of his arms and stepped away to give him back some personal space. He met Hudson's stare with his own certain gaze and said with perfect certainty, "Yes, it is. I know my crew. They aren't spies. Now, if the only way to prove it to you is for me to spy on them, so be it. But I'm telling you now: if there is a spy, it's not one of my people—and it's not Keiko."

Zek was in high dudgeon. He lifted his arms and wailed with steadily rising volume, "This is ridiculous! There's no good reason to trust her, and a perfectly valid reason not to. Why can't you be reasonable? Why won't you listen to the facts? *Why do you trust her?*"

"Because I love her," O'Brien admitted, without shame.

A collective groan rose from the group. Murmurs of "Oh, no" and "So, it's true" fluttered around him. Zek's voice shrilled above the chorus of dismay: "Love! The greatest of all natural disasters! The fastest way I know to get a man killed!" He pointed an accusatory, crooked finger at O'Brien. "No wonder you've gone soft!"

"I haven't gone soft," O'Brien protested, but part of him wondered if he might be lying this time. "I've just gotten a bit more *conservative* in my planning."

Behind him, Bashir whispered to Hudson in a voice just loud enough for O'Brien to hear, "When did conservative become a synonym for cowardly?"

O'Brien held his tongue and kept his eyes on Zek.

"For all our sakes," the old Ferengi said, "let's hope you haven't gone weak, O'Brien. Because now that the *Capital Gain* is ready for action, I've got her first mission planned—and it depends on the *Defiant* being strong by her side. The last thing I need is to go into battle and find out you've cut and run."

"Don't worry about me," O'Brien said, full of anger and wounded pride. "I've never run from a fight in my life."

"Good," Zek said. "Because it's time to hit the Alliance where it lives."

It was very late. The comm alert was harsh and loud.

Bleary-eyed, out of sorts, and woken from a deep slumber, Ro Laren cast aside her bedsheets in a single throw. The flutter of mustard-hued Tholian silk looked gray in the sleep-cycle twilight of her quarters aboard the *I.K.S. Negh'Var.* Mumbling curses, she shuffled across the room to the wall-mounted comm terminal. A scroll of data on the left margin of the screen indicated that the incoming signal was from Cardassia Prime; the encryption marker was from the Detapa Council. She knew exactly whose face to expect as she opened the channel.

The screen snapped from idly dark to blinding. Her eyes took a moment to adjust, then she recognized the face of her strongest off-world political ally, Legate Skrain Dukat. His leer was smarmy. *"Did I wake you, Intendant? My apologies."*

"That almost sounded sincere," Ro said. "You're improving." Without waiting for him to continue their verbal thrust-and-parry routine, she added, "What do you want?"

Dukat smiled like a serpent. *"Still not a fan of small talk, I see. Very well. I've heard from a mutual acquaintance that your predecessor has been spared by the mercy of Regent Martok."* He paused, as if anticipating some commentary by Ro. She flashed him a glare that impelled him to continue. *"It's also been brought to my attention that Intendant Kira has been entrusted to your loving care aboard the* Negh'Var."

Ro sighed. "Do you have a question you want to ask?"

"I was just curious how the two of you are getting along."

Her tone was laced with bilious contempt. "Swimmingly. Like giddy sisters. Couldn't be better. She completes me."

"That badly, eh?"

She rubbed the fog of sleep from her eyes. "I didn't have any choice about taking her onto my staff. Martok made that decision for me—no thanks to you."

"Did you really think I was going to use up political capital over this? Really, Laren, be serious. I can't afford to expend time and resources to block the Klingon regent from making a minor political appointment—no matter how odious you and I might consider it to be."

Ro combed her fingers through her hair. "Having her here complicates things," she said. "It might seem like only a minor annoyance to you, but it's not your back she's looking to stab."

"True enough," Dukat said. *"I certainly don't mean to say that she's not dangerous. Given her knowledge of how things work within the Alliance—and her knack for dirty politics in general—I'd have to say she could interfere in any number of ways."* He cocked his head forward, as if he could invade her personal space through a subspace comm channel. *"You have taken steps to marginalize her, haven't you?"*

"Of course," Ro said. She set the comm unit to wide-field display with tracking so that she could move about her quarters while continuing the conversation. "I gave her the worst job I could find. Paperwork, permits, budgetary red tape." Ro stopped in front of her replicator and pressed a quick key for *raktajino;* her preferred blend was cold and bitter. "It's the sort of job that makes people hang themselves," she added.

Dukat shook his head. *"I wouldn't count on that kind of luck with Kira,"* he said. *"The woman's like a disease with no cure. Every time you think you've stamped her out, she comes back. Assassination plots fall apart; schemes to send her back to Bajor in disgrace always seem to backfire. It's as if she leads a charmed life."*

After swallowing a sip of *raktajino,* Ro replied with a malicious grin, "You didn't see her when we picked her up at Qo'noS."

Ever attentive to salacious details, Dukat widened his eyes as he speculated, *"I take it she was the worse for wear?"*

"You know what they say about Klingons," Ro replied. "Speaking of which, I'm stuck on a ship full of them. When are you going to send me a Cardassian ship to carry my flag?" It was a loaded question; the decision wasn't up to Dukat, who continued to lag behind Martok in terms of his influence and prestige within the

Alliance. For decades the Klingons had lorded it over the Cardassians as the predominant power, in both military and economic strength. It was a longtime point of contention between the neighboring empires.

Unsuccessfully masking his irritation, Dukat shifted in his seat and smiled again. *"As soon as I can,"* he said. *"Until then, you should focus on keeping Kira under control. She's a tricky one; she'll constantly be looking for ways to manipulate you."*

"I know, Dukat," Ro said, becoming more irritated. "I've known her longer than you have. She and I have spent most of our careers making each other miserable."

"Good. It's a pleasure to meet someone who holds her in the same kind of contempt that I do."

Back in front of the display screen, Ro permitted herself a sly smirk at Dukat. "Oh, I don't know about that," she said. "An equal degree of contempt, certainly. But the same kind? I doubt that very much."

He bristled at her comments, which made his strained smile become crooked with doubt and ire. *"Why do you say that?"*

She let him stew for a moment while she savored another long sip of her *raktajino*. Then she set down the drink and folded her arms across her chest. "My problem with Kira is political. I don't like the way she mixes business and pleasure, or her habit of glorifying herself when other people do all the work. What's more, she was a disgrace to this office; she treated it like her own personal orgy. Put simply, she's a violent narcissist who consistently put her own pleasure ahead of the needs of Bajor or the good of the Alliance." Dukat was nodding at Ro's remarks, had been for several seconds. He stopped as she continued, "But you? I think your problem with Kira is personal. I know all about your little dalliance with her mother . . . and that you've had what can only politely be described as an unwholesome obsession with Nerys since she was a girl. And even though she's been notoriously liberal with her sexual favors, sharing them with men and women of just about any species . . . she has been pointedly unwilling to bestow any upon you."

"*That's enough,*" Dukat said. He was fuming now, his eyes blazing with fury. Just as Ro had suspected, his insecurities ran deep and would likely prove to be his greatest single personality flaw. *Good to know,* she decided.

In a more soothing tone of voice she said, "Now, darling, there's no need to get upset." She flashed a seductive smile. "Why would you want to waste your time with her, a lowly bureaucrat, when you already have me, the Intendant of Bajor?"

Her wheedling was enough to calm Dukat slightly, but his usual veneer of faux courtesy was now abandoned, replaced by his most abrasive authoritarian manner. *"Don't forget, darling, that the only reason you are the Intendant of Bajor is because I've expended a lot of effort to put you there. Bajor has been a puppet of the Klingons for too long; we're finally on the verge of shifting control of the Alliance to Cardassia, but if there's one person who can bring all our plans to ruin, it's Kira. She has to be kept in check until a believable 'accident' can be arranged. Do you think you can handle that?"*

"Don't worry," Ro said. "She's not going anywhere."

Dukat nodded. *"Good."* Once more his mouth curled up into an arrogant smirk. *"On a more pleasant note, have you given any thought as to when you might make another visit to Cardassia Prime? My bed has felt empty without you."*

A teasing smile softened the bite of her reply. "Which bed? The one in your home, in Coranum? Or the one in that little hideaway in Torr where you take all your mistresses?"

He shook his head at her, the way a father would reprimand a foolish child. *"Always the same refrain,"* he said. *"Do you ever have a waking moment that isn't colored with resentment?"*

"No," she confessed. She terminated the comm link, turned, and stalked back to bed, regretting once more her affair with Dukat. It had been a necessary sacrifice to secure his support, but as she was now reminded every time she saw his face, there was a bitter truth hidden in the phrase "stoop to conquer."

★ ★ ★

The only stink stronger than General Duras's body odor was his breath, which filled the air around Kira as the portly Klingon bellowed down at her, "You bothered me for this? For a jumble of trivia and old news?" He thrust her data padd back into her hands. "Get off my bridge, you ignorant trollop."

Begging did not come naturally to Kira, but she tried. "Please, General," she said. "There's a clear pattern, a connection. If I'm right, the rebellion is assembling a new stronghold, and possibly more. We have to—"

He yanked the data padd back from her grasp and poked at the information on its screen as he debunked it. "Missing deuterium freighter. You say hijacked by rebels; I say stolen by Orion privateers." Each jab of his index finger left a smear of skin oil on the padd's surface. "Antimatter tanker destroyed in transit. You say it was a fake accident to cover a rebel plot. I say it was bad maintenance. . . . Small arms go missing. You say rebel conspiracy; I say arms dealers. Stolen kelbonite—" He paused, seemed to reconsider. "That one *is* troubling, but it's hardly evidence of a major war effort by the rebels." Duras flung the padd away, across the bridge. It clattered across the deck and disappeared through a gap in the bulkhead. "Stop wasting my time, woman." He turned his back on her.

It was an insult for which, just a few short months ago, she could have had him stripped bare and whipped half to death. For a fleeting moment, her old temper almost flared. Her voice swelled in her chest, gathered strength, threatened to burst forth in its loudest, most imperious measure—

She caught herself. The privilege of pique was no longer hers. Raising her voice to a Klingon general would gain her, at best, hours of agonizing torture; if Duras was in a foul mood, he could easily have her killed for insubordination. She was no longer a person of influence; she was a nobody, and everyone on this ship knew it.

Reminded of her vulnerability she withdrew from the bridge without saying another word. She kept her eyes downcast, watching the gray-green deck pass under her feet as she moved in timid steps through the corridors of the *Negh'Var.* Until now she had not thought about all the ramifications of her servitude to Ro aboard this ship. To the Klingons, she was barely a person. *One word spoken out of turn, one glance at the wrong person in the wrong context, and I might end up with a* d'k tahg *in my back,* she realized. Suddenly, every Klingon crew member she passed in the corridors seemed threatening. No doubt, some of them had, at one time or another, been the victims of her wrath when she had reigned as the Intendant. They would be alert for any excuse to take their revenge.

The corridor narrowed as she neared the servants' quarters. Warm and humid air grew thicker with pungent food smells and the musk of perspiration. Inside, it was so heavy as to be almost unbreathable. A low chatter of idle conversations echoed through the ventilation grates from adjacent compartments. Most of the other residents of Kira's berth were here, whiling away their off-duty hours behind the flimsy curtains that gave their cramped bunk spaces the ambience of coffins. As she climbed to her rack on the top of the rearmost left row of bunks, she heard the Bolian slave on the bottom bunk chewing and swallowing; because his Klingon mistress never fed him, he was forced to steal food from the mess hall and eat in secrecy. Occupying the bunk directly above his was a Terran slave who spent her nights trying to muffle her sobs with her pillow. The woman would weep until the other slaves, desperate for rest, would beat her unconscious so they could sleep. From the bunk directly below Kira's came a regular cadence of heavy breathing and grunted exertions. She tried not to look, but as she climbed past she glanced inside. Looking back at her with a miserable expression was a young, lean-looking Trill man with blond hair. He lay on his stomach and covered his mouth with the end of his blanket, while a larger, far more muscular Terran man lay on top of him.

At the top, Kira rolled into her own bunk and pulled the curtain closed behind her. The sounds and smells and thrumming vibrations of the Klingon warship surrounded her, pressed in on her. She hated this place, this life. *This is as good as it's going to get for me on this ship,* she knew. There was no one of higher rank than Intendant Ro for Kira to aspire to serve. Even if one of the lower-ranking officers was willing to take her on as a slave, and perhaps eventually as a paid domestic servant, Kira had no reason to think that Ro would allow her to transfer. *No, she's having too much fun tormenting me. She won't let me advance, she won't let me transfer. All she wants me to do is die as her slave.*

That wasn't an outcome that Kira was prepared to accept. *There has to be a way,* she told herself. *Some other way out from under her thumb.* There seemed to be no one to whom she could appeal for help. Regent Martok had intentionally set her up to fail, so he was unlikely to help her now. General Duras was obviously not going to risk incurring Ro's wrath by supporting a slave. And she knew there was no point in trying to solicit aid from the Cardassians. Thanks to some skills that she had acquired during her initial rise to power years ago, she had been able to access a number of en-crypted transmissions to and from the *Negh'Var.* Now that she knew for a fact that Ro and Dukat were lovers as well as political allies, the battle lines seemed clearly drawn.

No point trying to build alliances with the enlisted crew, she reasoned. *They don't have enough clout. Most of the officers are with Duras; they won't turn.* She shook her head. Seeking an ally among the *Negh'Var*'s crew would be a waste of time. If she, a slave, so much as hinted to one of the crew that she harbored mutinous intent, she would be executed on the spot. The other slaves would be more likely to betray her than support her, both to improve their own standing with their masters and to avoid being caught in any cross-fire. No, if she was going to cultivate an ally to help her break free of Ro's control, it would have to be someone not on the *Negh'Var.*

Working from memory, she found herself at a loss to think of even one person on Bajor who would cross Ro in order to help her. *Too many burned bridges there,* she thought with regret. The most reliable ally she'd ever had, Regent Worf, had openly despised her. He was now somewhere light-years away, in the custody of the

Terran rebels. As she reflected on the few people she had ever trusted, however conditionally, she realized that all of them had disappointed her. Benjamin, Smiley, Antos, Ezri, even her own alternate-universe duplicate—they, and many others, had all betrayed her.

Energetic bumping from below shook her rack. She thumped her fist against the bulkhead, the universal semaphore for demanding silence. A moment later the thuds against her bunk stopped, but the muffled groans and huffs of labored breath grew deeper. Kira forced herself not to think about what she was hearing and just let it fade into the background, along with the rhythmic pulsing of the ship's engines. It worked for a few minutes, then the Terran woman started crying again. Kira sighed. *Let the beatings commence.*

Her thoughts turned again to Regent Worf. Though the rebels had taken him to Terok Nor after his capture, she'd heard rumors while she was on Qo'noS that he had been moved to a different site in order to reduce the likelihood of an attack on the station. Finding him would be next to impossible, but she wondered if there might yet be some political gain to be had from her close association with him.

Recalling some of her conversations with him, a new strategy occurred to her. She took her portable data-retrieval device from a pocket on the leg of her dingy gray jumpsuit. It had taken considerable effort to bypass the *Negh'Var*'s security lockouts, but she had succeeded in creating a secure remote-access channel for herself. It would enable her to conduct research and even send short encrypted text messages through the ship's communications relay without their being traced back to her or her workstation.

Moments later she patched in to the Klingons' data network. Within seconds she found what she was looking for . . . and she smiled. *There you are,* she gloated.

For now, she would weather Ro's abuse and play the part of an obedient slave . . . but that was about to change.

4

L ook sharp," O'Brien said. "Our timing has to be perfect."

None of the *Defiant*'s bridge crew responded. They were all too focused on their work, hunkered down in the darkness that filled the bridge. The lighting was normally subdued when the ship was cloaked, but for this operation its interiors were almost pitch-dark. Nonessential displays and interfaces had been powered down and noncritical systems taken offline. As an added precaution, they had dropped from warp speed back to sublight while they were still beyond the edge of the Cuellar system. From there they had navigated at one-tenth impulse speed to within a few million kilometers of the target, at which point they'd cut the power and drifted in. Thrusters had been fired in short spurts to make occasional course corrections.

On the main viewer, a Cardassian sensor station loomed large. It was a manned facility equipped with the most advanced signals-intelligence hardware that the Alliance possessed. Gray and organically twisted, it resembled a giant crustacean. The Cardassian name for the station was Vareth Dar, but the rebellion had nicknamed it the Watchtower because it was able to monitor ship movements and encrypted signal traffic for nearly forty light-years in every direction; its range extended from the Betreka Nebula to Terok Nor. As long as the Watchtower remained in service, there was little hope of the rebellion mounting a successful sneak attack against the Alliance anywhere within striking distance of Terok Nor.

O'Brien's orders were simple: destroy Vareth Dar. Achieving that objective posed a number of significant challenges. Even cloaked, the *Defiant* was not perfectly hidden. At close range, it would trigger numerous finely tuned sensors in the Watchtower's array. The station wasn't blind, nor was it defenseless. Its shields were formidable, strong enough to block the *Defiant*'s strongest barrage, and its weapons array was more than capable of pulverizing the ship if it scored a direct hit. Countless simulations had convinced O'Brien that a direct assault by the *Defiant* would be futile.

A coordinated attack by the *Defiant* and the *Capital Gain,* however, if executed properly, might have a chance.

"Sito," O'Brien said. "Stand by on thrusters. Nice and slow, now." The young woman entered the commands on the flight control interface and nudged the *Defiant* a few dozen meters closer to the Watchtower. O'Brien glanced right, toward the tactical console. "Tigan, you ready?"

"Yeah," said Ezri, her eyes fixed on her companel display, on which was superimposed a pair of manual-targeting crosshairs. Without the benefit of computer-assisted tactical systems, Ezri would have to guide the ship's phasers and torpedoes by eye and hand. Targeting scanners were a luxury the *Defiant* crew could not afford this close to Vareth Dar; one sweep would give away their presence instantly.

"Muniz," O'Brien said. "Anything on comms?"

"Nada," Muniz replied. "All quiet."

O'Brien watched the numbers tick away on the countdown, which was displayed in the lower left corner of the main viewscreen. "Thirty seconds, everyone. Stand ready."

Tense expressions surrounded O'Brien. Leeta stood tall beside him, her jaw set. In front of him, Sito hunched over her flight controls, ready to react on a moment's notice. Muniz sat with his eyes closed, tuning out everything except the passively intercepted signal traffic coming and going from the target. A bead of sweat trickled down the side of Ezri's face as she watched the target enter her crosshairs.

Fifteen seconds.

When the countdown reached zero—assuming Zek and his crew were on time—the *Defiant*'s crew would have only seconds to react. As soon as the *Capital Gain* decloaked, it would be detected by the crew on Vareth Dar, who would sound the call to battle stations. Thanks to a number of previous sorties the *Defiant* had flown past the station, O'Brien and his crew had compiled enough data to predict that Vareth Dar would raise its shields within four seconds of spotting an enemy vessel.

The final moments counted down. Three. Two. One.

Like clockwork, as the timer reached zero, the *Capital Gain* decloaked on the far side of Vareth Dar and accelerated to an attack posture. O'Brien gripped the arms of his chair. "Full thrusters!" Sito punched in the command and the *Defiant* shot forward to within point-blank range of the station. Counting the seconds in his head, O'Brien hoped that Zek's people remembered to fire at precisely—

"*Capital Gain*'s firing!" shouted Leeta. "The station's raising shields and powering weapons!" Blasts of pulsed phaser energy from the *Capital Gain* crackled against the station's invisible deflector shield. A volley of torpedoes flared against the shield bubble above the station's command center—and above the still-cloaked *Defiant*, which had maneuvered inside the station's shield perimeter before its defenses had activated.

Sito cut in, "We're in position!"

"Target set," Ezri called out, as more blasts from the *Capital Gain* flashed across the station's shields.

"Drop the cloak and raise shields," O'Brien commanded. One second later the bridge brightened as the cloak deactivated and all the bridge consoles surged to life. O'Brien sprang from his chair and pumped his fist. "Fire!"

Furious pulses of bright-orange phaser energy leaped from the front of the *Defiant* and tore through Vareth Dar's primary deflector shield emitters, a three-panel system much like the one in use at Terok Nor. Sito piloted the *Defiant* in a tight, fast circle around the station's core, giving Ezri a clear shot at each emitter's support structure. The last shield emitter disintegrated as the station's first retaliatory shots hammered the *Defiant*'s shields.

"Return fire," O'Brien said. "Target the command center." Ezri's shots became more accurate and more devastating as the *Defiant*'s targeting computer re-engaged. In just a few shots she obliterated the station's operations deck and communications tower. "Nice shooting," O'Brien said as more disruptor blasts from the station slammed against the *Defiant*'s shields.

"The *Capital Gain* is targeting the station's fusion core," Muniz reported.

"Sito, break off," O'Brien said. "Evasive, full impulse. Tigan, covering fire, aft torpedoes."

Engine noise grew louder and was punctuated by the thrumming echoes of torpedoes being released and the nerve-rattling concussions of enemy fire. Then a blinding eruption of white light filled the main viewer. Ezri swiveled her chair to face O'Brien, flashing him a wicked grin. "We did it! The Watchtower's gone!"

Whoops and triumphal shouts filled the bridge. O'Brien heard the engineers cheering over the intraship comm. Leeta embraced Ezri, and they clutched each other with relief and exhilaration. Though O'Brien had tried to discourage them from bringing their personal relationship with them onto the bridge, he decided that this was a special circumstance, one deserving of a slight relaxing of the rules. He made the rounds of the bridge, shook Muniz's hand, and gave Sito a fatherly pat on the back before he tousled her hair. "Well done, everyone," he said over the laughing and conversations. "When we get back to the station, the first round's on me. I'm proud of you."

"Thank you, General," Leeta said, and in quick succession the rest of the bridge crew did likewise, overlapping each other in their gratitude. O'Brien basked in the warmth and glory of the moment. *This is what it feels like to be part of a team.* He smiled. *Part of a family.*

A shrill tone on the communications console pulled Muniz away from the impromptu celebration. He checked the display, then looked at O'Brien. "It's General Zek," he said. "He's hailing us."

Adopting a more serious mien, O'Brien moved back toward his chair. "Stations, everyone." He waited until his crew had settled back into their chairs and resumed a more professional bearing. With a nod to Muniz, he said, "On-screen."

The starfield on the main viewscreen was replaced by the wrinkled visage of Zek, whose nasal whine O'Brien found just as grating over a comm as he did in person. *"Nice work, O'Brien,"* he said. *"Nice to see you've still got it where it counts."*

"My compliments to you and your crew, as well, General," O'Brien said. "It was a fine plan."

Zek seemed unable to smile without squinting. *"Thank you. Now we can move on to phase two, and—"*

"Phase two?" O'Brien didn't like the sound of that. "I don't recall there being a phase two in this plan."

The Ferengi responded with a shrug, then said, *"A last-second addition. Don't worry, it's nothing major."*

O'Brien made no effort to conceal his suspicion. "Care to be a bit more specific?"

"I'm sending you some coordinates on the fourth planet," Zek said, nodding to one of his crewmen on the *Capital Gain.* *"As long as we're here, we might as well destroy both targets. After all, as we Ferengi like to say, 'Never take one when you can get two for the same price.'"*

The data from the *Capital Gain* appeared on a monitor above Ezri's station. She studied it for a few seconds, then looked at O'Brien. "Sir," she said. "I think you should see this."

O'Brien got out of his chair and stepped behind Ezri. On her overhead monitor was an orbital scan of what appeared to be a Cardassian civilian settlement on Cuellar IV. As far as he could tell, there were no military facilities attached to the colony, no ground-based spaceport infrastructure with the ability to support military vessels of any kind. Neither visual scans nor energy profiles suggested any kind of weapons emplacements. The colony didn't even have any heavy industry to speak of—no mining, no refining, no manufacturing. It appeared to be a primarily agricultural community. He turned to face Zek. "I don't understand. Where's the target?"

Flabbergasted, Zek shot back, *"What're you talking about? Are you blind? The colony's the target!"*

"They're not armed," O'Brien protested. "They don't have any military assets, they're just farmers."

Zek retorted, *"So? So what? They're Cardassians! They're the enemy. This is my mission, I'm giving the orders, and I'm telling you to target that colony and fire, on my mark!"*

The silence was ponderous. No one on either bridge spoke as they watched the battle of wills. After several moments of forcing himself to remain calm, O'Brien replied simply, "No."

"Don't go all spineless on me now, O'Brien," Zek taunted. *"You were doing so well, why ruin it by turning into a—"*

"Save your insults for someone who gives a damn," O'Brien snapped. "I won't order my crew to fire on that colony—I won't *let* them fire on that colony. More important, I won't let you do it, either." The startled expression on Zek's face put a smile on O'Brien's. "That's right, you bloodthirsty runt, this is a warning. If you target that colony, I'll target your ship. If you attack that colony, I'll blow you to bits."

Zek shook with rage. *"Have you gone mad?"*

"The battle's over, Zek. We've won. Let's go home."

His lobes flushed with anger and frustration, Zek mumbled a string of low Ferengi curses. *"Fine,"* he said at last. *"We'll leave the colony. But this isn't the end of this, believe me."*

"I believe you," O'Brien said, his voice full of hatred. "Cloak and return to base. *Defiant* out." On cue, Muniz cut the channel, and the screen reverted to the dark serenity of the stars. O'Brien slumped back into his chair. "Helm, set course back to Terok Nor, warp seven. Muniz, raise the cloak."

The lights dimmed as the ship slipped back into its shroud. Then the warp engines throbbed to life, and the ship accelerated to warp speed on its journey home. Several minutes passed before Leeta discreetly sidled up to O'Brien and leaned over his shoulder. "I'm curious," she whispered. "Why didn't we just destroy the colony like Zek asked?"

"Because it wasn't a military target," he said without looking at her. He was in no mood to look at anyone.

"But the Alliance destroys civilian targets all the time."

Flustered, he turned his head and glared at the redhead. "Yeah, and if I wanted to do that, I'd join them. What's the point of fighting them if we're not gonna act any different?"

Leeta didn't seem to have an answer for that. She tilted her head and raised her palms in a gesture of capitulation, then backed away to leave O'Brien in peace.

It would be a few days before the *Defiant* and the *Capital Gain* returned to Terok Nor. O'Brien had no doubt that Zek would use that time to formulate an argument to convince the other rebellion leaders to oust O'Brien from power, or at the very least reduce his influence.

Making the others understand why he was advocating a more conservative approach to prosecuting the war against the Alliance would not be easy. It would be even more difficult if he was unable to refute their allegations that he had allowed a spy to infiltrate his command crew on the *Defiant*. To his dismay, the only way that he could think of to exonerate his people from such charges was, ironically, to spy on them himself. The very idea of it sickened him. *They've put themselves on the line for me a hundred times. And how do I repay them? By snooping on them like they're common criminals.*

Rationalizing that it was for their own good didn't make it any easier to excuse, but if Zek and the others succeeded in removing him before he could vindicate his crew, there was no telling what might happen to them under Zek's command. Determined to spare them that indignity, O'Brien swallowed his anger and resolved to do whatever was necessary to convince himself—and everyone else—that his crew was loyal, and that it was not harboring a spy.

Gamma shift. Last watch. Normally, O'Brien would have been asleep during this part of the *Defiant*'s duty cycle. Tonight he was ensconced in his ready room, reviewing comm and other signal traffic that had been sent or received by members of the *Defiant*'s senior bridge crew. There was so much of it, even for his small group of four top personnel. He had narrowed his review of files to the four of them because they had been the ones on bridge duty during each of the colony missions that Cal Hudson had alleged were compromised. One of the policies that O'Brien had always enforced strictly on the *Defiant* was the compartmentalization of mission-critical knowledge. If there was no reason for the engineering staff or the security detail to know where the ship was going or why, they weren't told. Except in rare cases, he limited bridge access to his senior personnel. He, Leeta, and Ezri took turns in command. Stevens and Sito covered the helm during alpha and beta shifts. The helm was often set to autopilot during gamma shift; traveling cloaked made unplanned encounters in deep space highly unlikely.

Manpower shortages had also played a role in how O'Brien chose to run his ship. Even if he'd wanted to have two or three full shifts of bridge personnel and engineers, there weren't enough qualified people in the rebellion now that Zek and Bashir had begun expanding their fleet. Many of the best people who had served on the *Defiant* had been poached by Bashir to take higher-ranking positions on one of the new ships.

Have to get to it, he chided himself. He rubbed the sleep from his eyes, sipped his lukewarm coffee, and settled on a place to start his overnight marathon of meddling in his crew's private business. *We'll go by rank,* he decided. *Top to bottom.*

Leeta seemed to have few incoming or outgoing messages. The bulk of her signal traffic was strictly internal on Terok Nor or aboard the *Defiant*, and most of it was brief text messages containing orders or schedules for other members of the *Defiant*'s crew. He had worried that he might end up sifting through endless kiloquads of embarrassing messages between Leeta and Ezri, but he was surprised to find almost none at all outside of their professional duties on the *Defiant*. Then he remembered that the two women shared quarters on Terok Nor. *Whatever they have to say, they can do it in person,* he realized. Leeta almost never secured any of her messages—which made the one she had chosen to encrypt all the more conspicuous.

It was a two-way audiovisual transmission from the comm unit in Leeta's quarters aboard Terok Nor to a residential terminal on Bajor. The recording had been recovered from the memory cache of the station's comm relay on O'Brien's orders, along with several others. While the *Defiant*'s computer reassembled the message for playback, O'Brien checked its log data. The call had originated on Bajor, but its content had been encrypted by Leeta shortly before she'd attempted to delete it from the station's comm system.

O'Brien tried to stifle a yawn but failed. He was blinking away the effects of exhaustion when a soft tone from the computer was followed by a synthetic-sounding voice that said, *"File ready for playback."*

He picked up his increasingly tepid coffee, leaned back in his chair, and instructed the computer, "Begin."

The monitor on his desktop showed both sides of the recorded conversation with a split-screen image. On the left was Leeta, on the right a middle-aged Bajoran couple, a man and a woman, both showing awkward, supplicative smiles. The man looked familiar; the woman bore a strong resemblance to Leeta.

"Hello, dear," the older woman said. The man beside her added, *"Hello, Leeta."*

On the other side of the screen, Leeta returned their faltering smiles with a frown. *"Hi, Mom. Hi, Dad."*

Her parents traded nervous glances, then her father spoke. *"How's everything going up on the station?"*

"*I'm fine, if that's what you're asking,*" Leeta said, her hostility plainly evident.

"*And your friend, Ezri,*" her mother said. "*Is she well?*"

"She's not my 'friend,' Mother, she's my wife."

The man masked his wife's consternation by interjecting, "*Congratulations, sweetheart. We didn't know.*"

"*How could we?*" his wife complained in an angry mutter. "*She never tells us anything.*" It was also news to O'Brien, who hadn't known until now that Leeta and Ezri had solemnized their relationship.

Leeta was obviously already losing patience with her parents. "*I'm not supposed to talk to anyone off the station, so why don't you stop wasting my time and tell me what you want?*"

"*The same thing we always want, Leeta,*" her father said. "*We want you to come home.*"

"*No!*" Leeta shouted as she pressed her hands against the sides of her head. "*Not this again? You know I can't come home, I joined the rebellion. If I come home—*"

"*We can fix it, dear,*" her mother pleaded. "*We—*"

"*No, Mother, you can't,*" Leeta said, almost hysterical. "*If I come back to Bajor, they'll put me to death!*"

Waving his hands, her father said, "*No, dear, they won't. I've talked to Minister Lenaris, he assures me that he can arrange clemency for you.*"

Leeta rolled her eyes. "*Let me guess—on the condition that I renounce the Terrans and help the Alliance recapture Terok Nor, right?*"

"*Well,*" her father said, "*naturally, there would have to be some concessions—*"

"*Tell me something,*" Leeta replied. "*What part of 'I've joined the rebellion' do you two not understand?*"

"*If it's about Ezri,*" her father said, "*we might be able to get her a pardon, as well.*"

Shaking her head, Leeta looked like she was on the verge of a homicidal rampage. "*You'll never understand, will you? You're part of a tyrannical empire—a passive part, sure, but still part of it. This isn't about Terrans, or Vulcans, or any one species. It's a fight about what kind of—*"

"*Here we go,*" her mother said, infusing her tone with bitter sarcasm. "*The lecture. Yes, dear, please do tell us all about how everything we know and stand for is wrong and terrible and how we're just such rotten people because we don't see the universe exactly the same way you do.*"

Her face reddened with shame, Leeta bowed her head. "*That's not what I—*" She paused, collected her thoughts. "*I'm not saying you're bad people. I know you're not. . . . But the people you follow are, and I wish I could make you see that.*"

Remorseful looks passed between Leeta and her parents.

"*Leeta, honey,*" her father said. "*I know you think you're doing the right thing, but you have to see the rebellion is doomed, don't you? How many of you are there, across the galaxy? Maybe a hundred thousand?*"

With contempt, Leeta replied, "*I wouldn't tell you even if I knew.*"

"*I just want you to see what a difficult position you're in,*" he said.

Adding disgust to her contempt, Leeta said, "*Don't you mean what a difficult position* you're *in? Less than half a year until the next election, and you're the candidate with a rebel for a daughter. That's what you're really worried about, isn't it?*"

Her father nodded as his eyes narrowed and his expression tightened into one of stern disapproval. "*As selfish as ever, aren't you? Not a care in the world for me and your mother—for everything we gave you, all we did for you. All you care about is your wants, your needs. Who cares who gets hurt along the way, right?*"

Leeta's sarcasm cut like a scalpel. "*Yes, Daddy, because that's the only reason I joined the rebellion: to hurt you and make you lose your precious seat in the Chamber of Ministers. I'm just such a* simple *girl, and you know me so well.*"

"*This is a waste of time,*" her mother said.

Her father nodded and mumbled in reply, "*You're right.*" Raising his voice, he said with cold authority, "*Good-bye, Leeta.*"

Tears of anger streaked down Leeta's face as she cut the channel. Both sides of the split screen on O'Brien's monitor went dark. A sigh heaved in his chest. He felt ashamed of himself, even as he resolved to press on.

Next up for review was Ezri. O'Brien had thought that Leeta was sparing in her use of the comm systems until he looked over Ezri's logs. As far as he could tell, Ezri neither sent nor received any signals except between Terok Nor and the *Defiant*. She'd limited her text messages to mission-specific tasks and information. The only significant use the young Trill woman had made of the station's information network had been frequent queries to its public news archives. Not wanting to take a chance on overlooking anything, O'Brien ran a program to seek out patterns in Ezri's news-reading habits. One common factor quickly emerged: she had diligently tracked a particular newsfeed from Trill for several months after taking up residence on the station. Then, less than two weeks ago, she had abruptly ceased querying that news service. On a hunch, O'Brien pulled up the last article that Ezri had retrieved.

It was a short text article from the Alliance News Network, Trill Sector edition. The accompanying photo showed a finely featured, attractive woman in her mid-fifties beside a burly man in his early thirties. The caption beneath the photo read "Yanas Tigan and her son, Janel. (Archive Photo)"

NEW SYDNEY, SAPPORA VII — Yanas Tigan, owner and operator of the Sappora system's sixth-largest pergium mine, was killed late last night with her eldest son, Janel, during a raid on her home by local police and troops of the Klingon Defense Force.

According to official sources, the Tigan Mining Consortium (TMC), a family-owned business, had been indicted as a "corrupt enterprise" for its role in aiding and abetting escaped slaves who wished to join the Terran Rebellion.

Tigan Mining had utilized its extensive drilling and excavation capabilities to engineer a vast network of subterranean passageways that linked several prominent locations throughout New Sydney. The tunnels funneled escaped workers to a remote loading site, where they could be smuggled off-world aboard TMC ore freighters. New Sydney Security head Yeroff Fuchida said that he believes Tigan and her son Janel may have helped more than three hundred slaves escape from Sappora VII.

"Obviously, it's difficult for us to be certain which escaped slaves were aided by the Tigans, and which were abducted by members of the Orion Syndicate for resale on other worlds," Fuchida said. "However, based on the last reported locations of several of the escapees, and the proximity of those sites to access points in the Tigans' underground network, we have a pretty good idea which escapees joined the rebels."

Suspicion first fell upon the Tigan family after reports from Klingon Imperial Intelligence linked them to the Terran Rebellion through Yanas's only daughter, Ezri Tigan, who is believed to be an active member of the rebellion aboard the occupied space station Terok Nor, in the Bajor system.

"We have an extensive dossier on Ezri Tigan," Fuchida confirmed. "Although we haven't found any evidence of direct communication between her and Yanas Tigan during the past year, we haven't ruled out the possibility that Ezri served as Yanas's contact inside the rebels' organization."

New Sydney Security and Klingon forces decided to take action against TMC after receiving incriminating intelligence from Norvo Tigan, Yanas's youngest child and sibling to Janel and Ezri. Citing "accounting irregularities" and the "suspicious deployments" of excavation equipment and resources, Norvo Tigan warned New Sydney Security that TMC might be involved in criminal activities.

After analyzing TMC communication logs and financial data provided by Norvo Tigan, security officials were granted a classified indictment. They secured a warrant for the arrest of Yanas Tigan and Janel Tigan and the seizure of all Tigan Mining Consortium assets. During the subsequent raid on Mrs. Tigan's residence, she and Janel allegedly resisted arrest and attacked security personnel and Klingon troops with deadly force. In the course of defending themselves, the security team and soldiers returned fire, killing the two suspects.

In return for his cooperation, Norvo Tigan has been cleared of all criminal charges and released. An investigation into what other business entities, if any, might have collaborated with the Tigans is ongoing, and is expected to require the cooperation of several off-world security agencies.

O'Brien closed out the news report. A quick search algorithm on the other articles Ezri had downloaded from the network made it clear she had been keeping tabs on her family through their local news. Most of it had been reports of a rather banal variety—business association awards, public recognition for charitable gifts, flattering remarks in the social columns. None of it had carried even a hint of the tragedy that had been to come. *Poor kid,* he thought with sadness. *To find out in the news that her mother and brother are dead, and her kid brother snitched to the Alliance. To see her own name in print as a wanted criminal. . . . No wonder she stopped reading the news.*

He got up from his desk and walked to the replicator. "Coffee, hot. Double strong, double sweet." The machine whirred and hummed melodiously as it produced his steaming beverage in a colorful swirl of energy. He took the mug from the replicator nook and returned to his desk. *Two down, two to go.* Continuing to work his way down the roster by rank, the next person under his microscope would be Enrique Muniz.

At a glance, O'Brien could see that he wasn't going to get off easy this time. Unlike Leeta and Ezri, Muniz had made extensive use of the comm system over the past several months. He had sent and received a combination of text and audiovisual messages, more than three hundred in all. Deciding that chronology was the least important concern at this stage, O'Brien sorted the files based on whom Muniz had been communicating with, and where those persons were located.

As far as O'Brien could tell, Muniz had at least respected the moratorium on communications with people on Alliance-controlled worlds. Instead, he had traded messages with fellow members of the rebellion—some of them on ships passing through the same sector as Terok Nor or the *Defiant,* some of them in the rebellion's semi-permanent installations in the Badlands.

How'm I supposed to whittle this down? O'Brien wondered. "Computer," he said. "Open all text-only messages sent or received by Enrique Muniz during the past six months. Show them in chronological order, oldest first."

"Working," the computer responded, and the messages appeared on O'Brien's screen, accompanied by a simple, icon-based navigation pane down the left side of his monitor.

The first message was sent to Muniz by a man named George Primmin, who was part of a group of rebels that had seized control of a small privateer called the *Vesuvius.*

> Hey, Quique. You still at Terok Nor? The rest of us sweatbacks
> finally took your advice and nabbed a ship. Write back if
> you're okay.—George

Muniz's reply had been sent within an hour of receiving the message from the *Vesuvius.*

> Prim! I knew you guys could do it! Yeah, I'm still sweatin' it
> out on big T. Stay safe.

Clicking swiftly through screen after screen of text messages, O'Brien saw that they were almost all as short as the first two.

It was like reading transcripts of conversations between people who lacked the attention span to write missives longer than a few sentences apiece. Muniz's brevity suited O'Brien just fine tonight; it made the task of reviewing his comm traffic go that much more quickly. Then he found himself reading a message that made him pause. In it, Muniz provided someone named Neeley, another member of the *Vesuvius's* crew, with detailed instructions for how to transmit a fully secure audiovisual message to Terok Nor by exploiting a loophole in the Alliance's communication relay network. Muniz was a talented engineer, even by O'Brien's standards, but he hadn't been aware that the man possessed that kind of skill.

"Computer," O'Brien said. "Show me all audiovisual messages received by Enrique Muniz during the last six weeks." This time the list appeared on his monitor without preamble. Surveying the items on his screen, he zeroed in on one sent from the *Vesuvius* by Neeley, at a time shortly after the instructions had been sent by Muniz. He selected the message and entered the command for playback.

"File restricted," the computer said. *"Playback denied."*

We'll see about that. "Command override: O'Brien, three-eight-five, alpha, theta, green."

"Override accepted. Decrypting file for playback."

After a momentary delay, a moving image appeared on O'Brien's screen. Blurry and dark at first, he realized that it was someone standing in front of a small portable video recorder that they had just set up. As the person backed away, he saw that it was a strikingly attractive red-haired woman. Her tall, slender body was wrapped in a heavy robe and blanket.

"Hey, Quique," she said. *"It's me. I, uh . . ."* She blushed, looked away from the camera at the walls of her quarters, and struggled not to laugh. *"I can't believe I let you talk me into this."* Staring into the camera, she went on, *"You know you owe me for this, right? Well, you're damn right you do."* A flirtatious gleam gave the lie to her narrow-eyed glare. *"Don't you even think of fast-forwarding until*

I get to say this: I love you, you big twit. And on that note—" She reached out from under her blanket and pressed a button on a table console. Resonant, bass-driven music began to pound from the speakers. With a salacious grin, she said to the camera, *"Happy birthday!"*

She jumped to her feet, threw off the blanket and robe, and revealed her outfit, a scandalously titillating leather ensemble that O'Brien was fairly certain even Intendant Kira would not have been bold enough to wear, not even in private. The blonde was dancing now, gyrating like an Orion woman, thrusting her hips and running her hands over her body, and as she began to peel away the first articles of her already scant clothing, O'Brien snapped, "Computer, end playback!"

All right, Quique's not a spy, O'Brien concluded. *Just a very, very lucky man.*

To be thorough, O'Brien made a cursory review of the rest of Muniz's files. The remaining text files were all harmless, and most of the encrypted video files were additional installments of "The Lisa Neeley Show," which O'Brien found increasingly compelling and difficult to turn off—until he thought of Keiko. Turning off episodes of "The Enrique Muniz Show," of course, had required no effort whatsoever.

And then there was Sito, he realized. She had joined his crew only six weeks ago, but her skill as a pilot had made her invaluable. He had worried that her youth and naïveté might make her unequal to the rigors of life aboard a combat ship, but she had surprised him, and everyone else, with her resilience. *Such a good kid,* O'Brien lamented as he called up her comm logs. *Hate doing this to her. Makes me feel like a bloody peeping Tom.*

Much like Leeta and Ezri, Sito had limited most of her communications to work-related matters. There was no record of her having had any contact with anyone off the station since her arrival on Terok Nor. But one file caught O'Brien's attention; it was an unsent text message, a draft that Sito had apparently been working on over the past several weeks. *Let's get this over with,* O'Brien decided, as he opened the file.

17 *He'mesh*

Dear Tera,

I don't know where to begin. First, I guess, tell Mom and Dad that I'm okay. I know they don't approve of what I'm doing, but I have to do this. I never meant to hurt them or you, it was just a choice I made.

There's not much I can tell you about where I am or what I'm doing, because that's all top-secret and stuff. I'm comfortable though, and safe. I'm still trying to figure out how to get this message to you. I can't send it directly, because we never know who'll be listening. I'm trying to find someone who might be going to the surface who could carry a printout of this letter. (If you're reading it, I guess I did!)

The rebellion's not like we were told on Bajor. The people here are good, and they take what they're doing really seriously. Don't believe people who tell you the rebels are just "criminals" or "malcontents." They've got some really big ideas about the future.

Have to run now—duty calls. More soon.

28 *He'mesh*

Tera,

I'm back. It's been a crazy busy time around here. You probably guessed that from the long gap in the dates, right? I figured. There's no point telling you what we've been doing. If it was something important, you probably saw it on the news already. And if you didn't, then I'm probably not supposed to say anything.

The biggest news is behind the scenes, as usual: I've been seeing a guy. Can't tell you his name (we're not supposed to make records of who's here, can't be too careful), but he's a decent man. He treats me well, and he's really smart. He's not the most popular guy, but he's steady, dependable. More about him later.

The hardest thing to get used to around here is the boredom. To fill the time, I've got a new hobby: gardening. The corner of my quarters has a bunch of new plants sprouting. You've probably already guessed they're all *jossa* flowers. They're the only thing I've ever been good at growing, so I decided to stick with what I know. I'm hoping to have blooms soon.

5 Yolava

Tera,

Okay, I know this is a long time between letters—I was offline for all of *Pel'hath*—but sometimes it just can't be helped. Since I haven't found a way to send this to you yet, I guess it doesn't really matter. By the time it reaches you it'll be more of a journal than a letter, anyway.

My garden is coming along. The flowers are all so pretty . . . it's such a shame you can't see them, I know you'd like them.

Remember that guy I told you about? Well, there's a new wrinkle in the story—I met someone else, someone closer to my age. The new guy is so handsome, and he just knows how to talk to me, you know what I mean? Problem is, he can be kind of a jerk sometimes. When he's nice he can be a lot of fun, but when he goes on a tear he can be dangerous.

So, ever a glutton for punishment, I've been seeing him behind the other guy's back. I thought I could keep it all casual, have my fun with the young guy but keep the steady guy as my safety. Didn't work out that way. And, in classic Sito Jaxa fashion, I've gone and done something royally stupid: They've found out about each other, and I know this is gonna get ugly pretty soon. Worst of all, I'm pregnant, and I don't know which one of them is the father.

I wish I was anywhere but here.

The letter stopped there. O'Brien looked at the date on the last entry; it was only days old, entered shortly before the *Defiant* had left Terok Nor. *Bloody hell, she's pregnant? That's just great. How can I take her into combat knowing that?*

Many times throughout O'Brien's life, he had uttered the words *I don't want to know,* but until this moment he'd never meant them so literally.

His first impulse was to relieve Sito of duty. *That won't work,* he realized. *Everyone'll ask why, and what am I supposed to say? I can't tell them she's pregnant, because how'm I supposed to know that? She'll know I've been through her private files—then everyone'll figure I've been through theirs, too. And they'll be right.*

He felt as if he were trapped in a corner. If Sito was pregnant, then for the safety of her unborn child she shouldn't be on active combat duty. But unless she volunteered that information, he would be unable to act on it.

He reclined in his chair, closed his eyes, and took deep breaths to ward off his impending monster of a headache. *Another glorious day in the rebellion.*

5

Captain Kurn of the *I.K.S. Ya'Vang* stroked the thick bramble of his dark beard as he listened to the Bajoran woman's proposal. So far, it consisted of little beyond wild speculation and conspiracy theories, none of which had inspired the Klingon commander with confidence.

"If I'm right," Kira Nerys said over the secure comm, *"then the rebels are gathering assets to build more ships like the* Defiant. *Possibly several more."*

He let out a derisive grunt. "You'll need to do better than that, woman." Shaking his head, he added, "All you've shown me is that you know how to spin a good story."

A fierce gleam and the hint of a smirk on her face made Kurn wonder if he'd just said exactly what she'd wanted to hear. *"What is it you're looking for, Captain? A connection? The missing piece of the puzzle that makes the rest fit together?"*

"Maybe I'm looking for a woman who doesn't speak in riddles," he warned with a jagged grin of his own.

She reached forward and sent a data file to him. It opened in the upper right-hand corner of his screen: a star chart centered on the intersection of four sectors of Cardassian-controlled space: Bajor, Cardassia, Almatha, and Algira. Bright red triangles marked several locations in interstellar space. *"Recognize the region?"* she asked. *"Do me a favor, Captain. Look at the map and tell me what a keen tactician such as yourself is able to glean from it."*

Kurn transposed Kira's image and the map on his screen, so that he could inspect the map more closely. One by one he called up the data linked to each of the highlighted locations, and then he began to understand what she was driving at. Though he had been generally aware of the positions of the star systems Kira had described in her account of various hijackings and disappearances, he hadn't really understood the truly proximate nature of their occurrence. Seeing it on the map made it abundantly clear that all the events that Kira had flagged had occurred in an improbably limited area.

"All right," he said. "I see how close they are." He switched Kira's image back to the primary position. "You think the rebels are targeting that sector specifically?"

"*I know they are,*" Kira said, growing bolder.

Alive with the rising thrill of the hunt, Kurn felt his pulse quicken and his blood rush hot on the back of his neck. "And that's where you think they're building new ships?"

"*Yes,*" Kira said. "*In the Trivas system.*" Another data file came across and appeared on his screen. "*The old Empok Nor station. The Cardassians decommissioned it years ago, when they finished mining the Trivas system's asteroid belt. Terok Nor was supposed to strip it for spare parts, but we never had time, so we left a few sentries on board.*"

"Punishment detail?" Kurn guessed.

"*Precisely,*" Kira said. "*With no one at Terok Nor to answer the sentries' call for help, the rebels could easily have taken control of the station and turned it into a shipyard.*"

The chain of her reasoning was locking together now in Kurn's thoughts. "The stolen kelbonite," he said. "They'd use it to shield the station's fusion core, hide its power signature from long-range scans." She was nodding, obviously pleased with his belated arrival at her way of seeing things. "I'll admit, it sounds plausible." Moving on to his next point of suspicion, he inquired, "Why are you telling *me*?"

"*Because telling Intendant Ro would do me no good,*" Kira said. "*If she did investigate, and it turned out to be nothing, I'd take the blame— but if I turned out to be right, she'd take the credit. Either way, I'd lose. . . . Regent Martok isn't interested in helping me—after all, he's the one who sent me to Ro. As for General Duras, I tried to tell him, but he's too afraid of Ro to make a judgment without her approval."*

"That's because Duras is a *petaQ*," Kurn said. "And Martok is an opportunist; my brother's throne was still warm when that *yIntagh* seized it for himself. Neither of which answers my question: Why should I help you?"

Her manner became as calculating as that of a Nilestran cobra. *"Because we both stand to gain from a partnership."*

"I don't agree," Kurn said. "My brother's capture disgraced the House of Mogh. If my family didn't have powerful friends, Martok would have stripped us of our lands and titles. I can't afford to give him a reason to do so now."

"Kurn, Kurn, Kurn." Kira flashed him a sinister smile, the kind whose exaggerated sweetness always concealed lethal venom. *"I understand that you're in a precarious position with Martok and the High Council. And that's exactly why you* can't *risk refusing my offer."*

His laughter was throaty and bellicose. *This woman lives up to her reputation and then some,* he decided. "I don't see why I need you at all," he said. "If I go the Trivas system, I can do so without your help. The honor of victory would be mine alone."

Kira stiffened her posture, but the fire in her gaze remained steady. *"And what will it gain you, Kurn? A small reprieve from Martok's wrath? A few extra years of watching your back before one of his people puts a knife in it?"* There was that maddening smile of hers again. *"Imagine how much stronger your position would be backed by a grateful Intendant of Bajor—one you helped restore to her rightful office."*

A slow growl turned in his throat while he considered her point. She was right about Martok; no matter how glorious a victory Kurn scored, Martok would remain his enemy and continue to impede his military and political fortunes. But if a strong off-world ally such as Bajor were to support Kurn, it might provide him enough leverage to gain a seat on the High Council, which would put him in a position to challenge Martok for the regency. At the same time, disgracing the current Intendant, Ro Laren, would weaken the Cardassians' sway over Bajoran politics and

keep the balance of power within the Alliance tilted in favor of
Qo'noS—but unless Kurn could guarantee that a Klingon-friendly
executive would take Ro's place, any such gain might be short-
lived. Grudgingly, he was forced to concede that Kira was right:
her best interest was also his.

"If I agree to a partnership," he said, "how will I convince General Duras to release the *Ya'Vang* for this mission? And how do you
propose to secure Intendant Ro's permission to accompany me?"

*"First, we're not to reveal the true nature of our mission to anyone until
after it's accomplished. Second, convincing Ro to release me to your custody
will be easier than you think."*

He began to see why she had a reputation for cunning. "I assume
you have a plan that addresses both our needs?"

"Of course I do, Captain," she said, with a seductive lowering of
her chin. *"Of course I do."*

General Duras leaned on one arm of his command chair on the
bridge of the *I.K.S. Negh'Var* and heaved a tired grunt. Intendant
Ro stood to his left. Together they faced Captain Kurn, commanding officer of the *Vor'cha*-class battle cruiser *I.K.S. Ya'Vang*. Kurn
had gone to tremendous effort to convince Duras to rendezvous
with his ship in the Rakal system. Meeting with any member of
the House of Mogh would once have been distasteful to Duras, but
to see the brother of the captured Regent Worf—former regent,
Duras corrected himself—come before him as a humble suppli-
cant had seemed like a privilege not to be wasted. Now that he knew
what Kurn wanted, he regretted his decision to let this *toDSaH* set
foot on his ship.

"You want *what?*" Duras barked.

With great patience and dignity, Kurn repeated, "Permission to
kill my elder brother, Worf, son of Mogh."

It was a brilliant gambit on Kurn's part. If Duras refused, he
would be acting contrary to Klingon honor customs, flouting
millennia of tradition. The blemish to his own honor would be a
grave embarrassment to his entire House. On the other hand, if

he permitted Kurn to carry out his insane plan, he would be enabling his sworn enemies to restore their own tarnished honor to its former luster. As usual for Duras, there was no winning.

Ro, as impatient as ever, interrupted Duras's ruminations. "He wants permission to *kill his brother?*" She shrugged. "He'd be doing the Alliance a favor. I say let him."

"It's not that simple," Duras said, unwilling to elaborate.

Ro nodded slowly. "I see. It's one of those complicated honor conundrums that keeps you people awake at night."

Duras was going to let a burning glower suffice as his response to Ro, but Kurn chose to explain the situation to her. "What I am asking for is permission to perform the *Mauk-to'Vor* ceremony," Kurn said. "One who has been dishonored has their honor restored by being slain with a *mevak* dagger by the one responsible for the dishonor."

The Bajoran woman looked and sounded confused. "So . . . you'd be restoring Worf's honor by killing him?"

"Not me," Kurn said. "The Council blames Kira Nerys for my brother's capture by the rebels. To lift his disgrace from my family, Kira must strike the fatal blow with the *mevak* blade. I need her temporarily transferred to my command, to help me accomplish my mission."

Eager to end the discussion and get Kurn off his bridge, Duras said, "Permission granted. Dis—"

Ro cut him off. "Absolutely not!" She took half a step forward and planted herself between Duras and Kurn. "Kira belongs to me, and she's not going anywhere."

A rough, hard growl rasped in Duras's throat. "Mind your place on my ship, Intendant." Ro turned her head slowly, her gaze coldly hostile and unflinching. Though her challenge was unmistakable, half a second later she gracefully stepped backward, behind his chair.

Turning his stare at Kurn, Duras asked, "Why can't you bring Worf here, to Kira?"

"After Worf was captured, the rebels took him to Terok Nor," Kurn said. "New intelligence suggests Worf is still there. To reach him and perform the *Mauk-to'Vor* will require stealth and subtlety— and the help of someone who knows the station's secrets better than anyone else: its former mistress."

On the edge of his vision, Duras saw Ro shaking her head and muttering under her breath. If Kurn's request vexed her, then it couldn't possibly be all bad. "As you can see," Duras said with dry sarcasm, "Intendant Ro cares deeply about Kira's safety. What kind of risk will your mission pose to her?"

"High," Kurn said. "It's to be a covert operation in enemy territory, employing no personnel other than myself and Kira."

"But couldn't she brief you here, in advance?" Ro asked. "I still don't see why you have to take her on the mission."

Kurn flashed a condescending smile in Ro's direction. "Safe here, she will have no incentive to be truthful and every reason to steer me into danger. If she faces my peril with me, her desire for self-preservation will keep her honest."

Finding no fault with Kurn's argument, Duras nodded and said, "Very well."

"You can't be serious!" Ro's outburst turned heads from all directions on the bridge. "All this prattling about honor—did you forget that Kira belongs to—"

"She is a slave aboard *my* ship!" Duras bellowed. "That makes her life mine—to give, to take, or to cast away. And you would be wise to remember, *Intendant,* that this ship serves Bajor only as a courtesy. It remains a Klingon warship, under my command." The face-off lasted for several seconds, then Ro turned away and stormed off the bridge under a dark cloud of indignation. As soon as the hatch closed behind her, Duras muttered a string of colorfully vulgar expletives describing her relationship to Gul Dukat. He looked at Kurn. "Is there anything else you want?"

"No, General," Kurn said.

"Then take Kira and get off my ship."

★ ★ ★

Kurn had wasted no time finding Kira after finishing his meeting with General Duras. Choosing to make a quick exit from the *Negh'Var* before the general changed his mind, Kurn led Kira through the cramped passageways to the transporter room. They ascended the platform and as soon as their feet settled onto the triangular transport pads, Kurn ordered the transporter operator, "Energize."

A white haze and a tingle of dissociation, and then he and Kira materialized in a smaller transporter room, aboard the *I.K.S. Ya'Vang.* He stepped off the transporter stage. In a single movement, he plucked a short, cylindrical device from his belt, lifted it in front of his face, and activated it. "Kurn to bridge. We're aboard. Raise the cloak and set course for the Amleth Nebula, warp nine."

Kira followed him as he left the transporter room. He was much taller than she, and his stride was so long that she found it difficult to keep up with him. She had considered the corridors on the *Negh'Var* to be dim and cramped, but the passageways on the *Ya'Vang* were even closer and darker than those on the dreadnought. The interior of the ship was also hotter and more humid than she had been accustomed to aboard Klingon vessels. *Probably because the only Klingon ships I've ever been on have had their climates adjusted for a Bajoran Intendant traveling on board as a VIP guest.* This, she realized, was probably what conditions aboard most Klingon ships were like.

They climbed a steep set of stairs up one deck and made a few hard turns. Kurn stopped in front of a green portal, which slid open with a deep rumble of servomotors. Beyond was a modestly sized compartment, large enough for a single bunk, a desk, and a private lavatory and shower. "Your quarters," Kurn said, motioning her inside with a sweep of his hand.

Kira stepped in and looked around. The room was spare and highly utilitarian, but it was clean and private. She managed a self-deprecating smile. "I hope I'm not putting anyone out."

"Not at all," Kurn said with a devilish grin. "My first officer prefers to bunk with the crew." He pointed to some drawers set into the bulkhead beneath the bunk. "There aren't many Klingon women your size, but I had the quartermaster alter a few uniforms that seemed close." Pinching a wrinkle of her gray jumpsuit between his thumb and forefinger, he added, "I thought you might appreciate something more becoming a once and future Intendant of Bajor."

She smiled salaciously at him, confident that he would be an even better ally to her than his older brother had been.

"Does everything meet with your satisfaction?" he asked.

"Yes," Kira said, eyeing her surroundings. "This will do nicely."

6

The bar on Terok Nor's promenade overflowed with angry voices. The senior leadership of the rebellion had gathered for a strategy meeting that was quickly becoming a free-for-all.

"Bloody irresponsible," O'Brien shouted at Zek and Bashir. "It was sloppy, and you know it!"

At the far end of the row of pushed-together tables, Bashir and Zek shouted back, their own replies almost lost in the hubbub of liquor-amplified tempers. "We did what had to be done," wailed Zek. Bashir added, "At least we were playing offense, instead of waiting for the Alliance to hit us again."

"Utter shite," O'Brien shot back. "You acted without orders, making tactical judgments without—"

"Without getting your permission?" Bashir cut in.

Nodding and glaring, O'Brien said, "Damn right without my permission, which, in case you've forgotten, is called insubordination." Almost all the ire in the room was directed now at O'Brien, who stood alone at the head of the group and weathered its disapproval with a stoic frown.

"Let's take it easy," urged Cal Hudson, while, across from him, Kasidy Yates pleaded, "We're supposed to be working together!"

Bashir retorted over the jeers, "And where is the court-martial, Smiley? Who'll be our judge? Our jury? Or should we just let *you* be everything—including executioner?"

When the indignation started to taper off, O'Brien spoke directly to Hudson. "They acted without telling anyone except their own crews what they were doing. They didn't let anyone else vet their plans—"

"And now we have a fleet of our own," Zek crowed. "Which just goes to show: ignoring you makes sense." A few of the gathered generals muffled their chortles in their sleeves or fake-coughed to make it seem as if they had at least tried to hide their laughter.

Lifting his voice, O'Brien continued, "Every heist they pulled was done within five light-years of the Trivas system. Plot 'em on a map and they make a nice little circle around it—or, as we like to call it in darts, a *target*." The laughing stopped. "They might as well have sent the Alliance a bloody invitation. It's a miracle they haven't hit the damn shipyard already." Staring down Zek specifically, he added, "And the *inexcusable* part is that if you'd consulted me first, I could've helped you get the same resources *and* cover your tracks. But this wasn't about what was good for the rebellion, was it, Zek? This was about what would make you and that shaggy dog of yours"—he nodded at Bashir—"look like heroes in here."

Pouring on the sarcasm, Zek replied, "Oh, you *wound* me. But I guess you're the right man to stand there and judge me for wanting to impress my partners in the rebellion; after all, you don't give a damn what they think of you, do you? That's why it was so easy for you to lose your nerve in the Cuellar system!"

Bolting from his chair, O'Brien clenched his fists. "I'll show you nerve, you—"

"He refused a direct order to fire on the enemy!" Zek cried. "Then he threatened to fire on *my* ship if we attacked an enemy target!"

Hudson and another man, Michael Eddington, intercepted O'Brien as he tried to rush Zek. Had it been Hudson alone, or Hudson and anyone else, O'Brien would have fought on. Eddington, however, had earned O'Brien's respect; he was the rebellion's best guerrilla warfare commander. For the sake of not embarrassing himself in front of Eddington, O'Brien backed off.

"It wasn't an enemy target," O'Brien explained. "It was an unarmed civilian colony. There was no reason to destroy it."

"Except that it was full of enemy personnel," Zek said.

"No, *civilians,*" O'Brien insisted. "Is that the kind of tactic we want to start using? Attacks on unarmed people?"

Hudson, ever the rationalizer of atrocities, said, "It's an *effective* tactic, Miles. It undermines the confidence of enemy civilians in their leaders. In turn, it weakens our enemies' control over their people."

"Besides," Bashir added, "if it was good enough for the Terrans of a hundred years ago, why shouldn't we—"

O'Brien lunged again and almost made it past Eddington. His baleful gaze fixed on Bashir, he growled, "Except that it *wasn't* good enough, you stupid sod. Learn some bloody history—a century of violence is what was destroying the empire."

An arrogant snort of derision twisted Bashir's face into an exaggerated sneer of contempt. "Spock's cowardice and weakness destroyed the Terran Empire—everyone knows that."

Twisting free of Eddington's grip, O'Brien said, "Yeah? Then everyone knows wrong. The Terran Empire didn't fall because it got too free—it fell because it got screwed by vicious, bloodthirsty bastards like you and your shriveled little friend."

"Gentlemen," Hudson said, his heavy baritone putting an end to the debate. "We came here to discuss strategy, not history."

There was heat and sweat on the back of O'Brien's neck. All he wanted was to strangle Bashir and Zek, no matter how counterproductive it might ultimately prove to be. "Fine," he said. "Let's talk strategy. I'm trying to wipe out an interstellar tyranny. Those two gits just want to set up one of their own."

Bashir hollered, "This is war, Smiley! Whose side are you on? Would you rather kill or be killed?"

"They have a point, Miles," Hudson said. "The Alliance wouldn't hesitate to wipe out an unarmed colony of free Terrans. And this is no time to be pulling our punches: the harder we hit them, the easier it gets for us to recruit new members."

"Hang on," said Yates, the attractive and pragmatic Terran woman seated opposite Hudson. "I have to say, I'm with O'Brien on this one. I'm not comfortable putting unarmed civilians in the crosshairs." O'Brien was grateful that Yates had sided with him. Though she was one of the few women in the rebellion's leadership, her opinion carried a tremendous deal of influence with the other commanders. "I mean, you can argue the Alliance would wipe out a free Terran colony, but it's not like they're executing Terran slaves to try and break our spirit."

"No," Hudson said, "but they are torturing and executing any escaped slave who they think was trying to reach us, as well as anyone they think is helping slaves reach us. And it's not because they think they'll learn anything from torture that'll help them find us. They torture runaway slaves for the same reason torture's always been used, anywhere and everywhere: to scare others into submission."

It was Eddington's turn to ask rhetorically, "Are you advocating we take up torture? To try and intimidate Alliance troops and civilians into not supporting the war against us?"

"Why not?" Bashir retorted. "A little fear might be good for them. Teach them we're not weak."

O'Brien returned to the head of the table. "Bollocks. If you need to use torture to scare someone, it's because you *are* weak. You don't have enough strength to negotiate, so you bully instead." A flash of memory: O'Brien remembered the sadistic glee with which Bashir had abused the captive Intendant Kira. "Unless, of course," he added, "you want to torture people because you *like it.*"

"Maybe I do it," Bashir replied, "because they *deserve* it."

It was late, and O'Brien was tired of yelling. He lowered his voice. "Is that all this is to you? Payback?" Just as he had learned by watching two different men named Ben Sisko, the other people in the room quickly hushed themselves to hear what was being said. "Is revenge a good enough reason to fight a war? I don't think so." He started walking around the table, his pace steady and unhurried. "Today it's revenge on the Alliance. Who gets it in the neck tomorrow? You? Me? When does it end?" He made fleeting eye contact with one rebellion leader after another as he continued.

"What're we trying to accomplish? Freedom? If that's all we wanted, we could just run—run till we get to where the stars have no names, and settle on some dusty little ball of rock. But how long would that last us? Till the Alliance finds us, or the next empire comes." He glanced sharply at Bashir. "Or we kill ourselves for some lunatic revenge fantasy." Rounding the far end of the table, he turned his back on Bashir and Zek and kept walking, taking his time. "That's not what I'm fighting for. That's not why I risked everything to start a rebellion. . . . I met a man who showed me a better way of life. He was proof that Terrans don't have to be barbarians, that power doesn't mean cruelty." He returned to his place at the head of the table and stopped, facing the group. "We can't just be fighting to bring back an empire that fell a hundred years ago. It's not enough to go back to being what we *were*. We have to fight to become something *better than what we are.*"

O'Brien looked from face to face, trying to gauge the group's reaction. Most of the others wore introspective expressions, but otherwise seemed to be trying to stay neutral. Zek was looking off to one side and mumbling Ferengi curses, while Bashir regarded O'Brien with a disappointed frown and a few somber turns of his head to convey his rejection of all that O'Brien stood for. The only person at the table whose reaction was completely unreadable was Eddington. He leaned back in his chair, hands folded together on his lap, saying nothing.

"Well," Bashir said. "That was a very moving speech. Unfortunately, it doesn't change the fact that we're at war, and that the only way we're going to win is by hitting the Alliance harder than they hit us, and more often. I'm sorry you don't approve of how Zek and I built the rebellion's fleet, but what's done is done, and complaining that we didn't do it your way frankly sounds like envy and not much else. So, unless you've got something productive to add, we need to get to our ships and begin planning our assault on Cardassia Prime."

Anxious looks passed between the rebellion leaders. O'Brien felt the balance of power shifting in Bashir's favor. Fighting it began to seem like a waste of effort. "Is that what all of you want, then? Are we done talking?"

"Miles," Hudson said, trying to strike a conciliatory tone. "We have to face the realities of our situation. There's a time and a place for idealism, and it's not on a battlefield. A decisive strike on Cardassia Prime will throw the entire Alliance off balance. It'll give us momentum—and it might even spark slave rebellions on some of the less stable planets." He got up from his chair and moved toward Bashir and Zek.

Several other members of the group followed Hudson's example. Among them, with apparent reluctance, was Kasidy Yates. Though she tried not to look back, she sneaked a look over her shoulder at O'Brien, who pleaded simply, "You, too, Kasidy?"

"I'm sorry, O'Brien," she said, and she sounded as if she meant it. "But I've been waiting for a ship like yours for a long time."

"Long enough that you're willing to slaughter civilians?"

Deep shame filled her eyes like a shadow. Unable to answer him, she turned away and joined the growing cluster that was following Zek and Bashir out of the bar. Her exit was a betrayal. In less than a minute, there was only one person left at the table with O'Brien: Eddington.

Noting the absence of the guerrilla leader from his group's ranks, Zek shouted back to him, "Eddington! What're you waiting for?"

"I'm not going with you," Eddington said in a quiet voice.

Consumed by ego and fury, Zek demanded, "In the name of the Blessed Exchequer, why not? You'd have a warship of your own to command! This is the moment you've been waiting for, the moment you've earned! Get off your ass and take it!"

Calm and unintimidated in the least, Eddington responded with a wan smile and a simple, "Good luck."

"Fine," Zek whined. "Stay here with O'Brien and write poems about this utopian vision of his. We'll be at Cardassia Prime, scoring the biggest victory of the rebellion!" The old Ferengi walked out of the bar with Bashir at his side and all of the rebellion's senior leaders except O'Brien and Eddington in tow. Kasidy lagged behind the others, as if she was grappling with second thoughts, but at the last moment she exited the bar, following Zek and his entourage to the *Capital Gain,* for transport to their new fleet at Empok Nor.

A dark moment of disappointment hung over O'Brien. He was effectively finished as the leader of the rebellion. Zek would be calling the shots now. With the power of a dozen *Defiant*-class ships under his command, Zek and Bashir would go on a rampage. Not for a moment did O'Brien believe they would stop after the strike on Cardassia Prime. Qo'noS would instantly become a target. After that, any world that didn't knuckle under to their demands would find itself the victim of a sneak attack by a cloaked fleet of the most devastating ships in the quadrant. It was a disaster on a scale that O'Brien didn't even want to imagine.

His glum ponderings were interrupted by Eddington. "What'll we do if Zek and Bashir actually defeat the Alliance?"

"I don't know," O'Brien said with a despondent shake of his head. "Start another rebellion?"

The leather of Kira's borrowed uniform fit her body more snugly than her body suit had, but she didn't mind because it also flattered her, boosting her décolletage and accentuating her every curve. She took Kurn's leers as compliments, and she found ego-pleasing amusement in the efforts his crew had to make to avoid being caught stealing their own glances in her direction. As far as they knew, she was Kurn's woman—and she played the part with enthusiasm, draping herself over his shoulder like a tendril of black ivy. Acting as his adoring consort and obedient plaything suited her purposes; it kept the rest of the crew at bay for fear of his wrath, and it made it so much easier for her and Kurn to conspire without making anyone suspicious.

Her breath rebounded from Kurn's ear and warmed her lips as she whispered to him, "We're close now."

Kurn knew what to do. "Helm," he barked. "Take us out of warp on the edge of the Trivas system."

"Aye, Captain," acknowledged Ronak, the *Ya'Vang*'s senior flight controller. Less than a minute later, the ship dropped back to sublight speed, and the stars on the main viewer retreated into themselves.

Kira nuzzled the tip of her nose softly against Kurn's ear as she mutedly advised him. "If you get within three billion *qell'qam*s of Empok Nor running at normal power, you'll light up every sensor on the station."

An amused grunt rolled inside Kurn's throat. He reached up and affectionately stroked his fingers through Kira's hair. To her surprise, she liked the way his hands felt on her skin. He lowered his hand and leaned forward in his chair. "Helm, set course for Empok Nor. Accelerate to full impulse for ten seconds, then cut all engines; we'll let inertia carry us in." Pivoting the chair, Kurn turned toward his first officer. "Krona, rig the ship for silent running."

The slight but wiry-looking executive officer nodded his understanding and began translating the general order into specific commands at each duty station. Step by step, almost every major system on the ship was powered down. Active sensors were disabled; the main computer was shifted to standby mode. Environmental support, replicators, turbolifts all were shut off. Almost immediately, Kira felt the air start to cool; it would soon grow heavier, thicker with carbon dioxide. Around the bridge, monitors went dark. Lights faded to anemic flickers. The hum of the warp core faded away, surrendering to the unnerving silence of deep space. A noncom marched onto the bridge and approached Krona. "Engine room secured, sir," the young engineer's mate reported. "Ready for snap restart."

"Good work," said Krona. "Go back and tell Hervog we'll need weapons online at the same time as the warp drive." The noncom nodded and ran back the way he had come.

Nestled against Kurn's arm in the darkness, Kira felt herself drifting inexorably into slumber. She was so tired; her limbs felt sapped of strength. To close her eyes for even a little while was tempting, but she had spent the past few months learning to stay on her guard, to remain vigilant against every threat she could think of, whether it had seemed imminent or not. Her head lolled forward, weighted down with drowsiness. She snapped it back upright, then blinked her irritated eyes against the ruby twilight of the *Ya'Vang*'s bridge.

Kurn's whisper was like a deep rumble in the earth, a low vibration that coursed through her. "It's all right to rest," he assured her. "You're safe here. . . . Sleep." His summons was all the urging she needed to let go. Propped against the side of his chair, his massive forearm a steady cushion beneath her head, she drifted off, releasing herself from consciousness.

She snapped fully awake. It seemed at first as if she hadn't slept at all, but then half-remembered nightmares lurked in her thoughts like shadows. She glanced at the chronometer in the lower corner of the main viewer and was taken aback to see that she'd been asleep for a few hours.

A chill now subdued the ship, but the mood on the *Ya'Vang*'s bridge had become charged with anticipation. Everything remained hushed and dark, but there was a new urgency to the crew's activity. Kira listened as Krona returned from one of the bridge stations to report to Kurn. "Passive sensors have detected energy readings inside the Empok Nor station, Captain. We've confirmed the readings are from industrial replicators."

Kurn asked, "Are you reading any power spikes in the station's fusion core?"

"No, sir. We detect no power-generation at all, but there are signs of low-level power consumption in the station's main habitat area. Hervog thinks that the station's power core might have been shielded to prevent its use from being picked up by ships outside the system."

"Shielded," Kurn said, as if he were thinking aloud. Of all the people on the bridge, only Kira knew that Kurn was feigning ignorance as he inquired, "What could shield a fusion core that size, Krona?"

"I asked Hervog the same question," Krona said. "His best guess is that the core's been wrapped in kelbonite."

A devilish smirk lit up Kurn's face as he looked down at Kira to share their private joke. "Kelbonite," he said. "Very clever." He looked back up at Krona. "It seems we've found the rebels' newest base."

"There's more, sir," Krona said. "Much more."

"Tell me," Kurn demanded.

Krona turned toward the tactical station at the aft end of the bridge. "Qeyhnor, put the passive-optical scan on-screen." The static curtain of stars was replaced by a fuzzy, dim image of the Empok Nor station. Twelve huge, box-shaped conglomerations of metallic framework jutted out from all the major docking sites along the outer perimeter of its docking ring.

Kurn leaned forward until he was perched literally on the edge of his chair. "What are they doing? Raiding it for parts?"

"I don't think so, sir," Krona said. "Qeyhnor, magnify." The image on-screen enlarged, revealing the telltale outline of a *Defiant*-class ship inside one of metal scaffolds. "It looks like they've turned the station into a shipyard. We count eleven finished starships docked there, and a twelfth spaceframe just starting construction." Krona cast a doubtful glance at the screen, then looked back at Kurn. "Perhaps we should summon reinforcements, Captain."

Instantly, Kira's lips were at Kurn's ear, her voice barely a breath of suggestion. "If you do, no one will sing songs in your honor," she warned him. "Martok will rob you of glory." Kurn seemed torn. His intense stare was fixed on the image of the improvised shipyard. She continued to nudge him in the only viable direction. "Reason it out, Kurn: What would the rebels have had to do to make that old, *decommissioned* station work as a shipyard? How much power would that take?"

Long seconds passed as Kurn considered what she had said,

and his crew watched him, waiting for his next order. Then Kira heard what she had been waiting for: a low growl of satisfaction from Kurn, followed by a sly grin on his face. "Maintain radio silence," Kurn ordered. "We don't need the fleet's help. We're going to destroy the rebels ourselves."

"Sir," Krona said, his voice lowered. "We are outnumbered eleven to one. Any one of those ships could be a match for us, in both speed and firepower. They might also have working cloaking devices like the *Defiant*'s."

To the crew's surprise, Kurn chuckled to himself. "It won't help them," he said. "Because it won't be the ships we're fighting—it'll be the station." He all but jumped up from his chair and marched toward the main viewscreen. Pointing at the image of Empok Nor, he continued, "Look how quickly they're building those ships. Think about how much power that must take, how overtaxed that station's fusion core is. Even if the Cardassians hadn't stripped it of shields and weapons when they decommissioned it, the rebels wouldn't have any power left to run them." Turning on his heel to face his crew, he declared, "One good torpedo salvo in its fusion core is all it will take to destroy that station—and the rebels' shiny new fleet!"

Roars of appreciation answered him, growls and cheers of inflamed battle lust. Within seconds, the crew was chanting Kurn's name, every utterance in synch with the stomp of boots on the deck and the pounding of fists against consoles. Kurn basked in the praise for a moment, then he held up his hands and motioned for silence. "Runner!" he shouted. A noncom stepped forward from the ranks to stand in front of him. "Take a message to Hervog: When I give the order to attack, I want to make the jump to maximum warp immediately. Go!" The runner sprinted away to take the message down to engineering. "Qeyhnor," Kurn said, "if we jump to maximum warp, we'll be in firing range in less than twenty seconds. You'll have that much time to ready a firing solution."

"You'll have it, Captain," Qeyhnor said.

Moving in long strides back to his chair, Kurn said for everyone present, "Stations. Prepare to attack, on my order." He took his seat as Krona turned from station to station, issuing specific instructions and readying the ship for battle. "Tactical," Krona said, "have the torpedo room load the first salvo manually. The station has no working weapons, so divert shield power to the disruptors. Helm, plot a course for a maximum-warp jump into firing range, followed by a half-impulse pass at the station. Make sure tactical has a clean shot at the fusion core. Communications, stand ready to jam outgoing transmissions from the station."

Moments later, the reports came back to Krona. The first officer turned to face Kurn. "All stations ready, Captain."

"Tell engineering to power up in thirty seconds," Kurn said. "As soon as we have warp speed, attack."

Krona nodded. "Aye, sir." He pointed at the communications officer, who relayed Kurn's message down to the engineering deck, then nodded a confirmation in reply. "Thirty seconds," Krona said, initiating the countdown.

Kira clutched Kurn's arm, giddy with excitement. The countdown felt slow, unable to keep pace with the flood of adrenaline rushing through her system. Twenty seconds . . . ten . . . then Beqar, the communications officer, called out, "Intercepting a transmission to the station! Beginning decryption algorithm."

"Hold the countdown," Kurn ordered.

As Beqar worked to unscramble the message to the station, Krona moved behind her and observed while she worked. "What's the message's point of origin?" Krona asked.

Her flurry of activity slowed, then she leaned back from her console. "Source, a ship en route. Based on the frequency shift, the vessel appears to be cloaked."

Kurn asked Beqar, "Have you decoded the message?"

"It's from a ship that identifies itself as the *Capital Gain,* under the command of General Zek," Beqar replied. "He says his ETA is nine hours, and he wants the ships at Empok Nor ready to deploy as soon as he arrives"—Beqar paused and turned to face Kurn as she finished—"with their commanders."

At first Kurn looked to Kira as if he was in shock. Then he laughed, guffawed with his head thrown back, at once triumphal and uproariously amused. His crew laughed wildly with him.

Regaining control of himself by degrees, he was still laughing in fits as he told the crew, "Stand down . . . return to silent running. . . . We do nothing until the *Capital Gain* arrives. But when it does . . . we'll kill them all." His enormous hand was firm and warm on the back of Kira's neck. He looked down at her with what she could have sworn seemed like genuine respect. He spoke loudly enough for everyone to hear, but his eye contact with Kira made it clear that he was talking to her. "Destroying the rebel fleet would be a great victory," he said. "But wiping out their leadership at the same time will make it a *glorious* one."

He's smarter than Worf, Kira realized. *More disciplined.* She smiled at him, projecting both pride and respect. For once, it seemed, she had chosen a friend wisely; she would have to get her claws into him, deeply and firmly. "We have nine hours until the rebels arrive," she whispered seductively to him. "How should we pass the time, Captain?"

Her solicitation turned his head. His piercing gaze seemed to question whether she was serious, or merely playing her part. She bit her lower lip and flashed him a "come hither" look that made it clear that her offer was genuine. He smiled, apparently quite pleased at the surprises his day was yielding.

"Krona," Kurn said as he stood up. "You have the bridge."

7

What do you mean it's impossible?" O'Brien asked Keiko while his dinner materialized in the replicator.

"Just what I said," replied Keiko, who was sitting on the sofa. "You can't prove a negative. It's logically impossible."

The bowl of beef stew was warm in O'Brien's hands as he picked it up. "How can it be impossible?"

"What if I asked you to prove you can't fly?"

He walked back from the replicator, taking small steps to avoid spilling any of his piping-hot meal. "Easy," he said. "I *can't* fly. Case closed." He paused behind Keiko and kissed her softly on the top of her head.

She tilted her head back, smiled at him, and watched him as he circled around and sat down next to her. "No," she said. "You have to *prove* it."

"What's there to prove?" Poking at the chunky broth to let some of the heat out, he inhaled the escaping vapor and savored the stew's aroma. "You want me to demonstrate it?"

"How would you?" Her question was rich with implications. "If all you do is stand there, I could accuse you of faking, of not really using your ability."

He lifted a spoonful of stew and blew gently across it. "So, what am I supposed to do? Jump off a cliff and fall to my death?" He slurped down the first spoonful and enjoyed its saltiness.

"That still wouldn't prove anything," Keiko said. "I could just say you died to hide your secret, and make up a bunch of reasons why you might have done it. That's why legal evidence is supposed to depend on proving what *is,* not what *isn't.* If I'm the one saying you can fly, it's up to me to prove that you can—because there's no way you can prove that you can't."

Between a third and fourth spoonful, he asked, "But couldn't you prove, say, that I'm not a Cardassian?"

"Not directly," Keiko explained with a teacher's gentle patience. "I could produce conclusive evidence that you're a Terran—and that, by exclusion, you are therefore not a Cardassian. What's key here isn't proving that you're *not* one thing but that you *are* another. See the difference?"

He nodded as he set down his bowl. "I think so." He took a sip of Bajoran springwine, which he found a bit too sweet for his liking, but which he also found vastly more palatable than any of the Cardassian swills or Klingon liquors that the replicators had been programmed with. "So what you're saying is, Bashir and Zek called me and my crew guilty, asked me to prove we're not, and that there was no way I could've done so?"

"Pretty much," Keiko said. "There are a hundred ways you can prove that someone *is* a spy, but there's no infallible way to prove that they're not."

"So I was spying on my own people for no reason," he said, bitterly upset with himself. "And why? Because Zek and Bashir had the gall to call them traitors." He put down his wine. "I'm such an idiot."

Keiko leaned close and put one arm over his shoulders. "You did what you thought was best for the rebellion," she consoled him. "It's not as if you did it for profit, or political gain. You just wanted to be safe."

He shook his head. "I'm still not sure that makes it right. I mean, who am I to play God and listen in on other people's personal business?" A heavy sigh left him feeling empty. "I wanted to talk to you about it, get your advice. But they were talking like they might come after you next. I didn't want to give them a reason." He reached out and took her hand. "What's done is done, I guess. The problem now is, what do I do about Sito?"

"That's tricky," Keiko said. "She's not even showing yet, so it has to be *very* early in her pregnancy. The Bajoran gestation period is only five months, and even so, Bajoran women tend to stay active right up until their babies are due."

"This isn't about her doing the work," O'Brien said. "I'm sure she'd be a fine pilot right up until she went into labor, and I'm proud of her for putting her own life on the line—but I'm not going to let her take an unborn child into battle. Nobody's asked that kid if it wants to be in combat, and I think it's bloody well wrong to put it there."

"Fine," Keiko said. "Relieve her of duty, then."

"How the hell am I supposed to justify that?" He let go of her hand and got up from the sofa. Pacing on the other side of the coffee table, he continued, "If I tell her that I know she's pregnant, she'll know I've been snooping in her personal files. And when the rest of the crew hears about it, they'll figure I've been snooping on them, too."

"You have been," Keiko interjected.

He shot her a scornful glare. "Then they'll start talking about finding a new captain, maybe Leeta, or Muniz. Next thing you know, I'm not only out as leader of the rebellion, I'm done as the captain of the *Defiant*. A perfect end to a perfect day."

"So, find another reason to take her off combat duty," Keiko said. "Assign her to train new pilots. Heaven knows we need them right now."

"True," O'Brien said. "But it'll still look like I've singled her out for punishment. It could still backfire."

Keiko crossed her legs and pressed a finger against her lips while she pondered the matter. Then she looked up at O'Brien. "You need to make your decision look impartial, right?"

"Right," he said. There was a surety to her manner; it calmed him enough that he stopped pacing to hear her out.

She nodded. "All right. Order physical exams for the entire crew. Call it a standard procedure, say the medics need to get some baseline medical data for future treatment, that kind of thing. Do it by rank, or by department, alphabetical, whatever. If Sito won't get examined, let her go for bucking orders. If she does get checked out, you'll have proof she's pregnant. Then you and the medics can have a sit-down with her, and you can reassign her to pilot training."

It was all so diabolically logical. The longer O'Brien considered it, the better it sounded. "I like it," he said. "Covers all our bases." He returned to the sofa and sat down next to Keiko. "Best of all, the medics could actually use that kind of information. It'd be a good idea no matter what."

"I'm glad you think so," Keiko said with a smile.

Once again he was reminded of how essential Keiko had become to his work, to his existence. It made him think of the strange turns his life had taken to bring him to this moment. "You know, it's funny," he said. "One of the most decent men I ever met in my life was the Bashir from the other universe—and the biggest jackass I've ever met is the Bashir from this one."

She chuckled as she snuggled under his arm. "Well, aren't the people from the other side supposed to be our opposites or something?"

"I asked the other Sisko about that," O'Brien said. "He didn't think we were opposites so much as . . . different possibilities. A lot of the same potential, but different results." He held Keiko a little bit closer. "Take me, for example. There and here I was a good engineer, a good mechanic. In that universe it made me someone important; here I was just a slave. Or look at Bashir; on the other side he was a doctor, and here he's—"

He searched for the right word. Keiko found it. "A jerk?"

"You can say that again," he said with a broad smile. He kissed her cheek, and they laughed together at Bashir's expense. Despite the fact that Terok Nor remained the number-one target of the Alliance, here with Keiko he felt safe. Protected. "Anyway, thinking about Bashir the doctor made me remember something he told me. My other self was married, he said. A family man." She looked at him, perhaps sensing that he was on the verge of saying something important. He pulled her tight against him, in a firm yet gentle embrace. "I never asked who the other O'Brien's wife was. I didn't feel like I had the right to know, and I didn't want to jinx it or get my hopes up. In case I ever met her over here, you know? But the way I feel, I don't know if the other O'Brien's married to another you . . . but I'd like to think that he is."

"Me, too." Keiko reached up and pressed her soft, warm palm against his face, and then she kissed him, long and slow and in a way that made the rest of reality fall away from his senses, made him forget for an instant that they spent every moment of their lives beneath the looming shadow of catastrophe. Then her lips pulled away by degrees, but her hand stayed where it was and she remained intimately close. She pressed her forehead against his. "I've heard Alliance physicists say that there are actually an infinite number of universes," she whispered. "If that's true . . . I hope we find each other in all of them."

"So do I, love," O'Brien said, grateful that, for the moment, they at least had each other in this universe.

Intendant Ro stepped onto the bridge of the *I.K.S. Negh'Var* and moved directly to intercept General Duras. Ro was certain that she noticed a hint of dismay in his averted glance. "General," she said. "Have we received any updates from Captain Kurn or the *Ya'Vang?*"

"No, Intendant," Duras said.

It became immediately apparent that he was not in an elaborative mood. Extracting information from him was going to require effort. "Weren't they due to check in four hours ago?"

Duras grunted as if clearing his throat and checked the chronometer. "Five, actually."

"Doesn't that strike you as cause for alarm, General?"

"Not really, no." He turned to her, half his face illuminated in the ruddy glow of a small station monitor, the other lost in shadow. "When a ship is on a mission like this, sometimes comm silence is needed."

"So there's no protocol for following up when a ship on a covert operation misses a check-in?"

A long exhalation of air through Duras's nose telegraphed his growing annoyance. "What do you want me to do, Intendant? Transmit an encrypted subspace hail toward Terok Nor, requesting an update on the *Ya'Vang*'s status? The rebels on the station might wonder why we're sending such a signal toward their best stronghold, but I suppose that's of no concern to—"

"Enough." She despised the condescending tone of his voice. "Let the *Ya'Vang* maintain comm silence. Notify me the moment they check in."

"As you command, Intendant," Duras said, without truly striking the tone of a subordinate. If anything, he made a mockery of her authority. He was the most insolent officer, of any species, that Ro had ever met.

Ro left the bridge and returned to her expansive but spartan suite. Its panoramic views of deep space were majestic but cold, the steady glow of starlight feeling almost surreal without the twinkle imparted by atmospheric disturbance.

Shifts of attendants swept into and out of the room, one group after another, bringing myriad flurries of official business and pending executive decisions for her review. Most of them she delegated to her subordinates; a few she graced with cursory reviews before scribbling her approval or waving them away to some unconsidered political purgatory.

The minutiae of work occupied her for a few hours until it was finally time for dinner. She had long since made it clear to her support staff that, whether she was dining alone or with company, she was never to be disturbed except in cases of dire emergency. Her evening repast was one of the few times of her day that she could be relatively assured of peace and privacy.

All her meals were prepared in her own galley, to prevent her food from becoming contaminated with any of the filth that the Klingons consumed. "If anything live ever reaches my table," she had warned her cook, "I will kill *it,* then I'll kill *you.*"

This evening's meal had met with her complete satisfaction. The appetizer, of salted Circassian figs and wedges of sharp Rakantha marbled cheese, had been followed by an entrée of Vulcan mollusks sautéed in Rhombolian butter and served on a bed of freshly cut seedling moon grass. A bottle of good Alvanian brandy had been set out for her after-dinner cordial, and she sipped the sweetly complex liquor slowly while considering the delicate nature of her situation with Kira Nerys.

There had been no choice but to let Kira go with Kurn. The Klingons, once they became obsessed on a matter of honor, were relentless. She had a grudging respect for Kurn's tactics, despite her dislike of the man himself. *He boxed in Duras like an old pro,* she reflected. *You'd think a warrior with political skills that finely honed would have risen further in the ranks by now, especially when his elder brother had been regent for years.* Then she realized the truth: it had been Kira's handiwork that had maneuvered Duras so adroitly. Kurn's appeal to Klingon honor, even his assurances to Ro that Kira's life would be placed in mortal peril—it all bore the mark of Kira's touch. *She must have coached him to tell me and Duras what we each wanted to hear. More to the point, he did it. So, if he's following her cues . . . what's in it for him?*

Ro pondered the mission that Kurn had proposed to Duras and she asked herself how its success might possibly benefit Kira. Its value to Kurn wasn't hard to figure out; lifting the dishonor of Worf's capture would preserve Kurn's wealth. It would not be enough to cleanse him of the political stigma, however; unless he somehow elevated himself to the rarefied status of Hero of the Empire, it was unlikely that he would ever be able to attain a seat on the Klingon High Council. As a mere starship captain, he would be unable to change Kira's fortunes for the better, so why would she aid him in killing Worf?

Helping Kurn complete the *Mauk-to'Vor* ceremony would earn Kira a small measure of approval among the Klingons, but not enough to offset the disgrace of her perceived role in Worf's downfall. *If I were her,* Ro wondered, *how would I have used Kurn to my advantage?* Making his mission a success didn't sound like Kira's usual means of action; betrayal was Kira's chief currency.

He needs her to land the killing blow on Worf, Ro remembered. *What if she doesn't kill Worf? What if she kills Kurn . . . and* rescues *Worf instead?*

Suddenly, Ro was certain that she could see Kira's plan revealing itself in her imagination. Worf, rescued by the woman who had been blamed for his capture, might be able to return to Qo'noS and challenge Martok for the regency. If he won, and regained the throne, he would almost certainly be very grateful to Kira, who would no doubt use her restored political influence to oust Ro and reinstall herself as the Intendant.

Over my dead body, Ro vowed to herself. *Or hers.*

A brutal bit of political calculus worked itself out in Ro's thoughts. If Kira's plan to put Worf back on the throne succeeded, the cost to Ro and her Cardassian sponsors would be catastrophic. But if Kira's mission failed utterly, what would it really cost the Alliance? One Klingon battle cruiser from a fleet of thousands, and a disgraced Bajoran ex-politician. Negligible losses by any standard.

The loss of the *Ya'Vang* might also provide the impetus to justify a more aggressive strategy for the recapture of Terok Nor, and with it the liberation of Bajor from a years-long standoff with the Terran rebels. A success of that magnitude could fortify Ro's power base for a decade or more.

In a moment of coldly reasoned spite, Ro walked to her desk, accessed the ship's secure communications system, and began composing a detailed and anonymous message to be sent on an encrypted channel to Terok Nor.

8

O'Brien hated being woken up in the middle of the night. His vision was blurry, his stomach was churning, and his clothes had been awkwardly pulled onto his body. Out of sorts, half awake, unshaven, and fighting against a leaden sensation in his limbs, he stepped off the lift into ops and walked toward Eddington. "What's the bloody problem?"

"Have a look at this," Eddington said, as he called up a screen of data on the main screen in the center of the situation table. "Just came in fifteen minutes ago."

Squinting at the bright jumble of text, O'Brien struggled to focus his eyes. The words sharpened, and he read quickly. "An attack on Terok Nor?"

"That's what I thought at first, too," Eddington said. He pointed out another section of the message. "Until I saw this."

It was a warning about the Alliance's target for a covert infiltration and assassination scheme. "What is this, a joke?" O'Brien groused. "We moved Worf to the Badlands months ago."

"Maybe the Alliance doesn't know that," Eddington said. "I raised the shields and ordered Luther to run a long-range sensor sweep to find any ships in silent-running mode nearby."

"Good work," O'Brien said. "So what are we talking about? A Klingon strike team or a direct assault?"

Eddington adjusted the display on the tabletop. "Neither," he said. "The message was specific: Worf's younger brother and Intendant Kira were going to be the only ones coming aboard to kill him. It didn't say why."

"Strangest bloody thing I ever heard," O'Brien muttered. "Must be some kind of Klingon nonsense." He tapped a few panels on the table's control interface and skimmed over the text-only message again. "No sender identity," he noted. "Looks like it got scrubbed clean on its way here." O'Brien turned toward the science station, where a fair-haired, weathered-looking Terran named Sloan was manning the sensors. "Luther—anything?"

The older man shook his head, his steely gaze fixed on his console. "Nothing."

"Keep looking," O'Brien said, then he turned back toward Eddington. "Maybe we should pass along a warning to our people in the Badlands. This message might have been meant for them."

From the tilt of Eddington's head and the hunch of his shoulders, O'Brien saw that he wasn't convinced. "It specifically identified Terok Nor as the target." Noting O'Brien's grouchy stare, he added, "But I'll send the message."

"Thank you." Suspicion had pretty much become O'Brien's default state, but this situation was making him edgier than usual. He reviewed the anonymous message again, mining it for clues. "None of our usual challenge-and-response phrases are in the text," he observed. "This wasn't sent by one of our people."

Eddington said, "A new recruit, perhaps?"

"*You're* optimistic all of a sudden," O'Brien quipped. "If you ask me, this reads more like an Alliance trap."

Calling up the sensor results on the display between them, Eddington said, "Well, if it is, it's the best-disguised trap I've ever seen." He enhanced the sensor results, revealing nothing but another blank screen. "There's nothing out there."

O'Brien rechecked the data. Eddington was right. There was no sign of any Alliance warship in the system. Even rigged for silent running, as the Klingons called it, their ships were not impossible to detect. Passive sensors might not register a ship operating in such a low-power mode, but active sensor-sweep protocols were still more than capable of pinpointing one.

"Why would someone in the Alliance send us this warning in the first place?" O'Brien asked. "If the threat is genuine, that would imply there's a traitor in their ranks."

Eddington chuckled. "Now who's being an optimist?"

"I didn't say I believed it," O'Brien replied. "For now, let's rule it out. What other scenarios does that leave us?"

"A disinformation campaign," Eddington suggested.

O'Brien nodded. "It's possible." He stroked his stubbled chin while he considered the matter. "But why bother? They have to know we'd check and see there's no ship out there."

"Maybe they think we're paranoid enough to believe they've built a new cloaking device," Eddington said. "One we can't see through."

For all their sakes, O'Brien hoped that Eddington's words didn't prove grimly prophetic. "Say you're right," he continued. "What're they hoping we'll do?"

"Panic? . . . Abandon the station?" Eddington rolled his eyes at O'Brien's *don't even joke about that* glare, then he added, "Maybe rally all our forces here to defend it?"

That made no sense. "Why in blazes would they want that?"

"Because," Eddington said, "to bring everyone here, we'd have to leave other strategic assets undefended."

O'Brien's face scrunched with confusion. "But we don't *have* any other strategic assets," he exclaimed. That statement lingered between him and Eddington for a long moment, and they both arrived together at the same conclusion.

In unison, they said, "Empok Nor."

"Bloody hell," O'Brien grumbled. "Luther, get me a secure channel to Zek and Bashir on the *Capital Gain!*" Under his breath he vented to Eddington, "Assuming the ego-twins haven't already gotten themselves blown to bits."

"We should be so lucky," Eddington said.

Zek loved sitting in the center seat of the *Capital Gain*'s bridge, but he hated the seat itself. It was too square, lacked adequate padding, and was too high off the deck for his feet to rest comfortably in front of him. *Built by Terrans, for Terrans,* he seethed. The circuit that automatically dimmed the lights when the ship's cloak was engaged would also have to be disabled, he decided. *How can anyone see where they're going with the damned lights half off?*

There would be time to make improvements once his ship docked at Empok Nor, which grew steadily larger on the main viewer. The blocky masses of scaffolding became more distinct. Zek swiveled his chair from side to side as he spoke with the other rebellion leaders who had gathered on the bridge with him for the arrival at the shipyard. "Eleven brand-new beauties, just like this one," he crowed. "Bashir, what're you going to name yours?"

An unusually wistful look came over Bashir as he said, "*Jadzia.* My ship will be the *Jadzia.*"

"How sentimental," Zek said. "Fortunately, you've got time to think of a better name. What about you, Yates? Got a name for your ship yet?"

Kasidy Yates grinned. "The *Terra Victor.*"

"Not bad, not bad," Zek said. "It's got a bit more fire than *Jadzia,* that's for sure." He smirked at Bashir's glare.

The station dominated the viewscreen. Nearly complete starships were distinguishable inside the construction frames. Cal Hudson seemed to swell with pride. "I haven't picked a name for my ship yet," he said. "Too many possibilities."

"Plenty of time before we ship out," Zek said. "Bashir, get ready to drop the cloak. Hudson, take the helm and get ready to dock. Yates, open a channel to—" A musical chirping sound emanated from the communications console. "What in the name of the Divine Treasury is that?"

"It's an incoming transmission, priority one," Yates said. "On a secure channel from Terok Nor."

More of O'Brien's deluded moralizing. Zek whined with exasperation then said, "Put him on-screen." Eddington and O'Brien appeared together on the main viewer, both standing in the ops center of Terok Nor. "What is it?"

"General Zek," Eddington said. *"What is your current status?"*

"Why can't you ever talk like normal people? Why can't you say, 'Where are you?' or 'How are you doing?'"

The question seemed to rile O'Brien, who looked ready to reply before Eddington cut him off. *"Is your ship still cloaked?"*

"Will you just come to the point? What's going on?"

Now O'Brien shouted, *"Just answer the damn question, Zek!"*

"Don't raise your voice to me! And don't give me orders, either!" It was always the same dynamic with O'Brien. He and Zek would scream at each other, bark orders at each other, and no one ever backed down. It was a perpetual struggle for dominance.

At the other end of the conversation, Eddington once again took quiet control. *"General Zek, have you reached your destination? Are you still* safely *under cloak?"*

The gravity of the situation began to sink in for Zek. "Yes, we're still cloaked," he said. "And we just reached—" He caught himself before saying "Empok Nor," because only at the last moment had he realized that neither O'Brien nor Bashir had uttered the station's name over the subspace channel. "What's going on here?"

"Zek, you're heading into an ambush," O'Brien said. *"The Alliance is waiting for you. Stay under cloak, turn around, and head back to Terok Nor immediately."*

All around Zek, the other rebellion leaders were looking at each other. A mixture of alarm and incredulity defined the mood. For his own part, Zek was flabbergasted at the audacity of the two Terrans' request. "Have you two lost your minds? Where did you get this ridiculous story?"

"An anonymous tip," O'Brien said. Eddington nudged him. Reluctantly, he added, *"From someone in the Alliance."*

The more they said, the less Zek believed them. "Someone in the Alliance told you that they were going to ambush my ship?"

"Not exactly," Eddington admitted. *"The tip said they were targeting Terok Nor. But we think that was a ruse, meant to—"*

"Are you kidding me?" Zek got angrier as he went along. "Someone threatens *you,* and you think that means they're out to ambush *me?* Have you two been drinking? Or are you just too proud to call for reinforcements?"

"We've already scanned the Bajor system," Eddington said. *"There is no attack on Terok Nor. But our analysis suggests that the Alliance wants us to move ships and personnel here, so that we'll have to leave . . . other assets undefended."*

From the tactical station, Cal Hudson said, "I'm running a long-range scan now, Mike. If there's an ambush in silent-running mode out there, I'll find it."

Zek sat back in his too-big-for-comfort chair and sulked. All the years that he and Bashir had worked to take command of the rebellion, so that they could fight this war the way it had to be fought, suddenly felt as if they had been spent in vain. Once again the others were taking their cues from O'Brien and Eddington. Bashir cast a simmering sidelong look at Zek that made it clear he was harboring the same sense of resentment.

"This is so like you, O'Brien," Zek said. "On the eve of victory, you find a way to hand us defeat. Cut and run, cut and run—don't you know any tactics besides retreat?"

O'Brien shook his head. *"Don't be a fool. If the Alliance has an ambush ready, you'll be sitting ducks. This is why I didn't want everything in one place."*

Propelled by animosity, Zek sprang out of the captain's chair to his feet. "Why do you have to be so negative all the time? Everything's doom and gloom with—"

"I have something," Hudson said. "On the edge of the system. Looks pretty big." Zek, Bashir, and Yates all crowded behind Hudson as he worked at analyzing the sensor data. "Based on the configuration and hull composites, I'd say it's a Klingon warship. Probably a *Vor'cha*-class battle cruiser, running in low-power mode."

Shaking his head, Zek said, "That could be anything! A derelict ship, a warp shadow, a sensor malfunction—"

"Get out of there," O'Brien said. *"Have your people on the station set their ships' self-destruct packages before they go."*

Zek shrieked, "Self-destruct packages? Defang the rebellion when it's finally ready to hunt? Have you gone insane?"

"*We can't let the Alliance capture our cloaking devices,*" O'Brien said. "*If they reverse-engineer it, our cloaks'll be as worthless as theirs.*"

From the sensor post, Hudson said, "I'll run an active scan to confirm our readings." A moment later, he reported, "It's definitely a *Vor'cha*-class cruiser."

"*Retreat,*" O'Brien said. "*Arm the self-destructs on the ships in port, then beam as many of your people off the station as you can in one shot, because you won't have time for two.*"

Fearful eyes looked up at Zek from every station on the bridge. He hadn't come this far just to let O'Brien bully him into sacrificing everything he'd worked to build. "Hudson, Yates: you're relieved. Take the other captains and report to the transporter bays." The other rebel leaders except Bashir filed out the aft doors. Half of them continued farther aft, to transporter bay one, while the others headed toward the forward turbolift to transporter bay two. Bashir remained at Zek's side.

"*Zek,*" O'Brien cut in, "*what are you do—*"

The old Ferengi cut the channel and continued issuing orders. He keyed the intraship comm from the command panel next to his chair as he sat down. "Zek to alpha-shift bridge officers! Report for duty." Keying in a different, secure external channel, he hailed the ops center on Empok Nor.

A male voice answered him. "*Go ahead.*"

"Tell the ships in dock to get ready to receive their captains," Zek said. The order was acknowledged, and he closed the channel.

The aft doors of the bridge opened with a soft hiss, and the alpha-shift bridge crew filed in and manned their posts. "Helm," Bashir said, "put the station between us and the Klingon cruiser. Tactical, get ready to arm all weapons. Ops, stand by to drop the cloak and help the transporter bays get the captains to their ships."

Everyone worked quickly. In less than a minute, the ship was in position. There was only one Klingon battle cruiser out there, and

Zek had command of a fleet. Running away was not an option. *Now I'll show O'Brien what leadership really means,* he gloated. "Drop the cloak," he ordered. "Signal the station to begin transport."

The cloak disengaged and the lights brightened. One minute later, the ops officer looked up and said, "All transports complete, the captains are aboard—"

"Incoming!" the tactical officer shouted. "The Klingons—"

"Shields!" Zek commanded.

Then the explosions started.

Captain Kurn watched the Empok Nor station on the main viewscreen of the *Ya'Vang*'s bridge. The anticipated hour of his targets' arrival had come, but all appeared placid. *No matter,* Kurn told himself. *Often the woods grow still and the wind falls silent before the prey appears. The hunter is patient. Readiness is all.*

Krona, his first officer, had wisely taken advantage of the nine-hour hiatus, as well. As soon as Kurn and Kira had left the bridge, though it had not yet been time for the shift change, Krona had brought up the second-shift team to serve during the expected period of downtime. Now, on the brink of action, the first-shift crew had returned to duty. Ronak hunched forward over the helm, eager to make the instantaneous jump to maximum warp. Qeyhnor had just finished running a weapons drill and reported all hands ready for battle. Beqar studiously monitored the station's signal traffic and general status.

Standing to the left of Kurn's chair, radiant in her adopted Klingon uniform, was Kira Nerys. She remained silent and maintained minimal but obvious physical contact with Kurn. He was grateful that she was not inclined to try fill this time with small talk, or inane questions, or pointless activity. Like a good hunter, she remained alert and quiet.

A low buzzing sounded on Beqar's console. She checked it and studied the results for a moment. Kurn let the woman work. When she had something to report, she would say so. Half a minute later, she turned her chair and said, "An encrypted signal is coming in from Terok Nor. They've updated their codes. This one will take time to break."

"Terok Nor is hailing its sister station?" Krona asked.

Beqar waved her hand side to side. "No. Empok Nor isn't receiving." She checked some more data on her console. "The signal is on an SLF channel."

Kurn understood: super-low-frequency subspace channels were used for communications with cloaked vessels. Someone on Terok Nor was trying to reach the ship carrying the rebellion leaders, and they had sent the signal here, to the Trivas system. Though unseen, their prey had arrived. "Battle stations," he said.

"Increased signal traffic," Beqar said. "I can't lock in the coordinates, it's too well masked."

Qeyhnor spoke. "Captain, passive sensors have picked up a minor increase in local charged particles. We're being scanned, and not by the station."

Krona looked to Kurn for direction. "Should we begin the attack, Captain?"

"Not yet," Kurn said. "Let's see if their scan actually detected us." Kira's hand closed a bit tighter on his shoulder.

The reports started to come in more quickly. "I'm picking up short-range comm traffic between all eleven ships in dock," Beqar said. "More signals between the station and another vessel close by—"

"I see it," Qeyhnor said. "It's the *Capital Gain,* sir. She's decloaked on the far side of the station." Working rapidly at his panel, he added, "All ships in dock are powering up their main reactors."

"Attack," Kurn said.

The first officer snapped into action. "Bridge to engineering: full power! Tactical, arm all weapons, target the station's fusion core. Communications, jam outgoing comm traffic. Helm, maximum warp on my mark!" Krona looked to Kurn for the final command, and Kurn nodded his assent. "Go!"

Ronak jumped the ship to maximum warp. Instantly, the ship went from cold, dark, and quiet to pulsing with heat, light, and energy. The station swiftly enlarged on the forward viewscreen. Kurn stole a look up at Kira, who smiled back with the wild gleam of a Klingon warrior queen.

"Out of warp," Ronak declared, "in three . . . two . . . one!" The gray mass of Empok Nor filled the main viewer. Inside its bulky blocks of scaffolding, the first glows of firing thrusters revealed themselves.

"Target locked," Qeyhnor said.

And the hunter strikes. "Fire," Kurn said.

Cal Hudson hurried onto the bridge of his ship with no name. "Report," he bellowed to his XO, a Bolian man named Zim Brott.

"Firing up the warp core, sir," Brott replied. "All hands are aboard except the medic."

Hudson settled into his chair. "If he's not aboard in the next thirty seconds, we go without him."

"Her, sir," Brott said with hesitation. "And she's my wife."

It was not an auspicious way to begin a working relationship. "Sorry. . . . Find her and get her aboard."

"Aye, sir."

As Brott stepped aside to the communications station, Hudson checked his command panels and confirmed that his ship was ready for action. "Helm," he said, turning the head of the young Terran woman sitting in front of him. "We need to break free of this scaffolding quickly. Can you keep her steady backing out at quarter impulse?"

"Sir, the flight specs call for thrusters only."

"Yes or no," he hectored her. "Can you do it?"

She looked down at her control panel, then back at him. With a diffident shrug, she replied, "I don't know. Maybe?"

His jaw clenched with anxiety. *I'd relieve her of duty, but we don't have anybody else.* "Just do your best," he said.

"Aye, sir," said the soft-voiced woman, as she turned back to complete her preflight systems check.

A series of distant, rumbling explosions was all the warning that Hudson and his crew had. Then a final blast ripped through their nameless vessel from stern to bow, turning it to vapor and debris in a single incandescent flash.

"Captain on the deck!" called Yates's first officer, a by-the-numbers Bajoran man named Tahna Los. Though the rebellion had no uniforms, he treated his own clothes as if they were his badge of office; they were always clean and pressed, and his shoes were diligently buffed and polished. His personal grooming was just as fastidious—he had the cleanest fingernails of any man Kasidy had ever met.

"Status," Yates said as she sat down in the center seat.

Tahna snapped to attention beside her seat. "Warp core online," he said. "All crew aboard and ready for action. Standing by to release docking clamps on your orders."

"Take us out, Mister Tahna," she said. "On the double."

"Aye, Captain," he said, then he turned and began issuing rapid-fire orders to the rest of Yates's handpicked bridge crew: Sakonna, a female Vulcan flight controller whom Yates had seen pilot a hijacked outrider at full impulse through a post-combat debris field; Reese, a hardened, no-nonsense Terran, whose uncanny ability to predict enemy behavior had made him invaluable as a tactical officer; Sarina Douglas, a shy and reserved Terran woman who had a knack for breaking codes. They were some of the most talented people she'd ever met, and all had been willing volunteers for the rebellion.

With this ship and this crew, we can't lose, Yates thought.

But in a flash of light and heat, they were gone.

"Incoming!" shouted Zek's tactical officer. "The Klingons—"

"Shields!" Zek commanded.

Watching the main viewer, Bashir winced at the flash of torpedo detonations against the far side of the station's fusion core, which disintegrated in a pulse of blinding energy that tore the station—and the eleven ships docked there—to pieces.

Deep, powerful explosions buffeted the *Capital Gain* and hurled Zek from the captain's chair to the deck. His aged body landed hard, and the shock of impact left him disoriented.

The crackling static on the main viewer cleared enough for Bashir to see the *Vor'cha*-class battle cruiser race past them and begin maneuvering for another attack run.

Zek was still on the floor, moaning. Bashir realized that the old Ferengi would not be able to keep up with the situation erupting around them. It was time for Bashir to take command.

"Damage report!" he demanded.

"Warp core offline," the ops officer responded. "Cloak offline. Comms are being jammed. Port shields buckling."

Stepping over Zek to take the center seat, Bashir spoke quickly. "Helm, go evasive, keep the Klingons to starboard. Tactical, fire at will. Ops, reroute portside shield power to starboard and tell engineering we need warp speed now."

"Here they come," the tactical officer said. "Torpedoes away!" On the main viewer, the torpedo volley went astray. Only one of the four warheads found its target, and it flared ineffectually against the Klingon ship's shields. "Firing phasers!" Raging trails of orange phaser energy lanced across the darkness, briefly strafed the Klingons' shields. Then the enemy ship was off the main viewer.

Thunderous detonations trembled the ship, which felt as if it were pitching and rolling on a turbulent sea. Bashir tried to keep the panic out of his voice as he said, "Helm, keep them to starboard!"

"Starboard shields weakening," the ops officer said. Then another scourging of disruptor fire made a terrifying screech as it raked the *Capital Gain*'s ablative-armor-clad hull. Fire spouted from sparking companels around the bridge, and the main overhead lights went dark. In the flickering glow of firelight, Bashir saw that the ops officer was dead.

"Shields are gone," the tactical officer reported. "Phaser couplings are blown. Torpedo room's offline."

The flight controller rotated her seat to face Bashir, her visage one of barely contained terror. "Engineering just ejected our warp core," she said in a quavering voice. "Main power's gone. Impulse is gone."

In front of Bashir, at his feet, Zek slowly pushed himself up from the deck, onto his knees. He looked around the bridge in shock. "Bashir, you idiot! What have you done to my ship?"

There was no point replying to Zek. His answer was about to come soon enough, either in the form of a final, catastrophic fury of conflagration, or a subspace demand for surrender. *Please let it end in fire,* Bashir hoped. *Let it be quick.*

To Bashir's utter dismay, the next sound he heard was the chirp of an incoming comm signal. Resigned to the inevitable, he pressed the touch panel to acknowledge the signal and put it on the intraship PA.

Moments later, a voice, deep and rough-edged, cut through the spatter of static.

"Attention, officers and crew of the Capital Gain. *This is Captain Kurn of the* I.K.S. Ya'Vang. *Surrender and prepare to be boarded."*

9

Kurn walked the decks of the *Capital Gain* hunched over and pulled in on himself. The captured rebellion vessel was every bit as spartan in its amenities as a Klingon ship, but its passageways were even narrower and its overheads lower. For Klingon warriors accustomed to wearing armor with bulky, broad shoulder pads, navigating the interior of a *Defiant*-class ship was a slow and awkward process. For Kurn, who towered over many other Klingons, it was an even clumsier proposition.

Krona was in command of the boarding party, which had beamed over to the disabled rebel ship more than an hour ago and made quick work of subduing its crew. Only a few rebels had tried to put up a fight. Most had abided by their commander's declaration of surrender. Now the prisoners were segregated in two holding areas; senior personnel—the rebels did not have officers, as such—were being held on the bridge, and rank-and-file personnel had been rounded up in main engineering.

Following in single file behind Kurn was a retinue that included, in order, Kira Nerys, tactical officer Qeyhnor, and a trio of armed shock troops. Ahead of Kurn, the portal to the *Capital Gain*'s bridge was open. He stepped inside.

At the front of the compartment were the rebel ship's commanders and bridge crew. Their hands were bound behind them, and all were seated with their faces to the wall and their tied wrists visible to their two armed guards. First officer Krona and second officer Garvig bowed their heads slightly to Kurn as he entered and took stock of the situation. "Report," Kurn said.

"The ship is secure, Captain," Krona said. "All enemy personnel accounted for and disarmed. Chief engineer Hervog has command of the enlisted crew in main engineering."

Kira slipped past Kurn and strolled slowly behind the prisoners. Kurn looked around at the charred companels. Smoke lingered along the ceiling, and a fine crystalline dust sparkled on the carpeted deck. Curious to know the value of this prize he was bringing home to the empire, Kurn asked, "How much of the ship is intact?"

"Severe damage to propulsion and tactical systems," Garvig replied. "Hervog says most of it's been slagged."

Krona added, "And the rebels managed to wipe their computer core before we could access it."

Kurn wondered sometimes if his men deliberately omitted the most important information he required as a subtle means of testing his patience. "What about the cloaking device?"

Garvig and Krona traded conspiratorial smirks. "Intact," Krona said. "Damaged, but Hervog says he has enough to reverse-engineer it within a few months."

Unable to suppress a broad grin, Kurn chortled. "Good work, men," he said. "Very good work." He turned back toward the forward end of the compartment, where Kira stood scraping her fingernails slowly on the backs of two prisoners' necks. Kurn called out to her, "Found a new plaything already, Intendant?"

"Better," she replied, with a sadistic glee that Kurn had not seen before. "Heroes of the rebellion." She tossed an invitational look over her shoulder. "Perhaps I could introduce you to them?" She looked to the two armed soldiers and pointed at the prisoners in front of her. The guards looked to Kurn for their orders. He nodded his assent. They stepped forward and yanked the two hapless rebels to their feet: a scruffy, spindly, dark-haired Terran and a shriveled, trembling old Ferengi.

It seemed like a joke. "*These* are the heroes of the rebellion?" Kurn asked derisively, as he stepped closer.

"My lord," Kira said, "allow me to present Julian Subatoi Bashir, and Zek, two of the leading generals of the rebellion." She pinched Bashir's chin between her thumb and forefinger and glared into his eyes. "General Bashir is also one of the rebellion's premier inflictors of pain and suffering." Then she looked at Zek. "And you . . . I've been waiting a *long* time to meet you."

"The feeling's not mutual," Zek said. The nasal quality of his voice annoyed Kurn greatly.

"Do you even know who your counterpart is in the other universe?" she asked Zek. "Would you like to know?"

"Not really."

"He was the Grand Nagus of Ferenginar," she proclaimed, as if that was supposed to mean something. "He was the leader of the Ferengi people, the chief executive of an economic empire, the richest Ferengi in the galaxy." Changing her evil gleam to a sinister sneer, she continued, "And what are you in charge of? A band of criminals. Pathetic." She gestured at the smoky rubble of the bridge. "We've decoded the message you received from Terok Nor. We know that O'Brien warned you to retreat. You should have listened to him. Instead, you walked right into a trap, one that you'd already seen with your own eyes! What were you thinking?" She shouted with mock outrage to the rest of the room, "This is the greatest tactical thinker of the rebellion? This is the vaunted Zek, the strategic genius of—"

"Oh, shut up already!" Zek bleated over Kira's tirade. "We both know how this'll end. Just get it over with, you whore!"

Kira spun and struck with the speed and grace of a serpent. Despite the fact that Kurn had ordered his people to make certain she remained unarmed at all times, a flick of her wrist produced a blade from the sleeve of her borrowed uniform. She plunged it into Zek's throat, mauling his carotid artery and trachea. Gouts of blood surged over the ragged gash in his flesh as he pitched forward and fell dead at Kira's feet. By then, one of the guards had disarmed Kira, but it was too late to do anything for the Ferengi.

Kurn advanced on Kira and locked his hand around her slender throat. "Why did you do that?" he demanded. "He could have had valuable intelligence!"

Defiantly, Kira pulled free of Kurn's grip. "Anything you could have learned from Zek you'll get more easily from *him,* and without all the whining," she said, pointing at Bashir. She batted her eyelashes at Kurn. "What's more, if you let *me* question him, I promise not to kill him. . . . Not for *years.*"

Ro became livid the moment that Duras had deigned to summon her like a common servant to the bridge in the middle of her sleep cycle. As she worked her way through the corridors of the ship, she grew even more agitated at the uncharacteristically boisterous mood that seemed to have infected the crew. Roars of celebration echoed inside almost every compartment she passed. Soldiers stumbled past her with half-filled steins of *warnog* or bloodwine, their breaths pungent with alcoholic fumes.

What's wrong with these animals? she wondered during her turbo-lift ride to the bridge. The doors opened, and a guttural chorus of male voices, lifted in half-inebriated song, assailed her as she stepped out. At the center of the song circle was General Duras himself, surrounded by his bridge crew and senior officers. *What's next?* Ro wondered. *An orgy?* She pushed her way into the midst of the raucous, chanting Klingons and snapped at Duras, "Explain yourself, General! Why did you send for me?"

Duras replied, "It's a celebration, Intendant! A glorious victory worthy of song!" Deep, droning voices resumed their chanting in sharp notes and minor chords, the lyrics full of hard consonants and rough subvocalized noises. The general waved his stein of bloodwine out of synch with the singing, like a deaf conductor trying to lead a choir.

"Whose victory?" Ro asked, shouting over the din.

Laughing maniacally, Duras answered, "Kurn's! Kurn, son of Mogh, scion of my enemy—but today I honor his name as a Hero of the Empire."

Ro didn't understand. "Because he killed Worf?"

"It was never about Worf," Duras said, as if she was stupid for ever thinking that Captain Kurn's stated objective had been truthful. "Kurn and Kira found a rebel shipyard at Empok Nor and faced more than a dozen *Defiant*-class enemy ships! All but one was destroyed. And guess what they captured on that ship." He grinned. "A Romulan cloaking device, like the one on *Defiant*." He bellowed to his crew, "To the crew of the *Ya'Vang,* who broke the rebellion, and put us back in the arms race! *Qapla!*" Another rousing cheer rocked the bridge.

Scowling at Duras and his rowdy underlings, Ro said, "Is that why you called me to the bridge? To tell me *this?*"

Shaking his head, Duras replied, "No, Intendant, of course not. I summoned you for a completely different reason." In the middle of a note, the singing stopped and all the Klingons on the bridge turned to face her. She was surrounded. "I called you here to place you under arrest."

Unwilling to back down, Ro retorted, "On what charge?"

"Treason," Duras said. "A crime that Captain Kurn warned me you would attempt, out of spite against your predecessor, Kira." He reached down and pressed a button on the arm of his chair. The text of the coded message Ro had sent to Terok Nor scrolled up the main viewer behind Duras. "You provided the enemy with critical, detailed, and classified information about a military mission. You put the lives of Klingon warriors in peril for your own political gain." The viewscreen went dark. Duras continued, "As an official of the Bajoran government, your conduct falls under your planet's independent jurisdiction." He looked to his communications officer. "Put them on-screen."

A moment later, the viewscreen hashed momentarily with snowy static and wavy interference. When it cleared, the face of First Minister Li Nalas was looking back at Ro. *"Is she with you, General Duras?"* Li asked.

"Yes, First Minister," Duras said. "The charges have been read and the evidence presented to the accused."

Li nodded. *"The Chamber of Ministers has finished its own review of the evidence. Intendant Ro Laren, come forward."* Prodded by disruptors against her back, Ro advanced in halting steps until there was no one between her and the viewscreen. First Minister Li's face, larger than life, eyed her with stern contempt. *"Ro Laren, by a unanimous vote of the Chamber of Ministers, you have been convicted of high crimes against the Alliance, in violation of the Treaty of Regulon. In accordance with the law, you are hereby ordered removed from office, stripped of title and diplomatic privileges, and remanded to Alliance custody aboard the* I.K.S. Negh'Var, *pending formal extradition to Qo'noS for a war crimes tribunal."*

Ro began to panic. "I have the right to present a defense," she protested. "It's a setup, the Klingons can't be trusted!"

"Actually," Li said, his manner so calm that it terrified Ro, *"the one who can't be trusted appears to be you—and, by extension, your sponsor, Legate Dukat. If his counsel is going to send us more traitors such as yourself, Cardassia's role in advising Bajoran policy will have to be . . . reevaluated."*

"Regent Martok has asked me to express to you," Duras said to Li, "his *personal* recommendation that you re-appoint Intendant Kira to her former office, in recognition of the great service she has rendered to the Alliance."

Li nodded. *"The Chamber will take Regent Martok's recommendation under advisement."*

"Thank you, First Minister," Duras said, and the main viewscreen blinked back to a vista of stars. The general gave a half nod in Ro's direction. "Take that *taHqeq* to the brig."

Two guards seized Ro's arms, and immediately she was dragged backward, away from Duras, toward the bowels of the ship and its pit of horrors. "Duras, stop!" Ro pleaded. "We can make a deal! You don't have to do this!" She wrestled in her captors' grip, but there was no breaking free. Her grunts of exertion became wordless shouts of rage as they neared the turbolift. Its doors opened. Duras and the others on the bridge all turned their backs on her as she was shoved into the lift car.

One of her guards smiled like a demon at her. "Welcome to Gre'thor."

As the lift doors closed, and Ro began her descent into a cycle of torture and abuse that would last for the rest of her life, her cries of fury became screams of terror.

10

The door signal buzzed. *"General,"* Sloan said over the closed-circuit comm, *"Sito Jaxa is here to see you."*

"Tell her to wait a moment," O'Brien said. He and Eddington sat beside each other at the table in the wardroom, reviewing information from a pair of handheld data padds. In the middle of the table was a tray on which a decanter of amber liquid and four glasses were neatly arranged. Keiko stood to one side and watched the men read. Looking up, O'Brien said, "Keiko, you really don't have to be here. Eddington and I can handle it."

"No," she said. "I should stay. The physicals were my idea. I want to see it through."

"All right," O'Brien said, not interested in provoking a debate about the matter. He looked at Eddington. "Ready?" For a few seconds, Eddington said nothing. O'Brien continued, "If you think I'm doing the wrong thing, tell me now."

Eddington sighed and put down his padd on the table. "No, you're doing the right thing. It's just a shame, that's all."

"No argument here," O'Brien said. He pressed a comm switch on the table in front of his seat. "Send her in."

The door unlocked and then opened. Sito Jaxa walked in, looking relaxed and casual. "You wanted to see me, sir?"

O'Brien and Eddington smiled warmly at her. "Yes, thanks for coming," O'Brien said. "Have a seat."

Sito sat down opposite the two men. "What's going on? Was there something wrong with my physical?"

"No, you're in perfect health," Eddington said.

"I'm sure you've heard the news about what happened at Empok Nor," O'Brien said to her. "About the loss of the fleet, and the other leaders."

The young blonde nodded. "Everyone has."

Eddington said, "Not exactly the outcome we were hoping for, obviously."

"No, sir," Sito replied.

O'Brien's brow creased with concern as he leaned forward. "Times like this," he said, "morale can start to suffer. It can seem like we're fighting a losing battle."

Sounding surprised, Sito replied, "That's not how I feel, sirs."

"Good," Eddington said. "We're glad to hear that."

Sito watched O'Brien as he picked up the decanter and a glass. "I wish I was taking it as well as you are," he said. "News like this makes me want a drink." He half-filled a glass with the liquor and offered it to Eddington, who nodded and accepted the glass. As O'Brien reached for another glass, he made eye contact with Sito. "Care to join us?"

"Yes, thank you," she said.

While O'Brien poured her drink, Eddington asked with a teasing grin, "You're not allergic to whiskey, are you?"

"No, sir," Sito said with a smile, then took the glass of spirits from O'Brien. He looked back at Keiko, who declined his offer with a wave of her hand. O'Brien poured himself a drink and leaned back in his chair. He, Eddington, and Sito sipped their whiskey, whose flavor was a complex medley of peat, smoke, sour notes, and sweetness.

Setting down his glass, O'Brien mustered a friendly grin and said to Sito, "Have you ever heard of the idea that it's impossible to prove a negative?"

The young woman nodded. "In school as a child," she said. "It's a basic precept of logical reasoning."

"That's right," O'Brien said, sounding impressed. "Smart kid, this one," he remarked to Eddington. To Sito, he continued, "My first officer told me the same thing not too long ago. It was the first I'd ever heard of it, but it made sense." He picked up the padd in front of him. "But if it's true, then I've got myself quite a conundrum."

Sito looked quickly back and forth between O'Brien and Eddington, whose unblinking stares were fixed squarely on her. Her glass was stopped halfway between her lips and the table; she appeared frozen in place. "Sirs?"

"Well, you and Keiko are both telling me it's impossible to prove a negative," O'Brien said, "but I've got a doctor who assures me that he's done exactly that." He gave his padd a gentle shove, sending it across the table to Sito. She glanced down at its screen as O'Brien added, "Your physical proves you're not pregnant."

Reactions competed for control of Sito's face, coming and going so quickly that each one barely registered before another took its place. First came confusion, then terror, then panic, followed by a poor imitation of anger. O'Brien imagined the rapid-fire sequence of thoughts that Sito must be grappling with. His simple declaration had made it clear that he was aware of the message she had been compiling, and that her medical exam had exposed her missive as a lie.

She took a deep breath. "Sirs . . . am I being questioned because I terminated my own pregnancy?"

Eddington just shook his head in disappointment.

In a low voice, O'Brien said to her, "Is that really how you want to play this?" He sighed. "Read the doctor's report. It's all there. You're not pregnant, and you never have been. All the tests were run twice, double-blind." He put out his hand and Eddington placed another padd in it. "What's more, you don't have a sister named Tera. Hell, you don't have a sister, period. And your mother died when you were nine."

Eddington leaned forward. "We checked your quarters. There are no *jossa* flowers planted there, as you wrote in your letter. Which leads to some rather awkward questions, wouldn't you say?"

"Sirs, I was just . . . that letter, it wasn't a real letter, it was just—"

"Fiction?" O'Brien offered with a sardonic grin.

Sito looked hopefully at him, only to be rebuffed by his discouraging glower, which asked with a look, *Who do you think you're fooling?*

Eddington folded his hands on the table and spoke with icy courtesy. "If I may, Miss Sito," he said, "I'd like to offer my interpretation of your letter." O'Brien handed him back the padd and sat back while Eddington worked. "Let's start with who 'Tera' is, shall we? I'm guessing that's your handler? Probably someone in the Ministry of Security on Bajor?" He scrolled through some more text on the padd. "'Tell Mom and Dad that I'm okay,'" he quoted. "A reference to the Alliance, maybe? Or to a joint effort of the Obsidian Order and Imperial Intelligence? 'Comfortable' and 'safe'—I presume that's your way of telling them that we believed your cover story. You wrote that we take what we're doing 'really seriously.' . . . A warning that the rebellion is better organized than expected, perhaps?"

As Eddington pressed on, dissecting Sito's every word choice, the young blonde shrank into her seat and became steadily more sullen and withdrawn.

"'Big ideas about the future,'" he quoted again. "Let me guess: you wanted to warn them about Zek's plan to attack Cardassia Prime." He scrolled ahead, then tapped the screen. "I have to admit, the gardening references took me a minute. But you were talking about the new shipyard at Empok Nor, weren't you? And that bit about *jossa* flowers being the only thing you were ever good at growing—you were trying to tell the Alliance that all our new ships were *Defiant*-class vessels, right?"

Now O'Brien leaned forward. "But the part about the pregnancy, the two men competing for your affection—that was my favorite part," he said with a devilish grin. "Eddington and I debated that one for all of five minutes. You were telling your handler about Bashir and Zek seizing control of the rebellion and putting me on the sideline." Sito averted her gaze, stared at the wall rather than look at O'Brien. "I'm the nice guy, right? And Bashir's the handsome one?"

"The pregnancy was the really interesting choice of words," Eddington said. "Your comment about not knowing who the father was made me think it was about seeing who'd end up in control of the rebellion. But then I saw your last line: 'I wish I was anywhere but here.' You were asking for extraction; you were ready to come out. 'Pregnant' was just a way of saying you'd obtained whatever information you'd been sent to acquire."

Heavy silence filled the room. O'Brien added with a sarcastic lilt, "Tell us if we missed anything."

Sito's hateful glare traveled from O'Brien to Eddington to Keiko and back again. "What're you going to do with me?"

"Way I see it," O'Brien said, "we have three options."

"We could send you back to Bajor," Eddington said.

"But with the access you've had," O'Brien said, "and the information you've acquired, that's probably not a good idea. Of course, we could just keep you locked up here on the station—"

"—or pack you off to one of our posts in the Badlands," Eddington interrupted.

"But sooner or later you'd get free, wouldn't you?" O'Brien said. Nodding, he continued, "Yeah, I can see it in your eyes. It might take you weeks or months, but you'd get out. Probably kill a few people in the process and hurt a lot more. Doesn't really make sense in the long run, does it?"

Eddington cut in, "And that brings us to our third—"

Sito pushed her chair back from the table and drew her sidearm. O'Brien and Eddington were still ducking for cover and reaching for their own weapons when a blinding yellow beam of energy struck Sito in the chest and vaporized her.

Keiko stood at the back of the room, her arm steady and her disruptor still aimed at the spot where Sito had been a moment before. O'Brien added "fast on the draw" to the long list of things he had grown to love about her. In a simple, fluid motion she holstered her weapon and walked back to the table. "Are you both all right?"

"Yeah," O'Brien said as he stood up. "Thanks."

Eddington stood and nodded to Keiko. "Nice shot."

"Thank you," she said.

O'Brien stared at the empty space where Sito had vanished. "This was my bloody fault," he said. "Zek and Bashir were right. I got sloppy, thought I was such a good leader that I could tell good people from bad with a handshake and a how-do-you-do." He shook his head. "I nearly got us all killed."

"The important thing," Eddington said, "is that we've learned from our mistake—and we're taking steps to fix it."

It sounded reassuring, but O'Brien still felt damned stupid for having put his people in this position. "I guess," he said.

Keiko faced O'Brien. "It's time to go talk to the troops," she said. "And whatever you tell them, it'd better be good. They're getting restless . . . and they're scared."

His face drawn from exhaustion and despair as he walked toward the door, O'Brien replied, "They aren't the only ones."

With the exception of a few essential personnel in ops, every member of the rebellion on Terok Nor had gathered on the Promenade to hear O'Brien speak. Recording devices were set to capture the moment both for posterity and for clandestine hand-delivery to other rebellion cells scattered across the quadrant.

O'Brien stepped out of a turbolift onto the upper level of the Promenade and slowly worked his way through the crowd toward one of the overpasses, which had been cleared of people and set with a podium to make him easier to see. As he pushed through the dense cluster of bodies, hands patted his back and slapped his shoulder in fraternal reinforcement. The clamor of voices was bright, echoing and re-echoing inside the torus-shaped space that ringed the primary core of the station. Waves of heat from the massed bodies rose from the lower level, imbuing the banner-draped thoroughfare with the scent of something vital, the breath of life.

Expectant eyes gazed up at O'Brien as he emerged from the crowd onto the overpass, followed closely by Eddington and

Keiko. Nervous silence spread through the crowd as he stepped onto the podium. He looked around and then down to the lower level. The faces that looked back were masks of cynicism and apprehension. They would be on their guard for evasions. Jingoistic lies had outlived their usefulness for these people; O'Brien could feel it. They needed to know the truth.

"You all listen to the comm nets," he said, lifting his rasping voice so that it would carry and convey the tenor of command. "So you all know what's happened. I won't tell you it's not a disaster, because it is. We lost a major base of operations. We lost a lot of good people. And there's a good chance the Alliance has one of our cloaking devices."

Whispers of panic traveled quickly through the crowd, like a fire racing through dry grass. O'Brien needed to extinguish that blaze of fear. "But this war is not over! The rebellion is more than one station. It's more than a handful of ships. Our movement is spreading. We're on dozens of worlds, and new cells are forming on dozens more. This isn't a battle to be won with conventional tactics—at least, not yet. This is a war of ideas."

He pivoted slowly as he continued, working the crowd, connecting with as many people as he could, second after second. "We still hold this station," he said. "And as long as we hold Bajor as our hostage, the Alliance won't move against us. This station, and every one of us who defends it—we're the thing that gives other freed slaves hope. They look to us to show them the way. To teach them how to fight back. How to resist. And as long as I draw breath, I plan to go on fighting, until we're *all* free!"

Cautious applause filtered up, emboldening him. "And that's what we're really fighting for," he cried. "*Freedom.* Not for payback. Not for power. But for *what's right.* We're fighting for a *higher purpose.* For a future when all beings live as equals under the law. For a society in which vengeance isn't the golden rule. For a galaxy where justice and mercy are united, not opposed. . . . Yes, we fight to destroy the Alliance. We fight against tyranny. But it's not enough just to stand *against* something—we also have to stand for *something better.* And that's what we're going to do, all of us, brothers and sisters in arms. We're going to build that better future, starting with ourselves. General Eddington and I have a plan, and when it's ready, the next phase of this war begins. A rebellion's not enough anymore. Starting today, this . . . is a *revolution!"*

Spontaneous applause surged like a tsunami. He stepped off the podium. *I don't deserve this,* he chided himself, even as he turned slowly to feel the tide of acclaim wash over him from every direction. *But they need this.* He followed Eddington and Keiko off the overpass and let them clear a path through the crowd to a portal that led inside the empty bar's upper tier.

The door closed behind him, muting the continuing roar of applause and cheering from the crowd outside. He passed Keiko and Eddington and proceeded downstairs, to the first floor. Moving quickly, he stepped behind the bar and chose a bottle of something blue and potent. As he filled a skinny shot glass, Keiko and Eddington stepped up to the counter and watched him. In a single tilt, O'Brien emptied the shot down his throat.

"Good speech," Eddington said. "It's just what they needed to hear." O'Brien nodded and poured another shot as Eddington continued, "So, I guess we ought to start hammering out the final details of that master plan for the revolution."

"Guess so," O'Brien said, then he downed another shot.

Keiko looked back and forth between the two men. It wasn't hard to guess the truth. "You don't really have a plan, do you?"

"Nope," Eddington said.

"No bloody idea," O'Brien confirmed. Exhausted and demoralized, all he could do was hang his head and wait for the booze to numb his misery by some small measure.

Eddington reached across and under the bar for a shot glass, took the bottle from O'Brien, and poured himself a drink. "I think I know where we ought to start," he said. "By not repeating the mistakes that Zek and Bashir made." He paused to pour the shot down his throat, then he exhaled sharply and gave his head a quick shake. He poured himself another shot, then gave the bottle back to O'Brien.

"They let it get personal," Eddington went on. "The fleet, the rebellion—for them it was all about being heroes. A cult of personality."

Keiko pointed at the bottle. O'Brien poured her a shot in his glass while Eddington continued. "Whatever we have to do to keep this going, we have to remember from now on that it's not about us—any of us. It never was. Like you said, O'Brien, it has to be about something bigger. Something better."

"Here's to that," O'Brien said, lifting the bottle in a toast and clinking it against their glasses. "To something better. . . . May we all live to see it."

The nightmare of pummeling blows ceased abruptly.

A door opened, admitting a slice of light.

The paingivers left, and the door closed after them.

Julian Bashir dangled naked from his bound wrists, which were secured to a hook along the overhead of his sweltering, oppressively humid cell aboard the *I.K.S. Ya'Vang*.

His interrogators had shown little interest in actually asking him any questions, being content simply to beat him for hours on end. *They're pulling their punches,* he realized. *Softening me up for someone else.* It was the only way he could explain why he wasn't dead yet.

Every part of his body hurt. He tried to assess his own injuries. His right eye was swollen shut; the view through his left eye was veiled in a reddish haze. Welts and bruises mushroomed across both sides of his torso, and his face felt puffy and half numb. Blood, salty and metallic, oozed from between his loosened teeth and dribbled over his split lower lip, which registered every drop as a fiery sting of pain. He was certain that several of his ribs had been cracked. His grip on consciousness felt tenuous at best.

Respiration was difficult; his nostrils were thick with dried blood, and mucus was pooling in his sinuses. He was content to breathe through his mouth, because the sickening, charnel odors that permeated this cramped, shadowy space were ones that he had no desire to smell again. Death. Blood, urine, and feces. Decaying flesh, broiled skin, scorched hair. This entire deck of the *Ya'Vang* bore the stench of a slaughterhouse.

A shrieking of metal as the door opened again. Light, dim and red, slashed into the cell and threw Bashir's long, twisted shadow across the floor. From another cell farther down the corridor came the sounds of a woman screaming in terror, and male Klingons laughing with malicious abandon.

Barely audible under the screaming and the low pulse of the ship's engines, the voices of Kira and Kurn were close by, right outside Bashir's cell door.

"Remember your promise," Kurn said. "Don't kill him."

A girlish chuckle. "I guarantee, you, Kurn. He won't die. At least, not today."

Footsteps, then shadows obscured the light from the door. Captain Kurn and Intendant Kira entered the cell and stood directly behind Bashir, who was too heavily restrained and too stiff to turn his head. "Look at him," Kira said with mocking sweetness. "So sad. He used to be so handsome. It seems like such a waste."

"What do you think he can tell you?" Kurn asked.

"Everything," Kira said. "He's going to tell me everything. Where the rebel bases are located. How they're defended. The number of people in each one. . . . He's going to tell me who sold the rebels their cloaking device. What the rebels' strategic objectives are. And so much more. Before I'm done I'll know everything about O'Brien and whoever else is helping him run that little rebellion. I'll have their life stories."

Kurn grunted his acknowledgment, then inquired, "What about the other prisoners from the *Capital Gain?*"

"Worthless," Kira said. "Execute them." The dry scrapes of shuffling feet matched the swaying of Kurn and Kira's shadows on the far wall of the cell. Kira asked, "How long until we rendezvous with the *Negh'Var?*"

"Sixteen hours," Kurn said. "They're holding station in the Almatha system until we arrive."

A purr of satisfaction from Kira. "And have we heard back from Martok?"

"The regent has agreed to designate the *Negh'Var* as your flagship as soon as you step aboard," Kurn said.

"Excellent," she said, in a tone that Bashir knew must have been accompanied by a lethal-looking smile. "My first official order will be to promote you to general, and name you as Duras's replacement on the *Negh'Var.* Any thoughts on what fate should befall him after that?"

"I'm sure there must be a garbage scow somewhere in need of a captain," Kurn said, provoking himself and Kira into gales of sadistic laughter.

When they finally regained their composure, Kira said, "Find one. I'll make sure it has his name on it."

"I will be in your debt, Intendant," Kurn said.

"It's my pleasure, Kurn," she said, then adopted a more seductive tone. "You and I are going to be close, my dear general. Very close, indeed. . . . Now, if you'll excuse me."

The shadows parted, then the door closed and darkness descended once more. The only illumination, harsh and white, came from directly above Bashir and spilled in a tight circle around his feet.

Sharp clacks on the deck. Footfalls in spike-heeled boots. Intendant Kira circled him in languid strides, looking him over like a butcher studying a cut of meat. She no longer wore the Klingon uniform in which he had seen her outfitted on the bridge of the *Capital Gain.* The Intendant was attired in her trademark black body suit, its surface form-fitting and almost mirror-perfect in its glossy sheen. Around her brow was a silver headpiece. From her perfectly styled hair to her expertly manicured fingernails, she was a living portrait of glorious vanity.

"Hello, Julian," she said. "It's been quite a while since we've been alone together, hasn't it?" With the knuckle of her index finger, she propped his head up. "I can't tell you how much I've been looking forward to this."

Kira withdrew her hand, and his head drooped back toward his chest. She reached out into the darkness and pulled over a rolling metal cart, whose top tray was covered with various quasi-surgical-looking instruments.

"I seem to recall you favored a brute-force approach to our encounters," she said. "Electrical shock, wasn't it?" She tsk-tsked and shook her head. "So crude. No style at all." Her hand hovered above the implements on the tray, vacillating between one with curving razor edges and another with saw-tooth blades. Then she selected one that had both, one at each end.

In slow, swaying motions, she waggled the tool in front of Bashir's one unswollen eye. "Tell me, Julian—do you remember what I used to say about violence being a *precision instrument?*" A sick glee contorted her face as she pressed the flat of her blade against his face and whispered in his ear.

"So is revenge."

About the Authors

Keith R.A. DeCandido grew up reading *Star Trek* novels and admiring the authors of same, never imagining that he'd grow up to be one of them. He still is half convinced that it's some kind of delusion he's been suffering. Still, they keep sending him checks, so maybe not. His previous *Trek* work includes writing eleven novels, one novella, ten eBooks, five short stories, and a comic book miniseries, and editing three anthologies, several novels, and the entire *Star Trek* eBook line. Some of the above include *A Time for War, A Time for Peace,* the *USA Today* bestselling lead-in to *Star Trek Nemesis*; several contributions to the popular post-finale *Deep Space Nine* saga; numerous entries in the *Starfleet Corps of Engineers* eBook series, which he also edits; the critically acclaimed *Articles of the Federation; The Art of the Impossible,* part of the *New York Times* bestselling *Lost Era* miniseries; two previous pieces of *Voyager* fiction, the first half of *The Brave and the Bold* Book 2 and the story "Letting Go" in *Distant Shores,* neither of which took place in the Delta Quadrant; editing the *Tales of the Dominion War* and *Tales from the Captain's Table* anthologies; co-editing *New Frontier: No Limits* with Peter David; editing the anniversary eBook miniseries *Mere Anarchy*; and much more. Coming in 2007 is *Q&A,* one of the post-*Nemesis* novels celebrating the twentieth anniversary of *Star Trek: The Next Generation.* When he isn't *Trek*kin', Keith is writing in the media universes of *Buffy the Vampire Slayer, World of Warcraft, StarCraft, Doctor Who,* Marvel Comics, *Serenity, Resident Evil, Farscape, Gene Roddenberry's Andromeda,* and much more. He lives in New York City with his girlfriend and two insane-yet-terminally-cute cats. Find out more at Keith's Web site at www.DeCandido.net.

Peter David is the *New York Times* bestselling author of numerous *Star Trek* novels, including the incredibly popular *New Frontier* series. He has also written dozens of other books, including his acclaimed original novel, *Sir Apropos of Nothing,* and its sequels, *The Woad to Wuin* and *Tong Lashing.*

David is also well known for his comic book work, particularly his award-winning run on *The Hulk*. He recently authored the novelizations of *Spider-Man, Spider-Man 2, Spider-Man 3, Fantastic Four,* and *The Hulk* motion pictures.

He lives in New York with his wife and daughters.

Massachusetts native **Sarah Shaw** is a lifelong *Star Trek* fan. Under a variety of pseudonyms, she has written fanfiction based on such series as *Buffy the Vampire Slayer, Angel,* and *The X-Files*. This is her first professional fiction credit, for which she is enormously grateful to editor Marco Palmieri, who graciously took a chance on her.

In addition to writing, she enjoys sleeping late, cooking with butter, tasting wines she can't afford to buy by the bottle, and supporting the efforts of Amnesty International and the American Civil Liberties Union.

She currently lives with her two cats, her rabbit, and her significant other.

Printed in the United States
By Bookmasters